JAN ROBERTS

A Blood Affair

SIMON & SCHUSTER
New York London Toronto Sydney Tokyo Singapore

SIMON & SCHUSTER
Simon & Schuster Building
Rockefeller Center
1230 Avenue of the Americas
New York, New York 10020

Originally published in Great Britain by HarperCollins Publishers.

Designed by Karolina Harris
Manufactured in the United States of America

10 9 8 7 6 5 4 3 2 1

Library of Congress Cataloging-in-Publication Data

Roberts, Jan, date.
    A blood affair / Jan Roberts.
        p.   cm.
    I. Title.
    PR6068.01446B56   1991
    823'.914—dc20   91-37818
                                                      CIP

ISBN: 0-671-74454-2

Acknowledgments

In the writing of this book I owe special thanks to Genevieve, who lived with it patiently and cheerfully and contributed so much, and Gillian and my son-in-law Thomas Pound of Film Associates New Zealand, for their unwavering support and encouragement.

Particular thanks are due to Susanne Jaffe of Simon & Schuster, for her help and editorial skill.

To the Blake Friedmann Literary Agency, London, my thanks to all of you.

For my daughters Gillian and Genevieve,

with love always—

One

He had the gun right on her, two inches from that beautiful nose, and there she was. A WASP, all blond and polished, silky skin; he just bet she had Chantilly lace on her little panties and creamy white thighs. All a man had to do was slide in between, take her slow and easy.

He could feel "Nailer" Meehan making a move behind him, feel him because you didn't hear Nailer, ever. Except when he was humming a tune. People don't expect to get mugged by someone humming "On the Sunny Side of the Street."

This was Freddy's, Luigi Frediano's Georgetown place, and piss elegant; the kind of hairdresser's with a jungle of trees sucking up the air and a cobra-smart receptionist at the front desk. While she was coming to terms with the fact that three hooded men had arrived and one of them was holding a gun at her head, the women under the row of hairdryers were just beginning to catch on. The heads gaping from their metal boxes looked like the electricity was running through them.

All except the girl.

But any second Sweet Thing was going to lift her eyes out of the magazine and find she was looking down the muzzle of a .44 Magnum. Funny thing is, women don't scream much. He'd bring the gun on them slow, right between the eyes, and they'd just sit there palpitating.

The hot air made the hair around her face blow out in silvery blond strands. She had on one of those little pink candy-striped smocks. All the women were wearing them, only she didn't have nothing on underneath. Nothing he could see. His eyes moved in hot jets down her long legs, up.

Then she was looking. He watched the shock in her eyes as they moved from the gun to his face. And outrage. He liked spirit in a woman. It was fuel to the flames licking up his crotch. He flicked his tongue in and out of his mouth. The obscenity of that red pointed tongue, the implication inherent in the gesture, made her go rigid, he saw her hands clench, pearly oval nails bite at the leather armrests. Nice and slow, he reached over and snapped back the dryer. She was still pretty, even with the curlers in.

He said it soft. "Get up."

The woman in the next chair whimpered. He stuck the gun at her temple, without once taking his eyes off Sweet Thing.

An air hammer was going in his brain. He screamed, "Get up."

The Pound Cake he had the Magnum's snout up against was mouthing words. "Go on, honey," her eyes were spinning with terror, "do anything he wants."

The girl went pale as death. She was looking along the row now, the women were staring back, petrified, their mouths lax, their eyes jumpy. They didn't care what happened to her, so long as they were safe. So long as they could get back to their big colonial houses in safe Chevy Chase and safe Bethesda.

They didn't care. Nobody cared. She was trapped with a group of women who cared more about their nails than her. Trapped with a violent, screaming mad dog whose face had nothing human in it; cut off from the world of normal rational people, from any kind of help, from law and order as she had known it.

You better believe it, Sweet Thing. He rammed the gun harder and Pound Cake made little animal squeaks of fear. "Two seconds and you get to wipe her brains off the wall."

The girl's eyes exploded into green splinters of fury. "You bastard." She said it low, but he heard.

"You're coming with me." He slid out a hand, seized her by the arm, hauling her up and twisting it behind her back. He put the cold muzzle at the nape of her young warm neck, where all the little downy hairs curled up against the apple-white of her skin. "Now walk."

There was a staff room in the back. When he got her to the door she jerked away. The pain made her eyes water. He shook his head, as if pitying her, then kicked open the door and shoved her inside. He got her face to the wall, slammed her up against it, and leaned on her some. It wasn't too hard getting her smooth little wrists tied in the handy length of cord he carried in his pocket.

"You'll get the chair for this." Her voice had a high-pitched quake of fear. He knew she hated hearing it, and laughed. That laugh had a sound more feral than human. As he ripped aside the smock exposing the triangle of bikini panties, she lashed back with her head and caught him a stinging blow on the nose. He swore, and knocked her back hard against the wall. She was quiet, momentarily stunned. With insolent deliberation he tore away the thin panties and freed his penis.

She felt it go through her. The pain. Pain—brought her back to consciousness.

A black tidal wave of pain. She hardly felt him jerk her around so that she faced him. Her mouth opened in disbelief. She sucked enough air into her lungs to scream. It was ripped from her body, a scream of convulsive urgency. She screamed so hard it paralyzed her senses, she couldn't see and she couldn't hear, and finally it died into a spasm as his gloved hand clamped her wide-open mouth. And that was when the real horror began, when she couldn't breath and he began to whisper obscenities, writhing against her.

Wet with her sweat and his, hair and curlers hanging dankly over her face, she began to pray. The image of the door opening in the dirty wall opposite was the last thing she remembered.

Lieutenant Malloy of the Washington, D.C., Homicide Squad was enjoying his lunch break when Sergeant Jackson telephoned from the exclusive Georgetown salon.

"Yeah, yeah. I know it." Malloy stretched on the sweaty sheets and scratched the hairs on his balls while he listened.

"What was all that about?" his mistress asked him when he dumped the receiver.

"Freddy's over on Wisconsin just got robbed, and one of the gunmen managed to find the time to rape a woman while he was at it."

"Jesus, you're not safe anywhere these days. Why do they want Homicide?"

"He got himself killed doing it."

*   *   *

Luigi Frediano massaged more than his rich clients' scalps—he had licked his way up the social ladder. But he could do hair like nobody else, and the society matrons adored him. Gaultier-wrapped in palest tangerine and honey, perfectly coiffed, he was on hand to escort his famous clients in through the black lacquered doors. He crimped and backbrushed and he listened to the secrets they poured into his ears.

When Lieutenant Malloy arrived, Luigi himself was standing in the banquette-lined entrance, waving his arms violently at the policeman assigned the job of preventing his wealthy clients from leaving, and worse, from coming in to keep appointments. The sight of him nervously touching a fuchsia silk handkerchief to his sweat-beaded forehead irritated Malloy beyond reason.

He was saved from Luigi's attentions by the plainclothes officer waiting for him, who escorted Malloy to the rear of the salon to the small room used by the staff as storeroom-cum-sitting room. It reeked of stale cigarette smoke and Chinese food. A table and a few chairs took up half the floor space. The body of a man took up the rest. He lay sprawled on his back, his head oddly at right angles, with the eyes open. Over his head was a dun-colored stocking; the rest of him was black. Black turtleneck sweater, black trousers with gaping fly, black shoes, black leather gloves.

Malloy squatted down on his heels in silent contemplation. "Run it through for me from the beginning."

Sergeant Frank Jackson, in his late twenties, had retained a fair downy skin that constantly embarrassed him with its peachy glow. It glowed now because Malloy made him nervous. He cleared his throat.

"Three armed men entered the salon at 1100 hours wearing masks—one of them had on a black ski mask, the other two wore flesh-colored tights over their heads. They grabbed the receptionist and threatened her, she buzzed for Luigi Frediano to come out of his office. Frediano then had a gun put to his head and was taken back in the office by the man wearing the ski mask. The other two held the staff and clients with guns. One of them forced a woman back here and raped her."

"Any witnesses?"

"They saw her being taken away at gunpoint, then they were

locked in the cloakroom. They heard screams, but that's all. One of the women fainted."

Malloy stared at the cadaver on the floor. "Who came in here while this guy was raping the girl? Can you tell me?"

"The other one?" Jackson said.

Malloy gave a hawking cough and decided he had to quit smoking. It had been a difficult week. "I don't understand that," he rasped. "I could understand it if he came back and had a go himself. I could understand if he got sore hearing her screams and came in here and made his buddy stop. But go on, don't let me interrupt."

"A client arriving for an appointment found the door locked and thought that was suspicious. She went into the coffee shop next door and made the call. She said Luigi would never close the salon like that without telling her."

"Where was Luigi when the patrolmen got here?" Malloy asked.

"Bound and gagged in the front office. The two gunmen could have used a rear door; it unlocks from the inside. They probably had a vehicle parked in the alley. Then we got here and found the girl and the body." Jackson's Adam's apple plummeted several times. "She didn't look too good, she was . . . conscious, but she wasn't talking—know what I mean—I don't think she could talk . . . Jesus." He gave the body a strangled look.

Malloy sighed. He had thirty years on the Force and he didn't understand the new breed of bleeding-heart cop. Next Jackson would be crying on his goddamn shoulder. "What'd they get away with?"

"Huh? Oh, cash. From the office safe. It had Saturday's takings."

"Yeah." Malloy got stiffly to his feet. "I want this whole place sealed off. I want to know who was here, names, addresses. I want to know everything about the girl, who she is, where she comes from, what she does, everything. And I want the whole damn place gone over top to bottom. Got that?"

Malloy was a grimly unattractive man with a face like a graveyard and chronically bad indigestion. That day it was particularly bad. He wasn't out looking for trouble and already he had one corpse, unidentifiable, some hysterical women none of whom had seen either the rape or the homicide—and his wife wanted him to take her to the theater that night.

He went out of the room and stood looking at the layout. Detectives were poking through everything and measuring distances, the fingerprint technicians were dusting the place down.

"Where in hell's Forensic? They going to take all day getting here?" Malloy snarled at Jackson after two smart-assed broads had been at him claiming diplomatic immunity and wanting the hell out. He went back into the room. Three minutes later Dr. Max Heller came in. Heller was the Medical Examiner for the D. C. police. The man had a fatigued look in his eyes that went beyond fatigue.

"That little guy out there, Luigi. He's got to be giving himself a heart attack," Heller said.

"Yeah," the Lieutenant said, and he smiled for the first time. "And I bet the press are pissing themselves trying to work into a headline the kind of blowjob one of Luigi's clients got here this morning. It'll ruin him."

Heller looked consideringly at the body sprawled at his feet. "What gives?"

"Three guys walk in by the front entrance. One picks over the office and scares the shit out of the little pussymouth, and the other cools his heels while his buddy helps himself to some beaver. Then the guy parting the curls gets his neck broken and the other two walk off. They don't take nothing but some cash from the office safe. It's screwy." He watched the Medical Examiner squat down on his heels. "Whaddaya think? The girl couldn't have done it. Or could she?"

"Nah. Not unless she's strong as an ox and got arms like a gorilla. No, this was done by a professional. Neck broken cleanly."

Heller looked over the rest of the body and at the exposed genitalia with professional interest. The rush of blood that had stiffened the erectile muscles had drained away, leaving the penis flaccid. He stood up.

"With a broken neck it takes five minutes to die. What happens is you lose consciousness, the body is dead, not brain dead. There is a neural discharge and you lose peripheral circulation. That's when your member deflates. You want a full autopsy?"

The Lieutenant had a lifetime habit of sucking his teeth. He stopped briefly. "I want this man taken apart. Track down his dental records if you have to, anything, but I want to know who he is."

Heller shrugged, resigned. "And you want the report sent to you direct, I know. Who's the girl?"

Malloy shoved a British passport at him. "Her pocketbook was found by the chair she had been sitting in. This was in it."

Heller opened the document and looked at the photograph inside, and whistled. "Beautiful woman. India. Unusual name." He rolled the name on his tongue. "India Grey. Born in Hong Kong, 1968. That'd make her twenty-two. Blond, green eyes, mole on right temple." He studied the photograph again. "I'd like to examine her before the hospital boys screw things up. Which hospital did they take her to?"

"Georgetown University. I'm going over there to ask her a few questions. She might be able to give us a handle on this mess."

While Malloy stood coldly to one side of the corpse, watching the forensic expert measuring everything and assessing, India Grey was already unconscious on the operating table, encased from head to toe in green sheets.

The nurses had hoisted her legs up from the hips and anchored her feet in stirrups where they hung strangely in the air. A black rubber mask, clamped on her face, rendered her only semi-recognizably human. Protruding from the mask were several tubes linking her to a mechanical device that hummed and whooshed. Stuck to the back of India Grey's hand was a rubber bung through which the anesthesiologist fed medication, from where it traveled efficiently via an intravenous needle into her bloodstream.

The doctor who sat on the stool between the stretched legs, cautiously probing through the slit in green, worried about his teenage daughter. The idea of some man making a sexual assault on her was intolerable to him. He finished making the repair on India's torn vagina in grim silence. About fifteen minutes later, when he left the operating room, Lieutenant Malloy and the City Police Medical Examiner, Dr. Max Heller, were waiting for him.

He didn't like the way Heller dealt with rape cases, and Malloy was just a plainclothes, hard-nosed cop who had made his reputation working undercover on the college campus sniffing out dissenters during the Nixon years.

"I'm Dr. Lewis," he said. "You wanted to see me?"

The Lieutenant stepped forward and flipped his badge under Lewis's nose. "You admitted a female under your care, name of India Grey. We need to ask her a few questions."

"She'll be kept under sedation for the next few days. Sorry. You'll have to wait."

Malloy frowned. "Well, jeez, I heard she'd been banged, not run over by a friggin' truck."

Lewis glared at him, but he contained his rage.

"We got a homicide here and we need some questions answered. Christ," Malloy growled, "you don't have the guy pumping you drop dead at your feet with a broken neck without noticing something going on. Now, when do we get to see her?"

Lewis looked as though he couldn't wait to get the Lieutenant on the table; he had the zoology department in mind. "How would you like your sex organs rammed and pulverized, then exposed to public view, drugged, fingered, photographed, questioned . . ." He took hold of himself with difficulty. "She was a virgin."

"Virgin?" Malloy repeated the word as though he'd never heard it before. "You think that could be possible?" he asked Heller.

"Believe it," Lewis told him.

"Sorry, sorry—there's not many of them about these days. When she came in, did she have anything to say? Because someone killed the maniac who was on top of here and she must have seen it happen."

"She was incapable of making any kind of coherent statement," Lewis said. "We asked her if there was anyone she wanted us to call. She gave us a name and a phone number. Those were her only words."

The name of the man India Grey asked for was Adrian Pugh, the chargé d'affaires at the British Embassy. The message from the hospital did not reach him until later that afternoon. Five minutes after calling the phone number and speaking to the doctor in charge of the case, he was hurrying through the embassy doors on his way to Georgetown Hospital.

The wind on that spring day was as bitter as his thoughts. India Grey was his cousin. He loved her. Always had. She was one of the few women whose company he didn't dread, and who didn't make his hands break out in a sweat. In many ways he loved her more than his wife.

By the time he arrived, India had regained consciousness. In the white bed in the private third-floor room, she stared at the nurse who was asking her questions.

India Grey was tall with a good body and a face that came to murder men's sleep at night. It was a striking face, pale, intelligent, well-formed, but it was the eyes under the thick dark brows that made it memorable. It was the glassy, flat look in them now that silenced the nurse.

India explored her bruised swollen lips with her tongue, and then moaned softly. It was the clenched sound of someone having her teeth drilled to the roots.

Her body understood—but her body and herself did not seem integrated. And from this knowledge that her body had, the separation was desirable. India's mind didn't wish to know the truth, and this idea, the only idea she could conceive of, was the one that took command. So the reality of not knowing where she was or who she was didn't really exist because she was inhabiting a place where it didn't matter anyway.

The doctors were obliged to inform Adrian Pugh that his cousin was severely traumatized and suffering from amnesia. Her memory loss, if only for the time being, appeared to be total.

On that same afternoon Max Heller was in a rubber "splash suit" at the center table in the autopsy room, carrying on a monologue as he worked. Over his head hung a microphone recording his words; when he wasn't talking he hummed happily. The body on the table had an incision that ran from the neck down to the crotch. Astonishing the things you found in bodies. The ass especially was a repository for all kinds of things—small tubes of vaseline, junk, syringes; anything a man wanted to hide was shoved up his ass. The shoddy surgery he came across never ceased to amaze him either. Nicks in the gut where the knife had obviously slipped, clumsy repair jobs, adhesions gumming the organs up, diseased livers. When Malloy arrived he was prying open the rib cage with a retractor.

The room itself had a hollow, gutted feeling. There were the long tables with marble tops grooved with run-off channels. Racks, pans, sealable jars, flasks containing fluid, drawers with cadavers in them, bottles with baby cadavers. Lights on tripods, camera equipment. Tables with arrays of saws, hammers and chisels, forceps, probes and dissectors, evil-looking, long, curving knives, several weighing scales.

The small scale for weighing tissues and organs was in use. Out of the corner of his eye, Malloy saw the technician brushing crumbs from a small electric saw. He looked, and sure enough, there was a neat little skullcap of bone at the head of the table. The gray matter had been neatly scooped from the cavity and arranged in a more or less recognizable shape in the weighing dish. He felt sick. Deep breathing wasn't any help. The smell was supposed to be entirely drawn out by huge extractor fans above the table, yet a sweetish odor reached his nostrils with each breath: the stench of congealed blood and preserving fluids.

The cadaver on the table was that of a male Caucasian roughly in his late thirties or early forties, with massive shoulders and biceps. What hair the man had was mousy and thinning and had been re-arranged so that it covered his face from the eyebrows down.

Malloy pressed a handkerchief to his mouth. "This the one?"

"The very same." Heller was delving into the thoracic cavity like a kid into a grab bag and studying its contents before choosing. "What d'you know. He had a coronary artery bypass. Nice piece of work, take a look."

"I'll take your word for it," Malloy said, looking away.

"Anything yet on his fingerprints?"

"Nope." He watched Heller reach inside the cadaver. There had to be something wrong with guys who could do that and smile at the same time. "Besides his ticker, what've you come up with?"

"First cervical vertebra—that's the ring of bone that supports the skull—snapped clean off the second." He gave an organ to the tech-nician, who weighed it and passed it back to Heller to slice through with his knife. "Poor bastard was iced right in the act of shooting his load."

Malloy had been avoiding looking at the slivered genital organs; looked at objectively, there was nothing too terrible, but it simply disturbed him. He frowned. "The girl knows what happened in that room and she's claiming loss of memory. Maybe a few questions will help give it a jolt."

Heller picked another body part out, looked at it, and put it back. "The slides Lewis sent over show sperm. But before I make out a report as expert evidence I have to examine her myself."

Malloy sucked his teeth hard. "Give me a couple of days. Maybe she'll get her memory back once the shock wears off. We're walking on eggshells here because already I got some bigshot relation of hers up my ass." He glanced at the big round clock on the wall. Six-thirty. "I got a meeting. The chief's sending down some heat, the CIA have their pricks up about the Russians again."

Russians. Who needed the Russians when every day he had psychopaths, weirdos, dope fiends who would crawl through the sewers, lie, cheat, kill, anything to satisfy their need? Con men, pimps, hustlers, he didn't need the CIA in under his feet bleating about Russians marauding through a hairdresser's shop scaring ladies, killing and raping. He stared hard at the body.

"It'd help a lot if we knew who he was."

Every time Adrian Pugh visited his cousin he was chilled by her apparent indifference. Her eyes in the pale skin, too deep in their sockets, seemed to be the barricades from behind which she watched. She clasped at wrists that still looked sore and chafed and didn't seem to notice any pain. She never spoke.

On the third day he came determined to prompt her into remembering something, and he fastened on the idea of building images for her. Images that would work on nostalgic childhood memories, anything that could reach and lead her back.

Adrian Pugh had the sleek impersonal look habitual to his office and to Royal Naval Commanders, and with India, that helped. There didn't seem anything in that smooth almost abstract face that could worry her.

She watched him mouthing words a syllable at a time—presumably in an effort to make her understand.

Now the face was closer, sidelong and insinuating, but still anonymous. The way he had of talking, as if she had lost all her faculties . . . his voice reached her from far away. She let it go on past.

She didn't want to remember. Because to remember was to feel—and she was afraid of feeling. She preferred to detach herself from that. And she had. Even pain seemed distant, not somehow connected with her.

So she wouldn't listen to the words which were making her rediscover pictures in her mind. She huddled away on the other side of the bed in a panic at these mental images. She refused to look at him, but her ears were catching every nuance of sound, every syllable.

He was telling her—in the same kind of voice the English are apt to use for people too unfortunate and too deprived to have a fluent command of that language—that she had known him since she was six, when he had gone to her birthday party.

He began to describe it, and she saw him standing at the front door holding on to a large pink-wrapped box with a ribbon tied in bows. It was her sixth birthday. Her cousin Adrian; a strange dreamy boy with fragile eyes and a hopeful manner. He was obedient and very polite and everyone disliked him, even the grown-ups. Even her mother.

Everybody except India.

Now she was beginning to remember and the pictures came faster, stuttering, like a silent movie. They materialized from a past that seemed quite independent of her. It was as if her role in it was purely secondary.

The birthday party Adrian referred to was held at four o'clock so that her mother, who was never coherent before noon, would have some leeway. Only, as it happened, four had turned out to be too late. Her mother was on the loose with a bottle of cooking sherry the cook had negligently left out.

India had been born in Hong Kong where her father was Colonial Secretary and her mother was already displaying a predilection for gin and extramarital affairs. When she consistently overstepped the mark and began openly inviting perfect strangers into her bed, they returned to England. Perhaps her father thought the gray weather might have a depressant effect on his wife's hormones. Unfortunately, this was not to be the case. After the birthday party, when her mother was absent with the sherry bottle and the man who had come to entertain the children as a clown, India was sent to a convent. It was a surprising choice, because the family was Protestant to the very core.

School, apparently, was hideous enough not to be forgotten for very long. It surfaced now in the illuminated images as poisonously as ever. The cold of the arctic bathrooms when the nuns yanked inexpertly at her long hair as she stood undressed, teeth chattering. They cut her hair off in the end: the uncaring grasp of those hands, the thick plaits shorn, dropping.

She remembered the horror of seeing the ropes of pale hair lying on the floor and feeling that long ago feeling of nakedness and shame. It triggered the same feeling in her now, a much queerer, more intense feelng of humiliation.

She remembered that she escaped from the convent three times. She always had the train fare to take her back to London, to her father, who would take her to Claridge's for lunch, but then, as certain as the train fares and the lunches, he would return her to Reverend Mother. During this time her own mother lived in a vortex of trained nurses. Later she was sent to a home, for treatment, from where she returned suspiciously subdued, her face bland. Nicely behaved, she tidied up, saw to it the ashtrays were emptied, the peanut bowls filled, attended dinner parties, and not once unbuttoned her blouse to the man on her left.

When India was in her first year at the university, her mother died. She came home to be with her father. She wanted to continue with her history degree, but she would no more have left her father when he needed her than commit one of the cardinal sins.

But hadn't she? Hadn't she left him?

India sat up in the night. She had left him. She had. She raked the white hospital sheets from her, intolerably obsessed with that one image.

She was leaving home, she didn't know why, but she remembered she was standing with her bag at the door of his room . . . and seeing him. He was weeping into his nicotine-stained hands, an awful, harsh, muffled sound , and his veins, swollen and blue at his temples as if he were suffocating . . .

And then, and then she was walking away . . . Why?

She couldn't see. When she wanted to, the memory twisted from her and she couldn't see, she couldn't see anything. It was not until the nurse reached her that she realized she was screaming.

Two

It was after midnight when Jack Donovan walked up the steps to the polished door of his Georgetown house and let himself in.

The brick and timber residence had come into being in the eighteenth century when George Town (as it was then known) developed into an important port on the Potomac River. Since, it had settled nicely into a pleasant tree-shaded street of the modern Georgian town that lies ten blocks square within the city of Washington, D.C. The 1930s had seen the house restored and renovated, but not much else had changed. The high-ceilinged, handsome rooms, the scent of leather preservative, fresh flowers, and money: it was the kind of elegant, colonial-style townhouse women burned to get across the threshold and become mistress of.

Jack Donovan had tulips growing in the teak boxes at the beautifully proportioned front windows. He hired his housekeeper's husband, Fitzroy, to keep the windowboxes and the tiny courtyard out back in trim and care for the weeping fig trees he had growing in big porcelain pots inside the house. Usually he stopped to inspect his trees for red spider mites.

Usually.

Tonight he went straight to his den and pressed the play button on his answering machine, then he turned up the volume, pulled the ends of his bow tie loose, and sat down to listen. He swiveled slowly from side to side in the leather bucket chair, letting his body relax with the motion. Eyes half-closed and sunk in thought, he bore a striking resemblance to a contented alligator.

Not that this in any way detracted from a charm of manner which drew people. He had the facility for putting people at their ease: he was an attentive listener and many discovered that they had said more than might have been wise to a young man who at thirty-nine was already a partner in the influential and long-established law firm of Kennedy, Winter and, now, Donovan.

Tonight? Christ, he was tired.

The $100-a-plate dinner he was obligated to attend in the name of party politics had gone on far longer than the food or company warranted. Tom Winter had managed to dodge out of it, but Richard Kennedy had been there with his wife Jane, who, when she came out of the powder room, sat next to Jack determinedly revealing some intimate details of her husband's sex life he would rather not have heard.

Well, hell, he'd begun to wonder what she had been using to powder her nose with, when he felt her hand under the table. Then she was clawing at the bulge in his crotch like she was mainlining it.

He was a sensual man and well endowed (maybe just a shade straitlaced about being felt up beneath the tablecloth at a public function by the wife of his partner, who happened to be at the moment addressing the dinner guests), and Jane even had earlobes that were sexy, but he thought she had gone too far this time.

The swiveling stopped as he listened to the answering machine intently. He waited, then he leaned over, punched the rewind button, and ran the section of tape through again.

The message gave information about the robbery at Luigi Frediano's salon and named the woman who had been raped, and was now a witness to a killing, as India Grey. He was told that the woman was still in the hospital acting less than normal and claiming she couldn't remember a thing about it, and Luigi was falling out of his asshole over the fact that a certain Lieutenant was giving him a hard time thinking the raid had been a put-up job. Jack had to get over there and find out if the woman was crazy or what, or if she was just scared shitfaced and keeping her mouth shut.

The message ended with the Washington address where India Grey was living.

Jack stared at the tape recorder.

The story had been virtually pushed off the evening news three days ago because of a panic about the partial meltdown—which had only just come to light—of a nuclear reactor in Maine. Only a brief mention of a robbery at an exclusive hairdressing salon and the fact that one of the women had been raped.

Jack tapped his teeth with a pen, then he swung his chair around to the computer on the side table. Ten minutes were spent typing in information until he had a go-ahead signal. Jack chose a data bank listing information on property and entered the access code. Minutes later he knew that the house India Grey lived in was an embassy residence owned by the New Zealand Government. It took him a further fifteen minutes to find out the name of the individuals residing there, and by then he was into pedigree information.

When the name Douglas Ross appeared, Jack sat back in the chair and looked at the profile he had on the screen. Douglas Ross was with the New Zealand Department of Trade, he was responsible for the sale of New Zealand lamb, and he employed a nanny by the name of India Grey.

While Jack was wondering how much India Grey knew and how much she was keeping to herself, the woman in question was pressing her face (the side that didn't hurt) into a hospital pillow.

Things were running through her bright mind, rapidly and noisily, but not in succession. She was closer to going crazy than she knew. Her memory was in overdrive. It was unearthing details she'd been happy to forget about for years.

But far from wanting to remember why she had seen her father in such distress, she wasn't even trying to think. All she wanted was to go to sleep.

Things had gone too far. Images, pictures, voices telling her the most distressing things imaginable—sometimes not even connected to the right pictures as if the sound was running on the wrong film track—it was destroying her. In the last five hours since Adrian had left she had remembered so much, in sick vivid detail.

But there was a compulsion too. There were things she had to know, look at again. Things that sickened her, that at the time made her take the only option that seemed open to her. Perhaps now she might be able to see them differently.

The reason why she was living in Washington, D. C., and not in London went a long way back. As far back as her last day at school.

Walking down the steps on that last day of days, hugging herself with excitement. Cars parked everywhere, girls waving to parents. She could see her hat now, sailing in the air with dozens of others to be abandoned on the sodden lawns. She had run giggling down the drive to where her father waited, pulled open the door to throw herself in and be hugged and kissed and then—

"Jeremy Hornby-Jones." The neat little man in the back seat held out a barely thawed hand: her father's private secretary. There had been a few of them. Her father had entered politics and the Commons, become important.

Jeremy Hornby-Jones had staying power. He was still there after her mother died and India was home where she had always wanted to be, with her father. People told her often how young (meaning the right marriageable age for India), debonair, and very charming they thought Jeremy was. Privately, India considered him a puffed-up, undersized little twit.

Two years later she came back to the house on Carlyle Square after a weekend away. They were expecting her on Monday, not Sunday at midnight.

She had gone to the kitchen for a glass of water, then quietly slipped upstairs. A chink of light escaped from beneath her father's bedroom door. She knocked softly and went in to say good night; often she would find him asleep behind his spectacles, an open book on his chest. That night, she found him lying naked on the bed with Jeremy Hornby-Jones.

But here, lying in the hospital bed with the memories screaming at her, the pictures in her mind which she couldn't make disappear just faded out. India had absolutely no recollection of what happened next. Had she shut the door and gone to bed? Had her father come out of the room in his dressing gown? Her only memory was of him knocking on her bedroom door the next morning.

It was all she could do to answer it. She had looked at him. A lock of pale hair fell engagingly over one eye, a white silk scarf showed in the rolled neck of his monogrammed robe.

"India, please," he pleaded, when he saw she was about to shut the door.

"All these years?" she asked.

"India," he implored, "I understand. You feel shocked. But given time—"

"All those young men when I was growing up," she whispered.

"Well . . ." he smiled, but without mirth, "not all, that would be excessive. Don't, please." He thrust a kid-clad foot in the door. "I'll send him away, I promise."

What she had always thought of as a liberal tolerance for other people's sexual preferences fell a long way short when it involved the father she adored. India could not come to terms with the sense of betrayal, the literally physical nausea she felt. She nursed a terrible hatred for Jeremy.

She had left home the next day. When she had gone into her room for the last time to pick up her bag, she had found an envelope propped against the clock on the mantelpiece. It was a note from her father wishing her well, and a very large check. India replaced the letter in the envelope and left it, then she carefully ripped the check into shreds and dropped them into the wastepaper basket.

Oh yes. She had left. She had left her father weeping in his room. It was him she had run to in the middle of some terrifying night when she was small. He who had given her the sanctuary of his arms and dandled her on his knee and made soothing sounds with his vinegary breath.

And now it was the middle of another terrifying night, and the nurse was shining the flashlight in her face.

"Another bad dream, honey?"

India shielded her eyes from the glare and realized she had been crying.

"Honey, I know what you're feeling. A real good friend of mine was raped. She thought she'd never get over it, but she did, and honey, you just have to believe that you will too."

India's memory went only to the point where she was at the door. It shied away from what had taken place in the room. She could not remember screaming until her lungs hurt, until she was breathless.

She didn't need her memory to know—it was all there in the

dreadful bruised feeling inside here, the way people looked at her.

Everybody knew. Everyone in Washington knew, probably down to the last prurient little detail.

No one, with the exception of Dr. Lewis and the night nurse, mentioned "it" by name.

Rape. Rape. India said it aloud; two or three times. Even the word carried an insult, a threat.

No one actually wanted to sit down by her bed and talk about the thing that had happened to her, as if the plain facts were too distressing, in the way that death is too distressing a subject to discuss with the terminally ill. The prescription was for an umbrella cloud of tranquilizers and palliative words.

The previous afternoon Adrian's wife Harriet had come in to see her.

"We all love you, India." She had pressed India's hand before quickly going on in a bright voice to discuss the baby and the terrible weather.

"There's no point in dragging the thing up if she can't remember it," India had heard Harriet whisper to Adrian at the door when he arrived. Harriet presumably thought she was deaf as well as dumb.

But there was a very inconvenient loose end that refused to go away. A man was dead, and even if Harriet could dismiss the whole thing as a freak accident, adding that the police were over-reacting, something had to be done. Someone had to tell India that her attacker had been murdered, and tell her soon before she heard a somewhat blunter version from another source. It was Adrian who stopped off at the hospital on his way to the embassy early on the morning of her fourth day there. He found India distraught.

"Bad night?"

"Yes," she said, her voice muffled by an outsize tissue. "It all started come back in chunks." She wiped her nose.

"Fairly indigestible," Adrian murmured in sympathy.

"Yes." Adrian knew nothing of the reason for her leaving home. She had told no one. The least she could do for her father was to keep his secret safe.

"But . . . you don't remember yet what happened in the room?"

"Adrian, I know I was raped—I mean, not precisely—I have no memory of it. What I know is more like secondhand."

"That's my cue, I'm afraid. You see, old thing, something happened in that room you have to know about. The man who raped you was dead when the police found him."

"Dead! God, don't tell me he had a heart attack, that would be too ironic."

"Not a heart attack," Adrian said with the casualness of a man worried about the reaction to what he was about to impart. "A broken neck."

"*What?* Oh my God," she said shakily, "are you saying he was murdered? That someone came in while I was there and killed him?"

"They think that's what happened, but they don't know for sure—except that he was dead when they found him."

"With me," India said in a wavering voice. "I was there, wasn't I?"

"Yes, well . . . yes."

"Murdered. You mean his body was lying—how was it lying? On top of me?"

"India, I think you should—"

"What? What should I do?"

"I was going to say perhaps you shouldn't think too much about this for now."

"No. I won't. I'm fine, I'm fine." She slid down on the pillows and stared at the ceiling.

"There will have to be some questions, I'm afraid."

"The police?" Her voice was shrill with dismay. She sprang up into a sitting position. Her gown was crumpled and twisted: "I don't want questions. I don't want to remember. Oh, Adrian, I wake up in the night and feel disgust and loathing—for myself, Adrian. I'm disgusted with myself. Can't you keep them away? Just until I feel a bit more together. It's not as if I can help them—I just don't remember."

"I'll try every way in the book to keep them out. And Dr. Lewis is holding them off as well." Dr. Lewis had in fact told him that an intrusion like that could be very damaging for India and would probably set her recovery back months.

The duty nurse was new, but she had her instructions. She looked at the badge Lieutenant Malloy proffered and shook her head. "Dr. Lewis said no visitors for Ms. Grey."

Malloy gave the usual grimace he thought passed for a smile.

"We're not visitors, Nurse." He reached over and picked up her phone and dialed an internal number. When a voice answered he asked to speak to the hospital's Chief of Staff. Thirty seconds later he spoke briefly and handed the phone over to the nurse, who colored and stammered, "Yes, sir," into the mouthpiece three times.

"We'll need a nurse to come with us," Malloy told her. He slung his coat over his shoulder and walked back along the corridor and joined Max Heller.

India Grey was sitting awkwardly on the side of her bed brushing her hair. She looked up in surprise when the two men, followed by the nurse, came into the room.

Malloy pulled out his shield and ID card and held them up to her. He exchanged a glance with Heller, who produced his ID and a word of explanation.

"We're investigating a homicide that was committed in your presence on March 30."

"I want somebody with me," India said. Her blond hair was disarrayed and her forehead beaded with sweat.

"The nurse will be here, but you can have anybody you like." Malloy smile was full of reassurance. "However," he continued smoothly, "this is purely routine. We came by to ask your help with one or two questions. All we really want is for you to give your version of the events as they happened in Freddy's on the morning of March 30."

India stared at him from a face devoid of makeup. She moistened her lips, which Malloy saw were drying and peeling. "I'll try," she said, and moved further along the bed away from him, so that her body was braced against the pillows. Her eyes warned him to keep his distance.

Malloy took the chair by the bed, moved it back a pace, and sat on it. He smiled agreeably and nodded to her to begin. When she was finished recounting her version of the event, he leaned forward a little. "The man who dragged you from your chair. Did you know him?"

"No," India said, a little startled by the question.

"Who killed him?"

There was a brief intake of breath. She shook her head. "I don't know."

"Did you go to the beauty parlor for any other purpose than to have your hair done?"

"No." Her hands pleated and unpleated the sheet.

"Did a man of unknown identity force you to have sexual relations with him?" She nodded. "You made no attempt to resist."

"I . . ." She was looking at him, appalled: a fixed disbelieving stare. He kept on the attack, not giving her a chance to think, hoping she would let something slip that would give him a link. Because, Christ, nothing added up. Nothing was taken from the clients, and most of them were loaded: furs, Rolex watches, diamond stud earrings. An armed hold-up, three men, and they only took cash from the safe which Luigi Frediano claimed was Saturday's takings. There was something going down.

"How did he have sexual relations with you? Describe what happened."

"I can't," she gasped. "I don't remember anything that happened in the room."

"There was another man. A man wearing a black ski mask. Who was he?"

"I don't know, I didn't see—"

"Was the man black or white?"

"I don't—"

"Was he young or old?"

"I don't know."

"The man who assaulted you spoke. What kind of accent did he have?"

"I couldn't tell. American, I don't know. His voice was brutal. And then he screamed the words at me."

"Who killed him?" He saw the film of sweat on her face. "Tell us, Miss Grey. Who was it?" Her expression didn't change, yet her look was different, you could see it in her eyes. Polite, oh very polite, but cool. Yeah, she wasn't just some blond bimbo who was going to let him push her around. She knew who she was, and how.

"Lieutenant . . ." She said it the way the Brits do, Le*ff*tenant, and she pronounced all the words so the last letter came out with a little clip. "I have told you everything I can remember."

He believed her.

He stood up and thanked her before leaving Heller to get on with his examination.

Malloy walked away from the room. It had been a long shot, but worth a try. And it still didn't add up. The questions were still in his mind. Was the raid done by professionals? And if professionals did it, they were after more than they allegedly got. But a pro wouldn't get mixed up in a rape case. Maybe it was just three punks having a go.

"Just routine," Heller said. He plucked a pair of rubber gloves from the trolley and smiled. The smile stayed on too long.

The nurse took away the pillows and got her to lie flat on her back with her knees up. "Doctor won't take a moment," she said primly.

A trickle of sweat ran down India's arms.

"Be over in a moment." The nurse patted her on the shoulder and began drawing up the gown. "Open your legs."

"No. Please, please. No." India held on stubbornly to the gown while the nurse's smile became forced.

"Give her the injection, Nurse, please," Heller said in a quiet voice. India looked at the trolley then and saw the hypodermic already drawn up. She went rigid with fear.

"Just a little prick," the nurse said cooly. The jab came instantly. "There you are, Ms. Grey."

Her fingers grew weaker and the gown was taken from their grasp. It was horrible. In her mind she was still fighting them, she knew everything that was happening, but she had lost control. Her muscles were congealing into jelly. The nurse propped up her legs, but they wouldn't stay propped, so she held them; her eyes were disinterested, like a spayed animal's.

Heller carried out the examination swiftly, and as gently as he could. She couldn't see his face, only the nurse's. She heard him say something and then his voice drifted away. There was a creeping numbness in her legs. Then it all became unreal.

Dr. Jason Lewis was fuming when he left the Chief of Staff's office at five that afternoon. India Grey was his patient. She wasn't ready for a police inquisition. In his fury he almost ran into some big guy in a trench coat. He mumbled an apology and stalked on.

"Ah, excuse me. Could you tell me where I can find Miss India Grey?"

Lewis was almost ten paces away by that time. He stopped and shot a look back. The man he had bumped into was walking toward him, hands in the pockets of his coat, nonchalant as hell. He looked like a journalist from the *Washington Post*. One of those cocksure types who would sniff out a story on the merest shred of evidence and keep on the scent until he had run his quarry to ground.

"We don't have a Miss Grey in. Sorry."

Jack grinned. "But you did, right." It wasn't a question.

"You already know, so why ask." Jesus, thought Lewis as he turned to go, how did he find out? They had a "No Information" red sticker stuck all over her file. There was a weird gripping sensation in his stomach. Christ, he was getting an ulcer.

The elusive Miss Grey. He was getting nowhere. Second time that day he had had the same type of answer. It looked like somebody was keeping her undercover. Maybe she did know something.

Jack ambled along to the phone booth to try the Ross number again. If there was no answer this time, he would have to work on the duty nurse some more, and he figured that wouldn't be too painful, the way she had of standing up real close with those big hard nipples poking right at him.

"Hello. Ross family residence."

It was a child's keen, piping voice. Jack cleared his throat. "Hi there. Who's this speaking?"

"Emily Ross, I'm six."

"Hello, Emily. Think you could ask India Grey to come to the phone for me?" Jack didn't have the remotest what he was going to say to the woman, if she did.

"Miss Grey went away. I've got a new rabbit."

"Gee, a rabbit. Where did Miss Grey go to, Emily?"

"I'm going to name him Pinky."

"A pink rabbit!"

Giggle, giggle down the line. "He's not pink, silly."

"He's not? I don't believe you and I don't believe you know where Miss Grey went to."

"Yes I do." Jack picked up on the kid's sharp note of triumph and smiled with satisfaction. Emily was braying the secrets out now. "She went to stay with Mr. and Mrs. Pugh because she's not feeling well."

It took him another five minutes to find out where the guy worked, besides a minute-by-minute description of what Pinky was up to with the other rabbit in the hutch. But when he did finally get the information he wanted, he thanked her and got off the line before he had her mother on, wanting to know who was taking to her daughter. What was she doing anyway, letting Emily talk so long to just anybody that rang up? Jack had very definite ideas about the rearing of children.

He rang up the British Embassy and asked to talk to Mr. Pugh. A snotty voice told him that Mr. Adrian Pugh had left for the day and, no, Jack couldn't have his home address.

"Don't worry, lady," Jack said when he hung up. "I can find that out for myself."

Harriet plopped baby Timothy into India's arms. "Be a love and hold Small for me while I do something about lunch. What do you feel like?"

After the business with the police, Harriet and Adrian had insisted she leave the hospital and come home with them. India was so knocked out with sedatives she barely noticed the transition. The bad feeling came only when the hourglass of tranquilizers ran out.

She gave Harriet a big smile. It was the slightly unhinged smile of a person recovering from anesthesia who finds that against all expectations she has made it back alive. "Really, I don't mind what we have."

India wanted to have a bath.

Her brain told her that was ridiculous. She'd already had two that day.

She must. She didn't feel clean.

The smell—his musky sweaty odor—had penetrated her skin.

There was no smell, except for the perfume she was drenched in, but she wanted a bath anyway. The urge, basic and compulsive, had nothing to do with common sense. It carried all the hallmarks of a full-blown obsession.

After lunch, when Harriet was snoring on her bed and the nanny was walking Timothy up and down the avenue outside, India seized the opportunity and ran the bath to nearly overflowing. It did overflow, slopping over the edges as she got in.

She gave a deep, relieved sigh. She floated. A sort of peace overcame her . . . She could lie in the clean, shining water for hours.

Her job . . . The job as live-in nanny to three schoolchildren, the job that supported her and enabled her to carry on with her graduate level classes in American history at Georgetown University . . . That job . . . The classes . . . seemed so small. Just dots in the distance. Her life, disappearing away from her.

Her life: it seemed unreclaimable.

Three

Although India's cousin Adrian had managed to keep her name out of the newspapers, he hadn't been able to stop the gossip suppurating from the lairs of those sleek wealthy women who killed time being pampered head-to-toe at Freddy's salon.

In the space of days, India Grey had become a hot property. There was something of the mystery about her. Her background impelled curiosity. There was a flavor of Tennessee Williams: "The mother—they do say . . . Booze and men, quite insatiable . . ."

If she had been married—but she wasn't. She was single, vulnerable, and she had the kind of beauty women claw each other about. The wicker peacock chairs on the huge screened porches whispered on the warm spring mornings as the ladies leaned forward over their morning coffee cups, the name of India Grey impaled on their tongues, their eyes watering with the absorbing question of rape. "My dear—"

Was she a Blanche Dubois, palely blond, eloquent and helpless, seized on by a grunting violent beast? Or was there something in the woman herself, something wanton, something she was stained with? Something of the essence of a whore. Men knew, didn't they? It was this question that tormented India. Fright had given way to shame and guilt. She looked at her face in the mirror and saw a whore. It was there in her makeup; she was her mother's daughter, wasn't she? The idea obsessed her. But in prayers, in litanies to the Virgin, she was too ashamed to speak the word and it remained there in her mind, poisonously reproachful.

And the worst thing, India was discovering, was that she couldn't talk about it. Especially she couldn't talk to Harriet, whose only advice so far had been for India to put it right out of her mind, as if such a thing was possible.

"It," unfortunately, was locked in (locked in with the guilt that something dirty in her invited men to unfasten their pants) and there was no actual memory of the rape India could drag out, examine, come to terms with, accept, dispose of. Or indeed do anything positive with.

India hated going out. She lived in fear of having people, strangers, stare at her. Men sizing her up, using locker-room language to discuss her and living a fantasy that women want to be banged over the kitchen draining board or on the hard top of an office desk.

She actually thought of going back to London and packed her suitcases, and then unpacked them again and lay on her bed.

She had the usual symptoms of someone clinically depressed; loss of appetite, loss of weight, and an overriding sense of failure.

She didn't, of course, talk to a doctor as she wasn't ill, in the proper sense. Americans had a mania for psychotherapy, but to the Pughs' English sensibilities the very word was suggestive of mental illness, bedlam, and the West Wing—no one mentioned it.

Then, coming down to breakfast one morning, India overheard Harriet complaining to Adrian.

"I tell you, she's becoming psychotic."

"For God's sake, she's disturbed, all she needs is time."

"How much time? Her mother was disturbed for the best part of thirty years," Harriet replied.

The remark unleashed anger. Not the kind that flashes out and is done with. The kind that burns away quietly—but burns. India needed that corrosive little remark to spur her on. She had lost the proper sense of who she was, and she began the struggle to find her own identity.

To help get rid of the feeling of worthlessness, it was necessary to be busy. India threw herself into the christening arrangements for Timothy. When Harriet went to Garfinckel's to get some dishy little frock that she was nearly "expiring with longing for," India went too. She clipped the boxwood and repotted the utterly neglected houseplants; simple tasks that helped her bruised mind find the courage to keep fighting, to get over the hurt, to hold her own.

"Bliss really, to have her normal again," Harriet commented over the *Washington Post* one morning at breakfast.

On the day of the christening, India dressed with care. The soft silky dress that Harriet had insisted on buying her clung all too revealingly to her figure, and was rejected for a wide-shouldered high-necked blouse and smartly cut skirt. She put on her coat, feeling the soft texture under her hands, remembering the time when her father had taken her to Harrods to buy it. The hat she borrowed from Harriet. It was a small circlet of fur, and it suited India, made her feel good about herself for the first time since "it" had happened.

Jack Donovan sat in Old St. John's Church in Georgetown, and fidgeted restlessly. They were taking their time about it. Why didn't the priest call the family up and dunk the baby and get on with it? He looked around.

Some gathering for a baptism. Directly behind him sat the official from the District Attorney's office who had returned him a favor and got him on the list. And here and there in the rows he recognized a face. A senator, a police chief, a Supreme Court justice.

The family sat on the other side of the church in the front row and from where he was sitting Jack had a good view of them. He tried to figure out who was who.

The guy in the English haircut sitting beside the woman holding the baby had to be Adrian Pugh. The two old folk, grandparents.

That left two other women. One had a florist's arrangement on her head, and the other he couldn't see for the wide-brimmed hat in front of him.

He angled his head, still couldn't quite get her in his line of vision. Then the yacht in front of him moved and he had her.

How about that. She was blond. Not just blond. Hair that held the pale blaze of winter sunshine and fell straight and heavy across the curve of her cheek to her shoulder. He could fall in love with a woman who had hair like that. Around her head was a circlet of fur. He hoped this was India Grey, and not the garden-patch beside her.

Now she was getting up and he saw she was tall and slender. Even in her big-shouldered beige coat that could have sheltered a couple of illegal immigrants, he could tell she had a great figure.

And the way she walked when she rose to go up to the front. He couldn't take his eyes off her; whoever she was, he had to meet her.

For the rest of the ceremony he didn't let her out of his sight. He rehearsed what he was going to say to her. Nothing he thought of seemed right, and it was suddenly very important that he say the right thing.

When the ceremony was over he tried to get to the door as fast as decency permitted, so he could be right behind her when she walked out. The family took their time; there was a bunch of people wanting to breathe all over the baby. If he was a parent, he would want to get his kid home before it caught a cold virus from everybody coughing and sneezing.

Then she was there, being swept past him in a crush of people all wanting to get out first to take pictures of the baby coming out of the church in its mother's arms.

They were almost through the doors and he was right behind her when the woman with the yacht on her head cut across, locked on to the arm of a friend, and he had these two overweight women lodge like the QE2 in dry dock right in front of him. His left shoulder was against the door, and he could see the tall blond woman he hoped was India slipping away through the crowd toward the curb. She would get in a car. He might never see her again. At this point, Jack didn't care who she was.

"Excuse me, ladies." He squeezed through, sidled around a wheelchair containing an octogenarian in full regimental uniform, and kept going. There she was. He was right behind her.

And that's when it happened. When she turned to suddenly avoid a reporter and he was face to face with her. The old boy in his wheelchair was cutting a swathe through the crowd and coming right at them.

He grabbed her arm—and she wrenched it back with her eyes blazing at him in a look that stopped his insides. Fear and anger and guilt, only doubled, trebled, all mixed up. The words he had planned to say stuck in his throat.

It all happened in an instant—the longest moment of his whole life.

Then she saw the wheelchair and moved aside. Green eyes, slightly slanted. And she had thick dark lashes and brows and wonderful dewy white skin. She smelled as though she had a bucket of scent on, but he liked that.

"I'm sorry." Was that him croaking like that? "I didn't mean to startle you."

"No, please. It's I who should apologize."

"I'm Jack Donovan. Can I give you a lift back to the house?"

What else was he to do? He had this tremendous feeling and in two minutes someone else was going to come and claim her and she would be swept away from him if he didn't move fast. Maybe it didn't have the finesse you would expect from a Harvard man, but what else? He couldn't stand there like a dummy.

The wind fanned her hair out from under the little fur hat; it was wonderful and silky and full of lights.

"Thank you, Mr. Donovan, but—" The voice was so quiet and nice, he was hanging on to her arm and looking into her eyes, and she hesitated, looking at him too and for a crazy moment there, he thought she was going to say yes. Say yes, and let him walk her away.

He could actually see himself helping her into the front seat of his Mercedes 500 SL convertible, tucking in the soft folds of her camel-hair coat before he shut the door.

"Excuse us." The one he figured as being Adrian Pugh was by her side. Same quiet, well-bred English voice, smiling, already drawing her away, polite as hell but not going to be held up by a stranger.

Jack stared blankly after them. She turned round once, looking at him, not smiling or anything, just looking.

It was a lost kind of look that went straight to Jack's heart. He knew then that he had to see her again. Then she got into the back seat, the tall fair guy got in after her, and the car slid away.

He walked back a block and got into his car. Jesus, he didn't even get the usual kick seeing all the dials come to life.

Before he left Georgetown he made a stop at Goldstein's on M Street. Behind the counter as always stood Goldstein's assistant, old and bent and as fragile as one of those antique chairs you felt would break the moment you put any weight on it.

He chose a sterling silver rattle and had it gift-wrapped, then back in his car he headed straight along M Street, turning up 23rd Street and then northwest on Massachusetts Avenue. It was an avenue of elegant villas; he slowed, looking for the number he had written down.

*   *   *

The Reverend Charles E. Norton had Adrian Pugh locked in a corner of his own living room, wedged in between a tufted club chair and a nest of antique mahogany tables with Queen Anne legs.

"So I estimate for the restoration of the roof alone we would need in the region of, say, a hundred thousand dollars. A conservative estimate. The thing is, we, I mean the Old St. John's Church Restoration Committee, we need someone to take up the cause, run a charity drive for us. Now if we, the Restoration Committee, could only—"

The words kept coming in a spray of Gilbey's gin which the reverend had been steadily, and without visible effect, imbibing, but Adrian Pugh's attention was elsewhere. His look of concerned interest was in overdrive while he tried to figure out who his wife was talking to. Same chap who had been with India outside the church. Probably one of the people Harriet had added to the list at the last moment. He was suddenly aware that the diatribe had stopped.

"Ah, yes. I think my wife is—"

"Exactly," the Reverend aspirated, "exactly who we, the committee, had in mind to organize a few charity lunches."

Jack Donovan wiped the icing from his fingers and proclaimed the christening cake magnificent. Helped down with a glass of Dom Perignon, it was. "Tell me," he asked Harriet, "was that your sister in church? Little fur hat, blond hair, sort of swings on the collar every times she moves?"

"Oh, that would be India. Adrian's cousin. Great girl. You don't think a bit much sherry—the cake—a bit much sherry?"

"Sherry? No, Ma'am. Adrian's cousin, is she here?"

"Goodness, she's here somewhere. Look around and find her, do. She's been awfully down in the dumps lately."

Jack went through to the room on the other side of the entry gallery, where groups of people were standing around talking and dropping crumbs on the Chinese carpets. No sign of India. The dining room, with the kitchen beyond, led off the room and he wandered through. In the kitchen two Mexican women were stacking a dishwasher; they took no notice of him. The kitchen table was covered with bottles. In the middle of the room a waiter was methodically lifting each glass from his tray and draining it blind. Jack passed on in his search, earning a look of bleary concentration.

*   *   *

Abigail Porter, who was a Vanderbilt and never once forgot it, circled closer. Her voice had its characteristic bite. "But you're looking just darling, not a teeny bit like a person in the dead center of a nervous collapse."

India hung on to her champagne glass. "Not a bit, I assure you."

"I know I wouldn't be out of bed yet if it was me, my first husband was so horny, my dear—" bony fingers clutching at India's arm accompanied the story with a tattoo of red-pointed nails.

India stared desperately into the woman's needle-prick pupils and wondered how she could get away. She felt exhausted, like a person who was drugged, well, she was drugged, and with the champagne—

A rough, warm, masculine voice was asking, "Abigail, I thought they had you off the booze?" And the man who had taken her arm outside the church was there.

Abigail's ivory matte finish almost glowed. She simpered, "Why, Jack Donovan, I declare, you're an old tease," then cried, "Goddamnit, Jack, they've got me off everything! No one's going to fuss over a little champagne at a christening party. Now let me introduce you to this divine creature. This is India Grey."

"We met." Jack enclosed India's hand in his own—his skin was dry and warm like desert sand—and released it again before the action could distract her. He was big and comfortable, and the warmth he exuded was an act of communication by itself.

His smile was drowsy-eyed and thoroughly disarming. His talk was as easy as his smile, and she must have been listening because she wasn't aware that most of the other guests had dwindled away until Harriet was upon them.

"We have dinner reservations and, er, Jack, please say you'll join us. And Abigail, you'll come, of course."

Abigail touched her forehead with a corner of a lace handkerchief and acquiesced. "Darling, I'd love to. But I let Cooper have my car and he hasn't arrived, I can't think what has happened."

Jack Donovan accepted the invitation and put his car at their disposal.

Harriet consulted India, a glance. "Why don't we go on, you know how restaurants are these days with reservations, and you come with Jack and Abigail. Could you do that for us, Jack?"

"Be my pleasure, Ma'am." The dark head inclined slightly, that hint of conspiracy, the deep voice vibrated with humor.

Oh, she should have left then. She tried to, politely, but Harriet wouldn't hear of it and her teeth smiled at India; the smile said, if India was going to carry on in this stupid fashion she would end up in the funny farm. And India knew she didn't stand a chance against Harriet. Few people did. They found after a while that life was more palatable if they just went along with her. India left to get her things.

The restaurant was a cheerful little Italian place on Connecticut Avenue, not far from Dupont Circle. Jack knew it. "They do this wonderful dish, steamed crabs with tomatoes, mushrooms, garlic, little pieces of bread fried in oil," he told India, adroitly claiming the place next to her in the wooden stall.

He looked lovingly at the menu. "They make the best minestrone in Washington," he said, "and wait until you taste their cannelloni stuffed with mozzarella, eggs, minced pork and veal and minced onion."

India smiled politely and vacillated over the printed columns. He leaned over and sought out a dish, running his fingers down the page. She felt the heat coming off his body, felt it closing in on her with a confused uproar of contradictory emotions—when he touched her, the shock paralyzed her stomach. She felt sick.

Jack, apparently, was used to women spoiled for choice and cheerfully took it upon himself to order for her. He seemed to know the waiter well and called him Carlo. When the pasta dish arrived and Carlo began ladling the clam sauce on top, Jack tucked his napkin in and began eating. He nodded, halting the delivery of his fork to flash Carlo a look of extravagant joy; *"Magnifico!"*

Suddenly India found her appetite again, her digestive juices released by the delicious aromas. The needle-edginess had quite gone. How could anyone be nervous about the man sitting beside her, who tucked his napkin under his chin, who had molten brown eyes dancing with little gold flecks, and whose eyebrows flew about like seagulls in a child's painting?

By the time the desserts arrived the two were talking like old acquaintances, the conversation had turned into a discussion of street crime, and she was feeling as relaxed and comfortable as a baby being lulled by its mother.

But somewhere in the last few minutes the subject had changed to the robbery at Freddy's, and the fine feeling of repletion and well-being was fleeing away.

"I believe they still haven't traced the man who did it . . ." Jack said, adding quietly, "I understand you were there that morning."

"Yes."

"Would it be impertinent of me to ask you one or two questions?" Jack asked. His brown eyes were expansive with sympathy for her.

"To what purpose?" India asked, her heart beating hard.

"Let's say I'm interested. It's not every day you meet someone who can tell it first hand. How does it feel being the one right at the scene?"

Leave it! Let it go, she thought. He doesn't know, don't get angry now and embarrass him. But the anger came flashing out.

"I was the woman who was raped. What do you think?"

He was looking directly at her.

She felt nasty, not dismayed at what she had said, but the way she had said it.

"Oh, Jesus—I'm sorry for bringing it up. I really am."

And then, while part of her reacted to the wealth of concern and the shock in his eyes and sincerely believed he was sorry, another part sat back and wondered if he hadn't maneuvered her to this point—whether or not he hadn't manipulated their meeting, just so that he could question her.

"Well," she said in the awkward silence, "I have no memory of it, so you see, I'm not a very good witness to ask, really." Then she turned a little aside. The moment passed, Adrian began talking to her, and soon it was time to leave.

Jack leaned over, "May I see you home?"

She declined. She couldn't imagine him forcing her to do anything against her will, but she wasn't ready yet to be alone with a man.

First the sheer black stockings, rolled and smoothed up the thighs and fastened to red silk garters. The French camisole in black lace, the floral kimono floating, gossamer-thin over bare shoulders. A stream of scent showering throat and wrists, the crème de la crème inner thighs—ravishing.

From the large red Moroccan-leather box came a blond wig. Exceptionally fine, healthy hair. The right color. Did anyone know how hard it was to get it just that color? Not too dark, not too pale and sickly looking. The only hair that came close was on the girl in the salon that day.

The memory brought out a cold sweat and the wig was placed on a stand. Well, cheer up, sweetie—pout in the mirror—mix another martini and put on one of those little ricky-tick hats, froth of net, perched to one side. Divine on all that loose hair. Darling, a hit.

Luigi Frediano was getting ready for a Saturday night of delights. Leaning over, pressing the play button on the tape machine, waiting for a moment so he could come in with the Ink Spots singing "If I Didn't Care."

Behind Luigi, in the mirror's reflection, a man in a gray suit and black leather gloves came soundlessly into the room. Luigi swiveled back to the mirror—the figure was gone. Humming, Luigi took the gold top from a long lipstick pencil, leaned forward, began drawing in his lips with Richezza Red. The man in gray reappeared in the mirror.

"Hey!" Luigi stopped penciling in, still leaning forward, the lipstick in his hand. "Fucking hell, Paulie, you give me the shakes sometimes, you know that? What are you, some kind of creeping Jesus or what?" Luigi pursed his lips again, this time the pout was truculent, letting Paulie know he was annoyed as hell with him. He gave a dab with the pencil, then his eyes slid to the man behind, wary this time. You never knew with Paulie. The way he crept upon you. His name was Paulie Fregara. He brought the money to put in the safe when the regular courier was away. He had his own door keys. Luigi didn't like that, or how Paulie just let himself in as though he owned the place. And he didn't like the way Paulie was always poking at his things.

The man's dull eyes stared at the wig. "That wig made of real hair?"

"Chinese hair. The best." Luigi puckered up again and began filling in with careful strokes. The lipstick was indelible, he didn't want to screw up and smudge it every place.

"Chinks have black hair." Paulie took the wig in both hands, studying it from every angle.

"It was dyed, stupid." Luigi was busy on the top lip, getting the points just right.

"Doesn't feel too tight on, get too hot?"

"Nah."

"Sure is nice." Paulie held the wig up, examining the mesh inside the crown. Luigi was concentrating on his lips, giving them a sensual pout, not watching. Paulie's long narrow face almost smiled. Suddenly he brought the wig down, ramming it on over Luigi's head, the back of the wig over his face; one fist tightly grasping the side hair, the other going for the long pointed scissors on the dresser.

Luigi's startled yelp was smothered in the dense underbelly of knotted roots, his reflex action a split second later was to grab at his $1,000 hand-sewn wig. It gave Paulie the fraction of a second he needed. He drove the scissors in above Luigi's daisy-strewn collar, slicing between the vertebrae and severing the spinal cord with a little clunk. He waited a few moments, grasping the wig tightly while Luigi flopped and jerked like a marlin out of water. The hair gleamed silver and gold in the light coming through the red silk lampshades. He waited, then slowly released his grip.

First he looked around the room, the big wide bed covered in rumpled satin sheets and cushions, rich brocade canopy matching the heavy drapes at the windows, peach-covered ropes and fringes. Paulie opened the closet doors, marveling at the sumptuousness of the clothes inside, dresses and furs exuding the heady aroma of expensive French perfumes. In another closet he found the clothes Luigi wore in public. Racks of designer suits, silk shirts, and sweaters in neatly folded piles according to color and season, silk pajamas, some striped, some spotted, a dressing gown with ermine tails. Racy-looking sporty clothes. Paulie stood there, just looking, then he got down to business.

Four

"I just saw our star witness. She is over at the hospital attending one of the counseling sessions Lewis gives rape victims." Heller walked into Malloy's office. It looked like a garbage dump. Between the desk and a couple of chairs and the filing cabinets were boxes crammed with more files, stacked on top of each other. There were files stacked on the windowsill along with a dying geranium. Heller counted at least six unwashed coffee mugs around the place. Malloy was sitting brooding behind his desk in his shirtsleeves.

"Forget the star witness bit." He picked up a file and threw it across. Heller noticed it had coffee rings on it. "India Grey is out of the case on account of her amnesia, and more especially because we got it from the top to lay off her." Malloy picked his teeth with the end of a paper clip. "You think she's covering, she might remember more than she's letting on? Scared maybe?"

"Maybe. She was knocked about plenty. You ever get around to reading my report you'd know that."

Malloy grunted. "I asked for a report, not a goddamn dissertation on the female anatomy. Okay, she's a virgin, she's got an exceptionally strong hymen . . . it gets torn . . . she bleeds . . . I get the picture."

"We hear anything on the stiff downstairs?" Heller asked.

"Nope. Zero. Same as we got on Luigi Frediano. I'd give anything to know what that little fat ass was playing at. Maybe he had a scam going and these guys come in and rip him off and walk away with the money. Maybe." Malloy gave the file on his desk a melancholy look. "The receptionist at the salon that morning swears the guy in the black ski mask had blue eyes. We pulled in thirty guys. The ones that don't have alibis don't have blue eyes. Blue eyes." Malloy scratched his testicles thoughtfully. "I ever tell you about this chick I met with blue eyes? Same color as blue ink f'chrissake, and she has all these blond curls up top and a pair of the biggest tits I ever saw. I go back to her place and I think, the hair and the tits aren't for real, and I'm waiting for them to disappear the moment we get in the sack. They're real, all right. But know something? The eyes weren't. She had contacts. I never knew what color her eyes were and I saw her plenty of times. They just never registered with me after that."

"With a topography like she had, wonder you saw them in the first place," Heller said.

Harriet opened the door and surveyed the flowers Jack carried with an appraising eye.

"Jack! How nice to see you again. Do come in. India will be back any moment. Do you mind coming along to the kitchen? Cook's got a migraine and I have six people for dinner. I'm simply frantic. Telephone's been red-hot all morning . . ."

She talked nonstop right through to the kitchen. "There's coffee in the pot on the stove if you'd like it. Harriet gave the contents of a saucepan a stir and lifted the wooden spoon to her mouth. She shook her head. "Doesn't taste as it should—it's a sauce for the spaghetti."

"Allow me." Jack raised the spoon to his lips and tasted.

"It needs reducing, and . . ." he looked for what he needed among the dried herbs. A good sauce needed alchemy, it needed to be voluptuous and possess depth, and it needed a good dash of fine olive oil . . .

Despite his preoccupation, Jack sensed the kitchen door had opened. He turned and saw India standing just inside the room and at the same time he was extraordinarily short of breath. She was wearing a suit with something soft underneath and a little string of pearls and he couldn't get over how he felt about her.

Harriet was clattering about with an assortment of vases. "I do think cook might tidy the cupboards. She leaves things in such a mess, I've got a good mind to let her go. Oh, India—Jack brought you flowers, so adorable."

India stood in the doorway, looking at the table where they lay. She walked forward, self-conscious, neck bent a little. Jack watched her open the package, carefully, so as not to tear the paper or damage the blooms. Then she thanked him and her voice sent a hot feeling right down his spine so that he had to turn abruptly and get back to his stirring.

"Well, I think we can leave this to simmer now." He was beginning to feel good; he took another sip and beamed. "Now that's beginning to taste like a sauce."

"There's the baby awake," Harriet said. "I'll have to go. You organize a fresh pot of coffee, India. Jack, it's most frightfully good of you. I do think cook might have got someone in if she was going to have a migraine."

Jack sat at the table and watched while India made the coffee. "I called you this morning."

"I had an appointment," she said. She had a voice like wild strawberries and cream, Jack thought. He could sit and listen to it all day, and all night if he had to. Except if he got her to himself for that long she wouldn't be doing much talking.

"Look, about last night, I'm sorry . . ." And he was. Why did he have to go and scare her off with that stuff about Freddy's? "And I'd like to make it up to you with dinner tonight. No strings, what do you say?"

"Forgive me, but it's just, well, it's difficult for me at the moment—something I'm not ready for. I need to get myself sorted out before I start going out again." Her gaze was straight and clear, but he saw the huge circles under her eyes.

"Sure. I can understand that," he said gently. "But look . . . if there is any time you need anything, anything at all, a friend even," he fished a card from his pocket and gave it to her, "you just have to call me at either of these two numbers."

India looked at the embossed card in her hand and nodded. She smiled. When she smiled her face just lit up. "Thank you, Mr. Donovan, you've been very kind."

"There's just one thing," he said with a grin. "Not Mr. Donovan—it's Jack."

*   *   *

That evening, India received a phone call from Douglas Ross. Shirley wasn't feeling well. The flu, probably. She would be okay in a couple of days, but if India could come back and give a bit of a hand, he'd appreciate it no end.

India knew Shirley would have to be dying on her feet for her to admit to being unwell and so she packed immediately.

Harriet thought she was mad. "They'll have you doing simply everything. You're a nanny, not a maid."

India emptied the drawers and began folding her clothes into the big Louis Vuitton bag which had been a present from her father. Only it had been Jeremy Hornby-Jones who went to Bond Street to select it. His writing on the card. Selected that as well. Her father never bothered with the little details; he delegated.

"At least wait until Adrian gets home," Harriet said rapidly. "Goodness, if it's money you're worried about, I'm sure we can help out. You only have to ask."

Not having much money worried India very much, but not half as much as having to ask for it. After two weeks not working, she had barely twenty dollars left. "I promised, Harriet. Besides, the children are waiting up for me," she said, and began dialing for a taxi.

The Rosses' tall, three-story Chevy Chase house was tucked away from the main roads and busy traffic in an area of gracious old houses, porch lights, and high shady trees. Harriet often declared she would kill for such a house, and wasn't it a pity it was so neglected and reeked like a zoo. "How Shirley can allow the children to have rabbits in the house, and let some dreadful smelly old hound sleep on the sofa . . ."

The interior did resemble a rummage sale, India had to admit, with each room as untidy as the last and seemingly giving refuge to some needy little animal that required care just short of intensive. Shirley Ross was a chronically tired woman with a leathery face that had seen long service in sunny climates. She was a committee person who worked tirelessly for the good of other people's children, and had three disturbed ones of her own at home.

The twins, James and Camilla, were seven-and-a-half and Emily was six. All three were hyperactive to such a degree that they had to be given an elixir at night that would have sent a heavyweight boxer to sleep for a week. The habit was well established by the time India joined the household.

The evening of her return saw the house in an uproar. Emily had put the baby rabbits—belonging exclusively to the twins—in her bath along with the plastic ducks and floating Carebear soap holders, to see if they could swim. Emily was sobbing in the closet under the stairs and wouldn't come out, and James and Camilla were threatening to feed her gerbils to the dog.

Douglas Ross, a good sort, but usually never at home when his children needed him, looked relieved to see her. He carried India's bag up to her room. "The doctor's been here. He thinks the trouble is exhaustion." He raised his voice so it could be heard above the commotion downstairs. "He says she's to have a complete rest."

With Shirley in her bed and defiantly on the phone, reorganizing her hapless committees, India ran the household. Success in this department didn't come immediately. Indeed, there seemed every reason why it never should, given the children's impetuous ways, the rabbits, noise, confusion, and a dog with a bad digestion. India herself quickly decided there were better ways of earning a living. So it was ridiculous the pleasure she got when Camilla and James brought home a gift they had made for her in their art class at school, and when she went to the top of the list, ahead of the pets, in Emily's nightly prayers.

But sometimes nothing was a comfort.

Homesick, more alone than she had ever felt in her life, she wrote letters, couldn't find the right words and ripped them up.

The nights were unending. She picked obsessively at the block in her memory and couldn't sleep. Then when she did it was restless, dream-racked, and terrified her with nightmares in which she was in a state of never-ending grief and humiliation, and always there was an image of a hooded man in black. In the dream she seemed to know who he was, but the knowledge faded before it could be examined.

In the mornings she was rocky on her feet with exhaustion. After the rush of getting the children off to school, while Shirley was still sleeping and Douglas at work, she shuffled out to an easy chair on the screened porch and sat nursing her coffee. It felt, in the hiatus of silence, that she was at a station waiting for a train to come and take her on a journey. Waiting for her life to begin again. Waiting, waiting.

Waiting for Jack Donovan to call her.

The strange, surprising thought lashed out at her: how could she think it? The man wasn't even on her mind.

A photographer was taking pictures from every conceivable angle and for every snap taken of the scissors protruding from Luigi Frediano's neck, three or four more were being shot of the red silk garter belt hitching the sheer black stockings to the lace camisole: Luigi Frediano was going to make the annual edition of the *Police Gazette*. Detectives were measuring distances, combing the satin sheets and taking samples from the jars of powder Luigi had lined up on his dressing table.

"Holy shit, whaddad he do with this stuff? Sniff it or what?"

"He shoved it up his ass. What do you think? You never seen face powder before?"

One officer stuck a set of bristly eyelashes to his top lip and fluttered his hand, "What do you think, darlings?" Falsetto voice.

"Jeez, that's an improvement. Maybe we should buy Frank a pair."

Malloy turned and scowled the detectives into silence. He was as far away as it was possible to get from the reeking body and the disgusting fluids congealing in a ghastly odor that was going to disturb his stomach for days to come. He tossed a couple more antacid tablets into his mouth and crunched them. His eyes were livid and glowering, his head lowered. With the flecks of white from the antacid tablets showing at the corners of his mouth he looked like a rabid dog.

Sergeant Frank Jackson nervously started up again. "Mr. Frediano was not a transvestite, ah, I think I have it established from a reliable source that he was a transsexual."

"Transsexual, eh," Malloy said, as though that kind of brilliant deduction made all the difference, solved the whole case.

Jackson squirmed in his shoes and colored to the roots of the scraggly blond whiskers sprouting from his upper lip. Oh yeah, the thing with the eyelashes had been aimed at him. He was the college kid with the degree, an outsider, a Limey. He had been born in England, but had grown up in the States. None of these fucking bog-Irish would know the difference between transsexual and transvestite, when personally he saw it as the key to the whole case.

He was right. Transvestites, transsexuals, homos, smackheads, junkies, cults were all the same to Malloy. In short, a load of shit. He didn't need to be run over with a lot of egghead language to know this wasn't your run-of-the-mill, untidy, amateurish sex killing, typifying passion run amok, jealousy and hatred. This was a very competent, clean, beautifully executed professional job. Malloy gave credit where credit was due.

The phone rang that evening while India was playing Monopoly with Emily and Camilla, and James was cutting photographs of a mob killing from the newspaper. Douglas came through from his den. "For you, India."

She picked it up in the living room, knew it was Jack Donovan from the moment he spoke, and at once had the twins' undivided attention with her flaming color.

"I asked Harriet for your phone number. I wanted to call, see how you're doing—" His voice brought him right into the room. It was incredible how plainly she could see him.

"Thank you, that was nice of you—" Silence. She wanted to talk. But she couldn't. She just sat there wide-eyed and breathless, her heart beating too hard.

Then Jack was saying, "I was at the restaurant the other night, remember the little Italian place with the fantastic food?"

"Were you?" Silence.

Who was he there with? India visualized some beautiful and fascinating woman holding his hand across the table.

Jack asked, "Do you have company?"

"No—I mean, just the twins and Emily. We're playing Monopoly."

James said loudly, "I'm not playing, it's dumb."

"James, shush."

"Well, you sound like you've got a good game going there, I won't hold you up."

She really didn't want him to hang up now, but she still said in an idiotic, stilted voice, "Nice of you to call."

He laughed, said something she didn't catch because Emily was screaming about something, said, "God bless," and was gone.

India replaced the receiver. If she never heard from him again she could only blame herself. How could she sit there and say nothing? She could have asked him about business, she could have—

For God's sake, all he did was sit next to you at dinner and that was because he wanted to ask you questions. And then he called back out of courtesy.

He didn't have to, though.

Camilla asked, "Who was *thaaat?*"

India shrugged, "A friend—Jack Donovan."

"Is he married?"

"Don't think so." He wasn't. She had checked. Harriet had it as gospel from her art appreciation group. It was common knowledge that Jack was considered an eligible bachelor who wasn't short of a girlfriend or three. "James, what have you cut out?" She looked at the two photographs spread out on the carpet. One showed, in close-up detail, the sprawled body of a man gunned down in the street.

The other showed a thickset man leaving a restaurant. The fleshy face under the hat was blurred, but there was no mistaking the arrogance of that look. He was surrounded by three men of lesser stature, but obviously bodyguards. One of the men looked straight at the camera, as if he suspected they were being photographed. His was the only face that stood out clearly. It was a long, narrow, and sharp in the way a ferret's is. Underneath the photo it said: "Salvatore Coltelli leaving Gamberoni's after hearing of the shooting of his son, Frederico."

"You gotta know who Salvatore Coltelli is," James said.

India did. Salvatore Coltelli was the head of the most hated and feared of the five eastern Mafia Families. A gangland tsar, Salvatore held himself to be more powerful than the law. He made a mockery of it by subverting justice, suborning judges, intimidating the families of witnesses. He was the king of organized crime and no one could lay a finger on him because he had more skins between him and those who executed his orders than on an onion.

India had read everything there was to read about the Mafia. It was her homework because she was studying the emergence of the Mafia in America's political and economic system, and its links with legitimate society, as part of her university course. The vice that was tolerated at the very heart of the nation, the brutal reality of the violence perpetrated by the Mafia and shown on television news every day, appalled her.

"He's a gangster, a hoodlum, James," she said quietly, knowing that Salvatore Coltelli was destined for a place on James's bedroom wall among the glorious great of the Organization. A full length blow-up of Al Capone was the most prized. James had once confessed to her that he believed he was Al Capone reincarnated. Sometimes India despaired for him.

Lieutenant Malloy was at his desk in Homicide surrounded by the debris of fast-food boxes, leftover bits of rubberized hamburger, onion rings—how many times did he have to tell them no onions—and used plastic cups.

He had the photographs of Luigi spread in front of him; he had the Chief walking up one side of him and down the other; the newspaper boys screaming because they couldn't get the pictures they wanted; and some Jesus freak, some Holy Roller, being interviewed in the squad room, confessing to the murder in the name of God, warning them the day had come when there was going to be hellfire and eternal damnation here on earth, that it had now become the Divine Right of the Soldiers for Christ Army to clean away the vermin that cluttered up God's House.

"Jackson," screamed Malloy, "where are the fucking reports? Do I have to type them myself?"

The door opened and Heller walked in, bringing the stench of his occupation. Jesus, it was right through his underwear, thought Malloy. Anybody else might perceive that Heller smelled faintly of violets. But Malloy had got the stink of Luigi's fat, gently decomposing body in his nostrils.

"Chrissy's working her little butt off getting them typed," Heller said. Malloy merely shrugged. "You think Luigi's boyfriend got jealous and stuck him?"

"No. It's too big a coincidence. It's got to be linked to the robbery." Malloy's stomach was burning the shit out of him. "We had one dead body, now we got two, both with their spinal cords severed, but not necessarily by the same outfit."

"How come it took this long to find Luigi?" Heller wanted to know.

"Because no one knew he had this other apartment he used as a love nest. Rest of the time he had a nice respectable place in Arlington. I got the boys going over it now. What I think here is, Frediano had something somebody wanted. Or maybe he was holding something at his salon and it was hijacked. What puzzles me, none of our contacts know anything about the first job. The three of them, they come out of the woodwork and one gets iced, and that leaves two, and they go right back to where they came from and nobody knows nothing." Malloy heaved his shoulders about like somebody trying to shift a weight. "And get this, on each occasion the place was turned over by a pro and nothing that we know about was taken. Nah. We got to find out who the stiff is in the morgue."

"Still doesn't explain why he was killed."

"Had something to do with the girl," muttered Malloy. His stomach was really burning up now. "How many of these antacid tablets can I take?"

"The stuff you get over the counter won't kill you, not before your ulcer does, anyway. See a doctor, for Christ's sake."

"When the fucking hell do I get time to see a doctor? They all work office-hours these days."

"That's more than I do," Heller was reminding him that he was working late. "Why was Frediano killed?"

"Like I said, he may have been holding the goods. Maybe he got careless with them. Maybe some people thought he helped himself." He was silent.

"If anybody knows anything, like you said, or if they're keeping quiet for reasons of their own," Heller said, "then the lovely Miss Grey might know too much for her own good."

"Yeah. What I was thinking. I would hate to see a pair of scissors sticking out of that beautiful neck."

Shirley was back to health and her good deeds. She decided India was looking decidedly peaked and took her to a doctor, who told India she was tense and gave her some pretty mauve and blue capsules to take at night and some yellow tablets to take when she felt depressed.

India sat in one of the two chairs and obediently took the pills. She would swallow anything, just so long as it stopped her dreaming and let her sleep.

Five

There was a voice, but a long way off. It made no impression on the cotton wool.

"India, Indiaaa, wake up!"

The cotton wool was in her head. India struggled to open her eyes and gave up. Too heavy. Then the cotton wool was blanketing everything in white silence again.

"Indiaaaaaaaaaaa!" The screech went through her ears and bounced off the back of her eyeballs, unhinging the lids.

Emily was standing by the side of the bed, her cross little eyes six inches from India's nose. Behind her, the early-morning sun filtered through the Venetian blinds, pale but bright enough to pick out the red in Emily's hair. She had on pajamas with Peter Rabbit hiding in Mr. McGregor's tool shed printed on the top, and unironed bottoms with prints of the Flintstone family. "India, my bed's all wet. Pinky did it."

Pinky always got the blame for Emily's wet beds. India opened her arms and moved over. "Come on, love, hop in." It was six o'clock in the morning, the usual time for Emily to make her announcement, and usually she went off to sleep until the alarm woke her at seven.

But not this morning. She hadn't come for a cuddle. She had something important to discuss. "India." She shook India's shoulder.

"Yes, love?"

"Don't go back to sleep, India. India, it's 'show and tell.' It's my turn and I haven't got anything to take . . ."

India couldn't help drifting back. Sleep was a monster, pulling her inch by inch, deeper and deeper into the cotton-wool world. Every morning she swore she would throw away the mauve and blue capsules, but every evening she thought of the night ahead and, fearing her dreams, took not one, but two.

Emily was breathing into her ear. "I thought it was your turn last week," India mumbled.

"I swapped with Mary Lou, remember."

The poisonous yellow tablets. She was up to six of those a day. What was she thinking? Never in her life had she taken pills. Well, then. No pills today, not yellow or mauve, not one. Today she was going to get back to her studies. She opened her eyes and reached out for the water glass. Her tongue felt too big for her mouth. She took a long gulp. Lukewarm, but it felt good.

"Emily. Why don't you take Pinky to school for 'show and tell'? We can put her in the cat's traveling basket and give her plenty of carrots."

"Oh, can I!" Emily bounded out of bed. India sank back into the pillows, listening to the noise fade into the distance, fade . . . Her eyelids dropped like stones. No! She opened them again and squinted at the sun-filled room. Then she struggled from the covers and groped with her feet for her shoes.

In the kitchen, James was eating peanut butter and reading the *Washington Post*. Shirley's look, as she rushed out the door to one of her meetings, indicated maternal pride. Others might read the tabloids; her son read a quality paper. She joined her husband in the car and discussed James's brilliant future career for the entire length of Connecticut Avenue.

Emily and Camilla had not yet emerged from the upstairs bathroom. India took advantage of the lull to pour more coffee. She sipped it looking over James's shoulder, curious about the smeary black photograph he was examining so intently. It was difficult at first to make out . . .

A fleshy woman sitting in a chair wearing a kimono and sexy

underwear, the mass of blond hair slightly askew and something sticking out from her neck?

"James?" She peered closer. "What on earth?"

"Scissors," James said.

"Scissors!" Her eyes made the journey to the caption: "Luigi Frediano . . ." Luigi? She scanned the rest quickly. "Found in secret apartment murdered . . . Proprietor of Freddy's, hairdresser's of established—"

Her eyes flicked back to the picture in utter horror. Not a woman—but a man wearing women's underwear and a wig.

"It is—it's Luigi."

The words fell out of her mouth while she stared at the picture; as people all over Washington were staring. The photographer, whose carrion instinct had captured the death-rattle of that final violent stroke, was made.

Luigi Frediano . . .

Murdered?

The week before, India had started back at her class in American political and economic history. The day after the papers ran the article on Luigi Frediano's death she was late getting home, so she picked the children up from school on her way. As Shirley and Douglas were not going to be home until midnight, she let the twins talk her into taking them for hamburgers. So it wasn't until early evening that she had time to sort through the deluge of junk mail.

There was a plain buff envelope addressed to her. India opened it in the kitchen and drew out the newspaper clipping enclosed within. She unfolded it, she had no idea what—

Her hands shook. It was the photograph of Luigi Frediano. Someone had taken the trouble to cut it neatly from the newspaper and send it to her. By the time India had finished staring at it she thought she could actually feel the blades in her own neck, and sweat began to break out all over her body.

She turned the envelope upside down and shook it. No note. Nothing. A typed label and no return address. She examined the postmark, but it was smudged and she could not make it out. She even checked the basket where the old newspapers were stored, to see that James wasn't playing a practical joke on her.

The article was cut out. But James would've—for his own collection.

"James! James." India called him in from the yard. "James, the photograph of Luigi? Do you have it?"

"It's on my wall. Why?"

"Oh, nothing, James. It's okay."

"You look sick."

"No. I'm fine. You run and finish your game." But she did feel sick, her head was throbbing; she felt as if she was still trying to claw her way out of a horrible dream.

Someone wanted . . . What? To scare her? Only to scare her? Or was she to be next?

What if Luigi had been murdered because the killer thought Luigi could identify him? She looked again at the photograph. It was obscene. Horrible. And she was meant to die too.

Panic leapt out and grabbed her. She began tearing the picture, not thinking, tearing it to bits. "No," she gasped, "no," and stuffed the shreds down the garbage disposal unit, switched it on and listened to it grind up the paper.

Switched off, the disposal unit died. The silence was deafening, a sucking silence—like the moment when a baby opens its mouth to get in enough air to scream. The next moment Emily screamed, and there was a momentary hateful exchange of insults.

"You stay away, you mutant!"

"I'm going to tell on you!"

He's out there watching . . . he's waiting . . . he'll come for you too, like Luigi—

"I'm going to thump you!"

India pushed open the window. "Stop it, you two! James, put that down and come inside. Both of you come inside."

She fought for control, but she needed help and she went to her bathroom cabinet to get it.

She had taken a vow, but she couldn't think clearly, she needed them.

They steadied her. That was the wonderful thing about the little yellow pills.

But not steady enough for the dead of night feeling when the children were in bed and asleep. She made a tremendous effort to push it to the back of her mind and get on with her work. But in the emptiness surrounding her in that big house, every creak, every rustle tempted her, terrified, to investigate. The back of her neck began to crawl.

India couldn't stand it. She picked up the phone and dialed Lieutenant Malloy's number, finally reaching his house.

"He won't be in till later but I can take a message for you," Mrs. Malloy said.

"It's all right, I—I'll ring him at work tomorrow. Sorry for disturbing you." She put down the receiver and looked at the card in her hand. Making up her mind, she dialed Jack Donovan's number.

Twice she came close to putting it down, and then Jack's strong confident voice was on the line.

When she put down the receiver down she knew he was coming. Then her knees felt as if they were going to buckle if she didn't pour herself a good stiff gin. She sat sipping it. The minutes dragged and she had another, because she was nervous. In all it was three stiff drinks before Jack was standing cheerfully on the welcome mat. Absurd how quickly his comforting presence dislodged the pall of fear that had hung over her since she had opened the envelope.

When they were both sitting on the sofa with a drink, he said, "Come on, tell me what's making you so frightened?"

It was a relief just to admit she was frightened, instead of trying to choke the feeling off by taking drugs. She started with a confused account of the photograph she had received in the mail.

"Let's begin at the beginning," Jack said. His smile was gentle.

She began telling him what had happened, perhaps more than she would have if she hadn't just consumed three large gins—four, if the one she was in the middle of counted.

She told him all she knew about that morning at Freddy's. How she was taken to the door of the room with the gun at her neck. "That's all I remember. But someone killed that bastard, and did it right in front of my eyes."

"And you don't remember at all?" Jack asked.

"No. I think I could cope with it better if I did," India said. She told him about the interminable nights dreaming dreams which started over and over continuously and never finished.

"I am in a strange place. Where I am there are people, but they are all going away from me. I have to run up and pull at their arms to make them turn around. I want to ask directions. Everyone who turns around is faceless. It's horrible. I feel so bad it hurts. And then suddenly there is a man I haven't seen before. He is wearing black. I don't run up to him and touch his arm because I am frightened. But he begins to turn as if he knows I'm there and I can almost see his face, I'm on the verge of knowing. And then I wake up crying. When I go back to sleep it all starts over again, exactly the same." She paused to gulp down her drink, as though she were dying of thirst.

"Do you know what it's like to feel a gun at the back of your neck? It's deadly cold. When I saw the scissors in the photograph that same feeling came back." India shuddered.

"I thought the picture was particularly horrifying myself," Jack said quietly.

"I think whoever sent the picture to me meant it as a threat. I phoned Lieutenant Malloy." She met Jack's eyes and saw the doubt in them. "Why? Don't you think—"

"Malloy's record of incompetence is a standing joke in the capital. Tell you what, why don't you let me have the picture and the envelope and I'll put a private detective on to it—I know just the man."

"I—don't think I could afford to hire someone private," she said with some embarrassment.

"Forget it." He took her hands. "I told you I was interested in this case. Now that I know you I'm even more interested."

"You think one of them killed Luigi, don't you?"

"It's hard to say, but trust me."

"All right. The picture got chewed up. I have the envelope, though." She got it for him and they sat studying the postmark.

"We'll get it enlarged—won't be much to go on but it's something. Anything more comes through the post, anything at all happens that's in the slightest bit unusual, tell me. Now forget this and let me worry about it."

"Ohhh," she leaned her head back on the sofa. "You've no idea how much better I feel." Jack poured her another drink and she sipped it down as if it were lemonade and asked for another.

"Think you want one?" He was teasing her a little, but she didn't mind. He had her hand in both of his and they felt warm and strong and so good to hold on to.

"Yes . . . makes me feel better."

"Darling girl, I'm going to see to it that nobody frightens you again." Before getting up he raised her fingers to his lips and kissed the tips.

She watched him go over to the liquor cabinet. He seemed so far away—she didn't know quite why this should be. "You see, can't talk to Harriet on the phone and Adr'n never at home." The words were coming faster than she could speak. It was very odd. She saw with relief that he was coming back and she reached out for the cool clinking glass, lemon bits and mint leaves floating on top, and took a sip. "Delicious."

"What time are you expecting them home?"

"Oh, 'bout midnight." Her head gravitated to his shoulder.

Jack looked at his watch. "Well, that's in twenty minutes' time."

India sat bolt upright. "You feel like dancing? Did I tell you 'bout the parties we had at home, everybody danced. 'Cept Jeremy Hornby-Jones. He sat and watched. Did I tell you about him?" She got up. Floated, really. "I could dance all night."

"All night," Jack said, getting up, "might be kind of strenuous, but I don't mind if you don't."

India flashed him an extravagant smile, and then slid quietly into his arms as limp as a strand of cooked spaghetti.

Ten minutes and they would walk in, and he'd be standing in the middle of the living room with their kids' nanny out cold in his arms, and as a lawyer he could see that wouldn't look so great. But at the same moment he was made senseless by the fact that she was in his arms. Jesus, he was blazing with excitement, and they were going to walk in any moment. He had to get her to bed.

Breathing hard, though not from the exertion, he carried India up two flights of stairs. Which room? Obviously the master bedroom and any room that had a kid in it could be discounted. Jack finally decided on one that looked like it had her things.

He sat her on the side of the bed and gently as he could with his large hands he undid the neck buttons of her sweater and drew it over her head. India gave a great sigh and curled up on the bed without opening her eyes. The moving contours of her breasts, the dark nipples visible through the lace bra, the silkiness of her skin; Jack wiped the heat from his upper lip and decided she wouldn't be too uncomfortable if the skirt stayed on. He pulled off her shoes and drew the covers up.

His cock was pulsing and his balls were tight as hell; it made walking painful. But walk he did. Right out of the room and down the stairs. He needed a cold shower. Christ, he hoped he'd got her in the right bed.

An hour later Jack left the house with three cups of tea and half a cream sponge cake swilling around inside of him, which on top of the rocket fuel India served was proving a gastronomic disaster. He helped himself to a handful of Tums and got into his car hoping Douglas and Shirley thought his explanation was kosher—about India not being well and calling him up to sit the kids while she went to bed. He drove off thinking about her. She was beautiful and she was a sweet girl, and she excited the hell out of him.

The night was warm and sticky and the leaves hung limp on the trees lining the deserted streets. Washington was in for a lulu: thick warm weather that clung like a wet blanket.He loosened his tie and switched on the air conditioner.

Jack never failed with a woman; in fact that confirmed a widespread view of him as the perennial bachelor. That women gave it as frequently and freely as they did, though, disappointed him. He despised their eagerness. One kiss and they were in bed waiting for him, usually on his side wearing a coy smile and his pajama top. All he had to do was brush his teeth and roll in under the covers.

His stomach was acting less like a kamikaze pilot, but his balls were beginning to feel as if someone was using them as an incendiary device. He had to think of something boring. He started reading the street names.

Chevy Chase had street names like Primrose and Brookville. Downtown, the street pattern was a regular grid where streets north and south were numbered, and streets from east to west were letters of the alphabet. The avenues cutting diagonally across the grid were named after various states of the Union. He was heading over to Wisconsin now and that avenue would take him from the Maryland suburb of Chevy Chase right on down to Georgetown. Whereas Connecticut ran all the way down to Lafayette Park at the White House.

No use. He had begun to think about his new porcelain dinnerware service and that got him back to thinking India had skin like porcelain—wondering what she would be like in bed, thinking of holding her naked body, skin rubbing against skin, tongue against tongue—it was too much. He grabbed his phone and punched out a number. After a brief conversation he turned off and headed for the Watergate Apartments on the Potomac River.

Livia Dannenburg had the mink-dragging walk of a high fashion model, the eyes of a snake charmer, and the ample bank balance of a second marriage to a former senator. She had met Jack Donovan at her own wedding reception, and had wanted him even before the limousine swept her and her new husband away on their honeymoon. These days she lunched with a coterie of girlfriends and was maintained by a succession of men, all of whom she called Sweetie. Rich, powerful men. But it was Jack she was playing for.

Now, she slid into two ounces of black silk and padded across the cream ankle-high carpeting into the black-tiled bathroom. From a cosmetic jar she flicked out a line of white powder and sucked it through a rolled bill in one single breath—felt the searing in her nostrils, the silent, purple explosion, saw her face in the mirror come into clear sharp focus.

She answered the doorbell and smiled with satisfaction when she saw the need on Jack's face and felt his erection through his clothes. Her mouth, the shape of it, the way it moved, kept Jack busy while her hands unzipped his trouser fly and reached inside his boxer shorts.

Jack took off his jacket and dropped it. Livia was already on her knees, her mouth—dependably red and moist with gloss—engulfing the tip of his exposed, erect penis, tongue flicking and twirling. Jack gasped, "Jesus."

Twenty minutes later they had progressed to the living-room rug—Siberian wool shorn from the breast of lambs—and from there to the bedroom carpet, where she turned and spread her ass in front of him in a way that released a pool of madness in him. Livia believed in doing it in one package. She held nothing back, kept nothing for later. By the time they hit the double, orthopedic mattress they had done it all, in every position.

"Livia," Jack asked, when his head was beginning to come back to him and he was sprawled across the satin coverlet, "say if you were raped, what would your attitude be to men afterwards? Would it put you off sex for life?"

"Raped? You mean, for real, like I didn't want it?" She sounded that incredulous. Jack smiled.

"It's the garbage collector and you don't want it," he said firmly.

"Uh huh, you haven't seen our garbage man. Sometimes I get up early just so I can watch him heave the trash cans up and figure out how he gets his jeans on."

His voice was dry. "Try and imagine him without an expense account."

"Well, sure I'd be mad, but I'd get over it. I might have to take a rain check the first couple of times, know what I mean?"

"What if you were raped and then you couldn't remember it?"

"I can't remember, so what's the problem? Hey, you going? I thought you were staying the night."

He leaned over and kissed her on the cheek. "Got a brief to read over before the morning."

Once Jack got home it took him not quite thirty minutes to read through his papers. When he finished he poured a glass of scotch and sat watching some foxy woman strutting her stuff on the late-late-late show.

But what he saw in his mind's eye was India Grey.

India sat under the sun umbrella and tried to make sense of what had happened. She had a vague recollection of Jack carrying her up the stairs and putting her to bed, and then leaving. She had lifted the sheets, seen that she still had on her bra and everything from the waist down. She wasn't naked. He hadn't undressed her. He had left her some dignity. Just to find that out—wouldn't such a situation prompt another, less honorable man into acting differently? Just to think that she could trust him. Trust was rare. But he had shown, hadn't he? And in spite of the embarrassment, she felt a pang of real happiness.

She watched the dog dig up the azaleas and never even noticed it. Why she expected him to call, she didn't know. There were reasons why he might be quite blatantly relieved if he never saw her again, all of them good: hysterical, neurotic, drinks too much. Her mind was crammed with them.

It had been two days now. Three nights, if she counted the night he had put her, disgracefully inebriated, to bed. The phone rang, but always for the others. It rang out of sheer perversity, shredding her nerves at the first ping. For her it maintained a malignant silence.

What was it she wanted, anyway? His friendship? Was that really all?

Yes. Why not?

Her body thought otherwise; it had known the comfort of those arms, his gentleness.

She thought tiredly that in a moment she must call the dog and go and collect the children from school.

The phone rang inside the house, the sound muffled and secretive as though in conspiracy against her. It would be for Shirley, one or other of her interminable committees.

But inevitably she held her breath, listening for Shirley's voice to call her. Silence. She let it out. The dead minutes idled by.

If she called him?

No. Never. She had some pride left.

"India?" Shirley appeared at the doorway.

Her fingers clenched the wicker arms, her throat constricted. "Yes?"

"That was Douglas. You'll never guess . . . We're being posted to Peking at the end of the month." She looked excited. Peking was a step up the ladder.

By the end of the month she would be out of a job.

It didn't seem to matter. Ridiculous and absurd though it was, the only thing that really mattered was the need she felt for a man who quite obviously was perfectly content without her.

"Oh, and that nice lawyer friend of yours called."

"Jack?" she asked faintly. "I didn't hear the phone."

"It rang just as I was putting it down. He's on his way up to see you."

Jack came and it was hard to know by his expression what he thought. He sat in a canvas deck chair, urbane and deferential, impeccably tailored, and reported a singular lack of success in identifying anything significant about the envelope she had given him. Even the postmark remained a mystery. He made it clear that they would keep trying, but suggested another possibility they might consider—that the picture sent to her might have been someone's idea of a practical joke.

India was thinking, that was all he came to say, when he asked her out to dinner. This time there were no reservations on her behalf. The prospect simply filled her with joy.

They went to the Italian restaurant on Connecticut which had the wonderful food, where this time India scarcely knew what she was eating. They talked, amid orange candlelight and wilting table carnations, until two in the morning, oblivious of the hour or the waiters' thudding glances.

She saw him for lunch and dinner the next day, and lunch the following. That night India went with Jack to see *Fatal Attraction*. The violent sex scenes brought back a punishing sense of shame and humiliation. Everything seemed wrong. She was edgy and nervous when they left the cinema.

On the way home Jack kissed her for the first time, but once and only and with extreme delicacy; there were sensibilities here he'd never known in his life before. He wanted to possess her, but he wanted her to come to him. Jack phoned the next day to say he would be away for a week.

A week! A week was a lifetime.

India sat thinking long after she had replaced the receiver. Was it business? It occurred to her he hadn't said. Of course it was business. She wondered who he saw. How many women?

Distracted, the noise and confusion of the impending household move to Peking barely penetrated. She was moody, restless, unhappy. She sat over her books in the evening, her mind elsewhere.

Shirley popped her head around the door. "How's the studying going? Like some tea?"

No, not tea! She wanted a shot of vodka, she wanted six months on a Greek island, she wanted Jack. She said, "Thanks, tea would be lovely."

Then he was back.

She met him at the Carroll Arms Hotel. He was waiting in the cool, dim foyer. She was exhausted from the heat and couldn't stop her legs trembling, but just to arrive and see him there waiting enveloped her in a wild happiness. Her linen dress was crumpled from sitting damply in the back seat of a taxi. He said she looked wonderful and scooped her up in his arms, his big earthy presence wrapping her securely in a tight cocoon of protective warmth.

"Miss me?" he asked.

"Yes," India said and closed her eyes, knowing she was falling in love with him, and knowing she wasn't ready—ready to love, but not ready for the act of love itself.

And also knowing that knowing couldn't stop it.

Jack had once tried the idea of marriage and was horrified at the reaction he had had: he'd been impotent for a week. Now he loved this woman and he couldn't get around the idea. It was just possible—unlikely but possible—that he could straighten it all out with her, without committing himself to the state of matrimony.

So do it, he thought.

But the more he thought, the more he knew he couldn't live with it. He was going to have to marry her.

Jack was in a bar on his fourth scotch. In his pocket was the royal blue leather box with gold trim. Inside it was the ring. A clutch of diamonds surrounding a perfect emerald and a whole network of gold. Thinking about getting married was one thing. Asking was another. He had never asked a woman to marry him.

What if she said no?

Failure was something alien to him. He never failed at anything. He didn't want to start now. Jesus wept, this was more difficult than he imagined.

He signaled the barman for another.

Jack couldn't find the car. He took a taxi. In the backseat he rocked sideways going round corners. At the address in Chevy Chase he climbed gracefully out, paid the driver, gave him a handsome tip, and fought the impulse to get back in.

Outside the front door Jack raked his fingers through his hair three times, then he pressed the buzzer. Shirley opened the door knotting the ties of a white cotton robe. He could see that she had nightcream on her face. The overhead light filled it with buttermilk brilliance. Her brown eyes lay on him accusingly. It appeared to be later than Jack had thought.

"I've come to ask India to marry me."

A wave of lightheadedness went through him—for a moment he thought someone else had spoken. Shirley was responding with a smile. She took his arm and led him into the house, much in the manner of a nurse escorting an escaped lunatic home.

Five minutes later India entered the privacy of Douglas's den where Jack waited. She was wearing a cream robe over green polka dot pajamas, and her hair had been brushed back and hurriedly tied with a ribbon at the nape of her neck. She looked the way a woman was supposed to look—covered up and demure and fresh and clean. For Jack, her image had the impact of a vision. An angel. His angel.

He hurried forward and took her tenderly by the shoulders and kissed her on both cheeks, then he sat her down in the big La-Z-Boy chair and got down on his knees and asked her to marry him. Not just asked her, he took her hands and his thoughts became a flow of urgent words, they had a dazzling insistence.

When he finished there was a deep silence. India looked dazed, but there was an excitement in her face as if she had wakened from a dream and found reality a lot better.

"If you want time to think it over?" he offered.

But then she was smiling and she was also crying and nodding her head and shaking it, shaking it because she didn't need any time to think about it, and telling him, "Yes . . . yes. . ." And there were tears pouring down her cheeks and he was scooping her into his arms. Wait until she sees the ring, he thought jubilantly.

India said yes. She didn't want time to think. She was in love, she trusted him.

Jack was everything that was good in her life.

"Three weeks!" Harriet put down her teacup. "Goodness, it sounds just a teeny bit disreputable. Is there any need to get married in such a hurry?"

India sat close beside Jack on the opposite sofa. "It's what we want." Her voice had confidence. She always had confidence when she was with him. The bad moments came when she was alone. The canker in the rose poised to corrupt and consume.

"I thought there had to be special circumstances for a marriage to take place in the Catholic Church in anything less than three months." Harriet brushed crumbs and the vagaries of the Catholic Church aside. "I mean, there's simply too much to do. Invitations to get out, and your father, India?"

- India was shaking her head. "There's no need for invitations, Harriet, we don't want anybody. Just you and Adrian and one or two close friends of Jack's."

"No . . .?" Harriet was thrashing about in uncharted waters. "Not even Jack's family?"

Jack took India's hand. He was smiling, he leaned forward slightly and, not unkindly, pinned Harriet to the sofa with his chromium eyes. "We want it very quiet, no family, no fuss. We will be married in the church at Chevy Chase Circle by the Right Reverend Monsignor Ryan Haughey. The Bishop is making an exception in our case and has given his permission."

The wedding. The church would be full of flowers and the women would say how lovely she looked, how handsome Jack was.

She would make the promise of union and mean it. She would say, "I will," and they would exchange rings and then . . .

The church was deathly quiet, a place of cool shadows and strange lights and delicate mysterious scents. India dipped her fingers in the holy water, genuflected, and made the sign of the cross.

One week . . . Jack waiting—waiting, but on the night he would expect his rights as her husband. He was hot-blooded, she knew that.

One week . . . Monsignor Ryan Haughey sitting before her, briskly barbering her soul in readiness for holy wedlock . . . in readiness for the act. She wanted to run, she wanted out. She needed Jack. She was popping a handful of yellow pills a day, two of the mauvy-blue ones each night. They soothed the hollow fear, held her together. Beyond that . . .? She knew she was heading for trouble.

"The thing is, Monsignor," she said, quietly desperate, "I love Jack, but I'm afraid . . . of the sexual side of marriage."

He was looking at her oddly, she thought he could be thinking of something else. His hands were fidgety. Suddenly they were grasp-

ing hers. Pale white skin, coarse black hairs, she couldn't help staring at them—as she had stared as a child at the pictures of the Virgin
of Sorrows whose bleeding heart was pierced through with daggers.

"Young brides often feel so. You mustn't worry, love conquers all.
Come, we'll kneel and pray together. God will help you."

Six

He lay on a wide bed with his head and shoulders propped up by a pile of pillows so he could watch the video. He was stark naked. The picture in front of him showed a black man shoving his cock into a girl's ass.

A shudder went through the man on the bed and his penis began to rise; he took it in his hands and began a frenzied pumping.

"Now!" he screamed.

A girl came out of the bathroom wearing a fur coat. She opened it slowly. She wore nothing else but black stockings held up by red satin bands and a pair of shiny red high-heeled shoes. She began gyrating towards him.

"For God's sake, Rosie . . . hurry!"

The girl stopped wiggling, gave a tired sigh, and got up on the bed on all fours.

"The other way. Face the other way so I can see the video. That's it, good girl." He took her by the hips and drew her back onto his penis, then he thrust.

He was nearly there, nearly, nearly, he grunted and strained, his face swelling and turning purple and then black, nearly, his eyes bulging, the blood vessels in them at bursting point, "Ahhhh, ahhhh, ahhhh, ohhhhhh." He slumped forward, his weight crashing down on the girl.

"Oh, Christ, move over, you're heavy. You're crushing me to death." She struggled out from under him, dragging the fur coat with her. "I'm going now, all right?"

There was no sound. His chest wasn't heaving the way it usually did. Then she clamped her hands to her face. "Oh sweet Mary, Mother of God!"

Jack rang India late on the eve of their wedding to tell her that Monsignor Haughey had suffered a massive heart attack and was DOA when admitted to the hospital. It would now be Father Michael Fitzgerald who was to conduct the marriage service.

Orange blossoms circled her hair. The dress was organdy, its scalloped points falling to her ankles wispy and delicate as a May breeze. She was radiant. Adrian told her she looked sixteen. The dark thoughts had vanished; it was as though the happiness in her had welled up and driven them out.

She went to her wedding in a resplendent black Embassy car with the Union Jack fluttering proudly on the hood and white satin streamers soaring and plunging in glorious sunshine. They drove slowly and majestically around Chevy Chase Circle before rolling to a stop in front of the church. The priest was waiting at the great vaulted door. The magnificent gold cope he wore over his white alb was carried with the courtly air only the very tall and graceful were able to achieve.

As India was handed out of the car, Father Michael Fitzgerald came striding forward to greet them. He led the way while she walked up the aisle on Adrian's arm, oblivious to anything but the man who stood at the altar waiting for her. The rest flowed around her, submerged, compressed in fleeting impressions; the controlled look on Adrian's face as he turned to leave her, Harriet with a handkerchief pressed to her nose, the crown of flickering candles, the shafts of light, the sweet air in which were mixed the potent scents of tallow and incense and blossom.

The altar boy took the gold cope, then the priest was before them in his stole and chasuble; the songs of praise, the words; and this man set apart at her side, whom she would live with for the rest of her natural life, love, cherish and obey . . .

"Repeat after me, I, India Kathleen Rothemere Grey . . ."

She held Jack's hand tightly and raised her head to the priest. His eyes were a startling blue. Not pale and yet not dark, but a blue so pure she would remember the color always. Did remember. Blue eyes in the slit of a black ski mask.

Her heart jumped, she stared at him. Jack was squeezing her hand until only her nails retained their usual shape and form.

Jack whispered, "Are you all right?" And piteously, "Darling?"

A scrap of memory. Her mind stuck on an image: a room, table and chairs. The man in the black hood. Tall. Much taller than she was. Slim. His movements graceful, ritualized.

The priest saying her name again, waiting . . .

The feeling she was dreaming, the dream confused, broken. The priest, waiting.

"India, look at me." The priest's quietly spoken words drew her back. She looked at him. An aristocratic face, the fine features beautifully proportioned. But the physical elements alone did not give him the power, that awesome ability to command a person's mind. It came from within. He had a presence, a terrible insistence, and he used it to draw her from the tyranny of those unintelligible half-images and return her safely to the moment.

"I, India Kathleen Rothemere Grey . . ." She spoke her lines, then, as Jack drew the gold band over her finger, she thought, I'm Mrs. Jack Donovan.

Father Michael moved gracefully among the guests, glass in hand. The grace was inborn, a part of him no circumstance could alter. Harriet's forced smile on his arrival had told how much she disapproved of priests. That had been an hour ago. Now, she was openly blossoming in his wake. "So charming," she murmured to India, watching him.

"Yes," India agreed with her. It had been a coincidence, that snatch of memory coming back at that particular moment. Still unnerved, she drank some champagne. Ridiculous to think that a priest was moonlighting as a burglar.

"Pity the Rosses couldn't have been here," Harriet said. "Have you heard from them?"

"A frantic note from Shirley. She's busy organizing a play group for the under-fives in her vicinity. James wrote; he wants a photo of Jack and me for his collection." India laughed and looked fondly at her new husband. "You can't imagine the company we'll be in."

At ten Jack put his arms around her. "Let's go home."

Home, now, was Jack's Georgetown house. They had made a decision to remain in Washington and take a long honeymoon in a month's time, when the pressure of Jack's work had lessened. India had met Wilma, Jack's housekeeper, and her husband, Fitzroy. She liked them both. She hadn't expected a third: a powerfully built man with the mean yellow eyes of a Rottweiler. Jack introduced him as Sonny.

Sonny got up from the kitchen table where he had been sitting, flexing his muscles—it made his shoulder jerk under the black leather aviator's jacket he was wearing—and shook hands politely. Jack explained when they were alone that Sonny would be living in the house and would accompany India when she went out. An idea with which India was immediately unhappy.

"But, he looks, he looks . . ." She didn't want to say, like a hood in a third-rate gangster movie, and upset Jack. "Don't you think he looks a little sinister?"

Jack took her in his arms, laughing quietly. "He's supposed to look scary. When I'm away on business, I want to know you're safe. I want you to have protection."

Jack was in the bathroom shaving. The maroon and yellow stripes coming off his pajamas like railway tracks moved together and parted in the mirror's reflection. Sick with nerves, jittery, frozen, India watched from the dressing room table in the bedroom. The champagne, the yellow pills, the three relaxing drinks before they came up to bed, had barely touched her. Except to give everything an enhanced three-dimensional look.

She had to get up, do something. She didn't want to get into bed. Self-conscious in her new satin bias-cut nightgown, she went over to the bathroom door and leaned against it. Everything had the intensity of a dream.

Jack was patting his face dry, humming at the same time. He came over and rubbed his cheek against hers. "Smooth?"

"As a baby." She gave him a smile as fragile as a meringue but his simple, casual action had calmed her. It's going to be all right, she thought. I love this man. She slid her arms up and around his neck and held on tightly.

"I won't hurt you," Jack murmured into her hair. His hands were doing magic things to her back: he was making love to her with his hands as she leaned against him in the doorway. He began kissing her face, her throat, then he lifted her nightdress and got down on his knees, his hands encircling her waist, and kissed her bare stomach. She was shivering. Her body was painfully nervous, and dry as if she had a burning fever.

He stopped. "I won't hurt," he pleaded. "I promise."

She ran her hands through his hair and took his head and pressed him against her. "I want you to make love to me—love me as a woman. I want it more than anything."

When he stood up his erection seemed to fill the space between them, reminding her. The back of her neck went rigid while the rest of her shivered. A flickering memory, her breath coming now in gasps, panting, remembering the man in the stocking hood. She looked at Jack and their faces ran together, until only one face, flat, distorted by the dun-colored stocking, remained.

When her head stopped spinning she was back in the room, face to the wall in the instant of that first scything jab. Pain pulled the strength from her legs. They buckled underneath her and she was sliding down the wall, pale concrete blocks scraping viciously at her face. Turned to face him and propped back she felt him thrust his knees between hers, scissoring them out. His hands were between her legs, brutal in the leather gloves, then he had them beneath her bare buttocks and she felt his hard hot penis penetrate her again, and then he was rutting—quick savage movements that made her gasp. This time pain made her beg. She offered him money, anything. Bargained with him. If he would just let her go.

Letting her go wasn't in his mind. She began to fight him, pounding at him hysterically, clawing at his eyes. She only knew she had to get away. If she had to kill him, she would. Her fingers scrabbled for an object, anything that she could hit him with, and closed on a cut-throat razor. The effect was miraculous. Immediately he began to back away. She crouched with her back to the wall, holding the razor in front of her.

Something was wrong. In the room, her hands had been lashed together with cord and tied behind her back. She couldn't remember freeing them. She couldn't understand it. Her mind was like a jigsaw puzzle where the remaining pieces didn't fit. She closed her eyes.

She stayed like that for a long time, crouched against the wall. The razor slipped from her hand. It was a nightmare.

I'll wake from it soon. India prayed, please let Emily come and wake me up with her stories and her fidgeting and her cold little feet.

Someone touched her arm and she looked up at a man's face. It was a nice face, well lived-in. She thought he said he was Dr. Nestor, but she couldn't be sure. He was murmuring to her as if she were an orphan. He dabbed something cold on her arm and she felt the sting of a needle, and then she was sliding away.

In her dream she was in the room once again—only this time she was crouched down with her back to the wall. And this time her hands were tied. She was dimly aware of the cord biting into her flesh. Her underwear was torn, she was wet between her legs, they wouldn't stop trembling. Gradually she perceived she was not alone. There was a man in the room she hadn't seen before. He was tall, dressed in black clothes with a black knitted ski mask over his head.

There, but why? She didn't seem to know. There was still a gap that hadn't been filled, some missing piece in her memory the dream didn't reveal to her.

But he was the man in black she recognized from previous dreams, the one who began to turn, and always she was on the point of seeing who . . .

She tried to talk, but she couldn't. Her tongue seemed too big. She had the oi'y salty taste of blood in her mouth.

He was drawing closer, and kneeling down right in front of her. Then, between one beat of her heart and the next, she was looking straight into his eyes. They were blue, blue and extraordinarily beautiful; it came to her without conscious reasoning that she would remember those eyes to the end. In the dream she knew him.

Very gently now, he covered her legs with the skirt of her smock, then he took a pocket knife from his black leather jacket and cut the cord from around her wrists. For a second longer the blue eyes stared into hers, and then he rose to his feet and slipped from the room.

India tried to wake up, but she kept dropping back into the well.

She drifted in and out of sleep. She heard voices . . . Wilma's, sometimes Jack's. She had to wake up because now she knew who the man in the black ski mask was. She had to tell Jack. And then she was awake, sitting up in bed trembling and covered in sweat.

The man who had cut the cords from her wrist was a priest. "His eyes, when I looked into his eyes I knew him," she whispered, dreading what was happening and already half-believing she was insane.

Because the man in the room, the man in black, was Father Fitzgerald.

But it was easier to believe in anything than to believe that. A priest? Involved in armed robbery? Easier to believe she was crazy and forget about it.

Except she wasn't crazy and she couldn't forget. He was that man, and she had recognized him in the middle of her marriage vows . . .

Her cheeks went hot. She put her hands over them and they were icy cold as she began to understand what had happened. Including the fact that she had become hysterical. What had she done? No, it was part of the nightmare. Please no, please . . . Not on her wedding night. No . . . but it was back. The mind-bending paralyzing scene. Now nothing else mattered. Only Jack mattered.

She had been asleep . . . hours, days. What had happened in that time? Where was Jack? Where was he?

She had to talk to him. Explain to him about her memory returning—talk to him until he understood the cause of her violent reaction. Make him understand that she loved him. That most of all.

The door opened and Wilma struggled in with a large tray. "Time you woke up. Fitzroy says to me—that girl been sleeping more'n a day and a half, if she don't wake up she'll fade away. You go on now and take her a big stack of your buckwheat pancakes and maple syrup with some of that nice crispy fried bacon. Yessir." Wilma calmly set a tray on the dressing table and began straightening the bed.

"Then, yesterday wasn't—"

"You slept all day yesterday, nothing but a little to drink now and then. Couldn't keep a cat alive. You jus' sit up now and eat your breakfast. Mr. Jack will be worried if you don't eat."

"Wilma, is he here?"

"Mr. Jack's in New York. Been calling all the time to see how you are. Be gone maybe until tomorrow. Says you got to rest up."

He's gone, India thought faintly, and then: "Do we have a number where he can be reached?" she asked.

"Sure, number's in the list by the phone. You can call him any time."

She looked and, sure enough, there was a card on her bedside table. She thanked Wilma for breakfast and had to make a start on it before the housekeeper was satisfied. But as soon as she left the room India picked up the phone. The New York number on the list was for an answering service. India called it several times over the next hour and left messages for Jack to call her.

The waiting became unbearable. But not for one moment did she think that she had hallucinated the whole thing, that incredibly her mind was expressing some kind of surreal vision which may or may not have stemmed from the actual memory at all.

No. What scared her, really scared her, was not being believed. Jack, everyone, thinking she was fantasizing about a priest, and just incidentally it had to be the priest who married them . . .

And thinking she was mad.

And just thinking about it, India had to confess she wouldn't blame them.

So for this reason, she had to make sure. She had to go and see Father Fitzgerald. Because face to face, she would know.

Seven

The priest stood half-hidden by shadows at a second-story window of the presbytery. Still and dark as a specter in his long black soutane, he watched the traffic move slowly around Chevy Chase Circle. A woman got out of a car and began walking in the direction of the church. He followed her with his eyes. He'd known that, sooner or later, she would come.

For Michael Patrick Fitzgerald, born in Northern Ireland, home had been in the Falls Road, Belfast. All of it gone when he was seven years old. Gone, blasted to smithereens by a propane gas cylinder. The cylinder ignited and rolled to the doorway by a rabid band of Orangemen bent on an orgy of destruction after a celebratory march. The explosion had killed his mother and father. But by some miracle, the blast whirled young Michael into the next street, where he was discovered wandering about dizzily by an older brother coming home from choir practice.

Even to death, he would remember going to see his parents' room and seeing only bits. Bits of furniture, bits of limbs. His mother's feet sticking out from beneath a pile of rubble. He had picked up one of her slippers and tried putting it on. His brother came and took him to their aunt's farm in Armagh.

His aunt taught Michael how to play the piano. It was she who had begun his education; and his uncle living in Boston, the Right

Reverend Monsignor Canon Fitzgerald, who had persuaded him to continue it. First the Jesuit school and then the priesthood.

But Father Michael Fitzgerald still dreamed about those days in the Irish countryside. Sometimes he saw his aunt's face, the deep creases in her cheeks, and when he was cold he remembered the warmth of her lap. He felt cold now and he shivered.

But the feeling went deeper than coldness, and the shivering was only something in his imagination. It was a warm June day with a humidity so high you felt you were wearing it. And below him in the quiet street, a car was pulling into a parking space. He watched as a man in a gray suit got out. For several long minutes more the priest did not move, but kept watching. Then he turned and walked rapidly away.

India rose from her knees and sat back in the pew. Here in the dim peace of the church the last of the nightmare was slipping away. Her mind had been hurtled through a chamber of horrors, she had dreamed, and the dream had been weirdly persuasive. But only a dream.

She was thankful that the priest taking confessions was not Father Fitzgerald, because she might have made a perfect fool of herself. A shudder went through her.

Come on, a priest! How could she possibly have taken the idea seriously? It wasn't credible. India thanked God that she had never called Lieutenant Malloy.

All the same, she would talk to Jack about it—she needed to talk to Jack. The feeling of being haunted, of feeling frightened . . . just to tell him, talk to him. As close as she felt to Jack, she had not confided in him, not yet, not the true horror, not really talked about the disgusting, dirty thing that had happened to her. If she had, she might have saved them both this misery. But she would talk, she would make it all right with him.

India sighed and was about to get up and go home. But then she saw Father Fitzgerald himself come through the door that led from the sacristy. And now, seeing him, tall and dark, his effortless grace, that memory returned and with it a sudden cold certainty.

Half out of her seat, she watched as the priest knelt down at the altar rail in prayer. When he stood up he crossed himself, and then he turned and looked directly at her.

India felt a shock race through her.

He knew she was there. Not only that, he knew why she had come.

He was walking down the aisle towards her, a priest walking down a church aisle, and she had gooseflesh on her arms.

Her every rational thought rejected it. But when he stopped a pace or two away and waited, and she was looking into the white intensity of that face, into those blue eyes, she knew. With absolute conviction, she knew this was the man in the black hood who had stood right before her in the room.

"You!" She thought she said it loudly, but she couldn't have. There were one or two others in the church, those who had come for confession—not one of them turned around or lifted their head to look. A wave of lightheadedness almost persuaded her she was still in the dream; the thought came to her that the room had no door and no way out, and, dreaming, she was trapped in it for ever.

"Come with me." The priest spoke gently but with authority. He turned and she followed him. He took her to a little room at the rear of the church. There were piles of books on the shelves, and a blackboard and chalk.

"Are you all right?" Pause, a smile. "Would you like to sit down?"

How could he be so calm? A flush of anger rose in her cheeks. Suddenly she spoke. "I recognized you."

"I thought you had."

Actually she had expected a bland stare and a bare-faced lie. It threw her. "Then you admit it—you, a priest. You take confession then you raid Freddy's with two gunmen who look like the scum of the earth and while you're going through the safe one of them takes me into a room and rapes me . . . Who forgives you, Father Fitzgerald?" Her face was deadly white, apart from red spots high on her cheekbones.

The priest grabbed a chair and sat her down on it—she must have looked as if she was going to fall—then went to the basin and returned with a glass of water. He got down on one knee and held it for her. India took it in both hands, but they trembled so badly the water would have spilled if not for his firm grasp.

"I know what happened," he said. "I see you when I wake in the morning, the very first thing," he whispered. "That dreadful crime committed against you will be with me always. I do not ask for forgiveness. I no longer have that right. Neither can I expect deliverance. Not in this lifetime, nor in the next."

India looked at him, dazed; Father Fitzgerald was in his own hell. It was in his face and in his voice.

Then she was seeing it again—the piece in her memory her mind wouldn't touch. Every time she thought about it, she felt the same unreasoning fear and her mind would go blank. But now—she remembered—in the room when it got so bad she wanted to die she must have passed out, because the next thing she was looking up at the man in the mask standing there.

But what happened before then . . . something . . . it was too dark to see, but—And then she answered her own question. The knowledge struck and struck hard, and just for a moment she was frightened, really frightened.

She looked at him then. "It was you. You came into the room and you killed him." She was aware of what she was saying, the kind of accusation she was making, and her voice lost substance, faded out.

The priest stood up in silence and his silence had the chill of a marble vault. She felt trapped by it, as if no words on earth could penetrate that elemental force.

"No. It was my partner who first heard you screaming. He was sure you were going to be killed and he went to your aid. It was an accident. He never meant to kill him. But if he confessed, who would believe it? Who except the Church. He confessed to me and I gave him absolution. Look at me, India. You are a Catholic, you know what that means."

"I know what it means," she whispered back. She knew. And shouldn't she also confess, because hadn't she wished him dead? Prayed for it, actually dared to ask God Himself, and so wasn't she just as guilty? That horrible thing that happened; there was no end to the guilty shameful feelings, the punishment.

"I know what it means, but how can I just walk away and forget it ever happened? How can I? You've committed armed robbery in which a man died violently. Someone has to be accountable. I don't mean to the Church, to God, I mean accountable to the law of this country."

"Perhaps I agree with you," he said softly. "Who else knows of this? Is there anyone?"

India hesitated. "No," she said, her voice low. "I had to make sure."

"And you came alone."

Again she hesitated. "Yes."

"Then, Mrs. Donovan, if you want the truth I will tell you who

should be made accountable. I will show you. And if you can recognize the truth and accept it, then you can judge if the judicial
system will do it or not. Come now to the window with me."

India looked at him in surprise, but she rose to her feet and followed him over to the one small window in the room.

"Look over there, by those trees," he said, and India turned her
head unwillingly.

"There you see a man who trades in violence of the most despi-
cable kind. The people who employ him steal from us. They're
greedy, Mrs. Donovan, powerful and greedy. They take our money
for their own gain." He gave India no time to reply, but turned to her
and spoke urgently, and the conviction and the passion of his words
lent them an almost hypnotic power.

"I am guilty of taking back only that which was stolen from the
Church, no more and no less. What I did was wrong. It can never be
condoned or sanctioned in any way, and for the terrible thing that
happened to you, I will be eternally damned. This I accept. But that
man out there commits crimes in the course of his work. He robs
and he kills, and he does it on command. Now tell me, is he one of
your bodyguards, Mrs. Donovan?"

"My what? I don't have—"

Then the question broke over her.

Sonny leapt into her mind. India, staring at the priest, was suddenly aware of her own feelings of unease at Sonny's presence in the
house.

"No," she said. "I've never seen that man before. I don't know
who he is." She didn't. But a cold irrational fear was growing. "What
are you saying?"

"The man you see out there is a hit man for the Mafia. He kills
people, Mrs. Donovan, and he does it on your husband's orders."

India couldn't speak, she couldn't even think. Her mind was
crawling over the edge of a precipice.

"Mrs. Donovan," how softly he spoke, "your husband is Mafia. He
is the youngest son of Salvatore Coltelli. And no one, not the judi-
ciary or any law enforcement agency, is going to make them accountable for the crimes they commit, because there is not enough
political muscle in the country to grapple with the power of the
Mafia."

*   *   *

Jack was on the phone, wincing, as Wilma told him India was missing.

"What the blazes . . . ?"

"Sonny don't even know she's gone," crooned Wilma, who didn't like that Sonny one little bit.

A charge ripped right through him; he could almost feel his teeth rattle. "Gone? You're telling me she was in bed one moment and the next she's gone! Where? She take anything with her? Packed and left? What?"

"No, nothing. She's not at Miss Harriet's place neither. She's probably just gone for a little walk in the fresh air."

"Holy shit, she's in no condition to be wandering around. Christ, who knows what's going through her head! Listen, soon as she comes in, call me. And Wilma, put Sonny on the phone for me."

While Jack was waiting to blast Sonny off the face of the earth, he seethed. He belonged to a crime organization with a global reputation for its pool of professional minders, and what happens? He's given one to watch his wife's back and see nobody touches her—and she walks out the door and disappears and the stupid fuck doesn't even know about it!

For Beniamino "Jack" Coltelli, born in Brooklyn, New York, survival had started in the back of Brooklyn cab. It was a messy birth and his mother had expired quietly in its throes. But Jack survived, the youngest son of Salvatore Coltelli.

Young Jack's ability with figures soon made him a favorite, and Salvatore Coltelli was quick to realize the potential. He saw there was a time coming when the blurring of the line between criminal fraud and sharp business practice would allow the important money to move into different fields. The field Salvatore had in mind was computer fraud involving a multi-million-dollar base.

In the 1980s he saw that it was possible to organize business on a worldwide scale and disperse the profits through a network of secret outlets, and do it all from home. His need, then, was to move in on the new technology: computer technology. He was confident that in the 1990s there would be few who could tell the legitimate businesses from the illegitimate ones.

He groomed his Jack for the job. So Beniamino "Jack" Coltelli became Jack Donovan. Donovan was a nice steady name. It was quiet and unassuming.

The days were past when gangsters wanted "respect." It was a quality that drew attention, and in these times attention could bring inspection. No. What Don Salvatore wanted for Jack was anonymity. And Donovan was a very good name for that.

With his name changed, Jack was enrolled as Jack B. Donovan at decent schools (good schools, not the kind where snobbery fixed your background under a scanner), and then it was Harvard and law school. After that, because Jack showed considerable aptitude and it couldn't hurt, came three years in the offices of a top firm of criminal lawyers in New York, before a coveted job in the prestigious Washington partnership Kennedy and Winter, and the additional responsibility of expanding the Family's profitable business dealings into the field of computers.

"Yeah, dis is Sonny."

Jack scored doodle lines on a yellow pad with his black pen. "You're not doing what I asked, Sonny."

"She's in her room one minute and the next thing—"

Jack listened, but not for long. He stabbed black dots along the line, and then said patiently, "She's missing, Sonny. You were sleeping on the job. Now get out there and find her, and don't fucking stop to catch your breath until you do." Jack hung up. He wrote a note on the yellow pad and looked at it thoughtfully, then he punched another phone number.

India was shaking like a leaf. She flatly refused to believe it. She couldn't—not that murderous organization, not Jack.

"Everyone in Washington knows him. He's Jack Donovan. His people are from Boston."

"But you never met his people."

"Jack doesn't get on with them. He left home and worked his way through college."

"All right, Mrs. Donovan, where is your husband now?"

"New York. He often goes there on business." She moved away from the window in a daze. "He doesn't discuss business with me."

"Is it Mafia business that keeps taking him to New York?"

"Stop it. Please stop," India cried.

"I'm sorry. I wish that I could," Father Fitzgerald said gently. "But I can't. You must know the truth before you can try to understand why I did what I did."

"The only thing I understand is that I love my husband. You saw what happened to me. Jack helped me pick up the pieces. How can I believe what you're saying without betraying all that? I feel that I've done that anyway. If it wasn't for me, he might not be in New York now."

The priest ignored her, fixing his eyes on the window; he seemed to be talking to somebody else. "It was my uncle who baptized Salvatore Coltelli's youngest son. Do you want to know what his first Christian name is?"

He continued when India turned her head away. "It was changed for convenience. So no one would know that Jack Donovan has his roots deep in a crime syndicate. A different kind of name because Jack practices a more sophisticated form of crime. He thinks it's all right to rip off millions as long as he's in an office wearing a suit. He operates a system of secret banks so there's always ready money. We raided one, we took our own money back. And now everyone is looking for it. Every link is being investigated. Jack searched you out, Mrs. Donovan—"

"Stop it!" India put her hands over her ears. Her head was pounding, she felt sick. Any more and she would turn and run. It was impossible to acknowledge anything the priest was telling her—the meaning was too enormous, it couldn't be contained. She couldn't accept it without denying so much else.

Who was lying? If it was Jack, he had lied to her all along. She turned slowly and stared out of the window.

"He's gone," she said.

"He's not. He'll be there somewhere. He followed you here. When you leave he'll follow you again. Everyone you see, everywhere you go, they'll investigate." He said more gently when he saw how shocked she was, "I have something to show you that will help explain my involvement in all this. Will you come? I want to take you to see the Church of Our Lady. We can go out a different way. We'll give our friend out there the slip."

She had come to accuse the priest of a crime, and had been totally unprepared for him to excuse himself by telling her that Jack was doing something far, far worse.

Jack? Had he contrived that first meeting? She remembered the questions he had asked her. She felt as if someone had kicked away her crutches, sent her spinning into the road and then run her over.

"What have I got to lose?" she said. Her voice sounded very strange.

Father Fitzgerald used a small side entrance. Outside, the sun was bright, hot on her skin. He led her along a path running by the presbytery wall until they came to a quiet shady back street where his battered old car was parked.

Eight

Salvatore Coltelli sucked the flesh from the head of a boiled pigeon and reflected upon the raid on Freddy's. Eventually he said, "Maybe we've been done by little stick-up men with no links, but that money will surface. It always does." Salvatore spat out a beak picked from his teeth, wiped his fleshy fingers on a napkin, and smiled. The smile wasn't pleasant. It was silky and dangerous.

Salvatore took any loss of income personally. Having one of their holding banks ripped off was a kick in the face. Fury had set in and he was an obsessive man. His second wife, Concetta, stood stiff and straight at his elbow, waiting to clear away so she could bring the dessert. There was a meeting at the house called for two o'clock and punctuality was mandatory. Excuses for lateness were bourgeois shit and the Don didn't deal in them.

The phone rang.

Concetta answered it immediately. She was smiling when she brought the phone around to Jack's side of the table, but her smile had a slightly worried twitch to it.

Jack tipped her a wink and took the call. When he put the receiver down she was serving him a helping of soufflé al cioccolato amaro, his favorite.

"Does Sonny know what happened to your wife yet?" Salvatore asked conversationally. Concetta's head turned. Jack hesitated before he sealed Sonny's fate, but only momentarily.

"No."

"Sonny is finished." Salvatore turned his pitiless eyes on his youngest son. Fredrico had been the first, then Angelo, finally Jack. When their mother died Salvatore had married a widow who was daughter to the head of the Detroit family. It had been a profitable union. But it would be a mistake to think that her son Tom and daughter Teresa, children of her first marriage, would ever play an important part in the Coltelli family business. Neither had been invited to the meeting being held at the house that afternoon.

"Finished?" Jack repeated.

"Don't leave it to Angelo. You deal with it." As Salvatore sat in his leather chair, knobbly-fat, balding, with a bland face, a casual observer might not suspect the presence of one of the most feared men on several continents. Until the eyes slapped you with terror.

The Don dipped his spoon into the extravagant confection Concetta had put before him, a rococo cloud of eggwhite and spun sugar floating in chocolate and liqueur. "Your wife is used to freedom of movement. It's important she understand her situation a little better. Otherwise it could be dangerous for her, going out by herself like that."

Obliquely Jack wondered how he could introduce India to the truth about his family. He had been hoping it wouldn't be necessary. His brother Tom had married a girl from the outside and the background details had not been important enough to cause trouble with his wife, Betsy. But Jack somehow knew India was going to see things a little differently.

"Talk with her, bring her to lunch," Salvatore said. Salvatore had mapped a very different life for Jack. But he deplored the fact that it might necessarily exclude him from knowing his daughter-in-law. Salvatore wanted her to be part of the Family—she would have children. The next generation; his grandchildren. He had a Sicilian's instinct to feel his way with things—when it came to women he knew the young spirited ones must be fed and coaxed. They soon settled down.

"I'm saying that she must know of the existence of the Coltelli family—not too much of the meaning. She is your wife, not your partner. But enough information so she can learn what is necessary."

India trusted him. That had never bothered Jack before, yet curiously it was beginning to. He lived in the same society of which

India was a part. And behind all that was his father—Mafia baron, omnipotent, dangerous. But India; there was an innocent, available quality about her which he found erotic—it filled him with a sensation, induced in him feelings which would otherwise be unreclaimable.

"Well, with all respect, we have to remember she's English, and the English see things differently," Jack said. Christ, he was thinking, the house looked like a goddamned fort the way it was set up with a battery of high-tech security devices. Even in Oyster Bay, Long Island, not every house had the impenetrable look of the Don's. India was certainly going to notice the armed guards at the electronically controlled gates . . . if the pack of patrolling Doberman pinschers didn't scare the living daylights out of her first. For the first time in his life, Jack felt torn between two worlds. His marriage was no longer just the convenient embellishment to his life he had always assumed it would be.

"When we visit, the dogs and the guards have to go," Jack said, determined.

The Don gave him all the reassurance of his cobra eyes and nodded. "Then she won't see the guards, and the dogs can be kenneled." He actually thought England was a backward country. As late as 1988 Scotland Yard was declaring they didn't have a Mafia problem. Mafia drug activity in England had been identified back in 1974. The English were one of the peoples in the world who didn't want to know, seemingly. It made it very easy. India would be the same.

Concetta came in to tell them the others had arrived. Salvatore got up and led the way through to his den. The Don spent hours at a time working on outsize jigsaw puzzles, the current one being a map of the world, which covered every square inch of his gigantic mahogany desk.

The den was serviced by an enclosed elevator that would transport the Don to any level of the house at the push of a button. On this occasion they went down and the door slid open on a basement room paneled with blond wood and lit solely by indirect ceiling lighting. A bank of computers and three enormous steel filing cabinets occupied the length of one wall, a large movie screen another. Two men sat on either side of the long, highly polished table. Except for a water pitcher and four glasses, the table was bare.

Seated to one side at the head of the table was Domenico Cechetti, the Don's *consigliere.* He was undistinguished, except for a nose that ran riot down his ordinary-looking face. No one could ever say what color his eyes were, or his hair, if any. He was neatly dressed, dapper almost, but people didn't notice, they only saw the nose. On top of this seeming ordinariness, Domenico Cechetti behaved with propriety, and to such an extent it was easy to forget he had a mind as swift and lethal as a shoal of piranhas.

On the other side of the table, but one chair further down from the head, sat Angelo Coltelli, the Don's second son and the family enforcer, a strongarm, and the underboss on the working side. Three hours a day working on his muscles pumping iron in a gym in Brooklyn had produced a well-oiled killing machine. It bugged him no end that Jack wielded the power. He breathed heavily just looking at him. Fucking lawyers. Angelo refused to see that Jack could steal more with one finger on his computer than he could in a year of collecting protection.

The chair beside Angelo and to the left of the Don's at the head of the table stood empty. Fredrico Coltelli, the Don's eldest son and heir, had occupied that chair and nobody made the mistake of presuming to sit in it. The death of Fredrico at the hands of a drug dealer had done much more than shift the balance of power within the Coltelli family. It was a plain signal that the business was moving away from the old guard and falling into the hands of the new Mafia, a flashy and viciously aggressive younger generation, not much keen on humility.

Until recently the American branch of the Mafia, the Cosa Nostra, had been subservient to the Sicilian brotherhood of which Salvatore Coltelli was the leader. But the heroin trade had ended that. Some of the other families in the brotherhood wanted a share of the profits to be had from heroin, the biggest drug market in the world. But not Salvatore.

Salvatore saw the hard drug market as attractive, but dangerous. Insider dealing and computer "long term" fraud opened up limitless possibilities without the aggravation—no street business, no slaughter, few risks. Fraud was altogether a much more enticing activity, especially now that there were interesting subsidy arrangements available through the European Common Market just waiting to be plucked.

But at the very heart, Salvatore was a family man. He saw, as few of the others in the brotherhood did, that the Mafia itself had been corrupted by drugs—that no organization could operate when discipline and standards had been swept away. In their place would be internecine slaughter, and there would be no profits from it in the end. Jack was to lead the family into the international money markets of the nineties. It was the only safe way to go, the only truly profitable way.

Don Salvatore motioned Jack to take the seat next to Domenico Cechetti and took his own place at the head of the table. When he spoke, it was about the problem uppermost in his mind; the missing money, a considerable amount of which had come from the Church Fund.

The Church Fund was very dear to Don Salvatore's heart. He had realized early that the Catholic Church was not properly exploiting the potential of the cash that passed through its coffers—cash that could generate profits if placed in the right currencies at the right interest rate at the right time. He demonstrated what might be done by setting up a trust which controlled the various estates and properties belonging to the Catholic diocese, a ruse which enabled the Family to skim off the money that otherwise would have gone to the Internal Revenue Service. The Family got what the IRS should have had, and the Church made a handsome profit. It was a neat arrangement.

There was, of course, the additional cash flow generated by the prostitution racket. Monsignor Haughey had been a regular contributor. Then in its wisdom, the Church had played further into their hands by choosing to use the dubious services of an "offshore" bank to deposit money raised by charity, from where varying sums were regularly transferred by computer to another account by an accountant on the Mafia payroll. The money was then withdrawn and moved into a holding bank as ready cash.

These were the secret banks Jack had set up, nearly all of them fronted by chic hairdressing salons and beauty parlors, part of an underground banking system designed to move huge sums of money to and from the mafia-owned "offshore" banks which operated out of the Bahamas. By using couriers, the system circumvented exchange control regulation. It also provided foreign currency to fund purchases of arms and ammunition difficult to acquire in the U.S.

It tickled the Don's sense of humor to think that the Church was playing a key role in a money-laundering operation that had an annual turnover of 800 million dollars. Now some of that money—the money from the holding bank for which Luigi had been responsible—was still unaccounted for, and it was a fact that upset him very much.

Don Salvatore's eyes were nearly closed in concentration as he ran through what was known about the raid, and the possible culprits.

"Luigi Frediano had to be in on it, had to be," Angelo began when the Don had finished.

Jack looked at him with such contempt that Angelo shut up. What kind of fool could hold Luigi's knowledge as of no account and send him to his death with his secrets intact? Without regard, without any act of negotiation. The thought of this sort of blind egotistical stupidity cast Jack into a black mood. But it was nothing compared to the rage he felt at his brother for sending the photograph of the murdered man to India. It was, of course, an attempt to scare her into going to Malloy with more information (the family had links with the Lieutenant's office) and Angelo had done it thinking that maybe India knew something and was keeping it to herself.

Angelo still did. That was why he had Paulie in Washington doing a bit of surveillance work. Sonny was a nice piece of muscle to have at your side, but he couldn't shadow to save himself, whereas Paulie was like a knife in your back. You never knew about it until it was there. If anything interesting came up in Paulie's report, Angelo was going to take great pleasure in telling Jack about it.

Angelo tapped his pen on the desk and said, "Luigi had people he owed money to running all over him. We know he had to meet a payment that week, or else." He drew a line across his throat. "We let every little pimp who screws up steal from us, we're never going to hold back the tide. Luigi did it, all right."

"The way he was staked through the neck," Jack said, "it looked like it was the work of the devil. Who'd you get to do that?"

Angelo shrugged and said, "That's my business. I don't ask about yours, so do me a favor."

Then Salvatore spoke. His pudgy hands were joined as if in prayer, and he appeared to be deep in thought. His voice had the consistency of an over-ripe fig: soft and oozing, and yet gritty. "I asked you all here today because there has been a new development. Jack will now tell us about it."

There was dead quiet in the room as Jack began to speak. He reminded the others by going over each important detail in the raid on their holding bank at Luigi Frediano's salon. Then he came to the information Chrissy Mangano had relayed from Lieutenant Malloy's office. Chrissy was Malloy's secretary. At work she called herself by her maiden name, Posnansky. Her husband Johnny Mangano was a small-time businessman who had neglected his debt to the Family. His imprudence was tolerated because of his wife's unique position.

"The man in the morgue is a known IRA terrorist named Patrick O'Fiaich. His identity was traced through hospital records. Apparently O'Fiaich had a fairly recent coronary bypass operation and the medical examiner played a hunch and checked around. The way the raid was carried out implies that the other two men were also IRA."

"How about that bastard?" Angelo said. "Using those rosary-rattling gangsters to do his dirty work."

Domenico Cechetti spoke for the first time. "We all knew Luigi Frediano," the Consigliori said smoothly. "He came into the business straight from high school after his father was killed. Don Salvatore gave him a start. Luigi proved that in business he was competent, he made a lot of money, he repaid the debt many times over. For a long time his loyalty was beyond question and then he began to have dealings with people who had a bad influence on him. He began to have expensive habits. To finance them he was stealing from the bank. Small amounts. He would have to be stupid to think he could go on bleeding us. Luigi wasn't a stupid man. It means that he must have had a plan to take everything and get out. Hiring gunmen to go in and shake the place up and make it look like they took the money seems feasible. Only a courier was to make a delivery of a further seven hundred thousand dollars the very next day. Luigi would have waited. Also, for him to make a deal with the IRA would be illogical to the point of insanity. He would never have committed himself to an act of folly like that."

Angelo had reached the outer limit of his political awareness and his eyes now contained a blank yawn of incomprehension. "They do the job, get paid for it like everyone else. What's the difference?"

"The IRA have a code," Domenico Cechetti said. "Even the most insignificant member, no matter how stupid, has a murderous loyalty to the cause. That is, to remove every trace of British power from Northern Ireland. The IRA are not interested in percentages. If there is money they'll grab it for their own political purposes. They're fanatics. They never back off."

"And if the IRA are involved and Luigi didn't invite them in," Jack said, "then something bigger than we thought is going down."

The door on the far side was opened by Concetta. A man came into the room. He was of medium size, height, and shape, with little round damp curls like snails sticking to his crown. There was a restless energy about him—if he had had a tail it would have been twitching. Concetta shut the door behind him.

Bernie Loeb was one of the couriers. Jack watched as he took the chair next to Angelo. He felt an urgent need to know more about Bernie. He'd had it ever since he saw him dining alone with Angelo in an intimate little restaurant off Broadway. He wasn't able to get the scene out of his mind, something in the way the courier had been leaning forward over the table, Angelo's broad, congenitally brutish face gazing placidly back at him. Jack had felt like a voyeur.

The Don asked Bernie, politely, how his mother was. Bernie said the usual things. Jack didn't bother listening. Talking away, Bernie drew out a black onyx case and selected a king-size cigarette which he lit with one of those lighters with a built-in wind shield that is much prized by the outdoors man. He held the cigarette aloft between two slender fingers, and Jack stared reflectively at the oddly effeminate gesture; it smacked him then, right between the eyes, that Bernie was homosexual. How had he failed to see it before?

Bernie wasn't around very often. The couriering kept him busy and away. Jack tried to think what Bernie's recent movements had been, then found he was wondering, almost idly, how they coincided with the new heroin trade rumored to be operating out of the Caribbean. The word had gone out that Salvatore Coltelli was behind it. Despite the Don's statements deploring the traffic in drugs, despite his strenuous efforts to keep the Family from involvement.

The fact that Bernie was in and out of the Caribbean didn't add up to much, but the secret purchase of a second home in Baltimore for $250,000, paid in full with cash, did. The first hint had come via the intricate network of contacts Jack maintained.

Both of them, Bernie and Angelo, were sitting back, puffing away, discussion about the raid on Luigi's having ceased by tacit agreement. Now the Don was into the business of Bernie Loeb's collection from a bank in the Bahamas. Jack forced himself to pay attention, but again he visualized the intimate little restaurant scene. Bernie Loeb and Angelo? Angelo?

He looked across the table at his brother sitting sprawled in his chair, shirt collar unbuttoned around his massive neck, tie loosened, big locker-room grin on his face. Oddly, it was the macho give-a-shit look that mocked, and made Jack wonder if this prize heap of over-exercised muscle was, in fact, gay.

Bernie was chain-smoking, lolling, but on edge. He was sweating. His eyes flickered now and again to Jack's side of the table. Like a nervous horse, he had picked up on a skin of feeling that made him agitated. It was not just that he was fucking Angelo; it was the heroin they were running. And if Jack ever figured out how they were doing it, they would both be dead meat.

The Church of Our Lady was in a decaying inner-city area India would ordinarily have avoided driving through at any cost. For one thing, the faces of the men with hate in their eyes, leaning up against the pock-marked graffiti-scarred walls, were all dark. She wasn't racist. God no, she was a liberal. But the truth was, her familiarity with these areas known as combat zones, and which made the no-go areas in London seem tame by comparison, began and ended with the charity projects run by the Reverend Charles E. Norton of the Episcopal Church of St. John, during Human Resource week. And only then as a favor to Harriet.

She stepped out of the car and into the thwanging thump of a ghetto blaster. Giving funky little slaps at it with his beringed hands was a guy in a pink stretch leotard and mirror sunglasses. Father Fitzgerald brought a few dollar notes from his pocket, gave half to a boy with white-bleached frizzy hair, and promised him the rest when he came out, if his car still had accessories like tires and an engine.

That settled, he led India to a building sandwiched between a run-down stone church, obviously the Church of Our Lady, and a shop that had windows covered in metal shutters. The two-story building they were approaching appeared to have been newly renovated, though the cyclone fencing completely surrounding it did nothing to erase India's profound unease. Father Fitzgerald got out keys and unlocked the little judas gate and stepped inside. He offered his hand to her. The steps leading up to the freshly painted door were swept clean.

India stopped on the threshold. "You're mistaken, you really are. All right—Jack had his name changed. But he did it to disassociate himself from his family. So he could make a fresh start." She had an expression of eagerness on her face. "That's it, that's what he did."

"If that is what you want to believe."

"There's no proof, is there? You don't have any proof."

"Well, that's the thing. It's almost impossible to prove the kind of imaginative schemes Jacks works on. That's the beauty of computer fraud."

"If people are being swindled they could complain, they'd bring in the anti-fraud squads," India pleaded.

"Jack doesn't deal with people—only big multi-million-dollar enterprises. Banks, companies with international reputations. They don't want to advertise the fact that they've been defrauded. They'd rather write it off. Now will you come in?"

"What is this place?" India asked as she went inside and looked around the half-gutted interior, which looked to be in the throes of major rebuilding although she could see no work in progress.

"This?" the priest's smile was grim. "This is a long-term shelter for people with . . . well, you could say people at the end of the line with problems government institutions don't want. It was scheduled for completion six months ago, only the money ran out. Come this way and I'll take you through. We're using the church hall as a day-care center."

India stepped over a tray of used mugs and old milk cartons abandoned in the middle of the floor. "Who comes here?"

"People with drug addiction problems. Mind those boards there."

"Drug addicts." India couldn't help recoiling slightly. Father Fitzgerald's smile had nothing to do with humor.

The hall at the back looked to be in much the same state as the church and consisted of two large rooms. One contained a television set which a few people were watching from an assortment of greasy armchairs; the other was a dining room and kitchen combined, and from it came a good smell of percolating coffee and frying bacon. A man in a large butcher's apron was adding eggs to the pan and whistling to himself.

"That's Mel Wooster," Father Fitzgerald said.

"Sunny side up or over easy?" Mel asked. The unkempt girl standing at his side with a plate seemed frightened, or confused, or both. At any rate, she was unwilling to speak. She just peered at the empty plate. Mel took it from her hands and eased on fried eggs and bacon. Then he took her to a table and sat her down. In her dusty patchwork dress she looked like a butterfly someone had squashed and thrown away half-dead. The others, all of them young and dreadfully thin, stared at India, but with a curious lack of interest. They looked like phantoms, suspended, holding on to life by just one slender thread.

Father Fitzgerald watched her staring. "Most of them have been strung out on heroin for years," he said. "Been in prison, bounced from one government clinic to the next. We try here to give some continuity—build up something that will create an atmosphere of mutual support. Unfortunately we don't have the facilities for overnight care."

"How y'doing there?" Mel came over to them. He had the smashed-in face of a man who had spent a number of unsuccessful years in the boxing ring, and a cheerful grin. Introductions over, Mel went back to his stove and cracked more eggs. He called over his shoulder, "Be fixing some fresh coffee in a couple minutes."

India watched as Father Fitzgerald said a few words to everyone in the room, then he showed her to a small table where they could talk without being overheard. She pulled up a chair and sat down. "But what happens? Where do they go at night?"

"Where do they go? Now there's a question. Some have places in homeless shelters. They're usually pretty squalid. Or else they camp out in the alleys. We have the go-ahead from the licensing authority for a board and care residence, so as soon as the building next door is completed and fully equipped, we're in business. We'll be able to provide clean rooms, regular meals, a clinic monitoring medication."

"You said the money ran out. What happened? Did you go over budget?"

Father Fitzgerald looked at her a long moment. "No. The money was there all right, in a special account."

She shouldn't have come. She didn't want to hear this. "What happened?"

Mel came over with a pot of coffee and a plate of pancakes which he put on the table beside them. More people had appeared and he ambled over to greet them. India stared at the pancakes as if they might suddenly get up and bite her.

The priest poured the coffee. "The money? The organization wouldn't overlook a lucrative source like the Church—would they now." He showed little emotion, but the accent, the tone, was out of Ireland. "The main problem stems from the Church's use of an 'offshore' bank. It has been exploited, vast sums siphoned into Mafia banks."

"You're saying that these are the secret banks Jack is supposed to run."

"Full marks. You're learning. Naturally the Church is trying to keep the lid shut tight on the whole affair to prevent a public scandal. What does it mean to us? The money is no longer there to complete the shelter. Not only that, we need regular funds to keep this place open."

She was aware of everything around them, but she didn't see anything. She looked at her coffee. It looked and smelled delicious—but she couldn't lift it to her lips. she didn't want to.

"I knew about the secret banks. It was just a lucky chance I found out that Luigi Frediano had Mafia connections. The salon was a front, the place was being used as a holding station."

India had a vision of Luigi clad in tangerine—she saw him quite clearly as though she had come from the darkness into the light. It was difficult to think of Luigi being connected with the Mafia. The picture changed and he was sitting in black women's underwear with his neck spiked by scissors. "Who killed him?"

"The Mafia. He had to be killed because they suspected he had set the raid up. Treachery is never to be forgiven. I think the man who followed you today murdered Luigi Frediano. The only name I have for him is Fregara. Not much is known about him and it's difficult to find out. He followed you. I thought at first he might have been your bodyguard."

"But why would he follow me?"

"Perhaps your husband doesn't trust you?"

"That's monstrous. There's no reason for him not to," India said. She bit her lip. "Until now," she added somewhat bitterly.

"Then there is someone else in the organization who doesn't trust you, an enemy of your husband's, perhaps."

India had been listening with a kind of blank horror on her face. She said slowly, "Somebody sent me a photograph of Luigi's body, the one that was printed in the papers. It terrified me. I told Jack about it."

"Were any more sent to you?"

The thought exploded in her. "No."

"You were under his protection."

India had sought Jack's protection. She just hadn't realized how much was on offer. How easily she had let him take her in, warm her until she expanded with joy, with love.

Father Fitzgerald was watching her. Finally he said quietly, "Someone called me when Monsignor Haughey was taken ill. He made a confession on his deathbed. The secrets of the confessional are inviolate, but I can tell you that through Monsignor Haughey's confession I learned of the Church's involvement with the Mafia— and with your husband." She didn't think she could stand it. The sweat ran down between her breasts. She thought of the man she had trusted, loved, married—

"I have to ask him. I have to hear what he has to say."

"India." He reached out a hand. " It would be dangerous to ask such questions."

"You don't know Jack. He's a good man. He wouldn't harm anyone."

"No?" Father Fitzgerald said harshly. "Then take a good look around you. Great God in heaven, who do you think supplies the heroin?"

India stared at the empty faces of the people at the tables around her. They were wrecks, half-rescued. Taken in tow by this priest who had become part of a desperate scheme to save them. Sick, she thought what the men must be like who dealt in this kind of misery, men with Florida tans and $5,000 sharkskin suits, sleek, well-barbered men living high on the proceeds from their filthy trade. Murderous bastards. Jack—

"I can't believe that he would . . . not Jack." At first she wasn't aware she had spoken.

"Then don't believe it. Forget it and go. Say nothing. It is your only hope of staying safe."

"Safe . . ." The word receded. It seemed actually to have died before being properly uttered, as if it represented a state of being already lost to her.

"It's your only chance. And mine." Father Fitzgerald gave her a gentle smile. "Talking to Jack about the things you know could get me killed."

India shivered. He hesitated before telling her one final truth. "You have to understand the outcome would be the same if you told the police. The Mafia would get to me. They're the ones with the hidden money and everyone—the banks, the police, politicians— everyone is working for them. Take money belonging to the Mob and you sign your own death warrant."

India couldn't move. She couldn't take her eyes away from his.

Their purity gave her the feeling that if she looked hard enough, she would be able to see right into his soul, just as it had been when she was a child, looking up into a high blue sky and thinking she could see through to heaven.

"In ordinary circumstances," he said gently, "I could not ask you to remain silent, because I have broken the law. You were right—I should be made accountable and punished for it. But for the sake of these young people, I ask you, I beg you, not to give the police my name." He was talking to her, quietly, in his good English with its undercurrent of Irish softness, and she was made aware of his faith; it was this quality in him that drew her, made her believe in his ultimate innocence.

Her eyes went to the junk-sick faces. She was seeing them now through the priest's eyes, beginning to understand his mission.

In the ordinary sense, he had committed a criminal act. But she couldn't think of him as a criminal, no matter how much evidence there was against him. She saw only that he had sacrificed everything in order to snatch something back from the avaricious men who had stolen it in the first place—not for himself, but for the needs of others.

The Mafia were capable of doing just about anything. But would they murder a priest? They murdered Luigi, but Luigi wasn't a priest.

With these questions spinning in her head and a feeling of having been persuaded into a game of Russian roulette, India gave her promise. How could she do anything else? She was not prepared to risk Father Fitzgerald's life or the work he was doing here. It was something she could not do.

But what if Father Fitzgerald was mistaken about Jack's involvement? She had to give Jack the benefit of the doubt. He had to have his chance to explain.

If she loved him, didn't she owe him that much?

Nine

There was a light on in the kitchen. India pushed open the door wondering if it was Sonny there, wondering what she would do if it was. But it was only Fitzroy. He had one of the cats on a square of newspaper on the table, dusting him down with flea powder.

It was late in the evening. On the way back from the Church of Our Lady that afternoon India had asked the priest to take her to her cousin's house. Not that she felt like company—she couldn't discuss what had happened with anybody—not a word of it—but neither had she wanted to come back here. She had phoned Wilma and Fitzroy (who were living in during Jack's absence) to let them know she was with family, and then stayed on to dinner.

"That Sonny." Fitzroy scowled. "Sits on the sofa all day, drinks Mr. Jack's liquor, acts like he owns the place. Wants you to think he's some big fella. But I see some of the bad trade he associates with. Oh yeah, he had two people in here yesterday I wouldn't want in my house. Wilma, she calls up Mr. Jack and she tells him she's not staying in the same house as Sonny, and Mr. Jack says that's fine with him because he was going to fly his ass right out of here anyway. And I'm sorry, Miss India, but those were his very words."

"Then . . ." India got the feeling she was inhabiting another world, one nobody had told her anything about. "Does that mean Sonny has gone?"

"Sure thing. He is *gone.*"

Thank God for that at least. India picked the cat up and rubbed his ears. She sneezed. "You know, Fitzroy, I think I'll buy him a flea collar."

"Mr. Jack don't like those collars on his cats. Says the toxins are harmful."

She remembered the scene that afternoon, and put the cat down. She felt like packing and taking a plane to London. Getting out *now.*

"He really has left?"

"Who, Sonny? Sure he has. And Mr. Jack will be home in the morning. We told him you're out visiting your folks. You feeling good now, Miss India?"

"Yes, thanks," she lied. "Good night." She wondered if she would ever feel good again.

She went upstairs. Everything in the bedroom held traces of Jack. She wandered about touching his things. In a red enameled bowl were his cuff links. She picked up a pair, heavy gold with beveled edges, her present to him on their wedding day. He hadn't worn them. Quickly she put them back. Jack had become someone she didn't know, a stranger she had married in a ridiculous bid for happiness.

Even the room felt like someone else's she had wandered into by mistake, as one did at a party, a room she could admire and then leave and go back to the comfort of home. She sat down on the bed and stared at the streak of streetlight coming between the drapes.

She *was* home, and thinking otherwise could be dangerous.

Paulie was slipping out of his lightweight jacket, his pearl-gray tie was knotted loose. He began rolling up his shirtsleeves. "You do great buckwheat pancakes," he said. Wilma beamed. She took trouble with her cooking, liked to have it appreciated. Paulie calmly began stacking the dishes. Jack noted the rapport with something like relief.

Paulie was replacing Sonny. For it to work, Wilma had to be completely won over. But Paulie knew how to handle himself. He'd be doing the dishes and helping around the place. Two days and he'd have Wilma eating out of his hand.

Paulie had met Jack off the early-morning plane from New York. Jack already knew the details. At first he had been ready to whack Angelo for stepping way out of line. When he simmered down he realized Paulie was more suitable for the job. And the vacancy existed.

He glanced at his watch. "I'll take some coffee up to India," Jack said.

India didn't hear his knock. She was in the bathroom with the water running. Jack went into the bedroom and put the cup down on a side table, careful not to spill the coffee, and went over to the half-open door.

He almost knocked. Except, when he saw her he forgot everything, even his hand which was still hovering in midair, because she was in front of the mirror washing her face and she didn't have a thing on. She had her hair pinned up and it was half falling down at the back. His naked lady before the mirror, breasts that danced as she moved, a bush of ginger hair between her legs. She had him feeling things he hadn't felt in years.

It was all there, glistening, warm, inviting. All he had to do was reach out and touch her—and she would scream the house down and try and kill him again.

The New York psychotherapist he has resorted to told him that was natural. He had said that after being raped a woman had difficulty relating to men, because at the back of her mind the man, any man, making love to her could turn into a rapist. So that was what had happened on their wedding night. In her mind she had turned him into a rapist. The psychotherapist also told Jack the emotional effects of rape could take a long time to heal.

All the same, Jack's eyes glazed over looking at her. He couldn't help himself. He kept remembering the night she had passed out cold in his arms, the hot, glorious feel of her. Nobody made him as horny as he got from just looking at India, not even Livia.

Then she turned off the taps, looked up and saw him.

"Oh." She yanked a towel from the rack and held it to her breasts. Her neck was red as a beet—she was ashamed of the way she had acted the other night. Ashamed and embarrassed.

They stared at each other for a long moment before Jack realized he had been moving towards her. He stopped. The razor episode had held the psychotherapist's undivided attention: to stop her going for the carving knife when she felt threatened he thought Jack should keep his distance, at least until after she had had the benefit of the psychotherapy he was going to give her. It sounded reasonable to Jack.

"Listen," he said. "I'll get my things and move into the spare room."

The way she was looking at him, as if he were a stranger, made him nervous.

"Jack . . . Oh Jack. Why didn't you tell me . . . ?"

"Tell you?" Jeez, she was het up about something. He loved the way little sparks came off her eyes, but he hoped she wasn't getting ready to have another fit of hysterics.

Gingerly, he asked, "Tell you what?"

"You see I know—your family—I know. You changed your name, didn't you?" She was losing control. Her teeth were beginning to chatter. God, please let him tell me he has nothing to do with them. If he says that he changed his name so he could begin a new life of his own, I'll believe him, I promise I will. I'll forget about this whole thing.

Jack was staring at her, just staring, and that expression, deadly, as if he hated her . . .

"You don't have anything to do with them—you don't own secret banks—say you don't—"

Jack's voice ground the words out in small chunks. "How did you find *that* out?"

He hadn't denied it! Her mind slipped, became dark. She didn't care then what she said. Instinct saved her when she was ready to blurt out the whole truth. The instinct for survival that makes a drowning man cling on to anything that will float.

"Sonny told me. He was drinking—your Old Napoleon. He was drinking, telling me these things. That was why I went out. I didn't know what to think. I wanted you to say it wasn't true, I—"

"Who else knows?"

"No one."

His eyes narrowed into a black stare, fixed unwaveringly on her face. The sheer grimness of it made her feel weak.

India said, "It's not something I would want anyone to know."

She sounded so convincing, he believed her. "Good, you're learning."

"It's not something I want to learn. You're not the person I married. You're someone else. Someone I don't know."

"Bullshit! I'm the same man you loved before. I haven't changed." He gave her an ugly smile. "I'm still the man you knew and professed to love when you screamed your head off the other night."

"Jack, I—"

"I could have married any woman I chose. I chose you." The words had the snap of a steel trap closing.

"Jack, we could have the marriage annulled."

He leaned forward slightly. "You're my wife." His face was tight, his tone uncompromising. "You belong to me now. You're not blood, but get this, you're Family."

She could feel the heat of his anger from across the space between them. He terrified her.

"You can have your own bedroom. I won't touch you. But don't lock the door against me. Not ever." He dug his hand into a pocket and pulled out a card and gave it to her. India looked at the embossed name. "If being the most expensive shrink has anything to do with being the best, then he's the best. See him. Get straightened out. You can talk your head off to him and it won't go further than that, he's in the Family. But no one else. To the rest of the world, you're my loving wife."

Up until then there had been a part of her that hadn't really believed it, but in that moment she knew it was all true. She knew one thing. Women who married into the Mafia stayed in the Mafia. It was a life sentence.

Jack turned on his heel and walked out of the bathroom. When he came back he was carrying her robe. He handed it to her. "Put this on and come sit down, your coffee's getting cold."

India dragged the robe around herself, knotting the tie with numb fingers. Jack was sitting in the Chippendale wing chair he'd had upholstered in Chinese red to match the red watered-silk coverlet now hopelessly crushed in a skein of sheets on the rumpled bed. India sat down, crossed her legs, and faced him with a look guaranteed to give any man tachycardia.

"India, listen to me. I was going to tell you. But I was waiting until you got to know them. India, they're not so bad, they're like any other family. Concetta, she's the Don's wife, she's looked after me since I was a baby. I love her like she was my own mother. She sends her regards. Papa too. He's looking forward to meeting you at lunch next weekend. Concetta's planned on having a big family get-together, and you're the guest of honor. Listen, you've got to forget all that rubbish the papers write about the Family. Half of it's fiction anyway. Sometimes I fall down laughing, reading some of the stuff they print."

India didn't speak. To belong at a rowdy happy table, laugh, quarrel—all her life she had longed to be part of a big family.

Now she was. All she had to do was forget who they were. Keep quiet, say nothing, never ask. As Jack's wife she would have everything. India was seeing a vision of what could be, and she shut it off. She would rather go back to London and a poky flat and work for her living.

"I never saw the funny side," she said. She took a deep breath and felt a little calmer. "Jack, I have to know if you work for them."

"A large proportion of my practice is taken up with Family business, yes. Mostly reinvestment income."

"Criminal income reinvestment."

"I handle legitimate enterprises, the same as I would for any other business, and like any other business it is not something I would discuss at home."

She wanted to ask if he was responsible for having people killed, but couldn't bring herself to. Was she afraid that he wouldn't deny it?

"India, there are matters I cannot discuss with you, matters that are not discussed with wives."

"Oh." There was a dry, bitter taste in her mouth. "There is something I have to ask you, and I must have an answer."

"Sure," Jack said gravely. "What is it?"

"Do you deal in heroin—does your family?" India knew that it was his answer to this question that would make her decide to leave him. Then—that day.

"No, we don't, and you have to believe that." He held her eyes; it was India who looked away first.

"Because I couldn't live with that," she said, and her voice was becoming harsh again with panic and scared dismay. "You have to tell me the truth."

"Truth is a very complex thing," Jack said blandly. "Sometimes we have to make compromises."

India let herself look at him.

"Jesus, all right, the truth is we don't deal in heroin."

"Very well then." She ran a sticky tongue over her dry lips. "Did you have a man follow me, a man in a gray suit?" she asked.

Jack's eyes narrowed perceptibly. "Why do you suppose that?"

"I saw him when I left the house. I went to church. I sat there a long time, thinking about the things Sonny had told me, and he was there waiting when I came out. He didn't notice me leaving. Probably because I didn't go back to the car. I felt like walking. The car's still there, actually . . . You had him spy on me, didn't you?"

Jack's eyes had become needles, for an instant he had seen something in her expression and wondered if she was lying. But only for an instant.

"You have to realize that my father has a lot of enemies and that everyone in the Family has to have protection. Yes, we had someone watch out for you. He's good, one of the best."

"Is he a hit man?"

"You've watched too much television," Jack snapped. "I run a business like any other. I don't have hit men on the payroll. Please, India, can I tell Concetta you'll come to lunch?" He was looking at her, not just looking but exploring. Assessing. India felt like a rabbit caught in a trap.

"And Sonny? Where is he?"

"Back in the pool. He wasn't suitable. Wilma didn't like him."

He rose before her eyes, took a small package from his pocket and dropped it into her lap. He bent and kissed her lightly on the top of her head before walking to the door.

"By the way," he said, turning around. "The man in the gray suit, his name is Paulie. He'll be taking Sonny's place."

India was staring at the package. She raised her head with a jerk. "No!" she looked as if someone had punched her in the stomach.

"Don't worry," Jack said a trifle uneasily, "he won't have to accompany you about. I discussed it with Papa and he agrees. But someone has to be in the house while I'm away." He opened the door. "I won't be home for dinner this evening and I'll probably be late." The door closed quietly.

She must have sat there for a full ten minutes before she began at last to unwrap the heavy folds of silver paper from the jeweler's box. She opened it and she was looking at the kind of diamond and emerald necklace Sotheby's would be happy to auction. It didn't take a jeweler's loupe to know they were serious stones. She picked it out—the eye-scorching diamonds shivering in her hands—turned it this way and that. The clasp was gold with a large cushion-shaped emerald embedded in its center. And then she saw the engraving. Round curly letters; she looked closely and spelled out the word *eternamente.* The Italian word meaning "forever."

The word began to sink in, the implication. "You belong to me now. You're not blood, but you're Family." Not even so much the words as the way he had said them, the cold fury in his voice.

"Oh my God." She flung the necklace, the box, the silver paper on the bed and wrapped her arms about herself. "Oh my God." She was shivering.

Suddenly she had a longing for the Ross household, the dull comforting routine, the children, familiar things.

A door banging shut downstairs startled her. India imagined a cell door slamming shut on her. Hearing another sound her gaze shifted focus.

As she sat there, impotently staring at the bedroom door, she heard it again. A footstep, a movement, someone on the other side. Not Wilma, not part of the usual household noises. Slowly she rose, and stealthily she stole across Jack's prized Aubusson rugs towards the door. A floorboard creaked underfoot and she paused . . .

Nothing.

Then she heard the faint sound of someone moving away. By the time she had gained control of her legs, walked forward and pulled open the door, there was no one there.

She hadn't been mistaken. Someone had been standing right outside her bedroom door. Jack had already left; she would have heard Wilma. Then she realized. That someone had to be the man in gray; the new man who was taking Sonny's place and whom Jack called Paulie.

Throwing her clothes on—anything that came to hand—she was dressed in five minutes.

She knew the instant she walked into the kitchen he was the one pointed out to her by the priest. Not only that, he was the ferret-like bodyguard whose face had been turned to the camera in the photograph young James had cut from the newspaper of the gangster Salvatore Coltelli leaving Gamberoni's restaurant in New York. The recognition froze India to the spot.

Paulie glanced in her direction, pushing himself up from the table where he had been sitting with a cup of coffee. "Ma'am." Polite, impassive, affable as they come. It did not help. India, looking into the twilight eyes—without trace of warmth or any emotion, so completely impersonal and yet predatory—saw him for all the priest had said he was, and now he was in their home and he would take his orders from Jack. The shock was severe.

Wilma came up from the basement carrying a wicker basket full of clean laundry, her slippered feet slapping at the kitchen tiles. Paulie slid into action. He was across the floor, had taken the load from her before India could blink.

"Don't you go fussing now, y'hear," Wilma said. But India could see she was pleased.

"You want the ironing board up as well, Momma?"

Momma?

"Yeah," Wilma said with satisfaction. When Paulie had gone to get the board, she whispered, "He's cute."

Cute? On Father Fitzgerald's information her new protector was a contracted killer, and here he was, flitting about their kitchen in the guise of a helpful gofer.

India felt the gun go off in her head.

All night she'd been over the ifs and buts. She did it again. If she hadn't gone to have her hair done that day. If she hadn't met Jack, fallen in love.

But it had all happened. She had married him, taken him for better or for worse, and the worst was that her new husband was the son of a Sicilian Mafioso who ran vice and pornography rings, who terrorized people, who could have men killed for money or power, or simply because they were in his way.

She had married a man who concealed his Mafia connections under a respectable title, and even if Jack was not, as he claimed, involved in criminal activities, she would have to be very naïve to think that the Family business—extortion, prostitution, loan sharking, labor racketeering—didn't generate a continuing flow of cash into his accounts.

Leave him, she told herself. Go back to London.

To what?

It didn't matter, she would be safe there. Wouldn't she? She watched Paulie set up the ironing board, angle it in a different position, more convenient.

He stood there, across eight feet of warm kitchen, tinkering with Wilma's iron, and suddenly he lifted his head and looked at her with his dead, secret policeman's eyes and it came to India with dreadful clarity: if she left Jack ever, she would not be safe anywhere.

Ten

There was not a soul in sight. The tall swing gates were electronically operated, electronically protected. They closed silently behind them. Jack pressed down on the accelerator of the Mercedes his brother Angelo had had waiting for them at the airport and glanced across the acres of green turf, looking for the Doberman pinschers.

Nothing.

No dogs, no armed guards at the gate. Concetta had taken a hand in the arrangements for India's introduction to the family, and Jack breathed a sigh of relief. He glanced at India sitting primly at his side, still disappointed at her refusal to wear the necklace, but knowing she was right. Maybe it *was* too flashy for Sunday lunch.

The driveway took them past an old stone carriage house bristling with ivy and electronic devices, accommodating four spacious garages at ground level and cramped quarters for the staff upstairs. The house beyond, built in uncompromising concrete blocks, rose from what could only be described as a concrete parking lot.

Don Salvatore was only happy when looking out on to bare spaces. Despite the dogs and a sophisticated alarm system which was practically fail-safe, he couldn't see the point of a lot of trees and bushes that might harbor would-be assailants.

In fact, the Don didn't like windows at all, which was why the ground floor had none and why the house looked so much like a fortress. As a concession to his wife Concetta, he had allowed windows on the two upper stories, just as he had conceded to her passion for growing rhododendrons. These were back where the Doberman pinschers were kenneled at the rear of the house, where the parking lot joined the lawns which stretched to the concrete wall encircling the estate.

The front door opened as the Mercedes rolled to a stop, and a woman with wavy dark hair and plump arms came out. India was staring at the house. Jack got out and kissed Concetta on both cheeks, asked her how she was, then, very much the attentive husband, came round to assist India from the car.

Lunch was to be served at one; it was ten minutes to the hour. Concetta hurried them, not a little apologetically, into the elevator. They were whizzed upwards, India wearing a glassy smile that looked as if it might fracture and fly into bits. When the door opened there were cries of welcome and they stepped straight into a large room.

Concetta smiled and nodded as Jack took India's shrinking hand lovingly but firmly and began the introductions by slapping the shoulder of a youngish man (mid-thirties, India guessed) with a crewcut.

"My stepbrother, Tom, and his wife, Betsy." Jack kissed her soundly on the cheek. Betsy wore almond-shaped glasses that crested near her temples, and a reddish gold beehive.

"I do declare," Betsy cried warmly, holding India at arm's length and studying her, "aren't you just the prettiest thing."

Jack was hugging a dark-haired woman who held a sleeping baby against her shoulder with a practiced hand; a tiny creature with stick-insect legs and arms in a bundle of cream wool crochet. The woman was his stepsister, Teresa; India hadn't even known of her existence. Teresa embraced her. "You sure are pretty."

It transpired that Teresa's husband couldn't be with them because he was working. India wondered what kind of work. No one volunteered the information and she didn't ask.

Tom told her he had a veterinary practice back in Lewisville, Ohio, and two children, who right then were with their grandfather helping fit in pieces of the Taj Mahal. His tone of voice said: "My life is the essence of respectability, my work is open and admirable, and the dear old man at leisure in his study working at his jigsaw puzzle with his beloved grandchildren is, despite a roster of corruption (entirely forgivable slips and errors of judgment any big corporate man could be guilty of), so lovable as to be entirely normal, the kind of granddad Norman Rockwell drew for covers of the *Saturday Evening Post.*"

The paneled room was furnished with big sturdy sofas and chairs covered in a kind of leather that was warm and surprisingly silky to touch; like lizard's skin, India thought as she sat down and glanced about. There were windows, which were wide open, and a pleasant breeze was helped along by old-fashioned ceiling fans.

A door opened and a short stout man entered the room with a giggling child on each shoulder. He was smiling broadly. His shirt, unbuttoned at the neck, revealed a brindled acre of curly hair. The man so clearly showing his delight with his grandchildren was Salvatore Coltelli. Behind him came a young man in a beige jacket with enormous shoulders and a black shirt buttoned to his massive neck. Angelo.

India, who on impulse had risen to her feet, stood stock still as if wishing for the chameleon's power of changing color so she might remain invisible. She was transported forward by Jack. Immediately Salvatore lifted the children down and opened his arms engagingly to her.

His smile was magnificent, his manners a charming display of pleasure at meeting her, Jack's dear wife. He apologized for not being there to greet her on arrival, explaining the delay: the jigsaw puzzle had proved too absorbing for his grandchildren to tear themselves away from—and such was his dignity that India momentarily forgot the circumstances of his life.

It was all so—she looked around the room—so ordinary. They seemed so nice, despite the sudden awful doubt when she offered her hand to Angelo and he looked as though one wrong move and he would have it off.

It was a shock to realize she could sit at the table next to Salvatore Coltelli (Jack was seated at the other end beside Concetta), drink his wine and laugh at his anecdotes, which were in fact very funny. She could not know the Don's peculiar charm of manner had the effect of subjugating all in his presence. He was famous for it.

The feeling of dreadful unease came back in the middle of Concetta's *sfoglia madonita,* a beautiful pastry stuffed with sweet cream cheese, perfumed with cinnamon and lemon zest.

Salvatore had been speaking about the global changes in the weather when he was suddenly looking at Teresa, "How's Rocco?" he asked benevolently.

"Fine, Papa."

"Your husband doesn't grant us the pleasure of his company today." Don Salvatore went on smiling.

"There was a problem, Papa. He had to work, he called to tell you . . ." Teresa's mouth was large, it was a mouth that blurted.

No one said anything.

"Listen to me, Teresa, dearest child, ask Rocco to come and see me this afternoon at five." He accepted another of Concetta's almond pastries.

"Yes, Papa."

Jack began pouring more wine, solicitously refreshing everyone's glass in turn. He topped India's up, beamed at her proudly, and moved on around the table. Tom had begun telling them about the arrangement he had with a local dentist who let him use the facilities, and the patient who wandered in to find an anesthetized German shepherd dog in the chair having its teeth cleaned. Tom maintained he couldn't understand the fuss that ensued.

Salvatore wasn't listening; he leaned toward India. "Jack has got a fine-looking English lady for a wife," he confided. He patted her hand and smiled at her. "You do us honor. I can understand his hurry. But this sudden wedding of yours was a surprise to us."

India looked up and encountered a piercing gleam in those eyes which seemed as soft and smooth as creamery butter. It was as unnerving as finding a needle in a down comforter. Added to that was a slight squint which gave her the feeling of being engaged by one eye while being examined by the other.

Something coiled and uncoiled deep in her intestines. "It was . . ." her mouth had gone completely dry, "we just . . ."

"I understand," he said gently. "I remember how these things were. Ah, God in his mercy works in a strange way." He blinked rapidly and made the sign of the cross. "Frederico was the eldest, his death came as a terrible blow to me. Now it is Jack who must take his place." He held her wrist and with his singular gaze on her India dared not breathe. "And you must, of course, realize how important this is to me."

He was staring at her the way he might a small caged animal on a treadmill. She felt a hand on her shoulder and almost leapt to her feet. It was Jack. He bent his head to say he was going out to make a phone call and to warn her they had to leave soon for the airport for the flight back to Washington.

She was about to nod when all at once she became aware of Angelo on the other side of the table looking at her with such hatred . . .

India drew in her breath, it was like being directly in the path of a moving glacier. This was a face, implacable, stone-hard, the face of an experienced killer.

These people were not friendly. The Don was devious as a parrot. His job was to label and dissect; Angelo's to kill. And Jack was the negotiator, the smiling acceptable face of a criminal organization. A shiver ran down the length of her body. She was scared. These men were as dangerous as she had imagined them to be, and she knew that all her life, as long as she lived, she would be afraid of them.

As the realization finally began to hit, smiling was like a death-defying high-wire act. But it was a dazzling performance. She smiled at the Don, at Angelo, she turned her smiling face up to her husband, whose hand still lay heavily on her shoulder.

"Of course, darling, you go ahead. I'll be ready to leave whenever you want." She dimpled, she held him with her eyes. Hers was a peculiarly English compliant charm and her smile had all the sweetness and simplicity of an old-fashioned country rose. She was Jack's pretty new bride and she smiled because she knew her life might depend on it.

India nosed the car cautiously around Dupont Circle, she wanted Connecticut Avenue . . . what a madhouse, oh Jesus, wrong lane, won't make it . . . go round again . . . an opening . . . NOW—she shoved the station wagon into high gear and squealed across two lanes of traffic.

God! Her heart still beat with a nervous twitch. She wiped her brow and settled down beside an enormous white Oldsmobile convertible encrusted back and front with chrome, the kind they stopped making about 1973, and became part of the relentless spill of traffic streaming up the long avenue to Chevy Chase.

Although it was not yet two, it was most likely that Father Fitzgerald would be finished taking the one o'clock confession. Since the priest's revelations on her last visit three weeks ago, she had avoided coming back. The church seemed ominous now. She found Holy Trinity in Georgetown conveniently nearer and much more comfortable.

But she was no longer the new bride very much in love with her husband, first shocked by what the priest had divulged, and then devastated. She knew the kind of man she had married, she had met his family, saw what her life would be like. Driving up the hill on this perfect sunshiny day it was indeed Jack she thought of; and of how to leave him.

India parked on Connecticut Avenue opposite the Chevy Chase Library, thus avoiding the free-for-all chaos of traffic speeding around the Circle. The day had become hot, stifling; she left her linen jacket in the car, locked the door carefully, and walked the short distance to the church. Under the broiling sun her crisp lawn blouse wilted and stuck like an extra skin to her body. Even so, she lingered extra minutes outside the entrance before entering the cool darkness.

Few people came at that time of day. Someone was playing a few practice pieces on the organ. She took the holy water on her finger-tips and made the sign of the cross, genuflecting before going to sit at one end of a pew. She bowed her head. A door banged and her eyes jerked open, the candles flickered redly into the semi-darkness, she could hear the muffled tread of footsteps. When she looked up the priest was standing by her side.

She leaned forward, clutching at the hard wooden rail of the pew. "Father Fitzgerald," she said, "I have to talk to you."

He paused a surprisingly long time and India was again made aware of an irrational coldness in the makeup of that beautifully shaped face, only to be swept up in the next instant by the gleaming vitality of his smile.

"Come, we'll go into the sacristy," he said, and led the way across the main body of the church. In the small room he offered India a chair, then sat down and drew out a cigarette pack. "Do you smoke?"

"No." She watched Father Fitzgerald take a cigarette, noticing how his wrists protruded from the black sleeves, how white and long, the extreme delicacy of the strong hands. She didn't smoke. But the pills? She was cutting down on them. They only served to increase her sense of unreality and in the end she felt even more depressed. Felt as though she were in quicksand, that was the scary thing about them. She knew she had to stop. One thing at a time.

"I was right," the priest said quietly.

"What do I do?"

Something. It would take money and she would have to borrow it. Adrian had his own financial problems. Her father was the logical choice. Could she? After throwing back his check? After the contempt? Tell him now that she had married into the Mafia and wanted money so she could run away?

Father Fitzgerald looked at her closely. "How much is Jack aware of?"

She explained what had happened. "I asked him about the secret banks . . . he didn't deny anything. Then I had to lie to him. I said that Sonny had been drinking and talked. Jack believed me. I don't know what will happen to Sonny—I daren't think." Then she told him about discovering Paulie in her own kitchen. She deciphered concern in his expression. It was a relief to talk; she should have come sooner.

"Did he tail you here?" the priest asked.

"No." She shook her head, adamant. "No, I made sure. But he frightens me. Really frightens me. And Jack, he's just . . . watching and waiting . . ." For what? But she knew. Jack was waiting for her to come to him. He wanted her. She told Father Fitzgerald about meeting the family.

"Salvatore Coltelli?" The priest propped his elbows on the table and studied her over tented fingers.

"Yes. At first I couldn't get over how friendly and nice they were, the ordinary things they talked about. I sat next to Salvatore at lunch."

She told him what had been said, and about Angelo looking at her. "I thought he was going to leap across the table at my throat, he had such a look of hatred on his face."

"Ah, well, you see, Jack did what his father always wanted. He married a nice respectable girl with an impeccable pedigree. You are a part of the plan, the grand design. Angelo resents Jack. After Frederico was killed Angelo thought he would be the one to take over as *capo da famiglia* when his father died. And who is to get it? The younger brother."

"I thought it was something like that," India said heavily. She seemed light-years away from the life she understood.

"What does Jack have to say about it?"

"I never told him. We don't discuss things."

"Not even in bed?" he asked gently. "Bed is where most couples talk."

"We don't share the same bed, Father." She turned red. "The marriage has never been consummated."

The priest nodded, and it struck India oddly that he seemed relieved. But then he murmured, "Perhaps in time," and made it sound encouraging.

"No, Father. I can't live with it." India gave him a worn smile. "Let's just say I found out more about him than the marriage can stand. I can't go on living in that house pretending to be his wife . . . I'm so alone. I thought I'd been lonely before, but it's nothing like this. Father, I need your help."

"You will never be alone," the priest said. "You have God with you. He will give you strength." He paused and then said deliberately, "Through him you will find the strength to stay in the marriage. You must help Jack to save his soul."

Her mouth dropped. It wasn't what she had meant when she had requested help. She wanted to leave Jack and she had come to enlist Father Fitzgerald's aid.

The priest's eyes leveled with hers over pointed fingers. In the suspended light from the stained-glass window, their beautiful distant blue had become as remote to her as glacial outer space. What he suggested was impossible. She had reached the point where she could only continue to do what she was doing if she knew there was a way out.

Always she had assumed that because he had burdened her with the truth, Father Fitzgerald would help her get away to safety. Even if it meant the most drastic of measures, she was prepared to take them. She could change her name, then go somewhere like, for instance, New Zealand—she could get a job as a cook on a sheep station in the high country in the South Island. They would never find her there. But she needed assistance.

The priest folded his arms on the table and looked at her benignly. "Have you not thought of helping others? It would take your mind off your troubles."

Troubles! India looked up at the stained-glass image of a shepherd ministering to a limp lamb as if calling his attention to her own suffering. She was in the midst of a disaster, in the wolf's den waiting to be pounced on, and Father Fitzgerald was talking as though she was having a minor disagreement with her new neighbors.

She laughed. A let's-be-serious laugh. "I really think I have enough of my own." The shepherd was looking down at her reproachfully, the pitiable lamb in his arms. She felt embarrassed. "Well, I mean, what could I do?"

"Work with us at the Center. Help us save the lives of those young people."

Father Fitzgerald got up and walked across to the door, he held it open. "Come and kneel down with me before the altar and we will pray."

Eleven

Livia Dannenburg walked into the office, skirted Jack's over-sized teak desk, and sank to her knees in straight-backed perfection beside his chair. She was dressed simply in one of those little suits that made her accountant whimper when he saw the price tag. It was the sort of tailoring that suggested everything and gave nothing away. But from where Jack sat looking down at the plummeting lapels, all he could see was a deep, distracting cleavage.

"Sweet Jesus, what are you doing? Christ, Livia, get up. The *Sunday Times* correspondent is due here in ten minutes."

Livia lifted Jack's unresisting hand and placed it inside her jacket. She had nothing on. Jack swallowed and felt an urgent need to adjust his clothing.

"Tell that humorless secretary of yours, if she comes in, she joins in."

"Livia, f'God's sake . . ." Livia was unbuttoning one of the two buttons on her jacket, any moment her breasts were going to plop out like ripe luscious fruit. Her perfume came to him in a wave, so warm and suggestive, so redolent . . . Jack had a vision of her lying down on the floor in front of him with her legs spread, wet open lips, pleading with him . . . He seized control of his brain. Livia wanted something.

"Stop doing that!" He grabbed her hand as it ran supple-fingered up the inside of his thigh.

"You want to take me to lunch?" Her hand slipped from his grasp and went for his zipper.

"Jesus, I can't, Livia—" His voice had gone hoarse. Down came the zipper. He was enormous. "I got—" The words turned into a moan. Livia was standing up and lifting her skirt. She was wearing a garter belt with little pink roses and pale, shiny, silky stockings. The second jacket button burst loose right in front of his eyes. "—a lunch meeting with Senator—"

Languidly Livia straddled him in the chair and eased down. He was fully erect.

"Caroline—" He pressed down the intercom button. His voice was reedy like a sick gull. "Hold all my calls." His hand dropped from the machine to the electronic switch that locked the door through to his office. Livia was moving very slowly, taunting him with her eyes. God, she was good. She was soft but firm, Jesus, she was firm. The intercom light came on red.

"Mr. Donovan, sorry, I was on the other phone. I didn't catch what you said. Mr. Cyril Ellis is here, shall I ask him to go in?"

All conceptual structures had ceased to exist for Jack. He was floating at the bottom of an ocean, he was—Livia leaned over and talked into the machine as if she were some cool, pragmatic schoolmistress who was in the process of helping a rather dull pupil with his homework. "Mr. Donovan will be another five minutes. Would you make Mr. Ellis coffee? Thank you, Caroline."

How could she sound like that? Sane, sensible, when his mind had gone to Jell-O. Jack's seized brain was only vaguely aware that something was going on at a higher level. Livia stepped up her pace and he exploded from the ocean bottom, up, up, Jesus he was melting . . .

Livia dismounted and walked through to the washroom, leaving Jack slumped glassy-eyed in his black leather tilt-back chair. She was back in a moment with half a crystal tumbler of Scotch. He took a sip and began pulling the threads back.

"You going to cancel that Senator—" Livia was putting on a pair of Paloma Picasso sunglasses, "—and take me to lunch?" She wanted to glide into the Ritz-Carlton with Jack on her arm so her friends could see he was still hers, married or not.

"What say we make it dinner instead, in New York?"

Livia began to relent. She had learned quickly that with Jack there was sometimes no second offer. "Done," she said. She leaned forward and gave his mouth a butterfly twirl with her tongue. Jack held her off.

"Don't start that again," he begged. But feeling only marginally reassured, he got up and strode into the safety of his private bathroom, locking the door behind him, to get himself back into shape.

Senator Thomas Edward Kelly (or Ned Kelly as he was better known on the hill) was second-generation American. His grandparents had been among those Irish farmers fleeing the potato famine. Too poor to pay the fares out of Boston, they packed into a fetid room with six others in one of the over-crowded Mick alleys on the waterfront. Ned's father grew up in a wild-eyed religious community with established rituals, rules, and conventions as rigid as any in the Old Country. Tribal rivalries and personal animosities ate into his soul like cancer. He killed himself working three jobs a day so his son could go to college.

Ned Kelly knew what counted: getting ahead, running things. Politics allowed him to grab a fragment of power. Ambitious, aggressive, he extended that fragment by making alliances, joining committees, and grasping the attention of the press and television. He was at home in the boiler-house atmosphere of Washington. Afternoon speeches, fund-raisers, back-to-back sessions with lobbyists, breakfast meetings, lunch and dinner—he was power-broking. He put up a moralistic front and was always running around giving the impression he was doing more to enforce ethical standards in government than anybody else. He was big on all the important issues: for law and order, against organized crime which was making cocaine as available as fast-food pizzas, pro-life and against abortion (if that was what the formula required). Less well known was his sympathy with the Provisional IRA and his maneuvers on its behalf.

A favorite watering hole was the Maison Rouge, where lunch for two costs a week's wages in Brooklyn, and the tab was usually picked up by the lobbyist with whom he was doing business. Today's venue, however, was the City Club, where Ned could be sure of a quiet table because he had clout with the chairman. Soon as Jack knew it was going to be the City Club he got himself wired for taping the conversation. You never knew, perhaps one day Ned Kelly would run for a higher office, and the Family could really benefit from knowing him.

The senator got to the point as soon as the rib steak had been eaten. "I got a situation here I need your help with. I need to buy some high-tech hardware. You know the kind, the stuff only selected army brass can get their hands on, and one or two nice bits the Europeans are turning out now." He looked Jack straight in the eye. "I know you help the CIA get what they want for the little wars they got going all over the world, and I'm not saying I know how you do it. All I'm saying here is, the Freedom Fighters in the IRA need something special."

Jack understood. Ned Kelly was telling him to get the weapons he wanted, or at his next press conference there would be a slip of the tongue, innocent but unfortunate for Jack. Jack would deny it, of course, but the effect would be the same.

Ned Kelly continued. My friends want some timers, the kind they use on the Continent—Memoparks is what they're called. Better get some remote-control devices with micro switches as well, voice-activated, I think they are."

"FX401s," Jack said. "What you're asking for is expensive. Prohibitively so, I would've thought."

"Just name your price, the money is available." The senator beckoned a waiter. "What'll it be, Jack?"

"Just coffee for me thanks, Ned."

"Try some of this." The waiter had brought a bottle of liqueur and two glasses on a tray. Ned claimed it had the deepest, the richest framboise taste of any liqueur in the world, and poured him out a large measure. Jack wondered what the hell the meaning of framboise was, and whether Ned Kelly had shares in Worldwide Distillers Co. He took a sip.

"Sure is smooth." Jack studied the label on the bottle. "We're talking cash up front, right?"

"Right."

"Nice to know there's people in town can back up a deal like this. Should I know them?"

"Jack," Ned Kelly said, "even I don't know who fronts that group. I'm dealing with an intermediary here. All you need to know is we got a large amount of money from an undisclosed source, and there's a big, fat commission in it for you if you get what's wanted."

*   *   *

Father Fitzgerald gave India two days to think about it, then he telephoned and asked if she could come and give them a hand at the Center the following day.

India rubbed her forehead—thinking, she didn't need this. She wanted to find her way out of her own mess, not get involved in other people's.

"It'd only be for a few hours in the morning," the priest said encouragingly as the silence grew longer. "Do you think you can make it?"

With a feeling of sinking into something that was bound to be unpleasant, she said she would try. Then he asked if she wanted him to come by in the morning and pick her up.

"No," she said instinctively. If she drove herself she could leave when she wanted. "Thanks, but it's easier if I take my car." Then she asked him where she should park and the best route to take, though she was sure she would remember the way from the last time.

She put the receiver down thinking that if she hated it, she needn't go back. One morning wasn't going to hurt her. It never occurred to her that getting there was going to be a problem.

It occurred to Fitzroy the next day when she went out to the station wagon parked in the street in front of the house.

"All I know is what I'm saying." Fitzroy shook his head mournfully. "You go down there and park this car in the worst crime sector in Washington, people gonna pass it around and everybody have a piece." He stood rubbing little needlepoints of light into the hood with a polishing cloth and giving India worried sidelong looks.

"Father says there's a place to park underneath the Center. Don't worry, Fitzroy."

"Mr. Jack's sure not keen on your driving down those parts by yourself."

India knew it. But Jack had left early that morning for New York and would be gone for a few days. She glanced back at the house with the feeling that Paulie was there at the window. There was no sign; there never was. But all the same, this feeling of being watched.

"Fitzroy," she chided gently and got into the driver's seat, "the Center's only, what? Less than a dozen blocks north of the White

House?" She paused, her hand on the ignition key. "Don't let Paulie know where I am. I don't trust him, Fitzroy. Please."

Fitzroy grumbled and rubbed off a smudge with his cloth. He didn't share Wilma's enthusiasm for Paulie's presence in the household, but he understood the need for security. There had been so many break-ins and muggings during the daytime that people were scared to open the back door to tradespeople. Everybody was taking measures. Most people got a dog, though.

India didn't drive off until he'd promised her.

All Jack's instincts told him the missing money was now in Ned Kelly's hands. That was the reason for going to New York. A driver was waiting for him at the airport to take him straight out to Long Island to see the Don.

"The senator knows about this?" Salvatore asked.

"He knows I can get weapons for the CIA the U.S. Government isn't able to acquire legitimately," Jack said. "There is nothing to suggest he knows my source or my connections or that we're milking the Defense contracts."

"We have to make sure." The Don patted in a piece of daisy-dotted grass to the Swiss mountain scene he was working on. "We know the raid on Freddy's was done by IRA people. Now with our own money they come back to us to purchase weapons." He smiled in satisfaction and fitted in part of the goatherd. "The senator will give us back our money."

Jack selected a piece of clear blue sky and began hunting for its place above the mountain peaks while he waited for the Don to boil down a plan on how it was going to be achieved.

"The senator is a mover and shaker," Salvatore said, "big on morality. Didn't I hear on the news he wants criminals who sexually assault young girls put away for life?"

"Sounds like him," Jack said. "He runs a forum on capital punishment for rape cases."

"Devoted to his wife and young children, and goes to church a lot, but plays down being a Roman Catholic," the Don mused.

"That's the ticket he's running on," Jack agreed. "There's a rumor he'll announce his candidacy for President soon."

Salvatore gazed dreamily at the peaceful scene he was constructing. "I'll have Domenico Cechetti work out the details. We'll make the Senator an offer—better for you to let us handle that end. Just be ready to pick up the money."

Jack nodded.

Then the Don was talking about India. How a sweet girl like that from a good family (she was perfect, she didn't have a thought in her head) was going to be a big asset to him. His eyes were all but lost within their halos of fatty tissue. Jack felt the stare rather than saw it.

"I want the next head of this family to be so far removed from the street business no one will be able to touch him," Salvatore said.

Jack understood what the Don was telling him. He, Jack, was going to be the next head of the Family.

He was the logical choice, and Jack knew it. Even as a young boy he'd had this conviction he would be the one to succeed his father, chosen over the older sons. It stood to reason—his name anglicized, the good schools, the assumption never spoken but there from the beginning that he would marry out of his Wop immigrant past into WASP society.

He had done that. He was moving into a hugely wealthy stratum of society and already he had more power and more money than any of them. By the time he was fifty he would be old money, leader of a new generation. The hoodlums, the Angelos of his father's empire, wouldn't even exist.

All that Jack understood. But would Angelo?

India leaned over the steering wheel, her hands tightly curled around it, as she looked for a street name. She was heading in the right direction, northeast, along a street of tan-colored apartment buildings with partially boarded-up windows . . . but surely she hadn't come through this district when Father Fitzgerald brought her?

She didn't remember it being so run down. Battered cars, just rusting heaps really. So many black faces . . . the graffiti . . . men lounging and watching her go by . . . the cool blank stares . . .

India made a left turn and was instantly aware of her mistake. The side street she'd taken ran between buildings that looked abandoned, and the way further on was blocked by people sitting on the ground playing some kind of game.

India didn't feel she should get out and ask them to move. She braked and began backing up. At the corner she swung the car around and ground her way out of reverse. She looked back along the street. There was a man watching her. He had a machine gun slung over his shoulder.

Oh dear God.

She kept on going. At the next intersection she thought she recognized the street. She turned left . . . two blocks, three, please God (she was feeling jittery) let it be this one.

Then she saw the corner and the Church of Our Lady and relaxed a little. The Center was a little further on.

Only it wasn't possible to stop because the entrance was blocked by vehicles, forcing her to drive past. Cars were crammed in all the way along the street and there wasn't even space for a scooter.

India double-parked and got out. She looked helplessly up and down the street. If the car got towed away she would never hear the end of it.

"Ya need any help?"

"No," India said, before she even turned around. And again even more sharply when she saw him. "No . . . ah, thanks. But no, um, no, I'm okay, I'm ah . . ."

"Sure? I'll park it, look after it for you while you're gone."

Did he think she was crazy?

He was young but mean-looking. Gold earrings and mirrored glasses, black jacket covered in studs, shredded jeans.

"I'm leaving it here and someone will be back for it in two minutes." She locked the door. "Less than that, probably." He was still standing there, running his fingers along the chrome strip. "Right back," she affirmed, and walked slowly away.

"I heard you was coming down to see us." Mel Wooster opened the door when she rang the bell. "You come right on in. I'm just making some fresh coffee."

India followed on his heels. "My car is out there," she laughed wildly, "And if we don't get it moved . . ." A phone was ringing. Mel gave her an apologetic look and went to answer it. India ran back to the door and look out. Still there, fingering the aerial.

Mel was at the wall phone. He replaced the cradle. "Sorry. Hey, about your car. No problem, I'll have Duane park it for you. Toss over your keys."

"Duane?"

"He's our valet service." Mel went out for a moment.

"He'll be careful?" India gave an embarrassed smile as he reappeared, "It's just that—"

"Sure, I know. Duane'll treat it like a baby." India had the alarmed eyes of a deer who scents the woods are on fire. Mel squeezed her hand and a smile strained his creased face to the limit. He was fiftyish, heavy and balding, and he was used to ladies arriving on the doorstep just one step away from becoming unglued. They usually smiled fixedly through an hour and then left. They never came back.

India squeezed his hand back. "And there's a man, a few blocks back, carrying a machine gun."

"Probably an Uzi."

"A what?

Mel grinned. "You'll get used to it."

"Used to it," India said in an almost nonexistent voice. "Shouldn't we inform the police?"

"No. They got their own problems. Come on and I'll get you acquainted."

The floor of the large room where meals were prepared and served ran with sudsy water courtesy of a student-helper vigorously mopping the crumbling linoleum. From the next room, heavily muffled by the building's thick old walls, came the faint sound of a television.

Mel took her over to meet a group of four people assembled in the area that served as the kitchen. "This is Doctor Bernstein, who takes a morning clinic here."

The doctor was pouring hot black coffee from a pot. "Call me Arch. Everyone does." He pushed a smile in India's direction, looking through half-opened, bloodshot eyes. He looked as if he hoped the coffee was going to get them all the way open.

Then Mel introduced the girls, who told India they were students from George Washington University. In the course of the conversation India learned they were earning credits off-campus toward their doctorates in the behavioral sciences.

A few people drifted in, got themselves a cup of coffee, then slunk into the television room. The students got busy with their projects. It seemed quiet. India wanted to know if this was usual.

Mel explained that it was "check day," which was apparently when the welfare checks came in. He told her the day after they could expect an avalanche of drug-related problems. "So if you want 'busy,' come tomorrow."

India wondered if Father Fitzgerald hadn't chosen this nice quiet day so she wouldn't be scared off. She said she would like to know more about the problems she was likely to encounter, and Mel said he would take her through to Father Mike's office so she could read up on some stuff.

India imagined something functional—a desk probably and a filing cabinet and the inevitable stack of dusty cartons, the plaster ceiling crumbling.

But the room Mel unlocked was quite different. It was freshly whitewashed and furnished simply but with grace. There was a big polished desk, comfortable chairs, well-filled bookshelves, and a low table covered in heavy tapestry. Framed photographs hung from the walls. It was a very civilized room belonging to someone who came to spend time in contemplation.

Mel opened a tall, deep cupboard and India saw it contained a large filing cabinet. He brought out several files and put them on the table for her to read. After he left she wandered about looking at the photographs on the walls. They were candid, street pictures in black and white, beautifully mounted. India focused on one in particular. A young black girl. She was beautiful. She stood out stark and clear from a background of unbelievable squalor.

India moved away.

She went back.

The pose was ordinary enough, and yet there was something explosively suggestive about the photograph.

For a moment she stood gazing at it, then she looked around the rest of the room. The desk had deep drawers richly carved with curling scrollwork, so inviting she felt a sudden urge to open them.

She turned away from the temptation and looked again at the photographs. Who had taken them? Father Fitzgerald?

Behind the desk was a high-back swivel chair upholstered in black leather. It looked outrageously comfortable. Venetian blinds covered the windows. She pulled the cord and look between the wooden slats at a vacant lot strewn with rubble and tires. Weeds drooped in the July heat, but the rusting air-conditioning unit set in the lower half of the window huffed in air that was deliciously cool.

She came back slowly to the table and sat down on one of the chairs. It was nice just sitting, peaceful. India picked up a file and began reading one shocking fact after the other. Little kids—kids six, eight years old—starting on drugs.

She read about children at the Head Start school at 18th and Diamond learning about crack before they started on the usual pre-reading program. Apparently they learned how to identify crack caps and vials as young as four. India thought of the play center she had attended at that age. Nothing more serious than coloring-in and finger painting.

The crack houses operated in one of the many city-owned abandoned buildings. The look-outs were six-year-old boys. India blinked. *Six!*

There was a picture of a youngster—he looked as if he could be twelve—with a machine gun slung over his shoulder. It looked about the same as she had seen earlier, and she supposed it was an Uzi.

Suddenly India was aware of the door closing quietly. She looked up, a little dazed. Once again she felt surprise. Father Fitzgerald had come into the room. He had on a faded denim shirt and jeans—and he looked so different from how he was in church. Relaxed, more fleshed-out somehow. He smiled at her and that smile went through her like a quiet flame.

Elsewhere, bodyguards sat in restaurants concentrating on getting through every course on the menu, gulping down food as though each morsel was going to be their last.

Elsewhere men believed their bodyguards knew what was going on around them, besides what was going down their throats. Domenico Cechetti was under no such illusion. While he spoke quietly to Jack he had his two bodyguards stationed out front and back so they could use all their faculties just seeing that certain people on Cechetti's list didn't eat at that particular restaurant that evening.

It was Domenico's conviction that he wouldn't be hit by anybody outside of the business and every strongarm and hit man was known to him. The possibility of someone putting out a contract on him and the job going to an unknown was remote. But it remained a possibility. That's why he varied the pattern of his movements, never ate at the same restaurant twice running, or sat at the same table. It was why he sat with his back to the wall, had an overall view of the place. He knew when someone noticed him, knew the instant when he was pinpointed.

There had been three attempts on his life. His native cunning had saved him. He was alive because he undervalued his bodyguards. As far as Domenico Cechetti was concerned, they were there to give out the message. Usually the message was understood.

Tonight, it wasn't his own safety that was on his mind. It was Jack's. The plain fact was, Angelo's attitude toward his brother was becoming one of barely controlled violence.

Domenico Cechetti reminded Jack as subtly as he could, not wishing to stir the waters of familial discontent any more than was necessary, of the need for greater security.

"A couple of goons following me around Washington is not the image I'm going for," Jack reminded him. "Anyway, India wouldn't like it. Listen, it's been tough on her. She gets raped getting her hair done, Angelo fucking scares the living daylights out of her by sending her Luigi's photo, then Sonny opens his big stupid mouth and tells her things."

Jack's accent had people thinking they were listening to William Buckley, Jr. Ten minutes talking family business with Domenico Cechetti and he sounded like a B movie. Jack loosened his tie. Where did Domenico find these restaurants? The place was like a sealed cave blazing with strobe lights.

"Air-conditioning broke down," said Domenico.

Jack undid his top shirt button. "Sonny's got it coming. I let him walk because I know he's up to something and I'm going to find out what that is. When I get through with him he'll be a fucking floor show and it'll be his last performance."

"You want me to take care of it?" Domenico asked.

"No. It's my job. You hear about that?"

"I heard. And I recall that Sonny has done a lot of work for Angelo."

"Yeah." Jack looked around for a waiter. Christ, there were only two and they both looked over eighty.

Domenico delicately forked a cylindrical tube of pasta. "Jack, listen. I want to talk about Angelo. He's mad—"

"He's crazy all right, a hoodlum. When it comes to my older brother I have to agree with India. He's perfect for running the street business because that's what he understands. Outside of being streetwise he has an IQ of about eight."

"He's mad about your inheriting," Dom continued. "It's eating him up."

"So what's new?"

"He's out to kill you is what's new."

Jack looked up. "You're kidding me."

"I never kid." In a rare show of emotion Domenico ladled a forkful of pasta into his mouth and chewed vengefully. "It's important, Jack," he said when he could. "Take my advice and keep your back covered."

"I knew Angelo was fucked up—" Jack muttered, suddenly losing interest in his meal. "But taking out someone of his own family?"

"You spoke to me once, things about Angelo you thought I should know about." The Consigliere fished a plain buff envelope from his pocket and handed it to Jack. "Read this later, it's a letter from Bernie Loeb to Angelo. No one else has read it. Do what you have to."

So far, Jack had dismissed Bernie Loeb with contempt. That is, until he opened the envelope and began reading the letter. Plainly Angelo and Bernie had an affair going. Jack has suspected it, but Christ, he'd thought, what had Angelo's sex life got to do with him? Angelo was free to do in private whatever he wanted. Jack could be as liberal when called for as the next man.

Only his jaw dropped open and he had to go right back to the letter's beginning to believe what he was reading. To try to regain whatever status he had lost, Bernie began by wheedling, then followed—the writing took on a desperate crabbed appearance as Bernie began imagining the wrongs Angelo was perpetrating against him—a litany of recriminations and insults, bitching on until finally lapsing into threats. It was grotesque, like eavesdropping on an argument that involved a person's most intimate acts.

Jack had no idea what the dispute was over. Bernie had been careful not to divulge anything incriminating. Nothing, not a hint about any operation or dealing, nothing that would bring a death sentence, although the contents could be dangerous as a timebomb in the wrong hands. Jack laughed fiendishly at what he was holding.

Until he actually read the letter, Angelo and Bernie Loeb had remained on the periphery. Now they were a great black mote in his vision.

It was clear to Jack why Domenico Cechetti hadn't taken the matter to the Don. It would kill the old man if he knew what his son was up to. The Don could see Angelo wasn't suited to leading the next generation of the Family, but he was still blood and his son. And Angelo was screwing Bernie Loeb—a wise guy, a little shit from a stinking back alley, who had grown rich on the Family because his mother had thrown herself on Concetta's good grace with some pitiable story and they had come up with a soft job for her son. Bernie made more money in a week than his entire family of six brothers and sisters made in a year.

The Don didn't expect gratitude. What he did expect was loyalty. Disloyalty burned him up. Jack looked at the letter and knew he would have to deal with it. He put the envelope away. It would be necessary to go back over some ground so when he was ready to move, he could deal with both Bernie and Angelo at once, in one sure final stroke.

Twelve

Duane bopped his head in time to the music crackling from his headphones. His earrings glinted in the afternoon sun.

"Is this your regular job?" India asked, shocked to find who was in charge of her car.

"D-dt . . . d-dt—flip hamburgers some nights—at McDonald's, d-dt . . . d-dt." Duane had driven the stationwagon up from the parking area beneath the center. Now he was zigzagging on the spot, watching India take a quick look at the front bumper. Watching her sidle over so she could see the passenger side.

Duane made his legs pay attention—they became still. "You don't have to creep around checking out the paintwork, lady," he said, with considerable dignity. "I played wet nurse to this car."

India blushed, and handed him the tip Mel said was the going rate. For a minute she thought he wasn't going to accept it. Duane took off his glasses. He reminded her of a young Tony Curtis, only meaner-looking, but without the sunglasses he didn't look like a threat any more.

Finally Duane accepted the note. "You can sell twenty-five rocks." He looked scornfully at India, suspecting rightly that she didn't know what a rock was. "Vials of crack cocaine . . . You can sell twenty-five rocks in maybe an afternoon and make five hundred dollars. Y'know that?"

India nodded and smiled. Her voice was as calm and pleasant as ever. "If you want to spend the next twenty years in the federal pen, go right ahead."

Duane stared, then he laughed hysterically. "Where you been, lady? No one goes away for mor'n five. And the cops are running around chasing themselves. They don't catch no one. Jesus. You can't hardly get past on the stairs in my building, people shooting up. Cops leave their car on the street to chase somebody in there, they know they're not going to have wheels when they get back out, and the police department don't like to be short on wheels. How many pretty babies has your old man got?"

"Excuse me?"

"Cars. How many others he own?"

India looked at him, her expression grave. "He owns a whole fleet, and if I hear you're out selling rocks I'll see he relieves the police department shortage of motor vehicles by donating the lot."

"Huh?" Duane paused. "You kidding me?"

"Nope."

"You going to be coming back tomorrow?"

It was India's turn to pause. "Yes."

"Okay then." He held out his hand. India held out hers and he gave it a friendly whack. "You got yourself a valet service, lady."

The white sky that afternoon seemed to lie on top of Washington like a lead blanket. Beneath, the city broiled in a stew of stagnant air and gas fumes. It made even breathing difficult.

Sonny was having the same problem in Florida, but not because of the weather. He was in a marina bar on the Intracoastal just out of Lauderdale, and a woman on the good side of thirty was busy working at picking him up. She told him her name was Gloria and her sexy red fingernails digging into his thigh told him a whole lot more. Basically she was stacked, with legs about up to her eyes.

It would have been perfect if she wasn't chewing gum the whole time she was talking to him. She was asking things like: How'd he *get* muscles like that? Sonny was used to hearing it. But what the hell. Even the way she chewed the gum was sexy. Her cherry-red lips made little smacky sounds. It was getting him going.

So when she said she gave massages and she worked from home, he got a hard-on. Underneath the bar her fingers started moving up his inner leg giving little slaps to the funky turned-up music. Sonny started feeling the beat.

"You think maybe you could give me a massage at your house?" He had trouble even saying it.

"Sure, big boy."

Jesus, she was corny, though.

"Honey," she smoothed her hair, touched the beads that strained around her throat, "I charge by the hour, but afterwards maybe you can massage me." She added that in a special husky tone.

Sonny tried an easy smile.

Money wasn't a problem. In fact, Sonny had plenty of money, more money than in his whole life, and he liked it down here. "I charge by the hour too," he told her and they both laughed uproariously at his joke. He ordered two more gin and tonics.

After the drinks they went outside and the sun pouring out of a clear blue sky nearly slapped them down. Sonny put on his mirror sunglasses.

"Your car or mine?" Gloria giggled. But she waggled her keys in front of his nose and kept right on walking to a fiery red sports model and climbed in. She sure likes red, Sonny reflected. He was surprised she could drive so well after the gins.

She had a nice place, too.

"Hey, you're doing all right," he said, admiring the setup. Big comfortable massage table, stacks of fluffy towels, oils, creams, and a real happy hour bar crammed with bottles.

"That's not all. Come this way." She walked ahead of him. The things she did with that hot little ass of hers, hips rolling . . . Gloria flung out her hands: "Taa dahaaa."

Sonny was looking at a big bath set in a wooden surround. The bath was two-thirds full of khaki mud. He asked her what she had mud in her bath for?

"It's not any old mud. That is mud from the Dead Sea. It's got minerals." She told him an hour in that was worth four hours working out in the gym, and mentioned a well-known film star famed for his muscles who used the treatment every day.

Sonny was impressed.

"'Course, as I said, it's expensive. Most guys I meet can't afford it."

"I can afford it. How's it work? You just get in there and sit?"

"I have to warm it first." She showed him the dial on the wall that operated the heater. The temperature gauge went from 1 up to 12. "I leave it on two mostly and put this wooden cover right over the top." She showed him a thick raft with a horseshoe shape cut in one end to fit around the neck. "Keeps the mud there at the top from cooling down," Gloria explained. "You have to have the heat to open your pores so the minerals can get into your muscles—four is about as warm as people can stand."

"Well, twelve must be hot as hell," Sonny said.

"I have to sterilize the mud every so often," Gloria said, running her hands up his legs. "Don't want any little bugs growing in there, do we." Her hands moved tantalizingly upwards. Sonny felt he had a brick in his trousers.

"I'll make us a drink first. Then I'm going to work on these gorgeous muscles . . . This mother's gonna be so relaxed," she cooed softly.

During the table work his erection got so engorged it was almost painful—yet he was so sleepy he couldn't do anything about it; he wanted to fuck her but he couldn't keep his eyes open.

Gloria stopped when she saw Sonny was out. His penis standing straight up began to waver, like an officer leading and just realizing his men behind him were beating a retreat.

Wasting no time she went through his clothes until she found the small diary buttoned into the breast pocket of his Hawaiian shirt. She photographed the contents with a small specialized machine that fitted into an average briefcase, pushing buttons happily. Loved that little machine.

She finished regretfully and returned the diary to the shirt pocket. Then she made coffee and drank it, waiting for Sonny to wake up. The drugs she used in his drink didn't take long to wear off, but long enough. There would be no aftereffects. Sonny would think her massage was so good she had wafted him off to sleep.

At first India thought someone had left a bundle of old clothing on the Center's doorstep, until it moved. A mat of black hair emerged and a face smiled distantly at her.

Oh dear God. India smiled uncertainly back. "Door's open if you want to go in." India turned the knob on the door and pushed it open invitingly. The head began to shake furiously and finally to disappear.

Lenny came to the door. Lenny was the high-strung boy given to nervous picking and scratching whom she had met the day before. He stood on the doorstep cracking his knuckles. "That's Malcolm," he said.

India went in to get help. Lenny followed on her heels. It wasn't much after ten, but the room was already buzzing with noise. She saw Father Fitzgerald talking with a group seated at a table. Lenny screamed, "Malcolm's back," and fell to cracking his knuckles with a vengeance.

"Stop that goddamn cracking. Goddamn son of a bitch," someone yelled.

"Shut up! Shut up! Cocksucker!" Lenny screamed and ranted. He seemed to go crazy. Suddenly the whole place was in an uproar.

Arch Bernstein popped out of the little room he used as a clinic, looking cross. "What the hell's going on?"

Mel Wooster turned from his grill. "It's Malcolm. He don't want to come in."

"Well, hassling him won't get anywhere," Arch shouted above the noise.

"No one's hassling him," Mel said, sounding pissed off.

Lenny's voice was disintegrating into quaking despair. He was like a horse in a burning stable whinnying in panic.

Never had she encountered behavior like this; crazy, incomprehensible. People who openly expressed their distress in public made her want to shrink away. India felt useless, out of place; a middle-class woman from the suburbs—that world of cozy privilege—better suited to arranging flowers in a hospital.

The priest came towards her across the room, a tall quiet figure. Pausing, he murmured something into Lenny's ear.

"Yeah?" Lenny wiped his nose on his sleeve and began to calm down. "Yeah?" he said, and then walked purposefully off. Father Michael came over to her.

"What did you say to him?" asked India in astonishment.

"I reminded him *Mister Ed* was on. Lenny lives for his television programs and *Mister Ed* is his favorite." He looked down at her and smiled his secret smile. Shall we go and talk to Malcolm and see what happens?"

Father Fitzgerald sat on the doorstep a few feet away from people passing in the street, talking to a bundle in a worm-eaten World War II army surplus coat. He seemed entirely at his ease.

India was not. She was already finding it hard to believe she had let herself be drawn into this pantomime. If the kid wanted to be antisocial and stay buried in his coat, she thought, then let him.

"I think Malcolm would like some cupcakes," Father Fitzgerald said. India gave the bundle a dubious look and encountered an eye staring at her. It seemed to say, why don't you go and get the stupid cupcakes like he said?

It seemed farfetched, but India got up and went inside and asked. Mel, at least, seemed to have recovered his good humor. "How're you doing out there?"

"We're having a picnic," India said, with a lightheartedness she did not feel.

She returned to the doorstep with three mugs of coffee and two Twinkies each—Mel was out of cupcakes—and Malcolm managed to consume all of his without once emerging from his coat. But then he stood up and India had never in her life seen anything more pathetic than this boy, standing holding a miserable brown paper bag containing his belongings in one hand, and his pants up with the other. Father Fitzgerald opened the door and he lurched inside.

Divested of his coat, Malcolm couldn't sit still. When he sat anywhere his legs would begin to vibrate. He was like an old boiler shaking away in a basement.

And then he gave her this smile, this wide toothless grin, and her heart went out to him.

"He started on crack," Father Fitzgerald said, "progressed to heroin. Rented himself out to fat old queens to get the money. Then he overdosed and almost died. They found him loitering face-down amongst the garbage bags and got him into a hospital just in time. He was walked through his tremors and several weeks later pronounced drug-free and discharged. Someone told him about the Church of Our Lady and he came here."

"What then?" India asked. They were sitting in Michael's office sharing a pot of tea, he in shirtsleeves, she in an old cotton print dress and sandals, bare-legged.

"It didn't work out. He was unemployed and on welfare. He was soon back on the streets, hustling and hanging out in pool halls. The cycle began all over."

Jack had the photocopies of Sonny's diary spread out on his desk. The page that most interested him had a rough chart with squares blocked in on certain numbers and against these were two capital letters. There wasn't much else to go on. Sonny appeared to have a very dull social life.

Nothing in the notes, none of the usual telephone numbers for medical and dental reference. Jack studied the chart. Then he had an idea. Gloria photocopies only the pages with writing on (and there weren't many of those), but some of these little diaries contained a lot of specialized information at the back. Like phases of the moon for that year—and tides. Jack began to feel sure the numbers corresponded to dates and times of high tides. The letters were initials.

Reaching for the intercom Jack gave his secretary a description of the diary he wanted and asked her to go out and buy one. Then he sat back and thought.

He was convinced Angelo and Bernie Loeb were the instigators of a plan to capture a slice of the drug market. They would never show themselves—Jack could make all the deductions he wanted, but he would never discover the links. He was beginning to know how it was done, though.

Angelo worked things from this end.

Loeb as courier worked the South American end.

And Sonny picked up and cleared.

It was all in the chart—dates, times. He could work those out. They were bringing the stuff in by sea. The initials referred in all probability to the distributors. Sonny would store the dope, they'd come and collect it.

Right, Jack decided, Sonny first. He was going to get the motherfucker. Angelo and Bernie: difficult. He'd have to get both of them at the same time, and after the Florida operation got wiped out they were going to be shitting themselves over who screwed them up.

Every so often Jack's brother Tom made a trip to Washington to see him. His wife, Betsy, looked forward to it. For one thing, it gave her an opportunity to prowl the boutiques on Wisconsin Avenue and M Street, Georgetown's two main streets that every day attracted a swarm of shoppers from outside the area. For another, it was a perfect excuse to call on India.

Betsy was resting on the sofa with her feet up and a hefty slice of coffee cake in her lap. Today she wore her bifocals in pink plastic frames. They were styled as lover's knots and made her eyes look curiously misplaced.

"You didn't know?" she was exclaiming. "I can't believe Jack never told you."

"He never mentioned a beach cottage," India said. She reached out for the blue and white china pot and poured tea into Betsy's cup. "Where did you say it was?"

Oh, something was going on. Jack didn't look happy. And India was, well, painfully thin. Betsy ignored the fact that she herself had put on rather too much weight during her marriage, the way she ignored the fact that Tom was cheating on her.

"Chesapeake Bay. It's just darling. I wonder why Jack never said."

"Chesapeake! Really." India put down the teapot. "I'd love to see it. Betsy, you ask Jack for the keys and then, well, let's go out there."

"India," Betsy said vaguely, "nothing's wrong, is it? Between you and Jack, I mean. You two are getting on okay?"

"What? Yes, of course. Sugar?"

"You are happy? India, I don't know how it would be if you and Jack weren't, well, happy. Papa Salvatore wants it. He's very concerned that the young people are happy. He'd be very upset if a marriage split up. Fact is, I don't recall anybody ever doing that. Well, there was that business with Teresa and Rocco, but—"

India eyed Betsy sharply over her teacup, remembering Jack's pretty stepsister, her strained face, and the absent Rocco. "What business?"

"Well, Lordy! Doesn't Jack tell you a thing? Rocco and Teresa were fighting like two dogs in August. Papa had to straighten things out . . ." Betsy emitted a little bird-cry. "Why, here's Jack now. Jack, you come right over here and sit beside me."

Jack was walking in the door. He came and kissed India brazenly with scornful unconcern—she felt the hard mouth briefly brush the corner of her top lip—then he went and kissed Betsy.

"Jack, you naughty boy, keeping the Bay house a secret," Betsy scolded.

Jack put his arm around Betsy's shoulders, squeezing her tight. His laugh was quietly malicious. He claimed he hated the beach. It was messy; people trekked in sand, it got everyplace. He couldn't sleep, the sudden noises in the night outside made him nervous. He and India wanted to buy a house in the Virginia hunt country.

This last was news to India. But she dutifully poured his tea. Looking up she smiled at them both.

"But I should love so much to go and see it. And Betsy would too. We could drive out now."

"Oh, it would be adorable," Betsy claimed loyally. "Where's Tom?"

"As a matter of fact," Jack assured Betsy, though his eyes were narrowed on India, "Tom is attending to some business. I'm only here to pick up the papers." He swallowed his tea. "How would you girls like to join us at the club for dinner this evening?"

Betsy said, "Now, Jack, I want to take India out to see the Bay house. There's scads of time. I know you and Tom. Business! Huh! You'll get into the bar and Lordy knows when we'll get to have dinner." Her implacable voice rolled on. "Jack, I swear, if you don't give me the key . . ."

It was surprising, Jack didn't look angry or forbidding, or even ready to lose his temper. He only sighed and looked at Betsy with exasperated patience.

"Okay, okay. If you go now you'll make it back in time for dinner. But drive carefully."

Betsy made short work of the beltway, the 64-mile freeway loop that circled the city, and drove the hour and twenty minutes to the Bay.

"Tom says you're doing some kind of volunteer work. How's it going?"

"I like it," India said. "I didn't think that I would. But I do. I like the people there."

It was true, she really did. Among other things it gave her something to think about. She wasn't just mulling over her own problems, hating Jack and being terrified of Paulie.

"There," Betsy said, "you can see it now."

The house was back a way, off the main road. They bumped along the dirt lane leading to it. The nearest neighbors lived further along, almost right on the beach where the lane ended. A row of gnarled old pines separated the two properties.

India loved the house on sight. Inside, there was a comfortable clutter of faded chintz-covered furniture, and everywhere drifted the scent of pine needles and the sea.

"The next-door people are real nice folks from Down East Kittery in Maine. Something in government," Betsy told India.

India felt she had come home. She felt safer in that house than she had anywhere for a long time.

"I want to come out here and spend every spare moment," she said. "It's wonderful, I can't believe it exists."

"I wonder why Jack doesn't use it any more," Betsy said. "Maybe he's worried about security. But now he has Paulie. . ."

"Paulie . . ." India's face tightened. "I don't want him out here."

"You don't like Paulie?"

"No—I . . ." Be careful, she's Family. "I'd just like to have this place as somewhere, you know . . ."

Betsy did. Men could be beasts sometimes, quite brutish. Sometimes Tom, well, it sickened her . . . Lordy, at times Betsy wished she could have a beach house to get away to. She felt a sudden sisterly feeling for India.

"Tell you what, I'll talk to Jack. Why, if he's worried about security, there's nothing stopping him putting in extra locks. And the kind of shutters we have at home, know the ones I mean? They're folded on the inside, you just pull them across. Don't worry. Leave him to me. Jack's a sweetie, but he can be stubborn."

When India entered the kitchen the next morning she found Jack had already left for the airport. Paulie was sitting at the table with the newspapers spread out, reading the comic section.

Jack had a gentleness and a fundamental decency, India knew that. Well . . . deep down she did. But the hired weapons man who sat in her kitchen reading the paper was something she couldn't live with. He was destroying her sanity. She had begun to have the most terrible, distressing thoughts imaginable. She lived in fear of him, fear of the watching eye and the soft tread. He was like the predatory-eyed wolf in her childish dreams, like a switchblade left open and lying carelessly on the hall table.

"Lenny's managed to gouge this great hole in his leg," Arch Bernstein said later that morning.

India stood by the examining couch while the doctor began unwinding Lenny's bandage. Before the clinic started she had been warned about Lenny's self-inflicted wounds.

"Tell us what you used, Lenny," Arch said.

"A nail." Lenny stopped picking at a scab to watch the bandage unwind with morbid fascination.

"A rusty nail," the doctor amended sadly. He lifted the dressing and looked closely at the festering wound.

"Have you been picking at this, Lenny?"

"Nah," Lenny lied cheerfully.

India felt a sweat break out on her forehead. Arch probed a swab stick into the infected center. "That looks necrotic—see that black area in there," he said to India. "That's dead tissue."

The July day was hot and humid and the rusting air conditioner at the window did nothing but push the warm air about—it wasn't even doing that. The close atmosphere made India feel frantic.

From the desk behind them the phone suddenly exploded in a series of rings. "I'll get that," Arch said. "Can you swab the wound, then try and clean out the center?"

India turned to the dressing tray laid out on a side table. She picked up forceps and cotton and dipped the ball into a bowl of solution. Lenny's fingers were itching to get into the wound. She turned her head and saw he was about to dig them in.

"Please, Lenny. Put your hands behind your back." She swallowed as a faint wave of dizziness came over her. "I'll try not to hurt."

She felt hot all over. She pressed the wet swab into the wound and gave it a careful little wipe.

Arch turned around, cupping his hand over the mouthpiece. "Give it a good clean out." India nodded. She disposed of the dirty swab in a paper bag the way he had taught her and picked up another swab.

This time she exerted some pressure. It didn't seem to hurt. Lenny was shivering, but it seemed with pleasure rather than pain. The whole inner core seemed to be moving. She wiped with the swab and a large piece of flesh came away and slowly oozed down Lenny's leg.

India dropped the forceps, clasping hand over mouth as her stomach lurched up into her throat. I'm going to be sick, she thought, and that was all she had time to think, because Lenny had his fingers in the putrid stream, hooking them into the gaping hole in his leg. The sight and stench, the wave of nausea beginning to swell up and up . . . She tried to swallow it down, will herself to take Lenny's hands from the mess. That mess was his own flesh . . .

She turned and raced for the door. One last frantic look behind, Arch's horrified eyes following her, the bloodied matter now coursing down Lenny's leg. She threw herself out of the room, pulling the door behind her, leaning on it with her hand still clasped over her mouth. The vision of Lenny's mutilated leg, the rotted flesh suddenly separating, sliding down . . .

A voice, a very gentle voice, said "India?"

She opened her eyes to see the priest standing there.

"Have you seen what Lenny's done to his leg?" Her voice a whisper. She still had the sensation she might throw up.

First he walked towards her, then he reached out and put his hand on her shoulder. It was comforting.

"I know. It's bad."

India had an attack of guilt. "I shouldn't have run out on him like that."

"Don't worry," he said. "Lenny will take it as a compliment. Come on, I'll make you some tea." He took his hand away from her shoulder. Withdrew his hand but not himself. They walked along the corridor and the talk between them was sociable and low-key, just as the feeling of closeness was real and acute. And then she was speaking too much, as if there was a need to cover a silence.

Yet he looked at her as he opened the office door and she could see that he was thinking it, too. She suddenly felt herself bare to him: and wicked and lovely and twice as beautiful.

Jack was picked up at Miami Airport by a man he trusted, Fingers Natale. Jack had an entire system worked out. Men who could pull off jobs, do whatever he wanted, and who would answer only to him. Fingers was magic. There wasn't a security combination he couldn't break.

They parked in a side road a safe distance from Sonny's house.

"You sure he's being taken care of?" Fingers asked. Sonny scared the shit out of him.

"I'm sure." Jack's face broke into a smile. "He's having the time of his life." And if he wasn't and wanted to come home early, Gloria would let them know by cordless telephone.

The house was back off the road behind a whole lot of scrub pine and behind the house was a barn and stables. There was even a couple of horses. Two dogs trotted up and gave an experimental growl. They looked too well fed. Jack talked softly, told them they were pussycats, and fed them some meat from a plastic bag in his pocket.

Once in the house they went to work. Fingers started on the safe which they found behind a photograph of Sonny sitting at the steering wheel of an ocean-going yacht. "Nice," Fingers said. He opened his bag and took out a number of ingenious instruments including a calculator and a baby computer capable of sheer wizardry, then he got down to business.

Jack went out to the barn and discovered what looked like a ton of top-grade Colombian marijuana behind a wall of hay bales. Jack estimated the weed had a street value of around two million dollars. He patted the horses and inspected their stables and found his way into a garage containing a Chevy van and a speedy-looking motor-boat.

When he got back to the house Fingers had the safe open. Inside was a list of distributors, pick-up times, dates, the lot.

"Jeez," Fingers said. "Sonny's got it all written down. Nice."

Jack checked the list with the calculations he'd made from the chart in Sonny's diary. "I was right. Alejo is making the pick-up tonight. You hear about Alejo?" Alejo was Cuban—mean, vicious when crossed.

"Yeah. Glad I'm not Sonny." In the safe was a stack of money. Fingers counted quickly. There was over a quarter million in hundred dollar bills.

Jack thought it was very cost-effective. There was enough there to pay for what it was costing him to do the job and a nice fat bonus for the men. He began speaking into his cordless phone. "Okay, come in, boys. Bring the moving van."

There were four of them, six counting himself and Fingers. He figured it would take thirty minutes to clear the marijuana. Then he'd take two of the biggest guys and they'd pay Sonny a visit.

Thirteen

Sonny thought, Angelo is going to fucking kill Jack for this. He was sitting up to his neck in warm mud and he had two heavies, one with hands like young bloodhounds, sitting right on top of the fucking board. He couldn't move. And Jack was standing over him with a bottle of Old Napoleon suggesting he drink the booze, seeing as he liked it so much.

"Whatta you mean? What's going on?" Sonny bellowed. "I never had Old Napoleon in my life."

Jack smiled. Sonny was a lying son-of-a-bitch. "I want to talk," he said smoothly. "Tell me things."

"Tell you what? I'm down here trying to make a decent living—"

"Up," was all Jack said, and Gloria put a languid hand on the temperature gauge.

"What . . . Hey, wait a minute there."

"Now are you going to drink this or not?" Jack asked with heavy patience. "Because if not—" He looked at Gloria. "Turn it up to six."

Sonny gagged. "Okay, okay, I'll take a little drink—I just don't want to get drunk, that's all."

"Why not? Why not have a good time?" Jack put the bottle to Sonny's lips. The guy with the big hands got out a knife and began paring his nails. Jack insisted Sonny keep on swallowing. "I know you like this stuff. Oh . . . Now every time you do that the temperature goes up.''

Sonny moaned like a foghorn, but he quit dribbling. Jack settled down to the questions he was itching to ask, starting with the pick-up time for that night.

But the edge was off Sonny's concern. To bring it back Jack asked Gloria to up the temperature to seven. Sonny started to flounder. His body underneath the solid weight made great noisy sucking sounds as he tried to get his hands and knees in a position so he could pry up the board . . . It weighed a ton. He collapsed, panting.

"No!' screamed Sonny as Gloria made a move. "I'll talk, I'll tell you—Jesus fucking Christ, just let me outta here.''

What Jack wanted to know was how the operation worked, times, dates, names. Did they deal in heroin? The quantity and quality. Little by little Sonny gave up his secrets. Jack believed India's story; he never thought to question it. The incident was past history and Sonny was paying for it.

Sonny didn't even *know* what had happened.

By the time the bottle was finished Jack had enough information to wipe out the Florida operation. His plan was to examine everyone involved, right down the line, right to the source. Angelo and Bernie. Let them sweat.

They hauled Sonny out as the mud began to make little puttering sounds. His face was glowing camp-fire red; a fourth of July firecracker waiting for explosion time. They took him back to his house and left a very drunk Sonny to face Alejo.

Meanwhile, in Washington, India was unwrapping a large parcel that had arrived that morning at the house.

The contents revealed a plush blue-and-cream Chinese carpet. A rug. Her father's wedding present to them. On the card: "To India and Jack, our warmest blessing." The parcel had been posted from Hong Kong. Her father was traveling with his catamite through Asia.

The rug was heavy and sumptuous; she trod on it with her bare feet, enjoying the sensual feel of the pile. It was so thick and glorious it looked odd, almost insolent, among the threadbare Aubussons.

She would pack it up and take it to the beach house. She planned to spend the weekend there while Jack was away. Perhaps leave straight from the Center early the next afternoon to avoid the Friday traffic.

Alejo was a skinny little man with a fat belly. Sonny was rocking on the spot trying to stand up straight and not belch.

"Shit," Alejo said. He dipped into the sack and held up another handful. "*Shit.*"

"Huh?" Sonny blinked. 'Huh?"

Alejo kicked him in the ribs. Sonny blinked some more, trying to understand how a little guy with so much belly could get his little bow legs up so high with such force. He rubbed the spot hazily, just beginning to see a warning light somewhere.

"Hay, you think I will buy hay. You have hay stuffed in your head."

Sonny burped. "Tha's not hay, sis top-grade mariwanna." Alejo started shouting words Sonny had never heard before, though he thought he recognized chicken and shit.

"I gonna kill you," Alejo told him in English.

"Wha's the matter, ole buddy . . ." Sonny meant to drape his arm around Alejo's neck and never got any further than that. Alejo's hand came flashing towards him and the blade went up and underneath the ribs and Sonny was still trying to figure it out when he slumped down on his knees into darkness.

On Friday afternoon the priest looked into the back of the station wagon and said, "How many weeks are you going for, anyway?"

India laughed. "It just looks a lot. Most of it's rug."

"I'd like to see this famous rug."

"You're welcome. You can come out and help me put it down,' she said, joking.

"I'm going to be out your way on Saturday—I've friends who live about twenty miles south of Annapolis. Write out your address and I'll come by."

The shingle boards were weatherboard and badly in need of paint. India planned to decorate the house herself. She needed to feel the pain of hard physical work. The rape had come close to murdering that part of her which was physical and outgoing. Too bloody close. She had crept into a shell and softened, like a clam.

If painting the house got too much for her, she would hire someone locally to finish the job. India chipped away the cracked and crumbling putty from around the kitchen windows and planned what needed doing first.

It was hot. The weather had changed from a gorgeous clear sunny morning to one of sullen heat and haze. She wiped her arm across her forehead and picked at her sweat-ringed shirt.

"Hi! You feel like a beer?"

India swung around, startled. The priest had come to the back of the house without her hearing him. He wore amber-tinted sunglasses, a faded blue shirt, old white cotton trousers, and loafers. He was laughing.

"Well, thank you."

"Welcome." He set down a six-pack of Miller Lite, pulled the tab from a cold beaded can, and handed it over. India took a thirsty swig and felt it run cool and good down her throat.

"Hmmm." She wiped her mouth with the back of her hand and settled down in the warm sandy soil leaning up against the shingle boards. "How did you find me?" she asked.

"You always find people at the back of the house." He came and sat down too. His smile moved in quick amusement as he looked at her; sweaty, smudged, white-caked hands. "On Saturday mornings you do, anyway."

India recalled the Father Fitzgerald who had stood before her, an image, tall and stern and remote on the day of her wedding (the one before that one was shut away and only half-remembered like a horrible dream). She couldn't see this man, sitting relaxed and smiling beside her, as that priest.

"Now where are you thinking of putting it?" Michael asked. He stood inside her bedroom door with the rug over his shoulder and looked around the room.

"I think where you're standing," India replied.

"Have you thought of lifting this old matting and just having the wooden floor?"

"I did. But it's a lot of work . . ."

"Not if you have help," Michael said cheerfully.

*   *   *

In the next hour they worked furiously to remove the dry old matting from the bedroom floor, and then, choked with dust but laughing hysterically, they struggled to toss it out of the window.

The matting hit the wild scraggly garden beneath them.

"Oh . . ." India stood up and stretched her aching back against the wall. It was hot, inside and out, the sweat running between her breasts. She closed her eyes. "Father, I wouldn't like to do that again."

"Don't call me Father." He said it quite gently. India opened her eyes to see him standing back from the window—just standing there looking out. His face so still, so tense. Behind him the Chinese rug was half unrolled; it looked smaller and paler by itself on the floor. From a long way off the sound of thunder breaking. A gull crying overhead. She saw and heard, but in that hot, beating silence there was only one separate feeling. It was dark and instinctive and it had to do with him, and him alone.

She brought her hands up to lever herself from the wall. She meant to walk past him, casually, go down the stairs and get another beer. Perhaps she didn't have the energy. Perhaps it required a superhuman effort. She didn't know, she would never know.

Michael turned his head slowly and started talking to her. One hurried move and those great dark dilated eyes would become as wary as a hunted deer, he would lose her. Everything depended on patience now.

He imagined he felt her heart beating, crazily, as it had when he found her in Luigi's salon, trapped and bloodied against the wall. Looking into her eyes had been like walking through a door into a place he had never been before. He'd understood then, that all the rules and all the laws laid down by the Church could not prevent him from knowing this woman.

At the hospital he had stood outside the doorway of room 214 where India Grey lay in bed asleep or barely conscious, just another priest going about his duties in a busy hospital.

A week later in church he watched her kneeling at the communion rail, her eyes shut and her hands curled into tight fists.

Her face on the day of her wedding was distant and hazy through the fabric of her wedding veil. The recognition in her eyes had been sure enough.

He knew when she came alone to the Center and when she was followed.

Now she was before him, his wounded mourning dove, and he was no longer a priest of the Church, he was just a man who realized the marvel of the woman. By God, accident or odd blunder of fate, he was already part of her, and love, need, sex, was written all over his face. No prompting of his soul could contest the fact or save him now.

She was so close, so close. He reached out for her and his lips came slowly down on hers and his fingers were reaching into her hair.

"No . . . No." She put her hands up to stop him.

He cradled her in his arms, his mouth open against her forehead. "No?" he asked.

"No."

Michael made tea in the kitchen. He didn't know she was glad he had kissed her—didn't know the soft, wonderful feeling, a warm and lovely thing she had almost forgotten—or that she understood why. Understood perfectly. The knowing was there in that deep part of her mind that was beyond her control.

She wanted to tell him it could never happen again but it seemed a waste of time. He squeezed lemon into her tea and added a teaspoon of honey. It whirled away, dissolving into the hot liquid.

She watched it. "What do you want?' she asked simply.

"I want to lie down with you," came the answer.

When she didn't look up, he said, "Can you get away next Wednesday?"

"'Yes . . .'"

"Then meet me here at two."

She was shaking her head and with each shake she said, "No."

"I'll be here anyway," he told her softly. "Here waiting, whether you come or not."

India had had her first orgasm the year she turned fourteen. It was all Miranda's fault. They were in the school dormitory, supposedly in their own beds after lights out. Only Miranda was in India's bed with the sheet pulled over their heads.

Miranda said that real living began with being a woman, and that you couldn't begin to be one until you had an orgasm. She said also that men passed over girls who hadn't had the sensation and become real women. "They just leave you on the shelf and you die an old maid," she told India. Miranda was an authority on the subject, having herself been instructed in secrecy by her stepfather. She got India to rub between her legs.

"Feel it?" Miranda kept asking, adding helpfully, "It's a pain, only nice."

India felt no such thing. Only hot under the bed covers, and sleepy. Miranda prodded her. "Press harder. You want to become a woman, don't you?"

The rubbing was making India sore. She was about to give up when suddenly there was a sensation she could not define. It was sweetness and pain, strangely mixed. The next instant she thought the old story about going blind was true.

Only worse. It was the beam from Sister Marie Celeste's flashlight as she pulled the covers back. "God help us," moaned Miranda.

They were led, shivering, from the sleeping dormitory, Sister Celeste clicking her tongue, spittle lacing her angry lips. They were led into the big, cold, stoneflagged room, the room where punishment was administered. One of the other nuns came when Sister Celeste rang the bell. She carried a leather belt. India had never felt the sting of its brass buckle, but Miranda had, and she promptly vomited on the floor. Seeing her friend in such distress, India collapsed and began to cry.

The girls were required to spend the remaining hours until dawn on their knees. Miranda, the lucky one in India's estimation, was sent home. As part of her punishment, India had to spend every night for the rest of the term on a hard wooden couch sharing the place where Sister Marie Celeste slept. She was required to rise at dawn every morning and kneel in prayer for an hour. Never, during that time, could she join in any of the social activities the other girls enjoyed. It was as bad as taking holy orders.

The nuns monitored her every movement. When finally she was allowed back in the dormitory, India couldn't think of touching herself without thinking of punishment.

*   *   *

She refused to discuss the ordeal. She adopted a pose of cool bravado, but in truth she was badly scarred by the experience. It didn't, however, stop her from growing up with romantic longings. Kneeling down to say her Rosary, her imagination would run amok with sweet thoughts of the man she would one day marry. She saw him a thousand times, felt his tender embraces.

Except there was no tenderness in the embraces, and with the first boy to put his hand up her legs came the old feeling and it was packed with punishment. The other girls said that once her knickers were down it would be all right, she would feel different. She didn't, she felt defiled. She suffered the boy's clumsy kisses, but recoiled in fear from the unpredictability of their strength.

In college she went through a series of dates in order to be one of the crowd. It was a relief when she was called home to be with her father and she didn't have to wrestle with some unreasoning male who expected at the end of the evening to spend the night in her bed.

All that had belonged to the year she turned fourteen had vanished.

But perhaps not all. Something of that lovely elusive sensation was back. Hot, forbidden. Shy at first and then not being able to stop, whispering Michael's name as the sweet feeling grew and grew—as first one and then another frenzied contraction rolled through her and she must surely surely die, and whispering jubilantly, ferociously into the darkness: "You didn't win . . . you didn't win, Sister Bloody Celeste."

Afterwards, lying limp, her head falling back on the pillows: "I won't go. I'll call him tomorrow."

It was Wednesday. All over Washington people were getting ready to go to work. India paced up and down the bedroom floor.

"I know he's a priest. I know he's taken a vow to remain celibate." She stopped and wrung her hands. "But he's just Michael," she whispered.

The phone rang and she grabbed it.

Harriet! India closed her eyes, sweat breaking out all over her body. "Yes—yes, Harriet, it's India."

"India, you sound so odd . . ."

India stared at the outsize carved-wood pineapples at the bed ends; she stared at the red silk bedcover flung over a chair, at the cats raking their claws through the silk tassels . . . Jack would kill her if he knew she was letting them fray the silk to pieces.

"I'm sorry, Harriet, but lunch, no . . ."

"Do your charity thing another day," urged Harriet. "Come on, we haven't done lunch for simply ages, and I want you to meet a friend."

It was divine providence. If she went to lunch with Harriet she couldn't meet Michael. Nothing would happen. She was safe again . . . in a little while she would forget all about this.

India's cab set her down outside the Hay-Adams Hotel. A party of glittering old women made a small bottleneck at the entrance. She glanced at her watch, impatient, but was forced to dawdle in behind them. Inside the lobby was a trio of tuxedoed musicians playing Mozart. India looked about, unsure of where to go.

Everyone looked so well put together, immaculately groomed, smiling, everyone smiling with their white gleaming teeth. Some of the women had great style and they looked very glamorous. India always took care to underdress; anything else was, well, overblown and therefore vulgar.

A stunning, dark-haired woman in glazed apricot silk walked through the foyer as if she owned the Hay-Adams. India couldn't help but notice her; the woman was very hard to miss.

Two minutes later India was passing by a quiet little cul-de-sac, having found the way to the restaurant she was lunching in, when she saw the same woman join a man who was talking into a phone at a booth. His back was to her, India wasn't really looking at him; she couldn't help, though, but observe the way his hand came around the woman's waist and slid over the silk-sheathed buttocks before he shamelessly, without hesitation, curled his fingers into the rich crease.

There was something so profoundly intimate (and so lascivious) in that gesture, that India, who wasn't prone to voyeurism, felt a small constriction in her throat. But it was nothing to the shock she got when the man turned his head to kiss the woman, and she saw it was Jack.

Harriet was darting little looks around the restaurant trying to distinguish famous from the merely beautiful when India walked in.

"Darling, I'd quite given you up. What do you think?" Harriet wiggled her head from side to side.

"New hairdo ..." As India sat down she glanced at the other tables ... Jack wouldn't, he wouldn't be seen here with ...

"It's a new place, French. They do a comb-out and a manicure. Very understated—well, you know how I feel about the way American woman do their nails—and quite reasonably priced ... India, sweetie, let me make an appointment for you."

Don't, prayed India, let Jack bring that woman in here.

Harriet prattled on. "You're not spending enough time on yourself and frankly, dear, it's beginning to show. Do remember, how you look makes a statement about Jack's status in society. You never can tell, a well-dressed wife meeting the right people in the right places might come in *très, très* handy. I just don't think you give enough thought to that aspect of your marriage, India."

That aspect? India was listening, almost afraid that she was going to tell Harriet Jack was Mafia and that she didn't care to be a perfect reference for him, and that anyway the marriage was sterile because she was a prude and her husband was, right now for all she knew, making voluptuous love to a woman in apricot silk.

"And you're so lucky," Harriet continued. "American men are generous husbands. Adrian has never understood the benefits of letting me have *carte blanche* ..."

Tell her, tell her now.

Tell her what? That her hormones had gone rampant, that fear and disgust of the sexual act couldn't, apparently, keep her from aching with desire for a man ordained as a priest in the Roman Catholic Church ...

Tell Harriet that already she was tasting guilt because not only was she about to (was she?) commit a terrible sin, there was the enormity of her need to explore the things that kiss could do to her—the cataclysmic nature of which put the significance of the woman with the apricot bottom and Jack and his whole family on the back burner.

To be in love and feel love, sexual love. She couldn't breathe without it, she'd drown if she didn't, and the knowing that she was going to was already part of her, as much a part of her as breathing, as the beating of her own heart.

"Harriet, you're not going to understand this ..." All sorts of words were colliding and interchanging in her head. Why not just tell her the truth? Not about Jack being in the Mafia, the more important truth. It was as if she were ill with a fever.

"What is it?" Harriet leaned her face over. "Are you sick?"

"Yes," India nodded. I want to go to bed with a man. He's a priest, actually, but that no longer matters. India thought she might have said it, except she knew she hadn't made a sound.

"Is it the flu? You look very hot," Harriet said sharply, and then, "Darling!" Harriet half rose from her chair as a petal-thin woman with fleecy hair and eyes like klieg lights dropped a kiss.

"Caroline . . . India, oh, you two know each other—just goes to show what a village Washington really is. Shall we order?"

She wanted to go to him—it seemed the only thought her mind would admit. "You know, I think that I do have the flu," India smiled dreamily at the two women. "Would you please excuse me?"

Patrolman Dick Murtry put his flashers on and took off after the pea-green station wagon bearing D.C. tags. A woman was driving, a blonde. She was now in a county that got its revenue from drivers breaking the speed limit on their way through to Chesapeake Bay.

It was quite a little routine. He'd inform her she was breaking the speed limit and she would make her eyes go all big and flutter her lashes some, maybe tell him what big shoulders he had, and he'd let her run on a little, then ask for her license and registration.

It was surprising the people that carried their license but left the registration at home. Failure to produce either was a fine. So there would be $50 for speeding for a start. If she couldn't cough that up she'd have to come with him to the county courthouse.

It being a weekday she was in luck, the courthouse was open for business. Weekend people had to wait in custody for Monday morning. After a couple of weekends cooling their heels waiting for the country judge to turn up Mondays, most got wise and carried fifty notes just in case.

When he had her pulled over Murtry got slowly out of his cruiser. This blonde was going to make his day. He hitched up his breeches and ambled over.

When India left the courthouse it was nearly three. Too late, a voice whispered. Go back. He won't be there. But she couldn't seem to stop herself. She drove as fast as the speed limit allowed, then past the county line she could not resist the insane impulse to press her foot down on the accelerator. Sitting upright, tense, gripping the steering wheel and glancing again and again into the rearview mirror, half expecting to see a cruiser with rotating lights behind her.

"He has to be there, has to be."

It began to rain and suddenly she was in the midst of a downpour. She had to slow down.

The rain was easing up as she pulled into the lane. For a moment her heart was in her mouth, then she came around the curve and saw that his car wasn't there and felt coldness rushing through her.

She sat behind the steering wheel for almost fifteen minutes, just sitting. She could hear cars and trucks passing on the road, but she knew it wouldn't be him now. He would have gone long ago.

Her thoughts told her she must have been insane to even imagine wanting to do this . . . told her that it was a good thing really that he wasn't here.

She got out of the car and started to walk over to the house. A voice very close behind her said, "Did you lose your way?" She turned and all her strength drained out of her legs.

Michael was standing a few feet away. His hair was damp and beginning to curl at his neck, the shirt open, the sleeves rolled. Beyond him the pine trees were sighing in the wind.

"Where were you?" she asked.

He came to her quickly. "Shall we go in?"

India felt an awful doubt—something clever and cold in his eyes and for the merest beat it was like seeing another person—fleeting, mistaken, and forgotten almost at once.

Once inside he pulled the door behind him and took her straight away into his arms. She closed her eyes. There was the scent of pine needles on him; he felt warm and wonderful. She let out a long sigh. It was incredible how right it felt. How safe, how gloriously safe.

"I had to make sure no one followed you."

Her heart was thudding against his. She shook her head. "No one followed me. Paulie stays in the house." She gave a tiny, breathless laugh. "He hardly ever leaves it."

Very slowly he began to undo the buttons of her blouse. She looked up at him, shivering. "Michael, I'm so afraid." He lowered his lips and she hung for a long time on his mouth. "I won't hurt, I promise you."

She believed him, no matter that she was crying hot tears. His hands moved, stroked and caressed her until she was ready. And then he was rubbing his erect penis slowly, slowly between her legs and she was tensing against him, against the hurt. Then, it was like waking momentarily from a dream. She opened her eyes to see his face, so close to hers. They stared at each other and she knew him, she knew this man, then she had her arms around his neck.

Later the orgasm carried her on its quick, terrible journey and she heard her voice cry out, "Yes," and, "Yes," and she was kissing him and kissing him again and again and again.

Fourteen

India lay naked with her head couched on Michael's shoulder. It still struck her as amazing that this man was breathing next to her. He was beautiful, slim, with the small hard buttocks and smooth sweet skin of a boy; in sleep his penis was curled up, lusciously warm like a mouse in a nest of silky sheeny hair.

When next she woke, Michael was standing by the window staring toward the neighboring property. In the early October evening the air hung piquant and gauzy with wood smoke over the trees. India watched from the bed. She loved him. Loved him with an absolute sense of possession, loved blindly. She lived for these secret meetings at the Bay house.

Michael moved restlessly. The eyes watching the outside were intense and unblinking, hands in the pockets of the paisley dressing gown—her present to him.

Looking at him in that robe it was easy to think that she had won him. That he would leave the Church and join the rebel priests who married and worked on the outside. She would go with him; they would go together. If only Michael would come and sit on the bed, take her hand, and tell her that was what he wanted too.

"Are they going to be all night with that bonfire they're making?" Michael asked.

India got out of bed and went to stand behind him. "They'll be leaving soon. They always go back to Washington on Sunday evening."

The deceiving, sneaking around part of it was awful. They were adulterers and there were times when thinking about it she was sick with shame. Standing there now with her arms around him, she thought that their guilt was harming them both. Could she end it now?

Could she stop a runaway train?

Michael was her life, her love, and it was being measured out in the minutes she could spend with him. She had longed for a whole night to spend in his arms—and tonight she could. Jack was away and for once he had taken Paulie with him.

She thought, too, that if ever Paulie suspected . . . and shivered.

"You're cold, darling girl." He turned quickly. His face had lost the serenity of sleep; there were shadows under his eyes. He works too hard, worried India. But it was more, more than that—she wouldn't think about it. Not now, not when she had him all to herself for this one precious night.

"I'm not cold, just happy." India drew her thumbnail slowly across a paisley pattern on his shoulder, and looked up at him.

He looked down at her radiant flushed face. "Do you love me?"

Oh Michael, she thought, and laid her head against him. "I love you so much."

Michael hugged her to him tightly. "Do you, do you darling girl . . ." There was something new and strange in his voice.

He eased her down on the bed, an arm behind her, the other closing her fingers over his rigid penis, taking her mouth, touching the tip of her tongue with the tip of his, pushing against her until she throbbed between her legs and her body arched upwards towards him. When finally he entered her she was trembling, unconscious of anything but her desire for him. Their lovemaking, as usual, was perfect.

And as usual, he got up immediately and went to wash his hands in the small hand-basin in the room. She had been indulgent about the habit at first because she adored him. Now it was another thing, like a cut hair embedded in her clothing, pricking, conscious of it but not . . .

She watched him as he picked up the soap and nailbrush and

suddenly it reminded her of being back at school. She had a recollection of soiling the sheets and mattress with blood because her
period had started early, the humiliation and the guilt. The nuns
making her scrub the unclean stains in cold water until they disappeared. It was a form of punishment. Obscurely she felt this was
what was happening now.

Michael, standing scrubbing his hands as if he were frightened of
the very smell of her, punishing himself.

She faded in and out of sleep, opening her eyes every so often just so
she could look at him. Then, waking, she found Michael's side of the
bed empty.

India sat up. "Michael?"

She slid out of bed, going instinctively to the window. She saw
him on the path walking towards the beach. It was raining. Why
would he want to go out in the middle of the night in the rain? The
answer came straight back. He's unhappy, you're tearing him apart
and you know it.

But she wasn't ready to acknowledge what it meant.

Instead, she pulled on some clothes and a waterproof jacket, fum-
bling with the fastenings, hurrying so she could catch up with him.

When she reached the beach the rain was slanting in from the bay,
wetting her face; she pulled up the hood of her jacket and looked
along the bleak stretch of sand. She saw Michael, walking fast and
almost out of sight. And then he was lost to the mist.

"Michael!"

She felt that he needed her, needed her desperately. Or did he?
Was her presence the last thing he needed? Fear began to grow in her
mind.

Or had it been there all along? Stumbling in the uneven sand she
began to follow him. The wind caught her jacket and it billowed out
behind her.

The waves slapped at the sand, slick and greasy in the rain. She
began running, calling his name, calling. It was in a hundred nightmares; the tall dark figure moving away from her and then turning
and always she was about to see who . . . Always the horror, the old
nightmare, the nameless dread, seeking, seeking—

She was running, heart beating, eyes bloodshot in the stinging
rain. He was just ahead of her.

"Michael . . . Michael . . ."

He stopped and turned around. For a moment she could actually see his face and it was full of misery and guilt and pain, and the way he looked at her, she felt his accusation. Then the rain swirled into her face and she couldn't see anything. She tried to call out and couldn't. Her knees were buckling, slipping away from her, and she was falling forward.

He helped her up, holding her, petting her, his hands clasping her against his wet shoulder, telling her it was all right. She was crying.

"Michael? Please tell me." She wasn't ready for it to end. She still hoped there could be something final between them, something permanent. The weight of it, the enormity of her hope, kept her from speaking out and making it easier for him. They were back in bed and he was cuddling her as if she were a baby, or a very sick person. Holding her clutched in his arms, stroking her hair, kissing her eyelids.

He said quite suddenly and very softly, "It's him. On and on at me. Always saying he wants me to do my duty, he wants me to do things." Then he was talking, almost incoherently. He looked like a man fleeing from pain, and that awful look of his shocked her more than anything else.

Did he mean God? The Church?

"Michael, who does?"

Michael looked at her then, and she was shocked again. She saw in his eyes an expression that wasn't Michael, and it scared her. Then they closed and he rolled on to his back. "My uncle," he said tiredly. "He hasn't realized his ambition for me. He won't die happy until I'm Monsignor." When he opened them again it was just Michael looking at her, terribly tired and a bit embarrassed.

He reached out a hand and smoothed her hair, the same Michael she had grown to know better than anyone. He kissed her softly when she didn't speak.

"Let's sleep now—please—lie in my arms."

His smile was so sweet and loving she felt herself letting go, drifting with it, letting it fill her with peace. He had that power over her.

*   *   *

"Don't go back."

"What?" India sat up in the bed; it wasn't yet dawn.

"Don't go back to him," Michael said. He gave her a mug of tea and sat down on the chair by the bed. His eyes were bright, bright blue. "You don't have to, you need never."

She stared at him, she didn't even taste the tea. It was what she had been waiting to hear, but her focusing thoughts were astonishingly clear. "Michael, think about what you're saying. One hour after Jack finds out, he'd have people all over the country looking for us—a day and there would be someone on our tail. Do you think they would ask us to come back?"

"There are other countries." He began to look haunted. His eyes hadn't lost their vivid blue, but the aching, obsessive doubt was back.

"Oh, Michael . . ."

"I thought it was what you wanted."

"I thought so too." She got out of bed and touched him gently. "But I know now it's not what you want. Really want. Is it?"

Something in his eyes, screaming in agony . . . the look seemed to pass right through her. She wanted him to deny it, and suddenly she was hollow with dread because she knew he wasn't going to.

He put his head in his hands. "It never felt like sinning," he said in a hoarse, broken whisper.

"Oh, Michael, Michael . . ." She got down on the floor on her knees and he pulled her roughly between his legs and held her tight.

"If I stay with the Church I'd not be able to see you like this any longer. There'd be no peace for us," he said, and his voice was shaken by both despair and betrayal.

"It's not wrong to love," she pleaded, drawing back so she could look at him, at his pale drawn face. She was going to lose him. She panicked then.

"We can go away, we can. We'll find somewhere," but even as she was saying it she knew; it was like holding a beautiful moth captive in her fingers.

The thing she kept thinking was, the Church had won. "I love you." She could feel the tears running down her face. "I love you . . ."

"I'm so sorry," he whispered. "So terribly sorry," and he was looking away from her.

She couldn't speak. She watched his face. He was different, changed in some infinitesimal way. His face had become expressionless, swept clean like a mask. At that moment the first awful feeling of doom swept over her.

That afternoon in Georgetown, India pulled to a stop in front of the house, badly scraping the white-wall tires against the curb and ending with one halfway up it. Not bothering to straighten the car or get out, she just sat at the wheel. In a matter of hours it was over. Her life no longer had boundaries. Without him she stood on a chill, barren plain, numbed and hardly alive. He of course had talked about friendship. But this other thing between them that above and beyond everything else had blazed with joy, the thing that had been uniquely theirs, was gone.

That night and every night thereafter, she went to sleep with the certainty that the bond linking them still existed, then woke in the early hours with a physical pain knowing she could never get him back.

It was like an illness. She thought she was over the need for him, when suddenly it would be back. Everyone actually did think she had picked up some viral thing that was going around. It made it easier to conceal her grief.

Gradually though, she got back to normal living again. At least she did things that were part of her everyday life; if that was what could be called normal.

One day she went to see the renovations for the new Center. The work had come to a halt with the men walking off the job because of some problem with the unions. It was frustrating. Government regulations forbade them to occupy the building until certain criteria had been met. So India was surprised when she saw a man, a stranger, standing at the bench in the renovated kitchen, stripped to the waist with lather on his face and a razor in hand.

"Would you be looking for someone now?" he asked.

"I'm . . ." India stared at the open case at his feet from where a crumpled shirt and sweater protruded. "Who are you?"

He gave her a lazy grin, then turned back to the mirror and began to scrape off the lather meticulously. "I'm Ken McWhinney," he said in a curiously soft accent (Irish, was India's immediate thought). "Who are you?"

She told him; her eyes were on the ugly scars cutting across his left shoulder. He turned and caught her staring. "Have you not seen bullet wounds before?"

"I'm sorry. No."

He went back to his shaving. "Then you haven't been to Northern Ireland."

Right again, India thought. "How did it happen?"

"The Army paid us a visit one night and they brought their machine guns with them."

"What army? You mean, the IRA?" she asked. He stopped shaving then and half-turned.

"No, the British Army."

"Then—you're . . .?"

"I'm nothing. That's what you are when you get out of the Maze. You've heard of the Maze prison?"

"Yes, I have."

"You've heard, but you don't know what it's like."

He was staring at her in the makeshift mirror and his air of heated righteous aggression set her teeth on edge.

"I was one of the lucky ones."

She watched him run the razor in a broad stroke down the side of his face. The eyes returned to her in the mirror.

"I escaped. I was brought straight to America. Father Fitzgerald's helping me start a new life here. He told me you'd understand."

It seemed to be getting worse, not better, the chaos now at the Center. They needed more room. They needed more money.

The drugs. The domestic disputes. The reports coming in when people realized that the toddlers next door had no one to look after them.

The mysterious men who came to see Michael and stayed closeted with him in the office and afterwards slipped quietly away without a word to anyone.

And now this man, McWhinney?

Michael's expression was cold. "He went to prison because of his political beliefs; he's not a criminal. Ken McWhinney would rather face death than submit to being classed as a criminal. Anyone with the least knowledge of Irish history would know that." Michael looked across at her. "I've got to do something for these men who are being persecuted in their own country. Somebody has to."

"All right then, but letting him stay here when the building's not finished yet? The bathrooms have nothing in them—no basins, showers, nothing."

"Why don't you invite him to your house? There's plenty of bathrooms." There was something in his voice that India had never heard before, and didn't like. It was spite.

"Michael, that's not fair."

"Yes," he agreed instantly. "I'm sorry, it wasn't. Forgive me." He gave her one of his transforming smiles. But it was rare. These days they had begun to bicker. Despite the end of their love affair, he didn't want to end the friendship, and neither did she. But some element, a meanness, had crept in that threatened to end it for them. The time when they had been so close to each other now seemed incredibly distant.

"India? Wake up, dreamy." Now his look was normal again, his blue eyes clear and straight with her. She laughed, but her throat felt dry and tight.

Michael was the only person India could trust. But just right now that seemed silly, dangerous; she didn't feel she knew him anymore. Sometimes, she thought, dealing with Michael was like dealing with two separate people.

She'd make cranberry citrus relish for the turkey.

"Ooooh, oooh—" Was a twenty-pounder going to be big enough with Johnny's folks coming? How many was that already? Eight?

"Ooo, oooh, aaah—" Pecan and rice stuffing, plenty of it. Why'd he have to invite them—usual excuse, "Momma's not up to doing Thanksgiving this year"—what a load of bull—

"Ooooh, aaah —" As if she didn't have enough on her plate. All her mother-in-law ever did was sit in the kitchen bitching and picking holes. She'd start right in about the pecan and rice stuffing— well, shit, let her. She wants something more traditional, let her stay home.

"Ready, baby, ready?" Malloy yelled in her ear, his straining face puce with exertion.

"Yeah, now. Hard. *Now* . . . *mmmmmm* . . . Oh oh oh!" Chrissy

Posnansky had learned how to fake an orgasm when she was four-teen. She locked her legs around his middle and undulated wildly.

"Oh Christ," Malloy said in a voice of plaintive agony and flopped down on her.

"What's the matter?" she cried back at him.

"I can't, Jesus, something's wrong with me."

Chrissy cursed under her breath. "You want me . . .?"

"Yeah."

She took the limp silly thing in her mouth. Sucking him hard again was hard work. All because her husband screwed up with the Mafia, Chrissy thought resentfully. She got him perked up and lay back again and hissed what he wanted to hear. "You big animal, fuck me, fuck me . . ." Malloy entered and began pumping her in silence. Chrissy gave one of her best moans and then Malloy sagged in a winded heap at her side.

"That was great, honey. Good for you, huh?"

"Mmmmmmmmnnnnn, you just blew me away this time." It was almost intolerable. She'd give it another six weeks, that was all. Johnny'd just better think of another way to get back in favor with the Family.

Pleased, Lieutenant Malloy reached for the remote on the night table control and brought the sound up on the television.

Chrissy was on her annual leave, three weeks gone just like that. She wanted to ask for another week to get Thanksgiving organized. "Joe," she purred, stroking Malloy's rubbery cheek, "think you could spare me from the office until after Thanksgiving? I want to—"

"Shzzz . . . listen to this, will ya."

". . . is the story that has shaken the nation," the news anchorman told reviewers. "Senator Thomas Edward Kelly — Ned Kelly as he is affectionately known to millions—has denied allegations of sexual abuse of eleven-year-old Tracy Waterman. In an extraordinary move Mrs. Waterman has sent her daughter, believed to be mentally re-tarded, into hiding. Mrs. Waterman's lawyer, Mervin Lanuzza, speaking on her behalf, says the action shows a mother fighting to protect her child from the indecencies of physical examination and questioning. Mrs. Waterman has been in Senator Kelly's employ as live-in housekeeper for a month while Mrs. Kelly is convalescing from an illness. This afternoon Mrs. Waterman called Senator Kelly a monster, claiming that he visited her daughter's bedroom with the purpose of sexually interfering with her. Senator Kelly said in an interview that Mrs. Waterman's accusation is monstrously false, and he promises to get to the bottom of the allegations. This is Jay Glover, CBS Evening News . . ."

"The bastard," Chrissy said.

"It's crap. I know Ned Kelly," Malloy laughed, "and he don't even like girls. The first time I met the guy he was in the john with a black boy's cock in his mouth—I was a patrolman on duty looking for someone I thought was in there and I barged in."

"Senator Kelly? You're kidding!"

"Nah. Not about naked little boys with erections. But this load of shit? Something screwy's going on. You know that raid on Freddy's?"

"I remember, sure," Chrissy said, reaching for a cigarette.

"We just found out who the second gunman was. The name's Meehan. He's known in the community as Nailer—IRA, same as the one that got himself killed, what's his name? O'Fiaich."

"Nailer Meehan," Chrissy repeated the name and committed it to memory. "How'd you track him down?"

"O'Fiaich was legit and he had a social security number. We turned it up in his hospital records," Malloy said, looking pleased with himself. "With a social security number you can find out anything. I had Jackson sweet-talk a girl working for a credit-research company. All she had to do was type in her ID and then put in the access code to the correct data bank. We got enough information on O'Fiaich to come up with a name. Meehan's."

"You're clever, you know that?" Chrissy lit a second cigarette and handed it to Malloy. "Where is he, Meehan? Or don't you know?"

"Ran out of luck there." Malloy scowled. "Meehan is Irish. He's part of the underground network of illegal immigrants living here. He's wanted in Britain for terrorist acts. The word out is they want him badly—and so do I. We discovered O'Fiaich ran a boarding-house, we think it is a safe house for an ASU—that's an IRA group operating abroad, an Active Service Unit. It was over on Decatur Street just off Florida Avenue. Ever since the raid on Freddy's the house has been closed down. We went through it and found traces of explosive in the basement."

"So what's all this got to do with Senator Kelly?"

"Kelly raises money for Noraid. He's even joined the IRA picket outside the British Consulate in New York. He was in Ireland last year looking up his family—that's what he said. The info that came back is that when he wasn't putting flowers on the family grave and visiting long-lost aunties, he was meeting with the Provisional IRA."

Malloy was sitting with the back of his head resting on the vinyl-covered headboard, staring at the television screen where two silent men were trying to kill each other; it had got to an interesting point and he was turning up the sound when the phone rang. He picked it up. "Yeah, Malloy speaking . . . Christ, WHAT! Suicide? Yeah, I seen it on the news . . . Listen, I'm on my way over." He dropped the receiver down. Chrissy's cigarette was burning between her fingers as she stared at him.

"What's going on?"

"It's Ned Kelly. He's committed suicide — supposedly. I got to get over there."

"Suicide! If the story about him wasn't true, why would he do that?"

"I can't tell from here, can I? The man's not breathing and he's sitting in his car with a big fucking bullet hole through his head."

The senator's home was a six-bedroomed mansion on Foxhall Road. When Heller got there in his unmarked car the entrance had been cordoned off; police vehicles and vans belonging to the television networks were parked bumper-to-bumper along the road. The networks were setting up cables and cameras and positioning their soundmen. As Heller drew up, reporters and photographers converged on his car. The crowd of onlookers came surging forward. Heller flashed his ID at a patrolman's face.

"Yessir!" the cop shouted. "Lieutenant Malloy's expecting you." Then he was flinging his arms about like a maniac getting them to move back. A minute later he was waving Heller through. "You'll find the Lieutenant in the garage around the back of the house, sir."

The driveway was pink gravel and crunched beneath the tires; Heller glanced at the imposing house as he followed it around to a double garage at the back. The metal door was rolled up and a patrolman stood at the entrance talking into his radio receiver. Heller braked to a stop beside two other police cars, skidding slightly in the gravel. He climbed out, annoyed at the cop's smirk.

The garage was roomy enough to accommodate three or four cars. Heller's eyes passed briefly over a station wagon to the Jaguar Sovereign surrounded by photographers and fingerprint technicians.

One photographer was straddled over the Jag's hood with his camera lens up to the windshield. Malloy had stationed himself by the open driver's door. He saw Heller and signaled him to come over. "The boys are finished taking prints."

The body was slumped at the wheel. Heller circled the car admiringly. "Beautiful, isn't she? Look at that bodywork." He peered inside. Leather seats, burr walnut veneers, beautiful.

"Yeah, but I dunno. Can't beat an American engine. They start when you want them to, no matter how freezing cold it is."

"You don't leave a lady like this out all night in forty below," Heller said, his eyes moving to the dead senator. "Who discovered him?"

"His secretary. He was bringing some papers. No one else was home except the kids, who were playing heavy rock in their room, and the Mexican maid, and she said the senator had gone out. She asked the secretary if he'd mind bringing in a carton of stuff from the station wagon because she couldn't lift things, her back was acting up. The secretary came out here and found Kelly in the Jaguar."

"No one heard the gunshot?"

"No one's said. The joint was jumping with the kid's rock and even the neighbors have been complaining about the noise."

"OK, let's take a look." Heller swung the car door fully open for a visual examination of the body. The head was thrown back and to the side against the headrest, eyes and mouth open in surprise. In the senator's right hand was a handgun.

"That's his gun?"

"We got to check it out."

Heller bent for a close look at the bullet wound. "Gun was rammed to his head, you can tell by the flame zone. The bullet exploded in the cranium and was blown out the other side of his head." He leaned across the body. There was gore and gray matter spilled on the soft leather hand-stitched seats, "Poor bastard had his brains blown out," Heller said.

"Suicide?" Malloy asked.

"Got all the appearances. He certainly had enough reason to kill himself. You guys finished? Can I get in?" Malloy grunted and Heller climbed into the back seat and sat forward with his right arm extended and angled to the side of the senator's head. "Someone in the back here, maybe, the garage is dark, Kelly wouldn't bother putting the lights on. Was the garage door open or shut?"

"Kelly's secretary says it was shut." Malloy was bent at the waist, hands on knees; he sucked methodically on an antacid tablet, watching Heller. "Kelly didn't leave a suicide note. He had the keys in the ignition. If a guy comes out to his car to shoot himself he's not going to bother putting the keys in the ignition. It's not like he was planning on going anywhere."

"A professional would have noticed the keys. You think the killer wanted to make it look like suicide but leave a question mark, a message, maybe?"

"Could be."

"What was Kelly mixed up in?"

"Military supplies—hardware, high-tech stuff. My guess is he was getting it for the IRA's military campaign."

"Who from?"

"That's what bothers me."

Johnny Mangano heard the footsteps out in the hallway. He got up quietly and looked through the small peephole in the door. The two men were at the doorway across the hall; the apartment used by Meehan (or the one it was thought he used) when he was in Washington.

Recognizing the men as plainclothes, Mangano swore under his breath. Damn cops will be running over the place like a pack of bloodhounds, he thought. Why doesn't Malloy just fucking advertise in the papers? He stood aside, cupping his hands and blowing into them. Two days in a freezing apartment waiting for an asshole on unsubstantiated information from a contact who sounded like an escapee from a loony bin. He moved back to the peephole for another look.

The men across the way had come to a decision. One of them stood back, then heaved himself at the door. Johnny walked away so he could speak into a miniature walkie-talkie and reach Angelo, who was positioned across the street, opposite the entrance to the apartment building.

"We got two mutts here breaking down the door."

Angelo's voice came through with a slight crackle; he was fuming. "Malloy's men. Saw them go in and know what? There's a great fucking Dodge van parked out here. Even the kids on the block know it's a police surveillance job. Meehan would have to be stupid to show now."

"And we know he's not stupid, right." From the window Johnny was watching a hot dog man set up his cart on the street below. He could see the steam rising from the pot and the long rolls being set on the hot plate—he could practically smell the onions frying. "So whatta ya think? No point in hanging around waiting for someone's not gonna show, and this place is freezing my balls off. Much more of this I'm coming down with double pneumonia."

"We wait," came the reply.

"Oh, jeez, Angelo . . . Listen, my business is going down the drain while I'm hanging out here."

"You can walk any time you like, Johnny. Then you have to explain why you can't make the repayments on your debt."

"Sure, Angelo, whatever you say. Over." Fuck the son of a bitch where he breathes. Johnny turned away from the window.

Jack waited in his car on a Baltimore side street. The night was deathly cold as a mist crept up from the harbor. He glanced at his watch; it was two-thirty in the morning. He opened the window and let the chill air hose over him so he wouldn't go to sleep.

A car turned in at the bottom of the street, a shadow in the pockets of freezing fog. Jack got out and walked down the street. The car pulled in and a moment later the driver got out. From the way he moved Jack knew he was tired, and careless. When he turned from locking the door and caught sight of a body his hand lunged in a reflex action to his coat pocket.

"It's me, Angelo." Jack stepped into the street light. "We have to talk."

"Shit! What is this?" Angelo stood motionless, a brick outhouse in a cream cashmere coat.

"My car's along the street further. We'll talk there."

"F'Chrissake, what's wrong with my car?"

Jack jerked his head. "This way." He wasn't getting into Angelo's car and then walking away from it with his back unguarded.

Angelo was breathing heavily when they got to the car. Jack motioned Angelo in and climbed in after him. "Visiting someone?" Jack asked.

"You wouldn't be here if you didn't know, so don't give me that crap."

"Bernie live here long?" Jack asked, keeping his tone light.

"You tell me. Listen, what is all this?"

Jack struggled. In the pallid orange of a street lamp his face was bland as cottage cheese. According to the last meeting he had had with the Family, the plan was to set Ned Kelly up in a ruinous scandal and then bribe him. All the Senator had to do was cooperate fully with the two things they wanted—the money back and the names of the two men who'd pulled the raid on Freddy's—and no mention would be made of the unfortunate incident relating to his housekeeper's daughter. But somewhere along the line Angelo had changed the plan and Jack didn't know how; killing the Senator was never part of it.

"Tell me about Ned Kelly," Jack said.

"What's there to tell? We underestimated him. He was going to make a press statement."

"Kelly would never have put his career on the line for the IRA."

"Yeah?"

"I knew the man," Jack said.

"You sanctimonious shit. He was running the whole American operation."

"You're a fool! He was a go-between. His sympathies lay with the IRA, but that was all. No way would he sacrifice his career for them. For Chrissake, he was going to run for president, he would have given us anything to stop a scandal ruining his chances."

"Well, I happen to disagree and I did something about it and know what? I got Family backing over it. You're not the lead dog yet, remember. Anyway, what's the complaint? We got our money back and your friend Kelly told us where to find Meehan—"

"When did he tell you that?" Jack asked quickly.

"When he had a gun to his head, that's when."

"And did you get Meehan?" Jack asked.

"No. Malloy had his men look over the apartment. Meehan won't go there again. But we know he's in Washington. We'll get him. Which reminds me . . ." Angelo smiled for the first time. "Have you thought about why he would go back to Washington?"

Jack looked at him as though he was a communicable disease. "So tell me."

"Only one or two people have ever seen this guy real close. India's one of them. More'n that, she probably witnessed him kill the guy that was raping her. She could put him away, if of course she ever gets her memory back."

"It's pretty hard to distinguish features through a stocking," Jack said evenly.

"Yeah, well, you think about it, she's your wife." He opened the door and got out, turning around to tell Jack, "In fact, you might even make a better job of remembering it next time you're seeing your mistress."

Jack could have killed him with his bare hands. He said, "I hear they pulled Sonny out of a yacht basin in Miami."

"Yeah." Angelo's voice seemed to have deflated suddenly. "Yeah, well, that's too bad."

"Word has it the Cubans are out for blood. They think Sonny was just a front man for people trying to muscle in on their territory."

Angelo snarled, "The Cubans should stick to trading cigars," and slammed the door.

Fifteen

A bottle of Chanel smashed against the wall. Livia stood in a black lace teddy with her feet planted wide and her hands on her hips. She was breathing in deep heaves and glaring at Jack. Her normally pale skin was white against the frame of dark tangled hair. Except for the deep breathing and the ice clinking in Jack's glass, there was silence. His face was tight with anger.

Clearly beginning to wonder if she had gone too far, Livia glided toward him. She stood up close, her pelvis thrust out, and she flicked the velvet skin of her lip with her tongue. "Sweetie, you promised we could go away this weekend." Her eyes were getting wild again. "You promised!"

"I didn't promise Thanksgiving weekend and you know it."

"Know what, Jack? Tell me what I know." She was scowling at him.

"You know that I always have Thanksgiving with my family." Jack was trying to be patient.

"What family?" Livia screamed. Jack looked at her and turned away. She came at him with her fists pounding his back. "You haven't got a family and don't talk to me about that stuck-up English cunt you married."

Jack whirled and grabbed a flailing wrist. "Don't," he snarled, "don't ever refer to my wife again." He let her go. "Ever." He set down his glass on a table and walked to the door.

In her fury Livia was almost grunting. "Fuck you!" she screamed at his departing back. "Fuck you."

India was hoping she was doing the right thing, hoping too that Jack had made other arrangements. Michael was sitting at his desk. She had invited him for Thanksgiving dinner.

The priest got nervously to his feet and began pacing the office floor between desk and window. "It sounds quite the cozy home now, inviting people to dinner."

India colored slightly and didn't reply at once. Was Michael jealous? "It was something you said, about having plenty of bathrooms. I thought . . ."

Michael turned, looking at her. He said nothing. India saw he was sick with desire for her, angry at himself, repulsed by his very emotions.

It was over and it wasn't. She could still go to her room and cry her eyes out; there was a part of her that would never be quite over him.

India told him stiffly she had invited Malcolm and Duane as well and that she was thinking of inviting Ken McWhinney.

"I thought you were dead against his politics," the priest said.

She was. She didn't want to feel sorry for him, but she couldn't help it. He was living in a half-finished building without heating.

Before she could speak he said, "You can forget Ken McWhinney. He's gone."

"Gone? Where to?" India asked, curious, but not really surprised. She had got used to people, strangers, coming and going. She presumed they were people Michael was helping.

"He managed to get a job in New Jersey. He's starting a new life there." She watched the eyelids droop, the secretive mouth; the conversation about Ken McWhinney was over. "I thought you'd be asking some of Jack's family. His brother Tom?" Michael asked. "He's always visiting. Are you sure his veterinary practice isn't just a front for criminal activity?"

"Tom is a good vet and he runs a busy practice." She liked Tom and Betsy. She shrugged. "You're right, though, Tom probably is linked in some way. He sees Jack often enough." India got up to go.

The priest was watching her. He said, "You know, don't you, that your babysitter is on duty these days."

"I'm sorry?" She stared at him. "What are you saying?"

"Paulie. He's right behind you. Comes with you, goes home with you."

"No, that can't be right. I never see him."

"Is he on the couch when you get in?"

"No. I complained to Jack about him being perpetually in the house. He arranged other work for him."

"Surveillance work. No use looking out the window. You were right—you won't see him. I wouldn't say he's the best, but he's good."

"Then how do you know he's out there?"

The priest went over to the window to stare out. "There's gang warfare going on out there, and don't imagine my being a priest or that we're on church property will prevent us from getting caught up in it. We have to know who comes and goes in the neighborhood and what's going on, and I'm telling you, the man we know as Paulie is out there. He follows you."

India stared at him, her mouth twisted. "I'm going to see Jack."

"India," he said. She turned. "Thanks for the invitation, but I have to turn it down. I'm sorry."

"Jack. Your wife is here to see you."

The little green symbols on the black screen of a computer terminal held Jack's gaze. He lay tilted back in his chair; button-down shirt with jaunty tie and plaid suspenders and sharply cut suit trousers. His feet were shod in gleaming Italian leather and they were up on the desk. "Who?" He swung his legs down and even before he plunged his finger down on the intercom button he was thinking: India, here! Something's wrong. What's happened? But he had Paulie watching out for her, nothing could happen to her—or could it? "Caroline, have her come in."

"India?"

The first sight of his wife standing just outside the door of his large high-tech office knocked at his heart. Her hair was newly washed and brushed and it gleamed palely in the sunlight coming through the window. She had a sensual innocence, a wonderful just-laundered look that reminded Jack of ironing day at Concetta's, the starchy, fresh, lemony smell of recently ironed clothes spread around the warm kitchen to air. India was glancing, as everyone did the first time, at the plate-glass window that faced south over the Potomac River and Theodore Roosevelt Island.

Jack pulled up a big leather chair for her and took the one opposite. She sat very straight—in opposition to the seductive cushioning, in opposition to him; the green eyes regarding him were fierce. Livia! thought Jack. Had Livia called her, said something?

"So . . ." Jack said, gingerly. "Thought this was your day at the Center."

"It is. But something happened, and I'm so upset I had to come straight away and speak to you about it."

Christ, it is Livia!

"You promised me I could go out without Paulie snooping on me. I don't want him following me," India said flatly.

Whew! Thank God it's Paulie, nothing to do with Livia. What was the asshole up to, letting India spot him? Now his voice was smooth and resilient, like the sumptuous leather chair India was sitting on.

"Oh, that." He leaned forward, a confident, optimistic smile that went nowhere near the careful brown eyes. "Just lately I was thinking you need protection when you go down there. Let's face it, India, I don't like you being in that area at all." He spread his hands. "Okay, Paulie's looking out for you, I don't get so worried." Sitting in the chair, ladylike, so ivorypale, fragile: his wife and he didn't know her, she would never let him get any closer than they were at that moment. Jack stared. The shadows under her eyes, she had seemed exhausted lately, but not the same beaten woman hunted by painful memories. Different. More determined. Tougher? Jack didn't know what or how, he just knew she had changed.

He said nothing to India about the man called Meehan. She was getting over that business, he didn't want it raked up again and have her worrying over being targeted by some crazy Irishman. Meehan was his affair now—and Meehan would lead to the other, Jack was thinking, the one in the black ski mask who knew the money was there in Luigi's office. The one nobody knew anything about. Who was this guy? Was he Irish as well? The word was out in the community and there were no answers coming back. Meehan! They had to get to him—

"I don't like Paulie," India was saying, "and I won't have him following me around. If you must know, I'm afraid of him."

"Huh? Of Paulie!" Jack's smile was droll; it said she shouldn't be afraid of Paulie, the man was a pussycat. "But, well, if that's the way you feel I'll see to it." He leaned over and patted her knee, a friendly pat he would have given one of his cats. He really wanted to take those small cool hands resting in her lap to his lips. He imagined he saw something in her eyes—perhaps it was the way the light slanted down. He often thought she was keeping a secret, that if he pressed her she would tell, that maybe if he took her in his arms—

"There's something else. Thanksgiving dinner. I'm having it at the house"—she never said "home," always "the house," and it irritated the hell out of him—"and I've invited some people."

"You've what?" Jack interjected. "You've done what?"

"Just a couple of the students who help at the Center and one or two of the, um, Malcolm and Duane, to be exact and—"

"I always go to my folks for Thanksgiving and it goes without question you'll come."

"Invite your father and Concetta to have it with us," she said, quite, quite sure that Jack wouldn't or couldn't, or both.

"I don't fucking believe this," Jack said, getting to his feet. "India, painful as it is for me to say this—I cannot be seen to have the Mafiosi sitting at my table. No one connected to them comes to my home and that means *no one*." He was glaring at her, working up a great righteous resentment towards her. "And what the holy shit is this anyway? You never wanted anything to do with them before!"

"It's just something I thought would be nice to do," India said calmly and Jack could see she was already slipping away from him. She'd get this determined look on her face and wild horses wouldn't budge her. How could she look so innocent, like you could say boo to her and she would cry and run straight into your arms . . . God-damn, he missed having his family come on visits. He missed having a family *per se*.

India stood up and began drawing on her leather silk-lined gloves. "Shall I ring them, or will you?"

Jesus. "Who the hell is Malcolm and—what was the other name?" Jack walked over to the bar. He needed a drink.

"They're um—drug addicts. Malcolm and Duane don't get many invitations. They're looking forward to it." Jack's hand shook as he poured a whisky.

Finally he turned his head. "You want one?"

The look in her eyes, that holier-than-thou look—as if he had said something indecent. Damn it, the mood he was in he would drink the rest of the bottle. Then he'd go and see Livia. Serve India right if he moved in with that bitch.

After she had gone he sat at his desk and drank the whisky, contemplating the glass, waiting to be warmed, consoled. He'd been a good lawyer. That could have been enough, he could have stayed clear. Tom had—though that wasn't strictly true either. Tom wasn't active in Family business but he allowed his veterinary surgery to be used as a holding bank.

He drank, swiveling in the big heavy chair. It was greed. Greed for power—and the slow drift into corruption. Times like now he imagined stairs leading straight to the bottom, to a damp cold cellar where there was a sweetly fetid smell. The smell of things rotting. Corruption. It bothered Jack that he could actually smell it.

The same way he could smell purity. It was the way India smelled. Jesus, sometimes he'd go into her room and take out some of her underthings from the drawers just to smell the clean beautiful smell. She was so beautiful you knew she was beautiful inside. Uncorrupted. He gloated over how pure and clean and good she was.

He'd tormented himself. All those weeks before they were married, wondering if he could control himself, waiting and wanting to make love to her. Their wedding night, the strap of her nightgown slipping from her shoulder, her hot eyes and the downy hair at the pit of her belly. He had been hard all evening and when he finally took her in his arms he felt he'd go crazy if she didn't let him. He was aroused now, just thinking about it.

He drank; and he thought of the revenge he would have on the man who had plundered and abused her. It drove him mad thinking of her being forced, that animal getting his filthy big dick up her. His! His angel. His eyes slitted in rage at the monsters who had permitted that to happen, made it possible. India was his wife now and he couldn't bear to think that it might happen again. It wouldn't, he would see that she was protected—when he was through kicking Paulie's ass.

Sixteen

She felt she was being watched. It was an odd feeling, persistent and distracting.

She was in Oscar's waiting to be served. All she wanted was country-style pork sausage meat, and some fresh cranberries, for the sausage and cranberry stuffing recipe she'd discovered in a back issue of *Gourmet* magazine. She felt on display standing by the window and moved to a new position where she could see the people going by on the street outside. She thought how absurd it was of her to do so. They were just shoppers, like herself, rushing to buy last-minute provisions for tomorrow's Thanksgiving.

"Which bird do you like, lady?" the clerk asked, looking at the turkeys in the window.

"I beg your pardon? Oh," she laughed and gave her order for sausage meat.

He came back with a neatly wrapped parcel. "You have a good Thanksgiving now."

India wished him the same. Outside on the street she checked her list again, and headed for the fruit market. At the corner she missed the light and was forced to wait for the signal to cross.

The crowd built up. People in a hurry jostling for position, the traffic streaming past only inches away. She was beginning to feel faint with hunger. It was because she had skipped breakfast—for some reason the smell of frying bacon had turned her stomach—and then she'd been too busy to stop for lunch.

All of a sudden the image of bacon curling in its own grease brought a wave of heat. India dabbed at her forehead. The thing is, she had been so ravenous during the night she had got up and at two in the morning she was eating grilled cheese on toast.

Funny how she had wanted it then. The mere thought of it now nauseated her. The cheese joined the bacon image. Smooth, runny, yellow, sliding revoltingly over the sides of the bread.

Giddily watching the car wheels whizzing past, fumes rising in a yellow haze. Warm bodies pressing up against her, smothering nauseating perfume, someone behind her, pushing . . . everyone turning and turning in space.

India lay flat on the hospital bed counting the days, calculating, trying desperately to remember.

The last time? The time before that? Michael always wearing a condom. How, then? She knew how, she remembered. That time. Michael not wanting to wait, urgent, thrusting his hard penis against her belly. Not caring, letting him because neither of them could stop. Then a week later feeling safe because her period seemed to arrive. Lighter than usual, hardly anything. Not a period at all.

India calculated she was eight weeks pregnant.

She was carrying Michael's child. She said it over in her head, waiting a moment as if to check she had got it straight. She had it straight all right.

She was in trouble. She was pregnant and she was married to the son and heir of a Mafia baron. Since her wedding night they had lived in separate bedrooms, and Jack had never made a sexual advance toward her.

What was she going to do? Oh God, what could she do? Oh Michael . . . Oh God. The sobs were dry, wrenching, despairing; they hurt, he wasn't there . . . the Michael she knew now was only a ghost of the man who had taken her body, caressed her, cradled her, kissed her with passion, with tenderness until she was giddy. That Michael naked, beautifully formed, unmindful of shame; that Michael no longer existed. She had watched him change. Bit by bit he had gone away from her, entered a cell of his own choosing.

The day he had told her he was going back to the Church, he asked if she understood. Yes, she understood.

So, what was she to do? What was the alternative?

It had been twenty-four hours since the accident, since a passing car had struck her a glancing blow as she fell. It was Thanksgiving Day, an odd day to be lying in a hospital with a headache because of a freak accident, nauseated by the heavy clinging scent of hothouse flowers because she was eight weeks pregnant by a man whose life she was no longer a part of. When the doctors asked, she had lied. She said her periods were normal, she had in fact only just finished menstruating; lied and hoped it wasn't standard procedure to examine women who fainted on the streets for pregnancy.

What she could do, India thought, suddenly cheered, was talk to Adrian. Her cousin would help, he would know what to do. She should have gone to him a long time ago.

"India! India."

A large cone of flowers preceded Harriet through the door of India's room. "You poor dear—where shall I put these?" Harriet caught sight of the long-stemmed roses on India's table. "Lovely. From Jack?" She kissed India's cheek and sat down on the bed. "When I think . . . you could have been killed! Jack said it was lucky the traffic was slowing to a stop."

"Someone was behind me, I was pushed."

"Pushed?"

"I saw him," India said, propping herself up on her elbow. "Harriet, listen, you have to help me. I saw him as I was falling, a man wearing a hat . . ." Harriet had on her earnest look. India thought, she doesn't believe me.

"India, dear," Harriet spoke to her in the same voice she used for baby Timmy. "You saw Harry Cleveland. He's the man who saved you. He reached out and pulled you back. You fainted, that's all. Exhaustion. Happened to me at my sister's wedding, so embarrassing—"

"No, you don't understand, nothing is what you think, Harriet . . ." Her skin was hot, she was babbling, she clutched at Harriet's sleeve. "You see the man outside the door, he works for them. Jack has him watch me all the time . . ."

India could hear herself, and she sounded absurd, preposterous.

Harriet was sitting and staring wordlessly at her. When she had come in India had noticed how pale and strained she was; she was positively white now.

"India, dear," she gave a furtive turn of her head and added more sharply, "Now stop it. They'll think you're paranoid or something. There isn't anyone outside your door." Harriet was stricken but composed. "I've talked to that nice Dr. Nestor. He says you are overstretched and I agree with him. You've simply run yourself ragged and all over some drug addicts."

Harriet said it politely and firmly. But quite frankly she was shocked. According to Jack, India had been most odd about Thanksgiving, quite off-course. Harriet sincerely hoped that India wasn't . . . The Waterford Clinic, the most exclusive private hospital in Washington, did after all deal with patients needing psychiatric care . . . not, of course, that there was any question in India's case. Emotional instability brought on by exhaustion was how Dr. Nestor described her state. And of course, as Harriet knew, India could be very highly strung with a tendency towards migraine headaches. Of course, the instability, that would come from her mother's side of the family.

"Harriet," pleaded India, "I have to see Adrian, would you ask him please to come? It's terribly important, Harriet. Harriet?" Harriet's face was creasing up behind a tight wad of tissues.

"Adrian . . ." Harriet finally said in a teary voice, "I wasn't going to tell you this because Dr. Nestor said not to worry you."

"Tell me what?" India asked, with a violent sense of impending doom.

"Adrian's had a coronary."

India tried to swallow, couldn't, her heart began to race. Harriet was poking her eyes with the tissues.

"It happened last night at a dinner party and—"

"Adrian's dead," India said in a horrified voice.

Harriet looked at her and told India through tear-blurred eyes that Adrian was not dead, he was in the Walter Reed Hospital and out of danger now, apparently.

"Oh." India flopped back on the bed.

Harriet asked cautiously, "What is it you wanted to see him about?"

"I just wanted to see him."

"Well, you have Jack, and you're very, very fortunate." Harriet looked as if she might lose all fortitude and break into sobs. She stood up. "I have to go back there, be with him. And Timmy . . . What if his father dies, poor little mite."

"Harriet . . ." Suddenly India felt terribly sorry for her. She got out of bed and put her arms around Harriet and kissed her.

"We ought to notify your father," Harriet said, appreciative but a little overcome.

"I had a letter from him. He's on a world cruise. His next port is Cape Town in about ten days."

It didn't occur to India until this moment how much she really needed her father. But it wasn't a simple matter of writing or phoning. He was far away.

Too far away.

At first India thought he was a hospital porter. She was looking more at the enormous basket of tropical fruits than at the rather weedy poinsettia plant, and then—

"Duane?"

"Yeah!" Duane stepped jauntily over to the bed. "Howya doing?" He set the basket and the poinsettia down on her bed.

"Duane," India said, staring at his uniform. "Duane, what are you doing here?"

Duane flicked at the smart blue trim on the lapels of his jacket. "Like it? They gave me all this jive about family only visiting, so I borrowed the gear and waited around until this guy outside the door—"

"In a gray suit, face like a rat?"

"Yeah, that's him. Sits in a chair outside. I waited until he was having coffee with one of the nurses and then I came in. Who is that guy?"

India shrugged and pulled a wry smile.

"Some hospital," grumbled Duane. "You have any trouble from him, you tell me, okay?"

"Okay."

"They say you got a concussion. What happened?"

"It was a silly accident. I'm sorry about the Thanksgiving dinner. I guess Jack canceled."

"Shit, don't give it a thought. We had dinner anyway over with the Mayor. Malcolm threw up over his. The food wasn't that bad, though."

"Then he's not really getting any better?"

"Malcolm's not exactly jumping up and down, but he ain't that bad either. Mel says not to tell you about him being sick and he says hi." Duane indicated the fruit. "Little something from us all."

India gave him her thanks and told him it was really sweet of them, and then she asked if Father Michael knew she was in the hospital. Duane didn't seem to know, or even to have seen him around. He was beginning to look around nervously. "Look, I'm outta here before someone gets on my case," he said. "You get better real soon, you hear."

India smiled as she watched him take a cautious peek around the door, then wave and go. She read the card attached to the plant. It had all the signatures, nearly all. She looked for Michael's and couldn't find it. The other card was deep down among the tropical fruits. It read: "For Mary Lou, get well soon, love Chuck and Barbie."

Meehan watched through the glass door. The glass was lightly frosted but he could pick out the vet's shape hunching over the sluice sink. In the surgery the dog was still on the operating table. He wandered over humming a little tune and prodded it. A muffled whinny from the vet's nurse caused the humming to stop.

"Will you shut up now." He looked at her. Fat all over, hips and thighs sagging over the anesthetist's seat, puckered knees. She was a picture. When they came in she had been holding a mask over the dog's nose. Right now she was tied to the chair with tape across her mouth.

The phone on the wall rang. Meehan stared at it, then he walked over to the glass door leading to the sluice room and swung it open. The vet was soaking wet. He was standing bent over backwards, blood streaming from a gash in his forehead, blood in his eyes, his hair clenched in McWhinney's fist.

"Tell us where the money is, Tom, and we'll stop," Meehan said in a reasonable voice. The vet screamed an obscenity at him.

"Put his head down the sluice. This time leave it down until he sees sense," Meehan said. McWhinney tightened his grip on Tom's hair and yanked him straight before plunging him back in the sluice where the vet's blood mingled with that of several unidentifiable objects that looked like a butcher's off-cuts.

Meehan and McWhinney became absorbed watching the bubbles

bursting on the surface. When they came less frequently, the struggling at an end, they let him up. Meehan yelled into the upturned face, open gasping mouth drooling liquid, "Tell us where the money is or we'll kill your nurse." He grabbed what stringy hair was available, his mean eyes glittering behind the stocking mask. "And then we start on your family."

Tom gagged, managed to splutter, "They're away," and leered triumphantly.

"Your nurse isn't," hissed Meehan, "and we'll kill you, then we'll wait for your wife and kiddies. Betsy! Now isn't that a nice name. Betsy. We know Betsy's out doing the shopping and we know she won't be long." He nodded and McWhinney started.

Tom tried to protect himself from the terrible things that were happening to him, the low blows, the knee in the groin doubling him up in pain, rabbit punches in his kidneys, that sent him sprawling on the floor. He saw Meehan's face, hazy. He saw the chilled eyes and he thought he'd had it.

"Floor safe . . ." His eyes shifted out of focus and rolled back in his head.

Meehan whipped him across the face. "Where? Die on us, you bastard, and this will happen to the kiddies." He held the vet's head up. "You're not that fucking dumb—tell us, and the combination." Tom mouthed something. Meehan bent closer to listen, then he let go and straightened up. Tom slumped on the floor. "Got it, come on."

McWhinney found the safe in the office under a section of flooring that lifted out. The safe was cemented in underneath. Meehan worked on the combination, opened it. He hefted the two leather bags out and took a quick look at the neatly banded stacks of notes inside. "Around what we expected. Let's go—"

"What the fucking hell?"

"It's the nurse got her feet loose. She's fucking kicking the place to bits," McWhinney said from the door.

Meehan went through to the surgery. He almost hit her, staring down at her pudgy face and arms, the tape across her mouth wet through with saliva. "Something we can use there in that anesthetic machine?"

"Like what?" McWhinney asked.

"Look in the drawer, there's got to be a mask. I don't know, you're the medical orderly."

"They use tubes on animals—wait, this'll do the trick." McWhinney brought out an oxygen mask and fixed it on to tubing connected to the halothane tank. The nurse drummed her heels and screamed behind the tape. Meehan got behind her and jammed the mask over her nostrils; it was like holding a walrus back in the middle of mating. The struggling slowly began to subside. "You seem to be on to the right stuff there," he told McWhinney. He slipped the elastic band around her head and fastened the mask tightly against her face. "Leave the gas running."

"You gonna kill her."

"That's her problem." Meehan noticed the dog on the table beginning to lift its head, wobbling and looking around. He walked over.

"Hello, fella. Whatta they doing to you?" He rubbed the dog's ears while looking at the shaved area on its flank and the neat sutures. Then he lifted the dog off the table, carried it over to a blanket spread on the floor and gently lowered him.

"Leave the dog, for Chrissake. Let's go." McWhinney had the bags and was standing at the door.

"Shut up." Meehan got a bowl and filled it with water from the sluice room, stepping over the vet lying insensible on the floor. He took the water back to the dog and put the bowl down beside him. Before leaving he patted the dog and smoothed its ears. "Good boy."

Tom recovered consciousness and lay blinking to clear his vision, then tried to get up. He was groggy with pain, both eyes swollen half-shut; he tasted blood in his mouth, it was trickling down his face. He got up on his knees, then pulled himself up with the aid of a heavy-duty plastic apron hanging on the wall, and staggered into the surgery.

The dog was lapping at a bowl of water. Tom turned his head slowly until eventually the nurse came into view. He lurched in her direction and stared at her dazedly.

"Oh hell!"

He pulled the mask from her face. But he couldn't get the tank turned off. Couldn't get his fingers to work properly. The place was beginning to reel. Finally he managed to shut off the gas. The nurse's head rolled forward; he picked up a dangling wrist and felt for a pulse. No pulse. No . . . Tom slid quietly to the floor.

GET UP! MOVE! DONT LOSE CONSCIOUSNESS.

He couldn't stand. He began crawling. The dog whimpered. He crawled to the office phone. As he scrabbled up from the floor by way of the chair he prayed the bastards hadn't cut the wires, prayed that Betsy and the children hadn't come back early. Whoever they were, they knew their names, knew what they were looking for. *They knew.* He punched his home number; no one answered. The next number was Jack's.

At the Georgetown house Jack replaced the receiver very slowly. Where the blazes did they get their information? How, for Christ's sake? Only he and one or two others in the organization knew where the secret banks were located. He got up and walked to the door, walked back to his desk; he was like a sleepwalker. Tom had said the one who talked had an Irish accent. Same bastards who did Luigi, had to be. Two this time. Meehan? Who was the other?

They had to be IRA.

Because of Ned Kelly the money was now back in the Family coffers. And the IRA bastards were out grabbing some more. Jesus.

One of the other syndicates behind them?

No. No one would touch maniacs like the IRA. But someone was tipping them off and whoever it was had inside information. Thinking about it filled Jack with murderous rage.

He was gathering up papers and thrusting them into his briefcase; he had to go to Lewisville to see what could be done for Tom and Betsy. As he left the study his face was dark with fury. India was walking through the front door, Paulie behind her carrying a load of stuff; bags, baskets of fruit, a potted plant.

Christ! The phone call had emptied his mind of everything else. India was coming home from the hospital. Was home. White as a sheet, dark circles under her eyes. He wanted a robust wife he could turn to, who would listen and be a source of comfort—well, not too robust and comfortable. Jack sometimes didn't know what he wanted his wife to be.

"Put that stuff up in her room," he told Paulie, glaring at India as if she might be the cause of all his problems. "How're you feeling?"

India shrugged. Jack thought she looked at him as if he were the devil incarnate. Was she trying to punish him or what? It slipped his mind that his face was like thunder and that he hadn't stopped glowering since he had heard from Tom.

"Look, I want to talk to you. Come into the study a moment, then I have to leave."

"Oh?" Her gaze veiled over, but she walked past him looking slightly more cheerful.

"Some business came up," Jack mumbled. "Sit down, will you, a moment. Listen, I talked with Dr. Nestor and I told him I wanted you to see this psychotherapist I was telling you about in New York."

"I'm not seeing any damn psychotherapist." She looked at him. "I'm sorry."

"And I'm sorry too, but that's the deal. You see this guy and get some help so you can stop looking like you've just been handed a bag of rotten apples, or Dr. Nestor will arrange for you to spend some more time at the clinic." He was thinking she wasn't going to answer him.

"Did Harriet phone and leave a message?"

"You heard what I just said?" Jack asked sharply. Her face sure as hell told him she wasn't thinking about it.

"Yes, I heard," India said. Her voice mocked him, the word "heard" was emphasized. She picked up the notepad that was by the phone and looked at the message written on it.

Oh, Jesus, Jack thought—he'd forgotten to tell her. This business about Tom had completely thrown him. He ran his hands through his hair and sighed. "Yeah, well, it's written down there—Adrian's off the critical list."

"Oh . . . thank God." She looked as though she was going to crack suddenly and start crying.

Jack hesitated. She was fond of Adrian; he wished he'd remembered and given her the message. "Yeah, well," he muttered, "pays to number cardiologists among your friends, doesn't it."

India looked at him. "You were saying something about being in a hurry to leave. Please don't let me hold you up." She looked at him with such loathing, Jack turned on his heel. He slammed the door hard on the way out.

Jack was going to kill her. Standing in front of the bathroom mirror pressing a cold washcloth against her eyes, she almost didn't care if he did.

She felt she ought to save him the trouble. God knows she felt like death. Especially in the mornings. Wilma would only have to put down a pile of steaming pancakes, streaming with yellow butter, and she would have to leave the kitchen and run upstairs to vomit in her bathroom. Languishing in her bedroom with a cup of tea and a dry biscuit was going to arouse everyone's suspicions.

She had to have an abortion. It was the only way. Anything else would be insane.

But how? There would be visits to a gynecologist to arrange a date, the operation itself . . . the actual surgery involved was minor but there would be a general anesthetic. How was she going to have that done at a Washington clinic when she was so guarded? Unless she went to New York.

And she could. She could because Jack had offered her the very chance.

"I thought over what you said and I've made up my mind."

It was early, Wilma hadn't even arrived. But Jack, back from Lewisville the evening before, was already shaved and dressed and at the kitchen table drinking coffee.

India reached into the refrigerator for a carton of white grape juice. She craved orange, the juice cold and tart, but it was too yellow first thing. "The psychotherapist you mentioned in New York—I'd like to see him."

Her expression was usually mute when she was talking to him. He never knew what she was thinking. Jack's eyes narrowed. This morning there was something, a brittleness in her tone; what was she up to? He shrugged, smiling, the brown eyes dangerous. "Do what you want. You've got his number, call and make an appointment."

He was still wondering about her change of mind, wondering why, but admiring the way her Valentino jeans hugged the curve of her bottom shifted his thoughts. "He likes to meet first and get acquainted," he told her. "Probably set up several appointments to run over consecutive days."

"That sounds okay," India said cautiously. It was perfect. She could see a gynecologist on the same day she went to New York for her first meeting, and then have the abortion when she went back for her sessions with the psychotherapist. "There are just two things. I want to stay in New York while I'm seeing him, that way it will be more intensive—"

"I'll get Caroline to book you into a hotel for two or three nights, whatever you need. What's the other?"

"Paulie. I don't want him with me."

"Yeah, but—"

"If he has to come to New York with me, I won't go through with it. Your choice."

Jack sat for a moment, hesitating. "Okay," he shrugged. "I want Paulie here in any case. What are you making there?"

"Tea." India swallowed hard as her stomach shifted to a new location. "Like a cup?"

"Thanks," Jack said. "Mind if I take a rain check?"

Why was she waiting? For what? The bleeding to start on its own? For Michael to renounce the Church and claim her?

If she started thinking what she was about to do—was it murder?—if she thought about that she'd lose control. She called the Center and said she was sick. If she saw Michael in the privacy of the office, not trusting her voice or her face to give her away, she might break down and tell him. And she couldn't do that.

But she had to see him one last time before she did it. Though she knew it was a mistake. A voice kept telling her: if he sees you he might suddenly realize, he might . . . To twist the knife deeper she took communion when she knew Michael was the officiating priest. At the altar rail she joined the other communicants and knelt down.

When he stood before her India raised her head. This was Michael, not an ordinary man, a priest, the father of the child she was carrying. She opened her mouth to receive the thin wafer on her tongue and saw his hand tremble, saw the heartstopping beauty of those blue eyes smiling down on her and then passing on to the next communicant and the next and the next, weaving their same terrible spell. God damn you, God damn you, Michael.

As soon as it was finished she was hurrying towards the door knowing she was going to have the abortion and knowing it was wrong, morally wrong, for a Catholic the gravest of all sins.

Seventeen

India registered at the Woman's Clinic on First Avenue and East Sixty-fifth Street under the name of Isa Davis. She was due there in one hour—this was the day for which the abortion had been arranged.

The psychotherapist had an office on West Seventy-seventh Street right off Central Park and she had been there for the appointed hour, longer, India fidgeted with her watchstrap; fifteen minutes longer.

An hour and fifteen minutes watching his half-smoked cigarettes get stubbed out in the onyx ashtray in the process of eliciting her life history. India thought he had seemed bored with the assignment, but now they had overrun the allotted time and her visit should be concluding there was a spark of interest.

"I never think anything is gained by hurrying." His sharp eyes were on her, missing nothing. "Is there any hurry?"

India feared he could know what she was thinking by reading her body language. He was staring at her as if he knew—he looked exactly like someone she might have met in Harrods' book department. But he was connected with the Family. He wasn't safe she couldn't tell this person the things she would never dream of telling anyone else. He would, she had no doubt, report it all to Jack.

"I'm not"—she had to leave, if she took a cab now it would take her every minute to get over to First Avenue—"in a hurry exactly, but . . . I do hate the smell of cigarette smoke."

"Ahhh, now this is interesting. Part of your trouble"—India had his undivided attention now—"is your lack of confidence. You need to assert yourself, learn how to say it, get the thing that you want. Assertiveness." His hand came down on a bell and immediately the door was opened by his receptionist.

"Evantine, clear away all the things pertaining to my filthy habit. India is learning to assert herself."

"Oh, please—"

"Don't spoil it."

India got up from her chair, saying rapidly, "I do have things to . . . shopping, things—thank you so much," seeing him still seated, studying her. In her panic to leave, how much was she giving away? The receptionist too, clearing the onyx ashtray, was giving her wondering looks. On the other hand, India thought, perhaps she was the only patient who had ever complained about his chain-smoking.

"I think we should carry on this afternoon; it might be valuable. I want to hear more about your mother—"

"Dr. Pautasso, I—"

"Because inevitably, the sexuality is first fixed on the mother—"

". . . have to leave now, thank you, it's been most—interesting."

"You're in such a rush I'd almost suspect a lunch date?"

"No, no . . ." India was almost at the door.

"Then would you do me the honor?" He followed after her, reaching for the door as if to open it, but not opening it, standing there smiling. "I'd like very much to take you to lunch."

"Thank you," she tried to speak lightly, "but I can't today. Perhaps some other time." He helped her on with her coat and opened the door. India thought that was an end to it—she was frantic to get downstairs and hail a cab—and said goodbye. She went out quickly into the hallway, to the elevator.

She pushed the "Down" button twice, looking upwards, waiting anxiously for the brass arrow to swing to her floor. The doors opened, she stepped in, smiled automatically at the woman with a small animal in her arms and pressed "Door Closed." Then she stood tensely waiting for the door to open again.

Out in the lobby, through the heavy circular doors, and out onto the street. "Taxi!" She stood at the curb with her hand raised for a yellow cab, not noticing the raw gritty cold. It was beginning to snow lightly; she was too agitated in her hurry to bother fastening her coat. The traffic sped past, ignoring her.

"Taxi!" Dr. Pautasso stood beside her. Immediately a yellow taxi swung over to the curb. "You can share mine." He took her arm. "Where to?"

India felt like screaming. She said calmly, "Bloomingdale's." She could get another cab. From Lexington Avenue, the clinic was only three blocks over.

He gave instructions, then settled back in the seat, swiveling his whole body toward her with a breathy chuckle. "Shopping? No wonder Jack's worried. Don't worry, only kidding. Is it going to be long, this shopping expedition of yours? Still like to fit you in for another session this afternoon if it's possible."

"It's not, I'm sorry. But we do have the next two afternoons," she pointed out. "You can make the sessions as intensive as you wish." Her eyes flattered him.

"All right, tomorrow afternoon, then." He sighed and began a loud discourse on infantile sexual development.

India's relief at seeing Bloomingdale's department store was so profound she barely thanked him for the ride. As soon as the cab was out of sight she ran over and gave the first free driver the address and got in.

The Woman's Clinic was an old building of red weathered brick. It could have been a residential hotel for women; it had the same slightly impoverished air of gentility. It was also expensive. She'd had to pawn the necklace Jack gave her.

This time the woman behind the registration desk knew her. "Mrs. Davis, and how are you today?" she asked, briskly bright.

The lilies on the desk, ashy white and wet and globby with pollen were making India nauseated. "Just fine," she said, and thought what a ridiculous thing it was to say. Her hands were shaking, she was sweating inside her coat and shivering at the same time, and she felt sick.

Sick because she was about to kill the life inside her, sick with fright, sick with hunger because she hadn't eaten anything because of the anesthetic she was going to have.

Sick, because the lilies reminded her of death and funerals. "How appropriate they are," she said, not realizing she was speaking out loud.

"Aren't they gorgeous!" The woman bunched the flowers, admiring them, and releasing a shower of sickly pollen.

An efficient young nurse in white led India to the elevator and from there down a corridor to a room overlooking the street. The narrow white bed, the antiseptic hospital smell. She was left to get undressed.

Taking her clothes off. Couldn't she have it?

Crazy thought at this stage.

Babies in bassinets, babies sitting in prams being pushed through a park; a baby no bigger than a clot inside her letting her know she couldn't do it.

The nurse was back and India was still standing at the bedside numb and dazed in her underwear—the nurse had to assist her. "Great, now slip the gown on, opening at the back. The Doctor will see you before we give the pre-medication. Do you want to get into bed now, Mrs. Davis . . . Mrs. Davis . . ."

The doctor came in. "I'm Dr. Brandon . . ."

Where was the doctor who had examined her the previous week? India felt anonymous in the white gown, unreal, somebody else going to have her womb curetted.

Why now? Why in heaven's name start thinking of "it" as a baby now? It had no identity, it was a nothing without her.

Nothing without her. She was all it had.

". . . the tests you had done last week in pre-surgical care are normal, no worries there, and you've talked it over with your husband, Mrs. Davis?"

"Yes," India said. What was another lie, she'd told so many.

"And you both still want the abortion?"

"Yes," said India.

"But you refused to come to our counseling service," he reminded her quite gently.

Oh Lord—a moment longer and she would be begging him to forget the whole thing.

"You'll have an injection to relax you—I suggest you use the bathroom beforehand. Don't worry if your mouth goes dry, it's supposed to. In half an hour you will be wheeled along to the operating room—you should be well enough to go home this evening. Have you arranged to be picked up?"

India stared in consternation. "Oh . . . yes." She'd cross that bridge when she came to it; anyway, one of the nurses could get a cab for her.

The needle that would carry the anesthetizing agent was already in a vein on the back of her hand; the doctor who would administer it sat comfortably on a stool at her side. He was young, smiling, wide-shouldered; he looked like a football star waiting to go into combat. Only it was a hypodermic syringe in his hands, not a football. India watched a drop of the clear pale solution ooze from the needle and run down the side.

"Anything you want to say?"

"Nothing, no."

"Okay—I'm going to give you an injection here, through the needle in your hand. It will make you go to sleep, you won't feel a thing. When you wake up it will all be over." These last words rang with an odd, ironic note, but his frank honest face beamed at her. He was ready to inject the drug, his thumb steady on the plunger. "I want you to start counting up to ten for me, Mrs. Davis."

"One, two"—she saw something, felt something, a need so desperate—"my baby, I want my . . ."

"Jesus Christ, what'd she say?"

"She wants the baby, she's saying she wants the baby."

India heard the doctor and nurse quite clearly, but she couldn't see them, and she couldn't speak. She wasn't able to explain, tell them she was making a terrible mistake, couldn't do that before everything went black.

"Isa! Isa . . . Mrs. Davis . . . she's coming round, Doctor."

India was beginning to surface, but the reason why these people were trying to waken her was still obscure. What had Mrs. Davis to do with her?

The baby! India opened her eyes and saw it was Dr. Brandon.

"Mrs. Davis, you haven't had surgery. Do you understand what I'm saying?"

"Yes, I'm keeping the baby . . . my baby . . ." murmured India. The doctor's face was disintegrating in front of her eyes and she drifted away from him. She dreamed there were precious jewels in her hands turning and flashing until in her imagination they became the necklace, and she was desperately trying to shove it away because the stones were burning holes in her flesh, not her flesh, the baby's . . .

"Mrs. Davis, Mrs. Davis, wake up."

And then she was awake again and the nurses were with her.

"No one's going to hurt your baby, Mrs. Davis." They lifted her head and gave her a sip of water and wiped the sweat from her forehead. "You're safe, your baby is safe," they told her.

There was a problem, it was real and she was aware of it, yet she couldn't seem to grasp its significance, she and the baby—not safe— had to do something—couldn't. Couldn't wake up, couldn't get out of sleep's grip.

She'd think later, work it out. She was the keeper of something precious, a tiny human being whose dependence on her was so overpowering and burdensome, there was nothing, nothing India felt couldn't be worked out.

The nurses were talking in the next cubicle. India was awake now, lying quietly on the narrow bed in recovery waiting to be taken back to her own room. A telephone began ringing, one of the nurses went to answer it. Silence, and then the nurse was asking: "Do we have a Mrs. Donovan on the afternoon list?"

India was listening, stiff with attention, the blood beating hard in her ears. Someone calling here? For her?

A nurse walked over to a board. "No one by that name on the OR list."

India heard the nurse talking into the phone, but couldn't follow what was being said. She closed her eyes. Someone knew she was here. But who? She had been so careful. Jack couldn't know, unless . . . Unless she had been followed. Dr. Pautasso? Someone who knew she was here, but not the reason. Checking up to find out . . .

Jack had had her watched. Paulie was here in New York and he knew where she was.

The curtains were pulled and the nurses appeared. "We'll take you back now, Mrs. Davis."

"Thanks. Who was that making enquiries?"

"Reception. They've got a man calling in insisting we've got a Mrs. Donovan in here."

"I'd have thought reception had a list of patients?"

"They do, only they get people calling in—boyfriends—husbands usually—wanting information. You'd be surprised, some women come in for a secret abortion. Am I right, girls, or am I right?"

"Ah, huh," a nurse answered cheerfully, "an' hubby dear don't even know she's pregnant, then holy shit, she finds he's got a detective on her."

"But reception wouldn't give out any information as to why a patient was in the clinic—would they?" India asked in a thin voice.

"Why, honey, if a woman comes to this clinic, everyone knows what she's in for. Say, are you the lady the man's looking for?"

India looked shocked, she stared at the nurse unflinchingly. "Most certainly not."

Not that the clinic's policy on information made much difference, India was thinking. Paulie would simply produce some money and a pile of notes slipped across the desk would ease out a fact or two.

"Here we are. You can get dressed now soon as you want, Mrs. Davis. You're free to go any time, just ring the bell and a nurse will take you down to reception."

"Thanks . . . and thanks for everything."

As soon as the door was shut India got up and went to the window.

Careful—don't disturb the curtains—she looked side-on, scanning the street below, alert for anything, any sign. A break in the pattern of busy people walking purposefully to and fro—she noticed the windows of the bar across the street gave a clear view of the clinic entrance. If Paulie was waiting, she thought, that is where he'll be. She'd begun to know the way Jack's man worked.

"Thank you, Nurse." India took the tray and looked hungrily at the tuna fish sandwich. Protein and fish oil. "It's got to be good for you, baby," she said aloud when the nurse had made her exit. "And so long as you're staying around, your diet is going to improve." She gobbled it down and drank half a cup of tea and then sat down by the phone. If Paulie had already rung his information through to Jack (she dialed Jack's office number, wincing), then the cat was among the pigeons.

"Hello Caroline, it's India, um . . . is Jack available? Oh . . . a meeting . . . all afternoon, good heavens — No, no, not if he specifically said not to disturb him . . . must be important, huh? Of course . . . yes, if you would, thanks. Bye now."

So, Jack had been tied up since the time she booked into the clinic . . . With luck, Paulie wouldn't have had the chance to speak to him—and knowing Jack, he'd leave the office and go somewhere for dinner. Which meant she still had a few hours yet before Paulie could get to him.

India went to the window again and stood drinking tea. Was tea bad for the baby? Too much tannin? She'd buy herb tea. But first . . . first she had to make sure if it was Paulie out there watching her movements.

It was six-thirty when India left the clinic by the main entrance and paused under the spill of light to tie her head scarf. The air was dry and cold, it hurt when she drew in a deep breath, but it was fresh and good. There was no sign of the snow she had seen earlier in the day. On the other side of the street was the lighted front of the bar.

Don't look, she told herself, don't, just act casual. She started along the icy sidewalk in the direction of Central Park. The traffic moved beside her, a vast anonymous tide rolling uncaring to the next intersection. There were few people on foot. Don't look behind. Not yet.

She turned along Second Avenue, walking rapidly, her breath hanging white in the frosty air. Over on the other side was a drug-store, the act of crossing the street allowed her one look back. No one. A couple walking in the opposite direction, the young woman in fake leopard India had passed. Wait—

There—across the avenue, barely noticeable through the traffic—a dark overcoated figure walking her way, stopping now at a news-stand.

India crossed, walked on without looking back and turned at the next corner. She continued along to the first lighted shopfront, the window displaying an idealized partridge in a gilded pear tree. She stopped just inside the entrance to look.

Through the right-angled panes of glass she was in time to see a man, dark coat, hat pulled well down, turn around and cross the street and keep walking. Was it the same man? India broke out into a sweat. Was it Paulie? He had been too far back in the shadows to tell. It was someone and whoever it was her feelings were the same as those of a swimmer who notices a fin cleaving through the water and knows it is a shark.

India spent ten minutes inside looking at objects for the avant-garde. Then she left the shop.

"A pot of tea, Earl Grey, and sandwiches, please."

"I'm sorry, we don't have Earl Grey."

"Anything then, it doesn't matter really." India's eyes were drawn again towards the window.

"We do have Darjeeling."

"That would be lovely."

"Or English Breakfast."

India turned slowly to gaze at the waiter. "Darjeeling will be perfect."

It was sheer madness to be sitting here now ordering food, except if she didn't eat something she might faint with hunger. Twenty minutes had passed since she took up her position at the window in the foyer of the hotel. From where she sat she had a good view of the street outside while the drapes obscured her from anyone looking in.

Perhaps she was mistaken. Mistaken or becoming paranoid. Perhaps she really was paranoid. India ate the pickle, the last edible thing on her plate. The tea tasted like watery coffee. Perhaps it was watery coffee. Across the street was a Pancake Parlor advertising an ice cream bar serving forty-two different flavors. She had an intense craving for fresh peach ice cream.

And then she saw him. Across the street, a man in a dark overcoat caught for a moment in the fierce white glow from the neon-lit windows. His hat was low, but there was no mistaking him. India was standing as close to the window as she dared, staring out, staring in horror at that familiar narrow shape in the white circle of light. Paulie. Watching thin-lipped as he entered the Pancake Parlor. She wished she hadn't eaten the pickles, she felt sick again.

"Father Fitzgerald is not answering," said the woman, beginning to sound reproachful. This was India's fifth call.

"Please could you try his room again?" India sat hunched on the bed holding the receiver in both hands.

"No answer."

"Please, when he comes in would you ask him to call the number I gave you?"

It was after ten-thirty. Soon Paulie would speak to Jack, soon there wouldn't be very much Jack wouldn't know. She wasn't going to sit and wait for that to happen; responsible now for another life, she had to save herself and her baby.

Which was why she had rung Michael. Not Michael the priest; Michael, the man in the black mask.

Once Michael had told her there would be a time, an hour, when she would need his protection, and need it badly.

When he had said it, had she known what he meant? Loving Michael the way she had, the issue of this other personality that was also Michael had become an abstract thing. She never referred to it. It was like owning a gun. It was kept out of sight in a drawer and never talked about. But it was there. She only had to open the drawer; she knew if she needed it badly, she could use it.

Had she known all this, all along?

But now when the time, the hour, had come, she was beyond examining her motives. She was ruled by the strongest force of all. Fear.

It was nearly eleven when the phone rang and she heard Michael's voice. She was nervous, her heartbeat running. She knew the mistake she might be making but she couldn't stop.

She told him.

"Where is he now?"

"Right across the street from my hotel, in Lulu's Pancake Parlor on East Seventy-second Street. I saw him go in. Then I came up to my room and found it was possible to watch the doorway from here. He hasn't come out in all this time. He's waiting—Michael, he has information I don't want Jack to know."

"Is it anything to do with us?"

India closed her eyes. "Yes." And it was true; the baby wasn't a lie.

"What does he know?"

India felt a rush of vertigo, she sat down. "He knows I went to an abortion clinic . . ." India heard the hissing intake of breath. "He was there, he followed me back to my hotel."

"Was it your husband's?"

"No," she shot back in anguish. There was a long silence. "Michael?"

"Stay in your room. Don't open the door to anyone until I ring back."

"Michael? Michael!" There was a click and the phone went dead.

Eighteen

Rosie Murphy was in the bathroom, naked, except for the silver chain and crucifix around her neck and the plastic bag covering the top of her head. She was standing with one leg on the stool applying henna paste to her pubic hair. Recently she had left Washington, D.C., to come and live in New York. She missed Washington. She thought of Monsignor Haughey. He had been a character, the Monsignor, and always generous. Besides her regular fee there had been regular handouts of cash. Rosie sighed. There was no one in New York like the Monsignor.

The doorbell interrupted her thoughts. "Bugger it." She crossed herself—you went to hell for saying words like that—but wasn't it always the way?

At the third blast she yanked on her stained satin robe and with a towel wrapped around her head she went to answer it. The small, functional studio apartment was heaped with clothes and piles of magazines. There were dirty plates, glasses piled on the Formica-topped counter in the area that served as a kitchen. Adroitly Rosie pushed a half-bottle of whisky out of sight. Her feet in plastic scuffs pattered on the linoleum by the door.

"Who is it?"

"Just let me in, for God's sake."

Rosie recognized Meehan's voice at once and unfastened the

chain, then began with the locks. She knew why he had come. If Meehan crossed the threshold into her apartment, it was for a job. She often declared she wouldn't mind so much if she got paid for her time. Lastly she drew the bolt at the bottom and opened the door a crack.

Meehan shoved it wide and walked in. "You'd think this was Fort Knox. Get dressed, we're going out."

"Now? I'm in the middle of doing my hair!"

"You've ten minutes. Wear something people won't remember afterwards."

Typical! The one night she took off to do a dye job on her hair. Rosie began rinsing the henna off under the shower, thinking resentfully it's hardly been on more than five minutes.

She only knew him as Meehan; she didn't like him. He came and went; like tonight, for instance. It enraged her. She had too many calamities of her own in her life to have this going on as well. It was only because of her brother. He'd been stuck in the Maze prison in Ireland for months, but if she helped the unit they would get him out and bring him to America. She had no choice.

Lulu's Pancake Parlor was crowded. It was always crowded; business was brisk. "It's him over there, by the window," Meehan told her quietly.

Rosie gave a discreet look over the top of the menu. "The one in the gray suit?"

"Yeah."

"He looks harmless enough. What flavor ice cream you having on your waffle?"

"Order what you want, I'm going downstairs to have a look around. He has to go for a piss sometime. Second thought make mine a hot fudge sundae. Keep an eye on him. You know what to do if he looks like leaving."

Meehan started down the stairs that led to the rest rooms. He was light and quiet on his feet; he noted everything. He had the ears of a trained professional and was able to judge distances by a sound.

The public telephone was beneath the stairs, the men's lavatory across a small hallway; the women had to walk further along a narrow corridor. What Meehan wanted was the service area. The years had trained him to check out such places as storerooms, service elevators, staffrooms, kitchen and back exits. Lulu's Pancake Parlor had a very convenient arrangement. A fire door at the foot of the staircase took him into a passageway. At the end was a room he could tell was the kitchen by the noise coming from it. But directly past the fire door was a narrow twisting staircase.

It led Meehan down to the basement. The dim light from a single low-watt bulb didn't bother him, he was like a cat. At the bottom a locked door held him up for no more than a minute. When the lock was forced he slipped inside, closing the door quietly behind him. He was in a storeroom directly under the kitchen. Lined along the walls were massive industrial freezing chests. He looked and found they contained tubs of ice cream. There was a dumbwaiter for hauling them up. Meehan presumed the staff must come down and load supplies on to it. He went back upstairs to the table.

Rosie, camouflaged in a large brown suede jacket, the suede like the inside of something live, was pouring maple syrup over three flavors of ice cream melting on to her waffle and worrying that her hair was kinky. It always went that way if she didn't have time to blow-dry it. She just hated her hair then.

"Take your time with that," Meehan warned her, sampling his hot fudge sundae. "It's only coffee after we're through eating."

By midnight the tables were starting to thin out, the staff beginning to clear up. Lulu's closed at one. Meehan ordered coffee and insisted on holding Rosie's hand, leaning over the table talking to her. The man known to him as Paulie was sharp as a knife, but he wouldn't be on the lookout for a couple of lovers interested only in themselves.

Meehan was stirring two spoons of sugar into his coffee when Paulie got up from his table. Meehan kept him in his peripheral vision and went on talking. It looked like Paulie wasn't going to make a visit downstairs, which was a shame because most of the staff had already gone home and there were few people about now.

Paulie was getting into his coat, buttoning it up, taking his time. The man was methodical. Meehan watched him arrange his scarf carefully, tucking the ends inside his coat. He looked at his watch. "Go on down for a piss, you bastard," Meehan muttered. Rosie made no answer, and slowly Meehan smiled—he had it all planned perfectly. Paulie was heading downstairs.

Meehan gave him half a minute then he followed. On the way he pulled on a pair of black kidskin gloves. He knew the instant he started down the stairs that Paulie hadn't gone to the men's room. There was extra light and it could only come from the phone booth; Paulie was underneath him now, putting through a call. Any creak on the stairs would give Meehan away.

He went down humming a tune, his tread that of a man whose purpose is to get to the john and then be off with his girl. Paulie's back was to Meehan, he turned, a brief look, apparently satisfied, he turned again to the phone and began dialing.

Meehan gave the men's door a kick. When it banged shut he was three feet behind Paulie and closing in rapidly. It all had to do with the element of surprise. One quick snap back of the head and Paulie was a dead man.

The sound of footsteps above froze him; he stepped back silently into the shadows of the staircase. Whoever was coming was coming down fast. A man's footsteps. Meehan tensed. Paulie was redialing. He only needed to look around and he'd see Meehan right behind him.

The footsteps came to the bottom, began crossing the hall to the men's, the noise and lack of hesitation serving to reassure Paulie. He didn't bother to look this time. The long hours of waiting had made him careless. He was yawning, leaning on his elbow, waiting for the person he was calling to pick up the phone. In disregarding the possibility that he himself was under surveillance, he was making the biggest mistake of his life.

Meehan watched the man go into the men's. He got his balance; he had two, three minutes at the outside. Didn't want a struggle going on when the guy came back out of the john. Everything had to look normal, and what could be more normal than two friends talking by the phone, one partly obscured by the other.

The men's door banging shut signaled the moment to move.

He stiffened his body as he spun into a lunge. In that instant some extra sense made Paulie turn—and turn faster than a whip, snake-like, face contorted. He held a knife, a thin stiletto.

Meehan was already on him, clamping his hand on the wrist, immobilizing the weapon, fingers going straight for the man's throat, digging in around the windpipe, tightening, crushing. The shock of the assault, the sheer brutal choking, rendered Paulie unconscious. He slumped back.

Meehan released his grip, yanked him upright on the chair and grabbed the receiver; it was still ringing. He was laughing into the mouthpiece as the men's door opened. Meehan kept up a conversation and waited for the footsteps to fade on upstairs. Just as he was thrusting it back the phone was picked up at the other end and a male voice answered. Meehan dropped the receiver back on the hook.

He had to hurry. He went to the fire door and opened it. The passage was clear. He went back and grabbed Paulie and started dragging him across to the stairs leading to the storeroom. With each second he expected someone to come down. He was breathing heavily when the fire door swung to. To save the noise of Paulie's feet bumping down each step he gave him a fireman's lift to the bottom.

This was a job for which he had to leave the place tidy, which meant he wasn't to leave the body around where people were going to trip over it.

The freezers were a handy place. Nice and deep. Meehan worked swiftly. He emptied one chest of ice cream containers and dumped Paulie inside. Was he still alive, or just unconscious? Meehan was taking no chances of having Paulie regain consciousness and crawl out of the freezer on him. Using Paulie's knife, Meehan drew the blade across the throat, bisecting windpipe, blood vessels and nerves in one precision cut.

For convenience, the body needed to be packed with something so the ice cream containers would sit nice and straight. Meehan remembered that one freezer was full of ice-cubes done up in party-size bags. He got several, ripped the plastic open and tipped out the cubes. They rained merrily down on Paulie.

Meehan began stacking the plastic containers. He managed to get them back in three deep, the rest he distributed in the other freezers. Then he closed the lid.

When Meehan got back upstairs Rosie was finishing off a banana split. There were two girls totaling up at the cash register and having an argument, and one or two people still at the tables. He nodded to Rosie and she stood up. He took her arm as they walked out.

She must have fallen into a heavy sleep lying fully clothed on top of the bed because when the phone woke her India felt dazed, not knowing what had happened or where she was. Then, remembering, she snatched it up. "Michael," she whispered, when she heard his voice.

"You've nothing to worry about. It's all been taken care of."

"How do you mean?" She was still groggy, couldn't fit things together properly. "Michael, My God, what is happening . . .?"

"I said, you're not to worry. Are you all right?"

"Yes, but I feel groggy, what—"

"Why didn't you tell me?"

India was only just capable of understanding the question. He means the abortion. She had to let him think she'd gone through with it. He must never know he has a child.

"I couldn't tell you," India told him quietly. "You had already decided what you wanted."

"I would have left the Church for you."

The vision came in a flash. She saw him at the basin washing his hands, turning from the physical act of sex in revulsion, in fear, almost. The pagan fear of woman that lay within the very roots of holy doctrine. Washing her from him, her very smell, as if she were tainted. Denying her. As if he could wash the guilt from his hands. Ashamed all along, but unable to look at her without feeling desire—and afterwards, a discreet hatred for her for exposing such weakness in him. This man was not going to take her and love her wholly and completely, nor was he going to be the haven she was seeking—had to have—so her baby could be born in safety.

"Leave the Church," India repeated, numbly. "You would hate me for it." She must have been crying because tears were running into her mouth, dripping from her chin.

"That's a terrible thing to say," she heard him say, and such was the desolation in his voice that India knew all she had been thinking was the truth and that he himself recognized it.

And yet she had loved him, loved him so much, and she was grateful. By some mysterious signal which did not correspond with his own struggle, he had been able to free her from her own abject horror of the sexual act and set her sailing forward without fear. Because of him, she was able to go on and know the joy of living and loving in a normal sexual relationship.

"India, are you listening? Don't ask questions now. Keep to your arrangements, do everything as usual. Forget you ever saw Paulie in New York. Remember, say nothing and come and see me at the Center when you get back. God be with you."

India put down the phone and put her face into her hands and sobbed, choking and coughing like a lost child, for now she was entirely alone and the weight of that state was, at that moment, more than she could bear.

Keeping to the arrangements as they stood was patently out of the question now. She could not go back to Washington. She was pregnant—she was carrying Michael's child. As she thought about that, the full realization of her decision taken earlier in the day burst upon her.

Jack was so immersed in the paranoia of the Sicilian macho ethic, India knew he would never let her go. A divorce would flout Holy Mother Church's laws and deepest feelings, but in any case, Jack would not allow it. She knew that, just as certainly as she knew he would never play father to a child his wife had conceived by another man.

There were clinics owned and run by the Mafia. She would be sent to one of them for an abortion, and returned, suitably lobotomized by anti-depressant drugs. It was how the Mob brought their wives to heel.

If she and her baby were to survive, she had to be the first to act. She must leave Jack and she must do it now.

Did she know what had happened to Paulie? Did she care? Driving out to the airport the next morning, India's only feeling was relief. She thought it might not be the wisest time to choose to leave Jack, but without Paulie in the background it was certainly the easiest, and no one was going to suspect her of anything to do with his disappearance.

She was going home, to London. But first she must go to Washington; she had to pick up her passport. India thanked God for the diamond and emerald necklace. The value was so immense that the startled manager in the pawn shop had made a generous loan—enough to pay the hospital bill, enough for the immediate purchase of the airline ticket. One seat was left on the plane, in the first-class section. It was fate. She would be on the British Airways flight leaving Dulles International Airport at 8:15 that evening, nonstop to Heathrow, arriving 8:30 in the morning, London time.

Her mind ticked over the details. The flight from LaGuardia Airport would bring her into Washington by early afternoon—Wilma's day off. In an empty house she could pack and leave again without anyone being aware of her movements.

Suppose Jack was home, then what!

No, thank God. Tonight he was speaking at some business function. Afterwards, India knew, he'd spend the rest of the evening with his mistress.

All the better.

Yet she felt a choked-down rage thinking of Jack with his mistress; it was an absurd thing to care about now—now, when she was planning to leave him for good.

India knew the instant she opened the front door that Jack wasn't home. There was no coat flung down on the chair, no scarf, no gloves on the hall table, and no sign of the cats. The house lay silent before her, only the dim night-light on, as was usual, at the bottom of the stairs.

India let her traveling bag drop to the floor, drew her hand to her chest, breathed deeply, and thanked God he hadn't come in yet.

Her hand had shaken so much putting the key in the lock—but it was all right. Although she'd missed her first flight because of traffic to the airport, she had managed to get on the next, and there was time enough for what she had to do. Five-thirty now, the taxi coming back for her at six. Tomorrow morning she would be in London. Tomorrow all this would be just a hideous memory.

India opened the door of the small cloakroom and hastily took down her camel wool coat—couldn't go without that! She dropped the coat over her bag and went to the stairs. Was there time to let the cats out? Suddenly she wanted to see them. It was sentimental but she wanted to say goodbye. She half turned to go to the kitchen; it was then she saw the study door ajar. India froze.

Had that door been open a crack when she came in? Yes, of course it had. She'd been nervous and upset and hadn't noticed.

She turned and fled up the stairs, the cats forgotten. She just had to get her things and get out. If Jack were to come in and catch her . . .

"India?"

India stopped, she could see an image of herself in the mirror on the landing, open mouth drained white, eyes bulging, incredulous.

She spun round. Jack stood big and triumphant in the doorway of the study. India stared at him and frantically wondered what she was to do now. She should have known he would ring through to Dr. Pautasso, then come home and wait for her. Wait in the darkness of his study. He knew everything, she thought, despairing. He *knew*.

"Jack?"

"Home so soon?"

"Jack, I—"

"Why don't you come down and tell me about it over a drink." She saw then that he held a glass in his hand. How long had he been sitting alone, drinking, waiting for her to come in? She mustn't let him see that she was alarmed in any way.

India walked back down the stairs. Her head was up, but the feeling was the same as drowning—caught in a dangerous rip tide, being slowly dragged down by the undertow. She had to keep her head, there was no escape for her if she panicked now. Paulie! Jack being here wasn't just to do with her coming back—it had to do with Paulie's disappearance. But he couldn't very well ask her, not after promising her she would be free of him in New York.

"The cats are still shut in the kitchen—I didn't think anyone was in," she said.

"The cats . . ." He said the words mockingly, as if she had said something of particular significance. He walked with her through to the living room. India, mesmerized, allowed him to help her off with her coat.

"Sit down, you must be tired." He was staring at her so intently India thought the folly of what she was doing must surely be visible. To her profound relief he turned suddenly and went over to where the drinks were set up on the sideboard. He picked up the decanter and poured her a scotch. "You didn't keep your appointment."

India remained standing. When she took the drink from the silver salver he gave a supercilious little bow. It made her angry.

"I take it you've talked with Dr. Pautasso?"

"We talked. I made a call to him this afternoon."

"Then he would have told you I phoned in to cancel the appointment because I wasn't feeling well."

"I called the hotel," Jack continued dismissively. "They told me you had checked out." He raised his eyes from the glass and looked at her.

"Yes," India shrugged, but she couldn't turn away, she had to return his stare—had to, though it felt as if her eyes were scorching.

"Why?"

"I decided to come back."

"Why?"

"Because I'd had enough of his questions, because—"

"Frightened maybe of getting involved, of having to look at yourself, frightened of what you might see?"

India winced. She lifted her glass and poured half a shot of scotch down her throat. "No," she said. "Not me. You!"

"Me? What about me? C'mon now, tell me about me, honey." And he stood before her with that grin on his face and she wanted to wipe it off. She felt so humiliated a virulent anger took possession of her.

"Yes, all right, I didn't like it, I hated it. I felt turned inside out—on display. But you, you are the one who's frightened of getting involved," she said, so low it was a whisper. "Of having a family—afraid of the intimacy involved in being a family—the kind of intimacy that makes a marriage."

He was laughing openly now. Let him, she thought, let him, she hadn't finished yet.

"Yes, I had a big problem. I was terrified of having sex. But that fear hadn't anything to do with being intimate with a man. It was purely and simply a fear—no, worse than that, it was terror. I was terrified. I saw a man's erect penis as something dangerous, something that would hurt too much. But you . . . You weren't really that interested, were you? You got what you wanted, a wife with a good pedigree. And all along you had a mistress . . ."

She'd hit home, a solid blow; the smile was off his face. He had stopped laughing, his face had changed. Reckless, fired-up, India pushed on.

"A mistress you could have uninvolved sex with. Who wouldn't make demands on you, demands you weren't able to meet. Go on, admit it, admit that."

His eyes were ugly, his mouth twisted into a scar; India's knees were turning to water.

And then the phone rang. The car service she had ordered to take her to the airport had arrived. The dispatcher was calling to let her know he was outside. All color drained from her face. She started forward. He was quicker, he took her by the arms and pressed her down into a chair.

"No, my dear. Let me handle this."

India sat staring after him. She felt as if she'd been injected with scopolamine and had woken up in the middle of an operation; she could feel everything that was happening to her, but she couldn't do anything about it.

She had to. She couldn't give in. The consequences of inaction now would not bear thinking about.

India got up and crossed rapidly to the door; she could hear Jack at the front door. The taxi company knew her destination; like a fool she had given it. A minute and Jack would have all the details.

If she could reach her room, get her passport . . . Without looking behind she ran across the hall and up the stairs. She'd leave via the fire escape. Was it possible? *Was* it?

She got to her room and closed the door, locking it, Jack's words coming in a flash: "Don't lock the door against me, not ever."

She went straight to the bureau, dragged open the drawer. Feverishly she went through her things, then at the very bottom she found the familiar passport—sweet heaven, how dear it was—stuffed it into the narrow leather shoulder bag hanging at her side. The strap crossed her body, the bag itself slim enough to wear under her coat; it contained too many vital things (money, credit cards, her airline ticket) to risk having it snatched walking the city streets. India remembered then that both her winter coats were downstairs.

It was freezing outside. India snatched a large square scarf from a drawer, her fur-lined gloves, put them on the bed and dashed to the closet. She pulled out a heavy leather aviator's jacket.

She heard the door crash open and let the jacket drop to the floor.

His eyes were black, narrowed, they went from the jacket on the floor to her. "How were you planning to leave? Oh, down the fire escape." He made a sound that could have been a laugh. It made her blood run cold. He was bitter now; the jeering thrusts had stopped. She stared at him, helpless and despairing.

"So . . . we're deserting the ship."

"I'm leaving if that's what you mean—now." To lend some credence to her words she bent down to pick up the jacket. In some inviolable part of her mind she knew that she must stand up to him, go downstairs and leave. He couldn't stop her. She had to believe that.

"There's something going on here," he said, and his eyes had a frightening glitter. "Tell me about Paulie."

India's hand shook so much that she had to do something with them; she began pulling on her gloves. "What about Paulie?"

"He seems to be missing—disappeared without a trace."

"Have you checked the city dog pound?"

Jack made it to where she was standing in two strides. "You know something. What is it?"

"How should I know anything about Paulie? I've only just arrived back from New York. I thought you were keeping him in Washington." Her gloves were on, she stroked the fingers, fighting to stay calm; time was ticking by, she was almost mad with desperation. "I don't know where you've mislaid Paulie—I didn't even know he was lost. Perhaps he'll come home by himself, wagging his tail."

She was goading him now, pushing him with a suicidal drive, but she couldn't stop. Not now. Not when, suddenly, she was washing about in her own anger. India, hands clenched in the thick gloves, wild-eyed, no longer afraid of Jack, said, "I don't care what has happened to that homicidal maniac—whether he's been blown to ribbons in one of your gang wars or whatever, it's of no interest to me."

Jack grabbed her by the shoulders. "That's it, isn't it? You've never been able to stomach who my father is. Well, I'll tell you something, sugar-lump, if it wasn't for him on the Commission fighting against narcotics and unnecessary violence, the drug syndicates would be in charge by now and law enforcement all the way up to the President wouldn't have a hope in hell of stopping them."

"What Commission? What are you talking about?"

"I'm talking national committee of Mafia godfathers based in New York, and if you don't believe they make the policy big business in this country runs on, then you're living in fantasyland." He was swaying towards her, a tough hard-voiced man.

"You've lived with it so long and don't even know," she said, almost weeping with pain and fury. "And they'll come for you as well. One day a hit man will walk into a restaurant in a mask with a MAC-10 machine pistol and leave your face down in your minestrone—"

Jack had her in his grip, shaking her. "Who told you about a MAC-10? Where did you hear about that?"

Her teeth were chattering, her eyes focusing and unfocusing on his face—she didn't know where she'd heard the MAC-10 machine pistol mentioned, couldn't remember—the name had come from nowhere . . .

"C'mon, it's about time you began remembering a few things, let's have it, come on."

His breath was hot on her, his flushed face inches from her own—his face—even in extreme anger it hadn't lost the superciliousness, the snotty head-boy reproving look, the smugness. Smug, smug, smug . . .

India clenched her fist in its glove and let fly with a right. "Smug, smug." Then her left fist, striking as hard as she could. "Smug," she panted, her blows glancing off his chin, uncaring of the pain in her knuckles, hair sticking to her face; gasping and panting she struck at his chest, shoulders, arms.

It wasn't doing any good, his body so hard, her own hands ringing with pain.

He was laughing, laughing at her. Maddened, she flailed at him with her arms, kicking, hair now in her eyes, crying, feverish. He caught her, lightly, but she could feel the violence in him; violence pitiless as the lash from the brass-buckled belt used by the convent nuns as an instrument of mortification and penance.

She wrenched from his grasp, staggered back, crashing into a table, hands scrabbling for the blue-and-white vase and flinging it with all her might—missing—the mirror behind him shattering.

"Seven years' bad luck," Jack snarled, startled with disbelief—his exquisite Chinese porcelain—furious with her, lunging at her.

She followed up with a heart dish from the 400-year-old pottery of Henriot Quimper, hair pins and odd pieces of jewelry showered onto the bed.

He was bleeding, a thin trickle of blood. She'd actually managed to hit him and cut his cheek. She wavered, breathless, as with astonishment he put up his hand and touched the sticky wetness. Suddenly India was sorry, she felt an extraordinary impulse to take his face in her hands and clean it with a soft damp cloth. But then his eyes were full on her, blazing, incredulous.

"Bitch," he said softly and there was something in his face she didn't recognize, a look—she began backing away, hair falling over one side of her face, the buttons ripped from her blouse and the material gaping—and even then, even then embarrassed, tugging, trying to hold the edges together.

If she could reach the street. She must try. She must—

India turned, half-tripped over an Aubusson, and he was beside her, swinging her up in his arms, his hands hurting her. She beat at him, used her nails. Biting, scratching. And then they were both sprawling on the bed.

They were rolling, Jack grabbing for her wrists. "Bite, would you . . . I'll teach . . . hey, Jesus," as they both slid off the silk coverlet, landing with a head-thudding crash on the other side of the bed.

Dazed, exhausted by the struggle, India felt a sensation of distance

and heard Jack saying, "You are my lady," before he kissed her fully
and hard on the mouth.

She was almost in a state of feverish prostration and didn't attempt to turn her head, didn't move, eyes fixed on the ceiling, half-
perplexed, dizzy with conflicting emotions—and all the time he was
caressing her with a calm skill, his mouth nuzzling, kissing her
again and again . . .

But she wouldn't let him, she wouldn't.

First came the involuntary and broken sobs. Then the feeling that
her strength was running from her, all her resolve, her pride, running
out of her.

Then she felt his hands tugging down her trousers, his fingers
slipping in between her legs and the crotch of her panties, caressing,
seeking, rubbing with his fingers until she couldn't bear the hot
quivering sensation. Kissing her with a hunger, an intensity, a com-
pleteness that obliterated reason from her mind. She had the feeling
that an abscess had burst inside her, unleashing all the anger, all of
the hurt, the kisses washing it all away.

She realized now that he was part naked, she could feel his penis
sharp between her legs and she was tensing against him, wanting to
cry out but only able to gasp. With each gasp he was filling her up
with his life, hot, coursing, advancing until every muscle in her
body was shamelessly yielding—yielding and moving and she had
her arms and legs wrapped around him, her mind free-falling in
space, vision gone, beginning to undulate along her whole length,
her tongue enclosed by his mouth, not able to breathe wholly without him, one person, one flesh. Being brought with each vibrating
beat, mercilessly, pitilessly, to orgasm, crazy and wildly crying out,
sobbing his name . . . Jack . . . Jack . . . oh Jack.

Nineteen

Jack made love with unbridled satisfaction. India had an excitement about her, an artless virginal sensuality, that caused his mouth to go dry and his heart to hammer and the need to move his stiff penis into her, deep into her, so terrible. Couldn't get over the sweet shock of every curve of her soft voluptuous breasts. He kept telling her wild, improbable, preposterous things.

Livia was passionate—he'd give her that. But making love to her was like being pulled alive into a burning wreckage. Okay until the fire went out. With India he felt he could never completely exist without her, he wanted to spend that night and every night, cradled at the mouth of her womb.

The whole of that night, in fact, they did spend together and everything else for India was relegated to a second place. No matter that the plane with its one empty seat was gone and half-way to London by now, India was oblivious. Jack took her body and mind and even as she struggled against him there was no escaping the process. His lovemaking was like nothing she had experienced with Michael; it was pleasure and violence that made her weep, it was excitement and surrender, it was totally unexpected.

He slept, she didn't. He never let her go. He gripped her tightly, his arms curled around her, one beneath her neck. He had fallen asleep kissing her, his mouth against her hair, his chest rising and falling with her heartbeat. Not until dawn, and then India slept.

*   *   *

She opened her eyes and saw her clothes and Jack's, strewn across the floor. Remembered the night and a soft, lovely feeling spread from her belly right up to her throat. She turned over and found herself alone in the bed. But what was so sudden and unexpected was the wild, disturbing sense of loss.

And then she saw the note.

Dear India,

You're dead to the world and I thought I'd leave you to sleep. So far you're not missing out on anything—it's sleeting outside and 10 below. Listen, I have to be away on business for the next few days. God bless and take care of yourself.

Love, Jack.

After the night they had spent? This was all?

From that violent confrontation to this lightly worded note, no explanation, just the quiet assurance of the "love, Jack" at the bottom? How could he? Was he really the kind of man who could love a woman and give himself totally to her in the night, then in the morning keep his distance and walk away? Leave her while she was still locked in sleep imagining herself in his protective arms, part of him?

Was he?

Hadn't he clutched her and called her by name, kissed and stroked and tongued her, in her ears, between her legs, kneeling over her—she had been his so completely.

Was it that way with that other woman? Was it? And if she couldn't bear the thought of him touching another woman, did that mean she was in love with him? Despite everything? What he was, his family, his mistress?

She had to think.

Because if she accepted Jack now—she accepted his family.

And the baby—what about the baby? India stared and stared at the note in her hands and swung between exhilaration and perplexity and outright terror. Even to contemplate telling him . . . And if he couldn't accept the baby then nothing had changed, not really. And if nothing had changed this was her last chance.

She had the opportunity. With Jack out of the house she could phone British Airways and rebook her first-class ticket—she could get away.

Phone now! Go downstairs and use the telephone in Jack's study so Wilma couldn't listen in.

India got dressed and went down but not to the study. To the kitchen to tell Wilma she was going out to the beach house to stay the night.

Here, utterly alone, she could think. India stood for a while at the kitchen window staring out at the deserted bay. The water and sky were a uniform gray. No sun, just the leaden clouds and the raw desolation of the windswept sandy shore. The neighboring summer houses were closed up for the winter, and their shuttered windows gave her an uneasy feeling.

There was no particular moment when she began consciously to think of Paulie—perhaps when she was putting the tea in the pot, standing then and looking out at the ominous sky—when she realized his absence was bothering her. But why now? Why was it so urgent?

Suddenly she understood she was not thinking of him at all, but of his dying, of Paulie dead.

She stood there with her hand tightly clenched on the teapot handle, water off the boil, tea leaves sitting in the cold pot, staring out into the gray. *What had she done?*

When India called Father Michael Fitzgerald the palms of her hands were so wet she had to continually rub them on her slacks.

When she heard his voice, just for an instant—a nightmare vision—

"Michael . . . I was hoping I'd catch you in the office."

"India, where are you? I called the hotel and they said you had checked out."

"I'm at the Bay House, Michael . . ."

"Are you in trouble?"

"No—no. I was ringing to thank you for helping the other night. I must have sounded hysterical."

"Think nothing of it. What are friends for?"

"That's just it, I can't help thinking—Michael, please tell me, what happened to Paulie?"

"Nothing's happened to him," the priest assured her. "He's okay. I had a friend go and persuade him to take a holiday."

*   *   *

Michael wouldn't lie to her, India was thinking, and perhaps it wasn't a good idea to come to this isolated house alone, she had frightened herself with her thoughts.

"Why are you at the Bay? Where's Jack?"

India felt easier now. She explained that Jack was away on business and why she had come out to the house. "I was leaving him, I had the ticket back to London. But then . . ." She stopped, aware that Michael wouldn't want to hear about that, and unconsciously acknowledging the embarrassment that was just beneath the surface of her relationship with the priest.

"But then . . . what?" Michael asked slowly.

She felt awkward. "Something happened between us that has changed everything." She was on the defensive now; the need to explain, justify, to him, to herself. Because she fluctuated hourly between anguish and exhilaration; she felt she was either blessed or she was losing her mind.

"In what way changed?"

"How we feel about each other. I know it sounds strange, but sometimes we love and it's so deep and terrible we deny it. We won't see that what we are feeling is love, we do other things and all the time it's there, helpless, and then something happens, some chemistry ignites it. Then"—she said it softly as if she spoke only to herself—"it's as if the tide is carrying me along and there's no stopping it and no knowing if I will drown and not really even caring."

"Jack won't change," the priest said brutally.

"I . . ." she sprang at once to his defense. "Jack is not his father—I should have seen that. He is just a normal man trying to live a normal life, and lonely, too. It's taken me a long time to know that."

Michael said something. India didn't catch it, his voice was so harsh, little more than a croak. She paused. He said it again.

"You don't understand." Then he was speaking urgently. "Don't fool yourself. Jack and his family are not two separate entities, they are one and the same: the Mafia. Live with one and you live with the other and there will never, ever be an acceptable way of whitewashing the fact. You can pretend it has nothing to do with you, or try and deny its existence, but it won't work. Get out while you have a chance. Stay where you are tonight, and tomorrow go straight to the airport. Do you have any money?"

India was listening in exasperated confusion, remembering the time when she needed him to tell her that. Instead he had prompted her to stay. To help save Jack's soul. It had been the last thing she wanted to do—then. It had seemed nonsensical, even. But she had stayed and now, somehow, she was realizing that she had never really stopped loving him. And regardless of what he was, or who his father was, Jack had a right to know that.

He had to know about the baby. If they couldn't work something out, then she would leave. But she would go with his full knowledge and support. India no longer believed, as she once had, that Jack would harm her. The belief had that quiet unshakable assurance that comes from erotic passion. She listened to Michael, but knew that the ultimate decision had to be based on her own judgment.

"I love him," she explained in despair, because she did, hopelessly. "Tomorrow I'm going home to wait for him, and I'm going to tell him so."

Michael Fitzgerald unlocked the drawer beneath his bedside table and withdrew a cloth bundle which he unwrapped on the bed. He took from it a Beretta automatic, a silencer and a fifty-round carton of ammunition.

He'd been interested in guns for many years, ever since he'd inherited his brother's sawed-off single-barrel shotgun. His brother Patrick was carried into the farmhouse one night in pain, with blood pouring down his face and chest and dripping in bright splashes onto his aunt's clean floors. His brother was in the IRA and had died in young Michael's arms, but not before extracting a promise from the boy to join the Cause.

"But why?" Michael asked, when the sod was turned back onto the coffin in the ground. He was a child. It didn't make sense. He wanted everything to go on in his aunt's house the way it had before. He didn't want to avenge the wrongdoers who had killed his parents and now his brother.

There were his aunt and uncle. But they were busy. The farm was poor, barely able to yield them a living, and it was isolated. Out in the fields his uncle worked alone. He didn't seem to want the company of the thin, delicate-looking boy who coughed incessantly and had to be put to bed with hot flannel and a mustard rub.

Michael desperately missed his mother and his home and their beds with proper bedclothes. He hated the flannel which itched against his skin, the lumpy, spiky mattress made from feathers plucked from his aunt's geese. He made up games and he fantasized a twin brother with whom he talked and conspired. In many ways his imaginary twin was stronger, insisting Michael do terrible things that would get him punished. Terrible things. But always justifiable. Later, with remarkable precociousness and malice, his twin told Michael he was the Angel of Death and said Michael had to punish the boy on the next farm—with whom Michael actually wanted to be friends—and Michael had rebelled. Said, "NO!"

But the twin pinched him, stabbed him, refused to let him eat, killed his kitten—he was unstoppable—until Michael agreed.

His aunt became worried. She saw to it her young nephew had lessons on the piano and that he spent less time alone. Michael indulged her because he found that his make-believe twin, of whom he was scared, didn't dare to come out in the open when she was around. It pleased Michael that the Angel of Death had to sit help-lessly in the background while he, Michael, played his pieces on the piano: But then the music took over and it too protected him and gradually the imaginary twin stopped hanging around. He simply faded out of Michael's mind.

"You promised your dying brother, and as long as Ireland is divided you're needed. This is war. You'll be a soldier. A soldier's not guilty who shoots someone on the other side. It's your chance to strike back at the British and their Northern Irish allies who keep the border there."

So "Nailer" Meehan had told Michael. It was Nailer Meehan who carried Michael's brother that night into the farmhouse. Nailer who gave Michael the *Green Book*, the IRA manual, to read and told him things the boy wouldn't understand until much later.

"And in the end, you do what you want to do. Isn't that right?"

Suddenly the voice of his imaginary twin was back. Not in any recognizable shape but stronger than ever and this time soft-spoken, well-mannered. "The only thing that can save Ireland now is fight-ing back," the voice told him persuasively. "It's gone too far. Forget civil rights, forget the law courts, join the guerrilla organization. If you have to fracture a few skulls to win the war, you've got to do it."

An honest, true man speaking to him, but, as Michael was to find out, he did have a terrible temper: "Get the scum and kill them. Fuck all that law-and-order shit, I say just kill the bastards."

Even the terrible time when he had killed his first man. "I just fired. He was there in front of me and I just fired at him. I saw his face, he was crying, and I killed him," young Michael told the priest in confession and he prayed every day for the man. The voice in his head said: "The man didn't deserve to live. He was British scum."

After basic training in guerrilla warfare, he was sent to London to join a cell of three IRA members whose orders were to start a bombing campaign. They were betrayed.

Walking home one night, Michael saw the police car when he turned the corner of his street. He knew.

He was the only one to escape. One of his mates was killed, the other two were caught and sent to prison. They never revealed Michael's name.

Michael had a room in Dockland Street off the Albert Road in case of an emergency. He walked there and waited for the *Dublin Queen* to come in, a cargo ship whose captain was friendly, to work his passage to America.

He wasn't the kind of man to get into a needless fight. But he was lured irresistibly by the voice urging him on to attack some troublemakers in a New York bar who called him "another dirty fuckin' Mick." His first night in New York he was nearly beaten to death. He arrived in a haze of pain, seeing double, at the Boston home of his uncle, the Monsignor Canon Fitzgerald.

The Monsignor took Michael in and looked after him. "The world needs trained, educated men," he told Michael, "not just another pair of hands." Eventually Michael went into the seminary, then became a Catholic priest.

Michael was to learn, but he never forgot. At heart he was a fanatic.

Nailer Meehan came one day when Michael was a priest at the Chevy Chase Catholic Church in Washington, D.C. Meehan came to remind Michael again of his promise to his dead brother Patrick. It was Meehan who brought the information about the Mob money being kept in the holding bank at Luigi Frediano's salon; Meehan who introduced Michael into the active network of cell members. The Provisional IRA in Ireland needed new weapons for its armory, so the raid was planned and executed.

India, as the wife of Jack Donovan, was a potential source of information. The priest saw that she was strangely vulnerable and in Jack's power.

The knife was double-edged.

Michael needed to keep her living with her husband where she was privy to information that could be useful to them. But not in Jack's bed. Intimacy and sexual closeness lead a woman to confide, and if that happened . . .

The thought haunted him. He was so close to achieving his aim. He planned, through supplying new weapons, to make the IRA into a world force more powerful than the Mafia. To that purpose he had set up the IRA cell which operated out of the Church of Our Lady Day Care Center.

It was not in Michael's plan to fall in love with her. But India awakened in him something soft, something he had long forgotten. He could not help himself.

In his room at the presbytery he took the gun from its cloth wrapping and held it in his hands. India was in love with her husband. He saw the danger to himself. His safety and that of the others depended on her being alienated from Jack. She could name names, identify people she had seen at the Center. She had become a threat to the cell and the whole IRA operation, as the man Paulie had been.

"No one must stop my work. Not even her."

The body he inhabited was empty, soulless, nothing more than an anteroom to death. India for a time had lit a flame. Now that too was extinguished. He had the terrible feeling that he was losing contact with reality. Sometimes it seemed to him that his thoughts were completely disconnected from his actions. More and more he was a disinterested spectator relying on his voices, and they told him— coldly and deliberately—to kill her.

Twenty

What else hadn't she understood?

India was sitting in front of her bedroom mirror staring at herself, eyes shadowy, as if she didn't see her own reflection there, but something else . . .

Abruptly she began brushing, quick strong strokes, her mind beginning to worry at the thing that was there in her memory, but wasn't there. Instinct told her it was the key. Each time she drove the silver-mounted brush through her hair, her hair crackled with electricity and sprang across the side of her face.

Three men. Michael had been in the office with Luigi. The two others in stocking masks were holding the salon at gunpoint. One had raped her. The other came into the room while he was doing it and killed him.

The way Michael had said. That stayed with her.

She didn't doubt that was the way it had happened, and yet . . .

And yet that fragment of memory, compelling, tremulous with meaning, telling her—telling her what? Still she couldn't see.

She shivered suddenly. She felt cold, and terribly alone. She switched the lamp on by the mirror and felt better; safer, anyway. What could harm her? She had the shutters tightly closed behind the curtains (because in the black cavernous night outside there was no

friendly pinpoint of light from a street light or neighboring house),
but sitting here in front of the mirror she knew something was
wrong.

India put down the brush. It was there in her memory, there . . .
Then she heard a sound that made her swing around and stare
through the open door. It had nothing to do with the wind whipping
the frozen branches against the wall of the house, nor was it the
tapping knock of the antiquated heating system. It seemed to have
come from the back of the house, where the kitchen window was,
which was right below her.

She sat listening, scared to move. Then little by little she began to
relax—no one could get in. All the windows had interior shutters.
They looked pretty, looked like wood, but they were steel. Jack's
security device. She remembered him saying it would take an anti-
tank grenade to get past them.

As she was taking comfort from this thought something hit the
side of the house where she was sitting, a jolt like a gigantic belch.
Her immediate thought was that she was being blown apart, and
that each breath would be her last. But after the first stunned moment of silence she found herself still alive and whole. When she got
her scrambled thoughts together logic told her the house wasn't
being blown up, it was being broken into. She stumbled to her feet
and ran to the phone.

"Police . . . Fire Department . . ." Her teeth were chattering, shock
beginning to set in. What number? Phone book. No—operator. Seconds ticking by. No dial tone. Jiggling the cradle. Then realizing the
line had been cut and whoever had done that . . . sweat trickled
down under her arms.

Her only thought—get out!

There was a back door leading from the kitchen. But that was
where the noise had come from. There was only one other way out,
the front door and then to the car. Could she make it? Was there
time?

The keys! They were in the kitchen. She felt ill, her stomach
stabbed with pain. She ran silently to the landing, staring down into
the darkness, her heart pounding so hard she could hardly hear anything else. Who was it? Somebody who knew she was here alone?
She wished she had a gun. Jack's suggestion she arm herself had been
scorned: *she* wasn't going to turn paranoid like the rest of America.

Her eyes growing accustomed to the dark, she saw the kitchen door was still closed. She'd go down the stairs and slip out the front way, run along the beach to the first occupied house and call the police.

She was on the stairs, half-way down, her slippered feet silent. A dozen more steps, then the front door, then run.

From downstairs she heard the kitchen door; the self-shutting spring needed oiling and it squeaked badly, it was squeaking now. She stood, paralyzed, breath stifled in the back of her throat. It was too late. She couldn't escape.

As she turned to run back up she stumbled. A beam of light fell across her. Frantic, unable to look around, she half-crawled and half-ran, stumbling, almost falling on the last step. She heard footsteps coming up the stairs behind her.

She was at the door to her room, slamming it shut, her breath coming in short gasps. Desperately she hung on to the knob. It began to turn, beating her, stronger than she was.

She looked wildly around the room, the terror of being trapped. Seeing the lamp on her dressing table, the solid base, no clear idea, just a last desperate attempt to defend herself. Letting go the handle, rushing forward, arms stretching out.

In the mirror she saw the door opening, a dark menacing silhouette in a black knitted mask stood there. Then she screamed.

For a moment she thought she had gone mad, she covered her ears and shut out the sound of her own screams. She was so frightened she wanted to crawl away and die. Because dead she couldn't witness what she was about to see.

That morning at Freddy's—screaming. Pulled brutally to her feet and screaming, "No! No! No!" His teeth baring in the fleshcolored stocking and his hand whipping tight as steel cord across her mouth. Her eyes going past him, past him to the opening door. Seeing the man in the black mask come in. She couldn't understand what was happening, her mind was so shocked—so filled with pounding blood. Nothing registered but the hurt and the disgust—the beast on her, straining, grunting, his ghastly face bobbing and bobbing, his tongue lolling—and behind him, behind him. . . .

Then the act—the man in the black mask stepping toward his victim, reaching out, one lethal movement—the neck snapping back, snapping like a rotten branch cracking apart from the trunk.

That single harsh cord—then silence. That was when she had fainted.

He had lied to her. Michael was the one who had killed on that day. Now he was here.

Her skin, waxen, dilated eyes, hair falling in damp strands across her face, India didn't see her own reflection in the mirror, she was looking at the dark figure behind her, at the gun which he held in his black-gloved hands. It was pointed down and at the floor. She didn't know anything about guns . . . she stared at it. She didn't turn, didn't attempt to.

"It was you. You killed him."

He said, "I had to. Michael's a sentimentalist when it comes to killing people."

India felt her bowels slide inside her, her mouth was open and her lips were stiff and dry. She moved them.

"You *are* Michael."

"If I was, you would have opened the door. You would only open the door to someone you knew. Like a priest, for example. That is how the police will see it. I couldn't take that chance. Entry had to be forced."

She knew then that he had come to kill her.

"Who are you?"

"Me?" He was smiling behind the mask, pale blue eyes. "Ah, but you're talking now to a proud one—you're talking to the Angel of Death."

"You're insane," India whispered—her voice like wind in stretched wires as she began at last to realize that she was listening to the delusions of a psychopath.

"Now that's what I don't like about people. They're hypocritical. You help them out, then they get squeamish about it."

"You had Paulie killed," India said, and she knew it then and the understanding amounted to agony. Paulie had been her protection all along and hadn't she asked Michael to get rid of him? And didn't that mean, in the bald simplicity of the biblical term, she had killed?

"Paulie was just one rotten apple that had to be taken from the barrel." He spoke in the thin flat voice she hated—and knew so well. "God has given me special powers to do a job."

"What job?"

"You have to imagine that God has created me as an instrument of His will, and you might say with the same discretion when it comes to eliminating people who oppose Him.'

"Michael . . ." She looked at him with stark horror, pleaded with him in the mirror—fighting for control over the chaos of his broken mind, thinking perhaps she still had a chance. If she talked, kept talking, didn't move. "Listen to me, to me, Michael . . . Don't listen to him—"

"Michael is dead," he told her. "Now I am to deal with you. Jack must be the next."

A floorboard creaked—the sound when someone shifts his weight. They both heard it. The priest started to turn, arms extended, the gun . . . In the mirror India saw Jack behind him on the landing.

As she screamed, Jack produced an automatic. There was a dull crack as he fired. The noise was still echoing in her ears as the priest staggered backwards, crashing at her feet. India saw he had been hit in the throat. Blood was crawling through his polo shirt. His eyes stared straight at her. She stood rooted to the spot. There was a sensation of a long time passing before she actually recognized he was dead.

"Michael," she whispered hoarsely. There had been a bond between them, there was a connection; the man who lay at her feet bore no resemblance to the Michael she had loved.

"I had to kill him," Jack said from the doorway. "I wouldn't let you die, I love you."

The room stank of gunpowder. Jack pocketed his own gun and in the act of walking forward to pick up the gun that had fallen from the priest's hand, India dropped to her knees beside the body. What happened next was a blur. The priest's right hand was at his neck.

"Aaaaaaargh . . ." In a surging maniacal violence the priest rolled onto his feet, ripping the ski mask from his head, and lunged, fingers hooked, reaching Jack, catching him off-balance, clawing for Jack's throat—the primitive instinct of a killer.

It was all so quick—the shock. He would kill. Jack. Jack. She saw the gun lying on the floor. She threw herself on it, picked it up—her hands shaking so hard it wobbled in all directions.

Covered in the priest's blood Jack was fighting for his life. He was fighting a professional trained to kill, a maniac with the strength of a wounded, crazed bear.

If she fired the gun she might kill Jack. She ran forward, jumping back as the two men rolled over and over, smeared with blood, tearing at skin and hair, grappling for each other's throats.

India hesitated. Now! She gripped the gun with both hands and struck down. In the split second before impact they rolled, she missed the priest and hit Jack a blow on the temple, and not only that, she dropped the gun. One moment it was at her feet and the next it had been knocked under the chest of drawers in the struggle and Jack was going limp on the floor.

"No!" India screamed as Michael tightened his death-grip on Jack's neck. She ran for the lamp. She grabbed the base and pulled; the plug dragged from the socket, leaving only the reading light on by her bed.

She must take the heavy weight and—"Don't make a mistake this time," she prayed, face twisted—kill him . . . somehow. India raised the lamp and smashed the base down on the priest's head. It hit with a terrible klonk. She snatched her hands away as the shock traveled up her arms and the lamp fell to the floor. She stood back. She was beginning to shake convulsively.

He moved! He wasn't dead yet. She wanted to scream and the scream was stuffed in her throat, choking her. He was beginning to raise his head, turning to stare at her, his face white, black, black eyes—staring at her.

He began getting to his feet.

They were incapable of killing him—he was the devil incarnate and he couldn't die. He was coming towards her—she saw death in the chill face, saw it and felt it. India thought she must surely die too. She must have closed her eyes because then she heard a thud and when she opened them she saw that he was lying on the floor.

"Jesus, what happened?" Jack lurched to his feet. He advanced drunkenly, his hands going from the swelling on his head to his throat. He stared down at the body on the floor.

India's knees were buckling under her. Jack grabbed her and sat her down on the bed. She felt him, solid and real at her side.

"He was an IRA terrorist," Jack said quietly. His arm was around her shoulder. India remembered a lot of odd things in a rush and groaned. He turned her gently towards him and held her.

When she pulled away from him at length, she stared at the body. She kept hearing the obscenity of that dull, crushing, klonk.

Suddenly she got up, went and knelt down and closed the lids over his eyes, shutting them forever. He'd opened the door for her, taught her to open new ones. He was the father of the baby she carried within her.

Jack came with a blanket and covered him.

She was crying softly. Jack drew her back to the bed. India said, "He was a priest too . . . a priest and he feared damnation . . ." She told him then that, seeing him in the black mask, in that recognition, she had finally remembered what had taken place.

Jack pulled a handkerchief from his pocket and wiped her cheeks. "When we knew it was the IRA involved in the raid I had Paulie cover you." (Paulie! She would tell him, India thought, but not now, not now.) "We tapped the phone at the Center looking for someone else, then I realized who we had."

"I called him this afternoon, Father Fitzgerald," India said. She looked at him, shocked, tried to say something else and didn't quite manage it.

"I know."

"Everything? About the tickets, leaving you?"

"Everything. The bit about how you thought you might get to love me. I came to take you home."

They stared at each other. Later he would want to know about the part she had played in Paulie's disappearance, but later. India was the first to look away.

"Help me roll him in the rug," Jack said.

India helped him. She was thinking in a queer, detached sort of way that the rug was her father's wedding present to them and now there was blood all over it. How upset he would be if he knew—always so fussy about stains on the carpets.

"I heard breaking glass, then there was an explosion," she said, looking at the black shoes, shiny well-polished priest's shoes, protruding from her end of the roll.

"He wedged some explosive between the shutters and blew the catch. His car's parked at the end of the lane. I thought that was odd when I came past, so I pulled in further along and got out to go and take a look. That was when I heard the bang. The noise you were both making up here, you didn't hear me come in."

They struggled to get the cumbersome roll down the stairs.

"We'll take him through the kitchen. It'll be easier."

"What are you going to do with him?"

"Put him in the station wagon and drive back to Washington. We can't risk having his body found in this vicinity."

"I wish you'd just go to the police and explain. It was self-defense, Jack."

"Screw the police," Jack said. "They won't do anything but cause trouble."

"It scares me—just the thought of trying to hide a body," India said.

"We're not going to hide it. Tell me something. There's a garage underneath the Center and Father Fitzgerald used it to keep his car there, right? From there you can get into the storeroom and up the stairs to the main room and the office."

"Yes," India said.

"That's where we'll leave him. You've got the keys. We'll leave him sitting in his office with the money."

"The money?"

"The money that belongs to the Church—it's a long story and I'll tell you about it when we get all through with this."

"This scares me."

"It scares the hell out of me, too. Jesus, the kitchen's a mess—wait a minute." His voice became urgent, he told her to go back.

India staggered backwards into the hall, she let the end of the roll go and slumped against the wall. She had a pain in her back, her white skin was even whiter. "What's the matter now?"

"There's a car parked out on the main road under the trees. I saw it from the window."

"It's probably a courting couple, they often park there. Jack—what if they turn into the lane, they'll see Father Fitzgerald's car. They might remember seeing it. They might . . ."

"If they're lovers they won't notice anything. Darling, go upstairs and stay there until I say it's okay."

India was mesmerized by the roll on the floor—she couldn't take her eyes away from it. She swayed dizzily. Jack looked at her sharply.

"Go up and have a shower."

She nodded and turned to go. She seemed dazed.

Jack took the gun from his jacket pocket and turned out the kitchen light. Then he positioned himself by the window where he could watch the car.

He waited ten minutes. The car moved away. He waited another fifteen. Nothing. There was no one on the road, the car hadn't come back. Most probably it had been a couple necking—steaming the windows up.

Jack looked at the heavy carpet containing the body neatly rolled against the wall. Who would have thought . . . a priest! Maybe he'd better make some coffee. The way India looked there for a minute he had thought she was going to faint on him. But Jesus! Jack shook his head admiringly. India wasn't going to make just a great wife for a Don—she was going to make a terrific one.

The first thing he did was close the battered shutters. The catch was blown apart but otherwise they were in one piece. Father Fitzgerald knew, had known, what he was doing; a modicum more would have blown the kitchen to smithereens, a trace less wouldn't have done the job. To make the place more secure he dragged the heavy Welsh dresser in front of the window. Next he drew the bolts on the back door, unlocked it and went out.

The night was bitterly cold and black; he could hear the bay. It was like the Arctic out here, no lights, no traffic on the road, nothing. Totally deserted. Why'd she come out to this Godforsaken place? She looked too pale. Sweet Jesus Christ he had to take care of her. He had to have her help him with the body, but after that he was taking her home, he'd make it up to her. He was about to walk away from the house, when he heard her call him. He turned abruptly and went back inside.

India was in the kitchen. She had on a red tartan dress with a lacy collar out over a knitted jacket. The jacket was cream with green holly leaves and red berries. He had never seen her wear it before.

"Like the outfit," he said. "Where'd you get it?"

"It was in the closet—something I used to wear here." The way it was said sounded as if coming out to the Bay house was a thing of the past. He'd sell the house, Jack thought. Get a place in the Virginia countryside. She'd like that. Maybe she could keep a horse and go riding.

"Listen, I'm going to make some coffee."

India looked at the roll in the hallway. "Please, I don't want anything—let's just get this done." Then she looked at him and winced. "Oh, Jack, take that jacket off, it's covered in blood. Here—" She went and got a plastic trash bag from a cupboard under the sink.

Jack peeled off the jacket. Before he stuffed it in the bag he took out the gun and checked his other pockets. He put the gun on a counter. "Coffee won't take a minute." He opened the refrigerator, took out the milk and poured enough for two cups into a saucepan. When Jack put the milk back he put the automatic with it—couldn't beat a fridge for a place to keep a gun out of sight and handy.

He put a hand to his mouth, he could taste blood.

"You're still bleeding." India dabbed at his lip with a tissue. "Come on, I'll help you get cleaned up."

Jack came down the stairs. He'd remembered the trunk stored away at the back of a closet and that it contained some of his clothes, old favorites he'd kept from college days. They were a bit tight, but not bad. He'd found his baseball hat and mitt too.

He had showered and India had treated his cuts with antiseptic. She had been so gentle he had to stop himself from whistling—it didn't seem right with the priest lying there. Finally he'd persuaded her to stay upstairs and let him bring up the coffee. He was thinking: she'd been raised to live a different kind of life, more social, lots of people in and out of the house, friends coming around. Home for Jack meant retreating into his fortress where he didn't have to cover his back all the time; a place he could put his feet up and lie back and watch the box. But if India wasn't happy, if she missed . . .

He stopped dead. There was a kitchen chair drawn up to face whoever came through the door and Angelo was sitting on it with a Browning automatic in his hand and a smile at one corner of his mouth. The automatic was aimed for the center of Jack's stomach and the range was point-blank.

Jack raised his hands in the air. "Okay, you got me," he managed to joke.

Christ Almighty, the back door! He hadn't locked the fucking door. It'd been Angelo out on the road—he'd been there all the time. He dropped his hands, careful to keep a humorous look on his face.

"Keep them up there." Angelo's thin dangerous smile went to the other corner.

"You serious?" The hell, he was serious all right, the asshole . . .

"Believe it," Angelo snapped. He stared at Jack. Those mean eyes knew something.

"So, you going to tell me what it's all about before you kill me?" Jack said, still jokey.

"You get at my pilots with big pay offers, get them to do a run to Colombia, they come in and you have them shot, no witnesses. You have their planes burned so their widows can't sell them."

Where the shit did Angelo get it from? "Christ, Angelo, lighten up and tell me what the hell's going on."

"Fingers Natale," Angelo said softly, and Jack felt fear in a way he had never known. "He got them all broken up. He was so upset about it he squealed. You shoulda heard him."

Jack was thinking, a few seconds and three bullets later he could be lying in a pool of blood on his own kitchen floor. He looked at Angelo, testing his will. Angelo's eyes didn't blink and except for the smile there was no other expression on his face. He had strength, but Jack had always thought it was the brute strength of a robot that did things according to some program and could be neutralized. Maybe he still could neutralize him.

"Come on, quit jiving, I'm making coffee here." Jack walked past him, over to the range. He switched on a burner. Angelo was caught by surprise, as Jack had intended. Jack had his back to him.

"You want a cup? We've got plenty of milk." He leaned over to the refrigerator, opened the door.

"I didn't come for any fucking cup of coffee."

His left hand was nearest to Angelo. He took out the milk and began turning. The door shielded his right hand.

Angelo was still sitting in the chair, Jack's new position had made him swivel around and he was slightly off-balance. Jack brought the gun out, leveling it at Angelo's chest. Both men fired simultaneously.

How could she lie on the bed and wait for coffee? India prowled the bedroom, feverish with impatience. How could she sit still, even, with the body down there rolled in her father's carpet?

"HHHHHHaaah." The house vibrated with dull staccato sound. It stopped, leaving India standing stiffly in the abrupt silence.

Then footsteps . . .

Then: "It's me, it's okay."

The voice came eerily distorted up the stairs. That's not Jack, she was thinking. It wasn't Jack's voice. It was the only thought beating in her brain. Her heart stammered. If it wasn't Jack, then . . . Her breathing became hoarse. It was Michael. He wasn't dead. Incredibly, he wasn't dead. In her mind she saw his white devil's face, the long thin hands . . . somehow, unrolling the carpet . . . he had killed Jack, he was coming to kill her.

He was coming, she heard his footsteps. It was too late. Too late to pray, even. No, it wasn't. She had to fight. Quick, unhesitating, she took the baseball bat from the trunk Jack had pulled from the closet, yanked the lamp plug from the socket, plunging the room into darkness, and made her way back to the door by instinct. She stood behind it with the bat raised.

Footsteps, then the door opening. This is it, this is . . . She was too frightened even to look, she had a grip on the bat so hard . . . NOW! She brought it down. There was a dull thud and a groan. She was crying, making small whimpering sounds, hitting out wildly. There was a hoarse cry as he crashed to the floor. She shut her eyes and raised the bat again for the final stroke.

Twenty-One

As Lieutenant Malloy cruised along the George Washington Parkway in his unmarked State Police car on his way to Central Intelligence Headquarters, he kept glancing at the bag of groceries on the seat beside him. The bag contained items he had purchased at the all-night supermarket.

He'd forgotten something.

As he took the CIA exit Malloy heard his wife saying as clear as if she were in the car, "Where's the Softies? I told you Softies."

He'd got Softies. Was it toothpaste? Toilet soap? Malloy put his hand in the bag and pulled out a box of doughnuts, selected one coated in powdered sugar and bit into it.

He stopped at the guard post, wiping his mouth with the back of his hand before he opened the window. The uniformed officer on duty stepped smartly out to ask his name. Malloy remembered the box of doughnuts on his knee and stuffed them back. All the guard saw when he bent down was Malloy's hand diving into the bag. The next moment Malloy was frozen in shock. The guard had a pistol at his head.

"Drop it," the officer snapped. "Take your hand out slowly and put them both up."

Malloy was breathing like a horse on a training run. He did as he was told. The guard put his hand in, unlocked the door and jerked it open. "Get out."

"ID's in my pocket," Malloy snarled, as he was spreadeagled against the car. The guard ignored him and kept running his hands over the contours of Malloy's body. He took the .45 automatic—standard Police Department issue—from Malloy's shoulder holster. Two other guards took the bag from the front seat of the car.

"Lieutenant Joseph Malloy?" the guard said.

"Yeah."

"What is your tax registration number, sir?"

"Eight two two nine four nine."

The information was checked against a list on the clipboard and checked again on a computer. Malloy was allowed to stand easy. The household shopping was repacked.

"Sorry, sir. There's been a theft of weapons from a couple of National Guard armories. We've been warned to expect a terrorist attack and when I saw your hand in the bag there—"

"Yeah, yeah, yeah," said Malloy.

"Sir, just drive on through to the visitors' parking lot—"

"I been here before." Malloy's glare encompassed all three guards.

As he drove off he suddenly remembered what it was. Shit, it was milk. He had forgotten the milk.

India tore the ice cubes from the freezer tray and dumped them on the tea towel laid out on the bench. Oh God, if she could just get through tonight. She fumbled for the brandy kept in the cupboard over the kitchen sink and turned to get a clean glass.

There was blood and gray matter in dribbles down the wall. She averted her eyes and clutched the brandy bottle to her breast like some token of faith.

With everything collected on the tray she picked it up, turning her back on the part of the floor where the body lay and sidling past. Her foot struck something soft and she was barely able to stifle a scream.

The fear now was very deep and she ran all the way up the stairs with the loaded tray.

Jack lay across the bed. India put down the tray and shook him. "Jack! Jack, please." He groaned. She took the ice wrapped in the towel and dabbed it on his forehead.

"Wake up, Jack, please wake up. I'm sorry, I'm sorry." She'd knocked him out. What if he needed a doctor, what then? Jack groaned and coughed. India tried to sit him up.

"God almighty." He blinked rapidly. She thrust the brandy glass to his lips. He took it almost sightlessly and gulped, shuddering and spluttering.

Please let him be all right. India clasped his head in her hands. "Tell me you're all right," she begged. "Can you remember anything?"

Jack was awake now. He said thickly, "I can remember being hit by a sledgehammer."

"I'm truly sorry, I never meant, I thought . . . never mind. Your voice when you called up the stairs, it didn't sound like you, that's all."

"My throat's all swelled up—that bastard tried to strangle me," Jack recalled, trying to clear this throat by coughing. "Still can't talk much, some hot coffee might help." He recalled more. "Oh, Christ." He looked at India, who was sitting on the side of the bed holding the ice pack, staring at him. "You must have been down there."

"I'll get you the coffee," India said. She would have done anything for him at that moment, anything. "I'll put a tablecloth over him."

Christ, he hated this place. Malloy walked into the seven-story, concrete building and was immediately under the observation of three security officers in civilian clothes and several he couldn't see: those in the central surveillance room monitoring his every movement on camera. A clean-cut type looking like one of the moral majority took him to the visitors' room where he was given a security pass. His handler and the pass got him through the various security checkpoints.

The agent he had come to see had his office in one of the drab anonymous corridors on the fifth floor, or was it the fourth? Malloy was escorted to a door by his nameless attendant (the pass on the chain around his neck had a photograph and a number, but no name) and wordlessly seen inside.

Buck Winterman was slouched in a swivel chair reading a manila folder. He was in his middle forties, and Malloy had known him since their days in New York's Fifth Precinct. Malloy was gratified that Buck's office was as shabby as his own—same green metal, gray Formica, government-issue furniture.

"How do you work in this rat trap?" Malloy complained.

"Good to see you, Joe." Buck got up and came over, made a few playful feints, then kicked at a chair. "Take a load off." Then he went back to his desk and shoved over some photographs.

Malloy sat down. "You mother!" he grumbled. "It's midnight, for Chrissake." He picked up the photographs and thumbed through them quickly, then examined them a second time. They were blow-ups; he scrutinized each one carefully. "Where'd you get these?"

"Classified."

Malloy snorted.

"Here, you better sign this." Buck handed over a form. "That means you can see what you're looking at right now. Stuff comes from the Brits. I'm hoping you might recognize someone in that bunch—could be useful to us."

"What's going on? The boys at the gate jumped me, nervous about a terrorist attack. They said there'd been a steal."

"Then they let out classified information."

"I guess the guy thought he owed me some kind of apology. Stop assing around, Buck. What's missing?"

"A few man-portable missiles and some new submachine guns with folding stock the army has been working on. Same standard modification to the Uzi, only these babies can be folded down so small they can be carried concealed on a person. Any terrorist organization would be interested in that lot, Iranian or Palestinian or Libyan. If the Provisional IRA is feeding them through their weapons pipeline they'll turn up in Ulster."

"Thought you had that line stamped out."

"Yeah, but we're not so sure now. If the weapons get to Ulster, at least we know where they are."

Malloy chuckled. "This time you don't know where they fucking are or who has them."

"Right. The chief was thinking it'd be nice if your department could get together with us on this one."

"Then it's official cooperation," Malloy said cautiously. Privately he was thinking, nobody in their right mind would cooperate with the CIA. He didn't mind meeting Buck somewhere and chewing the fat over a beer. This was different. He looked again at the photographs.

"Recognize anybody?"

"That's Senator Ned Kelly, or it was, should I say. And isn't that Danny Shanahan?" Malloy thought he recognized the front man for Sinn Fein, the Provos' political wing.

"Yeah. The one next to him, know who he is?" Malloy gave him a careful look and shook his head.

"That's Ken McWhinney. He's an assassin—one of the Provos' most experienced. He was one of the men the IRA had broken from the Maze prison earlier this year. You never seen him? We had a report he was here in Washington."

"Yeah? No, I never clapped eyes on him." Malloy turned to another photo. "This one—the young guy here?"

"Patrick Fitzgerald. Know him?"

Malloy shook his head. "Funny thing, though, he looks a dead ringer for the priest who runs this place where drug addicts can hang out during the day. What's his name? Father Fitzgerald . . . that's it, Father Michael Fitzgerald." Malloy sucked at his teeth thoughtfully.

"The Center's on my way. Think I'll pay Father Fitzgerald a visit."

"Is he likely to be there this late at night?"

"Place closes at eleven but the daily surveillance reports on the area note there's usually someone around until much later. The boys called in the other night because they saw a light on and he was there. It could be nothing, but what the hell. Gimme a look at the other stuff you got there in the folder. Shit, I'll sign the goddamn forms. Jeez."

"Leave it."

India couldn't leave it. They had hauled Angelo's body to the trunk of his own car and spent a terrible time trying to fit him in. But his brains were still on her kitchen wall and she was too distraught to think of anything else. She just wanted to get a bucket of hot soapy water and scrub it clean, every inch, and scrub away the stains from the floor where his body had been.

"The Cleaner will take care of it. Come on." India looked at him dumbfounded, but Jack drew her out the back door. "Where are your gloves?"

India pulled them from her pocket.

"Put them on and don't take them off." He turned the key in the two security locks. The station wagon was pulled up right to the back step. The problem of getting the carpet roll in was solved by lowering the back seat. Jack had placed blankets and pillows over the top. It looked like any family's car would returning home after shutting up their beach house.

"What cleaner? Who would come in the middle of the night to, to—clean up after *that?*"

Jack reached out and took her hand. It trembled; she seemed exhausted. He worried that she had to drive the Mercedes back to Washington by herself. He would drive the station wagon with the body, as they had discussed. She had seemed calm enough about helping him get the bodies into their respective cars. Now she was working into a state over the cleaning arrangements. Women! He felt a bolt of pain go through his head—it bothered him every time he moved his eyes. He hoped it wasn't permanent.

"Jack?" She looked at him, insistent.

He cleared his throat and winced as another shaft of pain jetted in. "Cleaner is just the name we use for him. He's in the business." Then he had to explain to her that the guy was really a scientist. "He can beat the Federal forensic experts at their own game—he used to work for the Feds so he knows what to look for. What he does is clean the place down to the door knobs and handles. He uses chemicals to get rid of the blood. When he gets done there'll be nothing that can lead to either Father Fitzgerald or Angelo ever being in the house."

She was still looking at him with that drawn nostrils expression, like she had just seen something dubious in her kitchen cupboards, but she didn't seem so anxious.

"You must pay him a lot not to talk," she said.

Jack nodded and rubbed the side of his head trying to shift the pain, which hadn't gone away this time. "Think you can manage to drive now?"

"Father Fitzgerald's car," she moaned suddenly. "We forgot about his car."

"No, we didn't," Jack soothed. "The Cleaner'll dispose of it. No one will ever see a trace. Someone may remember having *seen* it— but if the Feds don't have a car to analyze the dirt and grime on, they can't prove a thing." Thinking of Angelo, he added as a postscript, "The same goes for a murder victim. If they don't have one they don't have a case."

The business about Angelo would be kept in the family. They had contingency plans elastic enough to cover bodies riddled with bullet holes. A doctor on the payroll would sign a death certificate saying it was a heart attack and Angelo would have a nice quiet funeral. The police wouldn't even know about it.

"We gotta go, okay?" He kissed her and led the way to his car.

When she settled comfortably, he gave her some final instructions and then went and got into the station wagon.

Jack headed west toward D.C., taking Route 50, India a little ahead of him. Jack was worried. Not about the police finding out— about his father finding out.

No one shot and killed one of Salvatore's sons, not even another son, and lived. There was family honor involved, even if these days honor was merely a figment of a diseased imagination. The possibility that the old man would ritualistically take whoever killed Angelo limb from limb couldn't be taken lightly. Unless the mantle fell on someone else. Someone like Bernie. Now, that could be very conveniently arranged.

A lovers' quarrel and a shooting. Both killed. Salvatore wasn't going to come and inspect the bodies. He wouldn't take the word of anybody, but he would take the word of his consigliere, Domenico Cechetti. When he knew what had been going on he'd want the matter closed with the coffin lid.

Jack felt better having worked that out. But he needed a brandy, badly. He drove, though, as he always did, checking the rearview mirror every so often, making sure he didn't see the same vehicle twice. Jack didn't believe in coincidences. He watched a van that had been behind him for ten minutes, but he lost it when he exited onto the beltway that surrounded the city of Washington.

First Jack stopped at his house in Georgetown. He parked the station wagon and went inside while India waited. Jack made two calls on the safe line in his study. One was to the Cleaner, the other to Domenico Cechetti; to each he gave explicit instructions. When he was finished he opened the safe in the floor and took out several large bundles of used money and a letter. He stuffed it all into a leather holdall and threw in two pairs of plastic overshoes.

He looked longingly at the cabinet where he kept a bottle of very good brandy. He needed it to take the edge off the pain in his head, but shit, there was no time. Before leaving he pulled on soft leather gloves. A glance at his watch told him the time was 12:50.

As Jack drove the station wagon into the basement garage beneath the Center, India slid the double steel door closed. When it was sealed tight she padlocked it and groped her way to the light switch by memory. Then she ran to open the door to the storeroom that led to the upper part of the building.

At the car Jack turned quickly to open the hatchback. He flung the blankets aside and grabbed the rolled carpet, taking the shoulder end with both hands and hoisting it to his arms. India took the feet. But the weight! How heavy it was. She lugged the thing three steps and stopped.

"Can't we . . .?"

"Let's get into the storeroom before someone else comes wandering in," Jack said. He looked at the garage doors. "God knows how many people have keys for this place."

"Mind the step."

"Christ!"

"Are you all right?"

"Yeah—"

They stumbled into the storeroom. India lowered her end and switched on the lights. "My fingers are breaking."

"You're lucky it's not your back. Shut the door and lock it."

"Can't we leave him here in the storeroom?"

"No," Jack said. "The office is best." He was a meticulous man. He liked things to be neat and tidy and it seemed irresponsible to leave the priest lying on a basement floor in a storeroom. Deep in his Catholic heart, Jack knew it was an unfitting place to dispatch a soul (especially the soul of a priest) to meet his Creator.

India looked at the bloated roll of carpet. "But they'll know it didn't happen there."

"What didn't happen?"

"He was murdered. They'll know he wasn't murdered in his office."

"Just what do you mean, murdered? It was self-defense. And as I recall I was unconscious at the time."

"Oh—now you're saying *I* murdered him," India hissed. "That's what you're saying, isn't it?" She was on the verge of exhaustion, ratty with it. Her body ached all over.

"I didn't say you murdered him, for Chrissake. Let's get him unrolled—if you think that'll be easier—and up the stairs." Jack was tired, the pain in his head increasingly bad. Christ, why hadn't he had that slug of brandy?

"Well I do, the carpet weighs a ton."

"Yeah, you're right." He shoved aside some cartons to make room. "We'll have to get rid of the rug—carpet—or whatever it is."

"Get rid of it! It's my father's wedding present to us. What am I going to say when he comes for a visit and we don't have it?"

"Tough—Father Fitzgerald here is covered in fibers and we can't risk having them traced. It'll have to go with his car to be disposed of. Now, can you help unroll your end?"

"I can't do this."

"What do you mean, you can't do this?"

"I can't just unroll him and dump him on the floor," India insisted.

"I didn't say we're going to *dump* him. We're going to place him *gently* on the floor, then carry him up the stairs," Jack said, suddenly exaggeratedly polite. "Listen, if it disturbs you so much I'll carry him myself."

"What was that?" India's head surged up as she listened.

"What was what?" Jack hissed.

"I thought I heard something."

They listened, India swallowing with difficulty, Jack cagey. "It's nothing—someone going past—you think they can see the basement light?"

"No," India said. "You can't see it, there's no windows."

"Okay, but once we're up the stairs we'll use my flashlight. Give me a hand to stand him up. I'll carry him over my shoulder, you lead the way."

"What if someone sees the light?"

"Then we're up shit street. Okay, I got him. You get the bag, will you?"

"What bag?"

"The bag I—it's the leather holdall in the car, just get it."

Jack got his toe caught in the loose linoleum and tripped as he plunged through the doorway into the office. He staggered at breakneck speed towards the chair India had pulled out. There was a sharp creak as the corpse rolled from Jack's shoulder to the chair beneath. Jack ended up on his knees.

"Hold him, hold him. Christ, don't let him fall." Jack got to his feet panting. His mouth was dry and his spit was sour as hell.

She caught Father Fitzgerald as the priest slid forward in a flaccid embrace.

"Oh, no," groaned India, sinking down in dread.

"Hold him, hold him up!"

"You hold him!" India struggled to get free of the dangling arms.

Jack caught him by the wrists and shoved the chair in behind his desk. "That's got him."

"Why does he have to be sitting at his desk?" India whispered frantically, too upset now to remember what they had arranged to do. It seemed to her the priest whose arms they were arranging on his own desk wasn't dead at all.

"We agreed it'd look more dignified," Jack said. He grabbed an arm as it flopped over onto the floor. "Help me fold his arms."

"It's ridiculous. How's he going to look stiff, sitting up in his coffin with his arms folded like that?"

"India, I dunno—for Chrissake just hold him."

"I thought you knew about this sort of thing," India snapped.

"What the hell does that mean?"

"How to arrange corpses so they look as if they're still enjoying life," she whispered furiously.

"Just what in hell are you saying?" said Jack. "That I'm used to doing this sort of—"

"Jack," India cut him off in a shrill whisper, "I think I heard a car stop outside."

"Shit!"

"It's all right—it's turning around."

"Christ, let's get this over with and get out of here." He glanced at his watch: 2 A.M. already? Jack picked up the bag and tipped the money on the table.

India stared at it—wads and wads of money. The flashlight on the floor cast a brutish illumination. It dissolved the priest's face, leaving it malformed and fragmented in the dappled shadows. It was monstrous, so many monstrous things. "Oh," she cried. "Ohhh." Now in something close to real terror, India turned and fled.

Malloy pulled over. The Center was only another two blocks but he was doubled up with a pain in his gut. He groaned. A film of sweat covered his lip. Shouldn't have had that friendly bourbon with Buck before he left. For a moment all he saw was lights rushing through blackness—then the pain eased. Shit, tomorrow he was going to see a doctor. A station wagon drove past well over the speed limit; he didn't even see it. It took another ten minutes before he was able to sit up straight and start the car.

The Center was in blackness. Dead as a doornail, Malloy thought, as he sat in his car. He wouldn't even try the doors. Tomorrow he'd do the thing properly and come back with a search warrant. Then he'd go and see about his stomach.

Twenty-Two

Two hours later the station wagon was outside the Bay house and they were ready to leave. India got into the driver's seat. "We're never going to get away with this." Her voice vibrated with rising panic.

Jack leaned into the car. "Yes we are."

"No, we won't, because I can't go through with it."

"Yes you can—all we've got to do now is get Angelo parked. You follow me to Baltimore and pick me up. I'll drive us home and, finito." He kissed her on the cheek. "I wish like hell there was some other way we could do this, honey, I do. Now, you going to be all right?"

She nodded. Jack thought he had steadied her. But really she was willing to grasp now at anything that would bring the night and the horror to an end.

"Good girl." He kissed her on the mouth and right then wanted to make love to her, corpse in the trunk or not.

"Jack . . ." She held his face away, her eyes feverish, sweat in a film on her face. She looked really unwell. "It was seeing him sitting at the desk like that. I had the feeling he wasn't dead, Jack. That he is what he said he is—the Angel of Death." She was beginning to shake all over. Jack grabbed her hands and held on to them tightly. Her cheeks burned, but her hands felt like ice.

She was describing a vision of hell and in a moment he'd have that just-sailed-off-the-edge-of-the-world feeling himself. "Forget what he said. He was mad. Jesus, going around telling everyone he was the Angel of Death."

India was shaking her head, or was just shaking, Jack couldn't work out which. "If it wasn't for you—I mean—my God, he would have killed me. That's what he meant to do, wasn't it? He came here to kill me." Her mind couldn't accept it, and she had this terrible, disconnected, floating feeling, as if she were going to pass out.

"It's like a horror film. Just when you think the creature is dead, it gets up again and comes walking towards you."

Jack had to acknowledge that was a pretty fair description of the IRA. You got rid of one bastard and another stood up in his place.

"This thing is going to be over soon, then we can go home. You're going to be all right."

"Do you promise?" She managed to raise something that resembled a smile. He kissed her again and buckled her seatbelt before leaving.

He went over to Angelo's car and got in, glancing as he did at the house. The Cleaner was at work inside with his chemicals and vacuum suction devices, sanitizing what couldn't be disposed of by incineration. The fee for corpse disposal was extra, in some cases a lot extra. Jack hadn't wanted the priest and Angelo to disappear without a trace. Highly visible, their demise would convey a clear message. In the priest's case, the IRA would know they were being taken on. In his brother's case, it would signal the changing face of professional crime, the end of an era: Angelo's.

Jack drove off satisfied. Father Fitzgerald's car was gone. The Cleaner had seen to that detail first. Likewise everything that could identify them; he'd even insisted they dump their clothes—those wool fibers on India's jacket—the Feds needed only the smallest unrelated thing to start building a case.

Jack drove carefully; there were too many cops on the road to risk getting a ticket. Besides, he wanted to keep the station wagon in his rear view. Once he was on Ritchie Highway curving north towards Baltimore and India was right behind him, he became engrossed in his own thoughts.

It was time the Family mended its ways as far as the Church funds were concerned. Salvatore wasn't going to give up anything so lucrative. But Jack planned to channel some of it back to the project

India was working on, which he would allow her to administer so that she had something to keep her busy before she gave up doing that to have his children and run his home.

Jack thought that once he succeeded to his father's portfolio, he might build the scheme up into an international success with drug rehabilitation centers in Beverly Hills, Palm Beach, New York, London, Geneva, Tokyo, the financial capitals of the world. With all that money swilling around, the least the parents could do was put their kids into an expensive drying-out clinic. Perhaps he would even have a chain of detox units. It was a simple plan that would net a substantial few million, given the right administration, which would for all intents and purposes be the Church, of course. Jack didn't see where he could go wrong.

He groped for the bottle of aspirin in his pocket, and fiddled with the screw top. Fucking child-proof devices they had on everything these days. When he managed to get it open he spilled the lot and spent five minutes fishing between his legs.

His head ached, his throat felt as if it had been mauled by a bear, and he was weary of the whole messy business. Trust Angelo to creep up on him like an amateur. The chicken-shit moron deserved to die. He wasn't in the least grateful it was Angelo back there in the trunk and not him. Only losers wound up dead in the trunk of a car, and thank God they didn't intrude too often to stink up his highly specialized operations.

He went back to thinking about India.

He'd relinquished many deep beliefs since leaving college, oh yeah. But not the idea that a woman should be virtuous. And he had almost given up on that by the time he found India. She had made him believe all over again in the purity and goodness of a chaste woman. She was his conscience. When he got depressed he liked thinking how good she was. He was truly in love with her.

It was five in the morning and still dark when he drew up on the Baltimore street across from Bernie Loeb's house. As he was looking, the double gates at the side swung open. India was pulling up behind him, and Jack signaled for her to remain where she was. He hung a left and drove in.

Frank Bartelli closed the gates and followed Jack around the house to the garage at the back. The men were old friends. Frank was one of the élite, the one guard of the Coltelli family Jack trusted implicitly.

"Quiet trip?" Frank asked.

"Like a Sunday afternoon." Jack climbed out. The garage was warm. Bernie had central heating in his garage? Domenico Cechetti appeared at the doorway that connected the garage with the house.

"You find anything?" Jack asked.

Domenico was grinning. "We found his portable computer, a Datamaster Field job with a bubble memory."

"Good," Jack said. "When Bernie arrives get him to tell you the security code. Bargain with his life for it, anything you have to. When he tells you, check that it works, get him to verify all the information in the bubble memory, then kill him."

Jack went around to unlock the trunk. Angelo's melon face gazed out at them with affable reproach. Which was surprising considering the violent way he died, thought Jack, and the fact that a bullet had entered his head above the ear and blown most of his brains out the back of his cranium.

"The Cleaner doesn't know who we got here?" Dom asked. Jack shook his head. "Good. Then everything is set this end. We just wait for Bernie. You got the letter? We'll leave it on Angelo."

Jack handed him the letter and asked who was going to find the bodies.

"Frank has to make a routine collection, so it'll be him. First he calls to tell me, I contact the doctor and undertaker: they're qualified to handle delicate issues. Then I come straight here—Salvatore will expect that—then I break the news. By that time the doctor and the undertaker are doing their respective jobs."

"Can they be trusted?" Jack asked.

"They're my men," Domenico said quietly. "And I'll have my own boys waiting for Bernie when he arrives. Nobody in the Family is going to connect you with Angelo's death."

"I owe you," Jack said.

"Think nothing of it."

Jack would have control one day soon and the consigliere knew it. He produced the list Jack had asked for. It contained the names of Angelo's people who did his muscle work and made the hits. There were also the names of one or two who ran the shit operations and who were slick as weasel grease and as slippery.

Jack nodded. "Negotiate. If anyone smells like trouble, hit him." He turned away wearily.

Cechetti offered to make them breakfast, but Jack said he would rather go home.

"Better get some sleep in before you get a phone call," Domenico advised. "Salvatore's going to want to see you when he hears the news."

By twenty past five they were on their way back to Washington in the station wagon. Thirty minutes, a hot shower and a good breakfast, Jack was thinking. India's head lay back against the headrest.

"That was nice of you to give the money back," she said.

He'd just explained all about the money he had left on Father Fitzgerald's desk and how he was going to help the Church and not steal from it any more, and she'd lain there staring through the window as though it wasn't any big deal.

"Yeah, well . . ." Jack's first instincts were to drag all the information he could out of her. But he knew it wasn't the time. Maybe after breakfast. There was a lot more he wanted to know, details that would help the family move in on the IRA's operation. There was a whole armory of machine guns hidden away they wanted to get their hands on before the FBI picked up the scent. And there had to be a safe house somewhere.

"Oh," India moaned.

Jack looked over at her in alarm. "You okay?"

India's mouth was opened in a gasp; she made no sound. Jack checked the road and looked back at her, flabbergasted.

Her voice resurfaced. "Fine, fine. Just backache."

"It's all that heavy lifting. You'll be okay. Soon as we get in I'll run you a nice deep tub." Jack went back to the road and his thoughts.

The pain hit her again. She clenched the seat on either side of her with both hands and went rigid. Then she realized she was wet; she was sitting in a puddle. She felt between her legs. Then she looked down at her fingers and her heart stopped. They were sticky wet with blood. As a warm trickle ran down her leg the pain rose again to devour her.

"Jack," India reached forward and tugged at his arm. "Jack, help me."

"What is it, babe?" Jack slowed. India was clutching her stomach. "Is it appendicitis?"

"Please, can you get me to a hospital?" India mumbled.

Jack heard the word hospital and stepped on the gas. "I had appendicitis, hit me in just the same way." He reached out and squeezed her arm comfortingly.

"It's not appendicitis," India said in a low voice.

"What'd you say, sweetheart?" Jack changed lanes and streaked for the exit that would take him off the beltway.

India's voice was collapsing. Her legs were warm and wet now, she was sinking, she felt so weak. "I'm hemorrhaging." She thought, He'll find out at the hospital. I can't let that happen, I have to be the one to tell him. She felt very cold suddenly and very weak. She had to tell him now while she was still conscious.

"I'm three, nearly four months . . . " she tried to indicate the pool of blood spreading out beneath her, "pregnant," she said, before dropping into a dead faint.

Someone was shouting to her. Calling her name. Her eyes focused slowly. Everything was a blur. She thought she saw Jack's face behind a mask. People in green. The cramping pain deep in her belly was oddly distant. It was an effort to keep her eyes open and she closed them again.

She woke staring up at the fluorescent panels in the ceiling. A face appeared and said, "She's awake now." India didn't know if she wanted to be awake. She closed her eyes. When she opened them the face had gone. There was a dull empty ache deep in her belly. She turned her head slowly to the left. A red bag hung from a metal stand. She watched the drips and followed the crimson tubing down to her arm. Then she was aware of the doctor by her side dressed in surgical green.

"Where am I?"

"Casualty Hospital," the doctor said. "You were brought in by our Medical rescue team. Your husband called them up on his car phone. You were unconscious. He was pretty upset. You gave him quite a scare."

I bet I did, thought India. "The baby?" she asked without hope.

"Mrs. Donovan," he said gently, "we were not able to save the baby."

India turned her face away, mouth drawn tight, eyes fierce, stinging with tears. She heard retreating footsteps, then the murmur of voices and footsteps again, coming to the bed. India brushed a hand across her face to rub her eyes dry. She forced herself to look.

Jack had replaced the doctor. He stood stiffly at her bedside. "How are you feeling?"

"Fine." She felt his rage. He looked as if to touch her would amount to a kind of admission he didn't want to make.

The tears were bottled up but she was crying inside out of shame and sorrow, for the baby she had lost, for the man she was about to. She wanted to say how sorry. How terribly, terribly sorry. But his face was set and angry, his eyes like two hard stones. No woman betrayed Jack in the way she had.

He lowered his head almost to her face. "Who did this to you? I'll kill him."

She was as trapped in her own anger and misery and pride as he was in his. "We already did."

His forehead broke out in a sweat and his hands trembled, she saw the shock in his eyes. There, she had done the thing she had sworn not to.

"He feared eternity in hell as much as I do." India broke down then and cried in harsh, broken sobs. "I'm sorry, I'm sorry, what can I say?"

She loved him. She wanted to put her arms around his neck and tell him so. But it was too late for that, and anyway she lacked the strength to lift her arms. She wondered what would happen to her, but she really didn't care.

"Leave me alone." Pleading, miserable, sobbing, she turned away from him. "Just go and leave me alone."

That same evening Duane was punching a hole through the two separated layers of a plywood door. He put his arm through and pulled back the bolt. Walking inside, the room vibrated as a train rocketed past on the railroad outside the tenement building. He put the light on and a body stirred on the narrow stretcher bed.

"Mal?" Duane rushed to the corner where Malcolm lay in dirty blankets. On the table beside him was a syringe, spike, a cup of water, alcohol, some cotton wool and an empty packet. Malcolm tried to raise his head and failed. Duane darted to the washstand and wet a stinking face towel with cold water. He went back and sponged Malcolm's face.

"Pushing bad stuff," Malcolm said. His voice drifted. He smelled of death.

Duane extracted the packet from the mess on the table. He wet his finger with spit, poking it into the bottom corners, then gingerly tasting it. He gestured obscenely.

"You been to the Mortician," Duane accused.

"Yeah," Malcolm said.

"Jesus!" Duane said. The Mortician was a pusher specializing in dealing lethal concoctions. Only dope fiends went to him. Sick people whose need was such they would do anything to satisfy it. "I thought you was off that stuff. Jesus, Mal, you know that fat fuck sells shit, how else you think he got his name?"

Malcolm gave a little sound, like his breath was shutting off. His eyes stared and Duane went weak all over.

"Mal? Mal! Oh Jesus, Mal."

Jack was almost too distraught to eat, thinking about what India had done to him. He spent the day drinking and banging around in and out of the kitchen, getting ice out of the freezer and swearing under his breath until Wilma said she would leave.

When he was sitting in his study alone with a scotch, thinking that maybe he had finally had it with her, he started seeing the drowning look in her eyes.

When he went to sleep it felt like he was awake and thinking about her. He couldn't get over the way she had betrayed him.

In church he knelt in prayer. It only convinced him he would never feel the same way about priests. He went home and sat in his study and got drunk. India had betrayed him and he could no longer live with himself, or her.

By the next day the self-pity had shifted significantly to a state where he thought it might be possible. Yes, he could forgive her—he was just never going to forget.

Lieutenant Malloy had instructions not to stay too long. He could understand why. Mrs. Donovan looked ill with grief. He'd always thought she was nice, and he was sorry she had lost her baby.

He knew about it because one of his men was going out with a nurse on her floor. Gently (for him) Malloy asked his questions. Who had been to the Center? Did she know their names? Did Father Fitzgerald have any enemies, anybody who might want to kill him?

She stared at him with such shock in her eyes that he gave up and took the photographs from a manila folder.

"Is there anyone here that you recognize?"

"Yes." She pointed to Ken McWhinney's photograph. "I saw him there."

"And this one?" It was a photograph of Michael when he was young. Malloy pounced on her obvious discomfort. She told him it bore a resemblance to Father Fitzgerald, but she couldn't be sure as she had never seen him as a young man and she had no idea how he had got hold of it, and then began crying.

Malloy thought it was understandable. Father Fitzgerald had been very well liked at the Center. He excused himself before she got too distressed and he got into trouble with the nurses.

Jack walked past the hospital flower stall and stopped, deciding if he should buy some. Screw it. He walked on, stopped. He went back.

"The violets over there, please."

"Cold day. Think it'll snow for Christmas?" The man wrapped the violets in green paper.

"Might." Was it Christmas? Yeah, in about two and a half weeks it was. He pulled out some dollar bills and handed them over. At the newsstand he nearly bought a paper and decided against it because of all the news in it about Father Fitzgerald's murder.

Outside India's door he paused to straighten his tie. Then he went into the room to tell her he was going to forgive her.

India stared at him, dull eyes. "What does that mean?"

"It means I forgive you," Jack said, bitter at the resounding lack of interest—when he thought of what she had done, that lovely body. And all the time she wouldn't let him touch it she was with another man, so pure and innocent-looking and . . .

India didn't see any forgiveness. There was no love in Jack's face, only cold calculation.

"It's not that I don't care," she said quietly. "It's just that I seem to have gone beyond caring. It's too late. It's finished."

Her head jerked slightly so that her eyes looked past him to the window. The baby was dead, Michael was dead, and there would be no Jack. All she felt was sorrow and guilt and loneliness.

"I have to leave," she said. "Would you please do one thing for me?"

"What?" Jack asked, beginning to feel alarmed.

India's state of terrible calm was edging her closer to making the decision all over again, and this time it would be irreversible. "Please, get me an airline ticket back to London."

If she had thrown herself on his mercy and begged Jack for his forgiveness, pleaded to be allowed to stay with him—he would have got her a goddamned ticket back to London.

Instead she was responding like some voice-activated robot, saying, in that la-di-da accent, actually saying she was going to leave him. She had dishonored him and now she was going to dishonor him in front of his family. He knew his father was going to take the shame personally. Jack could hardly speak.

She was his wife and he would decide when she could go, or not. She was his.

Duane went out looking for the Mortician. He went to a place where he knew the drug trade was operating and he waited. Someone would deliver the junk and take the money back to the Mortician.

When that happened, Duane was right behind him, a boy with a habit who couldn't have been much older than ten.

When the Mortician came out of his apartment that evening and turned to lock his door, there was a knife digging into his back. Duane's voice was directly behind him. "You gonna go right back in there. I got something for you."

Inside the apartment, Duane pulled a cord over the Mortician's head and yanked it tight around his neck. Not too tight. He didn't want to kill him. Just enough to keep him quiet while he injected the pusher with his own dope.

"Funny stuff you been giving out lately," Duane said conversationally. "People are dying." He tethered the Mortician to a coat hook by the cord around his neck and tied up his arm ready for a shot. He hit a vein and a column of blood oozed into the syringe. Duane pressed the plunger down with his thumb. As the last drop was feeding into the vein and the Mortician's breathing had become a giant grating buzz, the door burst open and two undercover men from the Bureau of Narcotics had their guns trained on him.

"So, Mister Jack Donovan, where are we headed this morning?" Meehan muttered. He was parked in a white Oldsmobile Cutlass several cars further along the street from Jack's Georgetown home.

"Hello," he said, spotting the other man as he emerged from the house. "If it's not Frank bloody Bartelli himself. Things are hotting up if they're bringing you in, matey." Meehan chuckled. "Missing Paulie are we, Jack?"

Jack got into his car and started the engine. Bartelli stood at the window talking. Meehan saw him nod and move away. Then Bartelli walked off and got into a green Buick Regal further along.

Ken McWhinney came out of a deli with a bag of bagels and got in. Meehan expected Bartelli would wait and cover Donovan's back. But the Buick pulled out and was the first away. Meehan couldn't believe his luck. He waited until Donovan turned the corner at the end of the street and raced after him to keep the Mercedes in sight.

At about a quarter after eleven, Jack came into India's room and told her he was taking her home. "I only want the best for you and right now you're still weak, you need rest. The doctors agree home is best for now."

Right now she needed to be in a private clinic where she wouldn't last two days without seeing sense. Jack regretted permitting the Medical Rescue Unit to bring her to this hospital where he wasn't able to pull strings. But once he had her home and she got into one of her hysterical states, Dr. Nestor's expertise with the hypodermic would soon have her back to being a good wife.

"Home is London," India said. She had thought of going to Harriet, but Adrian was still far from well and they had enough problems of their own.

"I appreciate how you might think that," Jack said. He sat down on a chair and looked at her earnestly. "Look, we ought to talk. Before you go, promise me that?"

India nodded silently. She tried to comfort herself by remembering he had given her his forgiveness. But she didn't want to be forgiven, she wanted to be loved.

Jack was interpreting her silence as indifference. It acted on him like a cold wave. He knew he could keep her, but he also knew it wasn't how he wanted it.

"Look, I'm saying that if you still want to go home, then okay. It's a pity, though, because with Angelo gone the street business will be wound up." He neglected to say it would be franchised out and the Family would still keep the profits. "The old days are over—things are going to be very different." Jack expelled the air from his lungs. "The Family won't have gangsters any more, the hoodlums are finished." He didn't add that he was putting together an execution squad to do it.

"We're financiers now. Listen, we don't get involved with the drug market. I never explained it to you, but that was why Angelo came for me. He was up to his ears. I busted his dirty business for him. I had to do it because of the refusal by some individual law-enforcement officers to see what is going on. Because either they have a finger in the pie themselves, or they're taking a handout."

India was looking at him now; she had that soft look in her eyes. He knew he was getting to her. He got up and sat on the side of the bed and looked down at her. "So, please, will you come home and at least talk to me?"

Sergeant Jackson scribbled down the message and went through to Malloy's office. The Lieutenant was being nice to someone over the telephone.

"And you too, sir . . . Yessir . . . Wouldn't have it any other way. Haa, haa." Malloy turned crazed eyes on his young sergeant. "And give mine to your wife."

Malloy hurled the receiver down. "Raving lunatic, megalomaniac." He rubbed his face tiredly with his hands and mumbled something.

"Sorry, sir?"

"What?"

"I didn't hear what you said, just then, I—"

"Never mind." Malloy lowered his head and looked up at Jackson almost regretfully. "Just tell me why you're here."

"Police Officer Joe Fontane and his partner," Jackson consulted his notes, "Jean Heizer, reported sighting a white Oldsmobile Cutlass answering the description of the car we had from an anonymous caller—"

"Meehan's car," Malloy said, dangerously soft. "Where?"

"Ah, the officers reported sighting the car—"

"Where?" screamed Malloy.

"Stanton Park."

"Stanton Park is very near Casualty Hospital and Mrs. Donovan is being discharged this morning." Malloy was on his feet and moving rapidly around the desk. "Get every patrol car in the vicinity of the hospital . . ." He was already out the door.

"Chrissake, Jackson . . . You coming?"

India was in the wheelchair at the front door. Jack had her bag in his hand. He smiled down at her. "I'll get the car. It's parked in the street, not far."

"It's all right," India said. "I feel like taking a walk in the fresh air."

Jack glanced at her. "Sure?"

India was already standing up and thanking the nurse.

Police Officer Joe Fontane took the mike from its cradle in response to the call made a few moments before. "This is Seven K receiving, ah, white Oldsmobile Cutlass no longer in the Stanton Park area." Well, we can't see it, he muttered, lowering the mike.

"Seven, proceed to vicinity of Casualty Hospital. Be on the lookout for a white Oldsmobile Cutlass and if sighted keep in visual contact but do not—repeat, do not—attempt to apprehend."

"Roger. Moving down Massachusetts."

Sergeant Jackson was coming from the opposite direction. Malloy sat beside him barely able to contain his impatience. There was no doubt they were on to a terrorist network, but how did they operate? Who was bankrolling them?

Meehan was the link connecting the groups, Malloy was certain of that. Deadly, efficient, and a nuisance. Because this homicidal maniac had chosen to perpetrate his crimes on the turf Malloy considered his own, he now had not only his chief giving him hell, he had the Bureau on top of him too.

"I'll tear that bastard limb from limb," he told his silent and, he often suspected, disapproving sergeant.

They reached the car. Jack unlocked the passenger door and opened it. Someone was humming "On the Sunny Side of the Street." India climbed in. She tucked in the folds of her coat and looked up for Jack to close the door. On the edge of her vision was the man who was humming. He carried a Super Giant grocery bag in his arms . . . walking towards them . . .

In a sudden premonition of danger she said, "Jack," sharply. His eyes were on the door as he shut it and he didn't seem to hear her.

The man with the brown bag was looking right at them, at Jack, holding the bag with just one arm—

"JACK!"

Jack heard her, he was turning, aware now of the man behind him.

She clawed for the handle and slammed the door into Jack's back. It was the instant that Meehan fired.

India stumbled from the car and Jack turned, as if he meant to push her back in, out of harm's way. There was a surprised look on his face, and then he pitched forward into her arms.

She tried to say something, only she couldn't. And she couldn't hold him. They both went down. Then she realized he was soaking wet. She looked and saw the dark blot creeping upward from under his belt and staining his shirt-front crimson.

Twenty-Three

It was sheer chance Patrolman Joe Fontane happened to glance at the man holding the bag of groceries and saw the gun coming from behind.

His partner, Jean Heizer, was looking up ahead and had spotted the white Oldsmobile coming out of the next street. "There it is . . . WHAT!"

Joe had slammed on his brakes and spun the driving wheel. Instantly oncoming cars swerved to avoid being hit. The police car squealed across the road and slewed up on the sidewalk. At the first sound of brakes the man dropped the bag, turned and ran.

Coming in the opposite direction Malloy didn't see what was going on ahead of him; he too had spotted the Oldsmobile waiting to make a turn.

"Get him, get him. Cut him off."

They were already passing the corner where the Oldsmobile was sitting. Jackson hit his brakes. The car skidded sideways across the Oldsmobile's bow. The windshield shattered and Jackson's foot dropped to the accelerator.

"What the hell . . ." Malloy was thrown back into his seat. Jackson was draped over the wheel. The car careened forward hitting Joe Fontane as he ran in pursuit. Malloy opened his door.

Meehan sprang for the door McWhinney had open. The Oldsmobile shot through an opening in the traffic, skidded left, weaving in and out of both lanes. Malloy was on his knees where he had fallen on the street. He watched the car disappear out of sight. He could hear the ambulance siren. There was shattered glass all over the place. Joe Fontane was pinned under the car and Jackson was dead with a bullethole in his forehead.

India tore the scarf from around her neck. Folding it frantically into a wad she pressed it down into the seeping well of blood.

Jack tried to say something. She looked into his face and realized he would die.

She raised her head and shouted "Help! Somebody get help!"

Jack was still conscious. "I love you," he whispered in a voice that was no more than a croak. "I always have."

"Shush." Hunched over him, she broke down in tears. "Don't try to talk now, don't."

"India." His voice was going. She had to put her ear right to his lips to hear him. "Take the plane out of here. Get away before they kill you too . . . promise . . ." His eyes closed then.

That really did it. She held him in her arms and she swore to herself then that if Jack lived she wouldn't ever leave him.

Five hours later Jack was wheeled out of the operating room and into Intensive Care. The surgeon went straight into the room where his patient's wife was waiting.

"I'm Doctor Ed Martin. Your husband is going to live . . . Whoooa, you better sit down."

He helped her back into her seat. India was crying with relief and smiling in gratitude at the same time. He dropped down beside her, a tired man with a thin, cratered face. "Would you like me to explain what we've done, or wait till later on?" he asked.

"No. No, please, I want to know."

"Your husband is a sick man, but he's going to pull through. There were quite extensive internal injuries—some damage to the liver which he'll survive." He paused. "It's the damage to the spinal cord that is worrying us."

"Yes?" India croaked.

"Mrs. Donovan, there is a chance that your husband may not walk again—he may be paralyzed from the waist down."

India wept quietly. Ed Martin looked guilt-ridden.

"I'd like to see him."

"I'm sorry, right now it's maybe not a good idea. Your husband is being attended to constantly and he's wired up to several different monitors. It could be very distressing for you. Tomorrow, when we've had time to further assess his condition."

"Please, Doctor Martin, I want to be there when he wakes up." Her face grew stubborn. "I have to. It's very important. Please."

"Tell you what. I'll have one of the nurses take you through the minute he regains consciousness. How about that?"

"Thank you, Doctor."

"You'll be okay in here. Least it's quiet. There's reporters, police, detectives, everybody, still out there. It's bedlam."

The nurse came and got her in the early hours of the morning. India was at his bedside when Jack called her name. It was the very first word he uttered.

"Jack, darling. I'm here." She leaned forward to kiss him and his hand found hers and hung on.

"I thought you'd gone," he said in a cracked voice.

"No. Never. I'm staying with you."

"India. It was Meehan . . . dangerous . . ." And then he faded back into unconsciousness.

It was as Ed Martin predicted. Jack had come out of surgery with his legs paralyzed and India thought she would gladly have been the one to die, if that meant Jack could have the use of his legs back. It turned her right around. She had to do something. The man who did this, Meehan, couldn't be allowed to go free. With some urgency she set about recalling everything, anything, that could have relevance.

She came up with a name and a New York address. An envelope Michael had left on the desk. She could never remember him ever doing that because usually he kept all his correspondence locked away out of sight, except this one time. For that reason, India decided, it had stuck in her memory. Though it was more likely the fact that the envelope had been addressed to a woman, because the name, Rose Murphy, jumped into her mind, and she saw the address as clearly as she had on that day. It was conceivable that it was one that Meehan used, or that Rose Murphy might know something that could help them find him.

She could go to Lieutenant Malloy, tell him everything she knew, and let the law and the judicial process take over. It was her natural inclination.

But she couldn't go to the police with something that could link Jack to murder, conspiracy to commit murder, and an organized crime syndicate. Because if Michael knew about Jack's connections, then she must believe Meehan did as well. If Meehan was pulled in he might try and trade his freedom for evidence against the Mafia—against Jack.

She decided to give her information to Jack's own people. It was the logical thing to do—the only thing she could do.

From the Family came a cry of grief and outrage for Jack's useless legs. Angelo's funeral was postponed once more—it was getting to the stage when he was almost deep-frozen. Salvatore spoke to India on the phone. The whole family had been wronged. His people were more effective than the state, they would find Meehan—he would pay as nobody else ever had.

"India," the Don said, "Jack will have the best security available. He will have a team of doctors and physiotherapists. You also will be protected. I have personally instructed Frank Bartelli to look after you." India listened unhappily. "Angelo—my beloved son—the funeral will be private. Family only. In ordinary circumstances Jack would attend."

"I'm sorry that he cannot be there," said India.

"You must take his place."

India felt a chill crawl over her. "Perhaps, considering his condition, my place is at Jack's bedside."

"Jack will understand. It is important the Family see his wife at Angelo's funeral."

*   *   *

India took two other phone calls that morning before she left for the hospital. The first was from Jack's partner, Richard Kennedy, offering the firm's support, and whatever help she needed. The voice was wholly solid with sympathy and goodwill, and she wondered if Richard Kennedy and Tom Winter had any idea of the kind of market force that was behind Jack.

The second call was from Duane, who told her he had been arrested and taken in on an assault charge and the victim had since died. Duane said he was using up his one phone call on her and she had to help him.

When India hung up she went and did something she never did at a quarter to ten in the morning. She poured herself a shot of Jack's best Napoleon brandy, and sat down on the sofa Paulie had made his own, to think.

She had to get things straight in her head. If she was staying with Jack she would have to be clear-eyed about it. She sipped the brandy slowly. She couldn't kid herself. It she stayed she would be living with the Family, and she recognized them to be dangerous, criminal, and completely ruthless. The question left hanging was not whether Jack fell into the same category (she knew that he did) but whether he meant it when he said the street business, the "organized crime" side, was over with and things were going to be different.

Something about it, however, she couldn't firm up in her mind. People didn't change. And they didn't give away a business that generated millions of dollars' worth of gross profit. Something else was planned.

India mulled it over a long time. Belonging to an organized crime syndicate like the Mafia was morally indefensible. She accepted that.

But if she were to look at it from another way around, if by educating herself in computers the way Jack had, she could outdistance them . . . India reasoned that she had time on her side. The Don was getting old, his consigliere past retirement age. In the long run Jack would have all the power, and by then she would be indispensable to him . . .

She would love Jack and try to make the marriage work, and she would accept the Family, but she would use their resources for people like Duane and Malcolm; by working within the organization she would subvert what it was doing.

India decided she had better study law and business administration. She had to be qualified for what she was taking on.

Before she went out to buy the most beautiful and extravagant black hat she could find, India called Richard back to ask the name of the best defense lawyer in the country (money being no object), and then she phoned Harriet.

Twenty-Four

The priest led the procession. Just behind the closed casket India walked beside Salvatore Coltelli. Behind them came the rest of the mourners.

In the bitter wind at the graveside, the priest intoned the litany and the small family group repeated the words after him. The priest then closed his breviary.

India watched as the simple casket was lowered into the grave. She remembered the look of pure hatred Angelo had given her across the table, the feeling that if he could, he would blow her away like so much dust.

Ashes to ashes, dust to dust.

Not me, Angelo. You!

She breathed in the keen air. Her face showed strength, an obduracy; she had survived, she would survive. And in thinking that, she felt some of the cold proud power in the man standing beside her. The crime boss, her father-in-law.

"What kind of crazy question is that?" Jack was saying. "I can wiggle my toes."

"Wiggle them," commanded his surgeon.

"I can feel them. I'm wiggling them."

Ed Martin shook his head and made a note on his clipboard, then he pulled a pin from behind the lapel of his white coat. "Tell me if you can feel this."

Jack got impatient. "What are you waiting for?"

"Can't you feel me pricking you?"

Jack couldn't. Not the faintest twinge.

He said with cold dignity, "Will you stop it? I'm not a pin cushion."

After the funeral Concetta went with Tom and Betsy in their car for the ride back to the house, and India sat beside Salvatore in the back of the steel-plated custom-built Volvo.

The car itself was quite ordinary-looking, until you got into the enclosed back. The oxblood leather seat as big as a couch permitted the Don to recline in old-fashioned comfort. In the middle, the fold-down armrest had a touch panel that operated the alarm system, doors, and windows, overriding command signals from the driver if it was necessary. There was a bank of screens on the left-hand panel beneath the dividing window, a stereo sound system, and a liquor cabinet.

Salvatore touched a button now and a small table lifted out, absolutely flat. On it was a jigsaw puzzle. He explained to India that puzzles helped him think while he worked out problems, and at the same time they helped him relax, which in turn lowered his blood pressure.

He touched the panel, somewhat regretfully it seemed to India, and the table slid quietly away. "It has been a very bad time, India," he said, and sighed.

She agreed with him and turned down a drink as the cabinet appeared in view. It vanished.

India waited, knowing full well there was a reason she had been invited into this inner sanctum that Jack's father shared with so few. Could it be that it had something to do with power? Angelo's going (and she was preparing to burn rather than be sorry over that one) had eliminated one more power base. Tom was only interested in his experiments on animals. He had no will to win—he could be whipped but, as with a horse, that wouldn't make him a winner. The Don was relying on Jack. And Jack, as perhaps his father knew, was relying on her more than him. Perhaps only for a short time, and then depending . . .

It all had to do with power, and for the first time she was realizing that she could deal from a position of strength.

"This business of Father . . . what is his name?"

"Fitzgerald," India said, with the feeling he knew it very well.

"Ah yes, Father Fitzgerald. Very sad." He turned his head for the first time and looked at her with his terrifying eyes.

"Yes, it is, and the problem he leaves behind is even sadder." She gave him one of her most truly innocent smiles. "Father Fitzgerald told me someone was stealing the Church money. It's true," she said, nodding as he adopted an expression of belligerent virtue. Then she outlined her basic plan to take over the Center, with Church permission, of course, and to administer the new rehabilitation Center, which she was going to allow Salvatore himself to finance . . .

"It will take a great deal of money," she said. "Then there is the trust fund I want to set up for Duane. I would like to send him to college—after we free him."

"Duane?"

She laid her arm delicately on his coat sleeve. The surprising frailty of his hands convinced her the old man's health was beginning to fail, and that as she was Jack's wife, he would want to see her happy. She smiled at him. "Oh, I must tell you about Duane. He needs our help." She went on to explain how much help that was.

"Perhaps you are taking too much on," the Don murmured, but without much conviction. His lips, like his hands, India noticed, were blue. A heart condition?

"No. It's Jack's idea. Before the accident —" She touched the wispy handkerchief to her nostrils.

"Yes, yes, but—"

"Jack thought of me as a partner in the true sense of the word. He outlined many of his ideas and plans. His intentions . . ." India broke down then, but recovered.

"When this terrible thing happened I went to see Richard Kennedy and Tom Winter. Tom is Jack's own lawyer, as you know." (He was Jack's own lawyer for the legitimate side—India was quite certain there was a criminal lawyer, a gutter fighter, one of the Mafia's own, ready and waiting to do combat on Jack's behalf should the need arise.) "I had them draw up a power of attorney—Jack wished me to have authority to act on his behalf should that be necessary. Jack signed it yesterday. I know that if anything happens to Jack, he would wish me to carry on . . ." Her eyes behind the veil of her exquisite little hat overflowed with tears.

"It's terrible to think about, but Jack is a very sick man, as you are aware, and in his weakened state, necessary, don't you think?"

India looked away and blew her nose. "When I saw him lying there in his own blood, it made me realize how quick, how deadly the bullet is. How transient life is. It made me think I could be next, and before I did I would like to be sure I had done what Jack asked me to do."

"Have my handkerchief, India. Let me think about what you have said. Tell me about how you are going to run this Center."

Jack was never sick a day in his life. Now he had doctors coming at him from every direction with their needles and lights, prodding and hammering at him with rubber mallets. He was pushed under complicated-looking machines, he had dye injected into his nerves and arteries so photographs could be taken. He was growing very upset.

"Doctor Martin says the nerves are damaged and they'll take time to heal. He rates the chances of your walking again very high," India said.

She was at Jack's bedside on his fifth post-operative day, when the nurses had taken out the nasal-gastric tube and left him clean and shaved and sitting against a stack of fluffed pillows. All that remained of the extraneous equipment was the bottle feeding him fluid intravenously and the drain running from his abdominal cavity to a jar underneath the bed, which the nurses monitored as constantly as the drip going into his arm.

Jack laughed sarcastically. He didn't put a great deal of stock in "your surgeon says." He'd had everyone from the top neurologist to the lowliest intern around, and they all had something different to say.

"You shouldn't have tried to knock me aside. You should've just let that bastard kill me," he told India.

"Jack, you don't know what you're saying," said India, distressed.

"I'm sorry, I'm sorry. But I'm not spending my life in a fucking wheelchair."

India wanted to tell him about Salvatore's offer, but when she mentioned Angelo's funeral he raged at her.

"That shithead. I hope he rots in hell."

Jack didn't want to hear about anything she had to tell him. He was ill-tempered, sarcastic, morose, demanding, and frightened. When he wasn't railing against his fate he was busy making notes on all the people he thought wanted to kill him. Half the time he didn't seem to realize who he was talking to. He took it for granted India would stay at his bedside. He seemed to have forgotten he had given her almost total control over his affairs. India thought it wasn't the time to tell him she had enrolled in a crash course in computer know-how, and that she would be spending much of her time at his office.

Jack had fallen as low as a patient could. "One fucking careless moment and some bastard nearly wiped me off the face of the earth," he would snarl, and then revert to self-pity. "Shit, why the hell didn't he make a job of it?"

It was very depressing.

After India went to her bank to deposit the very generous check Salvatore had written her, she went home and burst violently into tears. Then she pulled herself together and got to work on her new computer. She had a lot of homework to do.

Next day the morning papers reported the story of the body found in a freezer in a New York pancake house. The man was said to have died under suspicious circumstances and the case was being investigated.

Twenty-Five

It was a cold brutal fuck, the woman against the wall. When Meehan ejaculated he saw a girl with blonde hair getting raped. Afterwards he went to wash his penis and zip his pants. The woman got indifferently into her underwear.

On the run, Meehan had the instincts of a sewer rat, and went to ground as easily. On this occasion it was to the bed of a woman friend. He lived in bed, ate in it, slept in it, watched the TV. He only got up to go to the bathroom, and to fuck. Always against the bedroom wall, so he could see the girl with his cold, undreaming eyes.

When he had to go out it was as a middle-aged woman. Nothing was so anonymous as a woman of a certain age. Put on a dyed wig of curled, medium short hair, head scarf, and plain specs, and no one looked. If they did, it was right through you. But the kind of disguise depended on the area he happened to be in.

Meehan had some favorites. One was selling hot dogs from a street cart. You could stand there all day and watch what was going on. He'd even sold hot dogs to cops who were out looking for him. His disguises were always simple, ordinary. For each assumed character he had documents. Beautiful forgeries done by an old Jew down on his luck: driver's licenses, street vendor's licenses, letters and other stuff people carried around with them.

If he was picked up, he wanted to pass inspection. Passing for a woman had certain disadvantages if it came to the crunch. But the police weren't looking for a woman. Neither was the Mob. Anyway, he wasn't in New York where they seemed to be searching for him, he was here in Washington.

Meehan had to be. He had to find something.

"Where did you hide it, Michael?" he asked of the priest every time he woke from sleeping. Malloy's dicks had been over the Center like a dose of salts. The Mob had been there. They had even searched the priest's room in the presbytery. They were hoping to find something that would lead them to the treasure, as well as lists, names, addresses. Michael committed everything to memory; he never wrote anything down. He never trusted anyone.

Only he and Meehan knew where the weapons were hidden. And the money? Only Father Michael Fitzgerald had known where that was. Fuck the bastard, Meehan thought.

There had to be a key. All Meehan had to figure out was where the priest had hidden it.

The Center was the only place he was sure of, but where? He'd searched every inch.

Unless the girl knew? Meehan couldn't be sure of the answer to that. Michael had been pretty weird toward the end. Men did strange things thinking they were in love.

"I'm in love with the girl myself," Meehan sneered. "And she knows it." Knew somebody was watching her every thought and movement.

Only she'd been wrong in thinking it was Paulie. Half the time the lazy shit would be sitting in some café, or in bed, when he was supposed to be watching her back. He'd track her down to the Center all right, then slope off to his woman.

Watching her had sent contractions up Meehan's rectum. The day before Thanksgiving he'd been standing right behind her. So close he could feel her edgy, like a mare with a stallion sniffing at her. He could have screwed his cock up her in that crowd.

But did she have the key, or know where it was hidden?

It was time he did something. Maybe frighten her a little. Maybe, his testes shifted, maybe get her up against the wall like O'Fiaich had done.

The Center had its Christmas party on the afternoon of the twenty-third. Mel Wooster, in a Santa Claus costume numerous sizes too large for him, waved his hands, welcoming Jack in his wheelchair up the newly erected ramp. Jack beamed expansively and offered a magnum of Moët champagne to his delighted host while Frank Bartelli recovered himself from the exertion of pushing his boss up a startlingly steep gradient.

"So this is the new Center. Very nice," Jack said.

"It's nowhere near finished," Mel said. "But what the hell, we decided to have the Christmas party here anyway."

India joined them. She bent and kissed Jack. "We moved everything over last night."

"Except Father Fitzgerald's desk," Mel said. "It's one big gorgeous desk, but she don't want it." Why would she want to get rid of a good piece of furniture like that? His expression asked.

"It's . . . too big and ornate for the new office," India said. She smiled, but she felt very tired. And harrowed. What with Jack cantankerous one minute and sweet as pie the next, and shifting all their things over to the new building. Mel was right, she hadn't wanted Michael's desk. In fact she couldn't get rid of it fast enough. She kept seeing him sitting there, arms folded in that clumsy, bungling position . . . She had arranged for it to be collected by a buyer early the next day. Before she went home she wanted to clear it out; she was going to be busy the next day preparing a big family lunch.

Jack affected a jaunty, give-a-damn-about-this-wheelchair-shit air and greeted everyone warmly, as befitted a representative of the new Center for Drug Rehabilitation's principal sponsor. He wondered how she had twisted Salvatore around her finger when it was a known fact the old man never listened to women, and never wrote a check unless he saw the profit figures on the bottom line.

"Which is the one we spent a fortune on in bail money keeping him out of the can?" he murmured to India, when the party was in full swing and just about everybody present had swarmed over and acted like it was his brain that was defective and not his legs.

"Duane. He's the one who came and offered you the Christmas cake."

"Oh, yeah."

Jack had been forced into making intelligent noises when Domenico Cechetti visited him. He thought maybe he'd talked coming out of the anesthetic or something. Domenico seemed to have the idea it had all come from him and India was doing something noble carrying on for him. The sun apparently was shining out of her asshole these days. Shit, he couldn't even remember signing anything. But he kept quiet, not wanting to appear stupid. The fact was he couldn't care less about the Center, because just at present, his paramount concern was being a damn cripple.

They all pitied him. And they were junkies! Shit, you had to like that one.

He wanted to escape back to his private room at the hospital where he would be spared the awful humiliation of it all.

"You look tired, Jack," India said. "I'll get Frank to take you back."

He thought, thanks a whole bunch. "Push me into your nice new office," he ordered.

When they got there, he said, "Now shut the door." They stared at each other and it took more than a few seconds for India to understand what he was telling her. She went red.

"The door," Jack growled, "and better lock it."

India went and shut the door, locked it. Jack gazed at her with desire in his eyes. "Come here." India swallowed and felt very hot all of a sudden. She walked over slowly. He reached out his arms and she bent and kissed him softly on the mouth.

"Lift up your skirt," murmured Jack. Nervously India looked behind her as if she thought assassins were about to hammer down the door.

"Now take them off," he said.

"My . . .?"

"Yes."

She did it, trembling.

"Come here. Kiss me."

She kissed him on the mouth and felt his fingers advancing between her legs, pushing upward into her soft flesh. "Unzip me," whispered Jack.

Without saying a word she did as he told her.

"It's only my legs are useless." His hands circled her waist and turned her around so she could sit down on his quivering erect penis.

Frank folded the wheelchair and fitted it into the trunk of the Mercedes. "You want me to come straight back for you?" he asked, as India came from settling Jack into the back seat.

India told him she didn't and asked if he would mind delivering a box to Harriet on his way home after dropping Jack off at the hospital. "There's some things I have to do here. I'll get a cab home later. Don't worry, take some time off."

The Washington Society for Joy at Christmas was giving out presents and showing videos for the entire evening at their club headquarters and promising as much pizza as you could eat, and at five o'clock everyone still left at the party packed in Mel Wooster's old van, unable to resist the come-on.

"Leave the mess, we'll fix it up in the morning," Mel shouted from the driver's seat as they were leaving.

"I will." India waved them off and locked the big front door.

She was crossing the big room in the old building, empty now of tables and chairs and without the welcoming coffee smells, on her way to the office. Her footsteps resounded eerily on the wooden floor. She shivered and her pace quickened.

She reminded herself the building was secure. She had had new security locks fitted on all the entrance doors. There was an alarm system wired up—not activated right at this moment, but then she didn't want another false alarm and patrolmen rushing in and giving her hell about it. Just thinking about them doing that cheered her up. It was so damned quiet. The tune he was humming on that day, she remembered the tune.

Stop it. No one is going to step out of the shadows. They pull in every male who just faintly answers to Meehan's description. He won't dare to come back to Washington.

The office door stood wide open—as she had left it when the filing cabinet was hauled out—and India put her hand to the light switch before going in. The cylindrical tubing on the ceiling flooded the room with white.

So bare, all the furniture gone except for the desk, and the swivel high-backed chair. Michael still existed here. She still saw the things he kept on his desk, unexpected beautiful things. She crossed the floor. The desk and the chair, good, comfortable, sturdy. Mel thought she was mad not to keep them.

India went around and began pulling out the top drawer. She emptied the contents into a cardboard box on the floor to sort through later.

She worked on down, taking each drawer out, turning it upside down and shaking. The middle drawer looked as solid as the rest, same grainy wood, but as she turned it to shake it, something inside shifted. She gave the base a thump and a layer of wood that perfectly fitted the bottom fell out. And with it, an envelope.

A plain, blank envelope. India picked it up and turned it over. It was sealed. She hesitated, then she tore it open. Nestled in the bottom was a short, flat key, quite small. She took it out and saw the three numbers engraved on the side. It lay in the palm of her hand, distinctive, startlingly familiar.

There was no time for association or discovery, or thoughts of any kind.

A woman stepped in through the door. An oldish black woman who wore a baggy coat and a hat over her frizzy graying hair. One of the mothers who came to help with the party, India thought. She even thought she recognized her.

What happened then was a bad dream. As India opened her mouth, the woman's arm came up and took deliberate aim. There was an automatic in her hand with a long black silencer.

"Aren't you the clever one," the woman said, and it was a soft, low, Irish voice.

India's open mouth had dried out—she couldn't even swallow, couldn't speak, couldn't make a sound.

"Now you know what I want." The woman said it with a kind of insinuating familiarity. She smiled then. The smile was curiously obscene.

"Give it to me."

India stared at her. The room went into a gravelike silence. She had almost forgotten the key in her hand, almost forgotten the gun, she kept thinking . . .

The woman took a step forward. She was directly under the fluorescent lighting, and India thought her skin looked odd, blanched. The same way people look when they go white underneath a deep tan. And then India realized it was a white woman wearing dark makeup. She stepped backward in a sudden panic, pushing the chair behind her. The woman was right on the other side of the desk, the gun unwavering in her hand.

"If it's money," India said, "I don't have any here."

"It's money all right, and I believe you, dear. Now give me what is in your hand."

India blinked. Her fingers tightened around the key.

The woman snarled, "Listen, cunt . . ." and the words that kept coming out of that coarse mouth were so ugly India stood and gaped in shock, in pure disgust. Later she would wonder if it was disgust that made her do it. She popped the key into her mouth and swallowed. She nearly choked for lack of saliva and her eyes watered viciously.

"You stupid bitch!" the woman howled. "Are you nuts?" She dropped the gun on the desk, one nimble bound and she was on top of it. India flung herself backwards, falling down into the chair. It slammed against the wall. As the woman's hands came clawing for her, India spun around and slipped out, and the woman smashed into the chair. India hurled the carton at her, pads, ink bottles, erasers, files, screwdrivers rained down.

"I'll kill you," the woman screamed, her eyes going to the automatic lying on the edge of the desk. Grunting, she catapulted from the chair back across the desk, arm outstretched for the weapon. She had her fingers pawing for the gun butt when India knocked it to the floor.

The woman had momentum, she dived off the table. But India was picking up the gun—and seeing the woman's hair come off with the hat. Meehan! He was nearly on top of her. She tried to run. Meehan just missed her. He crashed on the floor, winded, but his grasping hand caught her foot and sent her sprawling. The gun flew out of her hand and spun toward the door.

Sobbing, India wrenched her foot free of the shoe and crawled for the gun. Meehan came grunting and thrashing headlong over the floor after her like an enraged primeval beast.

He lunged and caught her by the leg.

"Ahh, Ah." She kicked and flailed with her other foot. He clamped that too, pinning her down. She was groping for the gun, plunging her nails into the wooden floor to drag herself along. Her fingers began closing on the handle.

She got it!

India heaved herself around and squeezed what she thought was the appropriate part. Her hand jerked out of control and Meehan dropped his head down on her legs. Had she hit him? All she could hear was her own hoarse breath rasping in and out of her throat.

Was he dead?

Slowly Meehan raised his head.

India trembled so violently the gun veered from one direction to another.

"Give me that."

"No." She was almost too horrified to move. The gun rattled in her hand.

He was creeping up, his outstretched hand coming nearer and nearer.

"No. Go back. Go back, I'll shoot," she whimpered. "No . . ."

He reached for the gun—she saw the crazed determination in his face.

She clamped her other hand on her wrist to steady it and shot him, watching his face explode into a cloud of blood and clotted matter.

She pulled back, wrenching her legs out from under his body, then saw she still held the gun and dropped it. On her knees, half crawling, she stumbled away. She looked back and could see everything under the white light in documentary detail. She ran, making little gasping noises. She staggered into the bathroom and fell against the basin. She turned the cold tap, sluicing the water over her face, her hands, wetting wads of paper towels until they were soaking and sponging the blood from her red pullover. There was blood on the collar of her shirt. She felt the key like a stone inside, around the region of her diaphragm.

It wasn't in her mind to call the police. She wanted Jack.

She grabbed her coat, more to cover herself then to keep warm. Leaving the lights on, she ran out into the street and hailed a cab. She'd forgotten her purse, everything. She wasn't thinking properly, she felt unreal. Halfway to the hospital she remembered she only had on one shoe, but that only vaguely. Featureless shapes rushed by on the street outside; she didn't take anything in. When they got to the hospital she opened the door and ran. The driver sat dumbfounded, then he leapt from his taxi with an angry yell.

A small group waited silently for the elevator. India couldn't wait. She weaved through the people in the lobby to the heavy fire doors. Shoved through and up the stairs, running, one footstep beating a tattoo, the other silent on the cold marble-like surface.

She'd killed a man! Shot him in the face. Oh God, oh God. Jack would know what to do. He'd take her in his arms, he'd . . .

Feet and hair flying she ran, along the corridor past nurses and patients, and two orderlies pushing a trolley, until she came to Jack's room. Her lungs felt as if they were bursting.

India opened the door and nearly fell inside. She looked toward the bed—where Livia, her long silky legs gracefully displayed, lounged comfortably, glass in hand, waiting to toast Jack with the champagne he was pouring. Stupefied, India's eyes went from Livia to Jack, sitting in his wheelchair holding the bottle, to the ice bucket at his side, and back to Livia.

"Get out," India said, almost too quietly but perfectly audible. She advanced, watching Livia in sudden alarm begin to uncurl her legs. India stalked towards the bed and all the while she had the sensation of standing aside and watching herself, horrified.

"Get out, do you hear me? Get out, get out, get out!" Her voice was hysterical, she was panting, Jack frantically trying to maneuver his wheelchair. Her hands were clenched. Livia scrambled off the other side of the bed in unseemly haste.

"India, darling, don't," Jack said, finding his voice.

India looked around. His face pleaded with her. Beyond his chair hung Livia's voluptuous Russian sable coat glistening in all its primal erotic glory. The temptation was too sweet; she brushed past him and snatched the ankle-length fur in her hands.

Livia's hand flicked out, her voice was a howl. "Stop her, for Christ's sake!"

"Come and get it, dear," India said and turned for the door. She remembered the dirty laundry chute further along the corridor.

"India!" Jack called vainly.

India was stuffing the coat into the chute's greedy steel cylindrical throat even as she heard Livia's footsteps come racing out of the room. The heavy fur plummeted down like a broken corpse.

Livia's hands flapped in desperation like the wings of a bat. Her mouth was a frozen "oh," the sound strangled in its infancy. Then she saw the Nurses' station and bolted for it, shrieking, "Get security! Emergency! Don't just sit there! Get Security!"

All at once India felt sick. What had she achieved? What victory was there for her in her childish action?

People were walking past, looking with uncertain eyes and then averting them—as people did when confronted with someone who looked as if they might behave irrationally. She longed to lie down in a quiet, dark room and have someone soothe her to sleep. There was no chance. An angry taxi driver was waiting for her. The police would come and take her away.

Jack skidded to a stop outside his doorway. He was having trouble getting turned around. India walked right past him, heading back to the elevator. He had Livia to help him now, when Livia was through looking for her coat—which Jack had probably given her.

"I LOVE YOU!"

Startled, India looked around. She saw Jack sitting in his chair, she saw people standing in doorways, along the walls, looking. She saw the curiosity on their faces. She began walking away, fast.

"I LOVE YOU!"

She started to run. No use, India panted, she reached the elevators and punched at the DOWN button. You think that's all there is to it: "I love you." Then back to your extra-curricular love life. Thanks a lot. But not this time.

The doors opened and two women laden with flowers walked out. India flew in and stabbed at the buttons. The ladies outside gave little shrieks. Jack sped past them on humming tires. India jammed a quaking finger on the OPEN button just in time to prevent the doors closing on him. Jack barreled into the elevator. He was grinning.

"This thing's not bad when you get the hang of it."

India put out a hand making a stop sign. "Don't," she said, shaking her head, but with a queer numb look. She repeated weakly, "Just don't."

The doors had closed; they were starting down. Jack reached from his chair and pressed the emergency stop. The elevator halted almost instantaneously with a cacophony of whines.

"We're taking five," Jack said, reaching out and grabbing for her hand to pull her to him.

"Jack . . . ," she said, staring glassily, "I shot him."

Jack looked at her.

"Meehan. I shot him." She was sniffing and wiping her face with her hands. Jack took the box of tissues from the side pocket of his chair. He pulled her down on his lap and wiped her face. "You better tell me what happened," he said.

Jack called his father from his hospital room. He kept looking at India proudly as he spoke.

"She did what?"

Jack had to explain. Salvatore was pleased.

"You married a fine girl, Jack. Do you want any help? I can have the best criminal lawyer fly down there."

"I've got a good man on his way here now. There won't be any problem, except maybe Malloy will be jealous. Shit, Meehan must've had to fall over his men to get anywhere near the Center."

"Never mind about Malloy's men," Salvatore said softly, and Jack felt sort of sorry for their own guy who had let Meehan slip through.

When he got off the phone he sat back and looked at her, thinking about his father's words and realizing how lucky he was. He said, "Soon as we get Malloy sorted out, let's go some place."

"How do you mean?"

"A honeymoon. We haven't been on one yet."

"Your mistress won't like that."

"Won't she?" Jack said, and grinned. "Livia was here celebrating her engagement to Lord Beckon-someone-or-other. She's going to live in England."

"Is she? She is!"

"We can hop on a 747 to Honolulu and stay at the Halekulani on Waikiki Beach. We'll have to take Frank, though, to haul me about."

India put her arms around his neck. "Just tell me when." She was pleased, really pleased, but also she was thinking of the three numbers she had seen on the flat little key.

"Don't you have a key with the number 747?" she asked softly.

"Yeah. My locker number at the Chevy Chase Country Club. I only use it when I go to play squash. You should go there sometime, wives can use their husbands' membership. The key's on the ring."

"I might, sometime. Is it very difficult getting a membership?"

"You're my wife," Jack said, and looked hurt.

"I mean, just anybody?" She meant a priest. Not that Michael, so far as she knew, ever played squash.

"It used to be very exclusive. Now anyone with the money to pay the fee is in." He wheeled over to his table and took a bunch of keys from the drawer. Jack liked to have his keys handy, even though there were some he wouldn't have much use for again. "Here . . ."

He handed her a small flat key with the three numbers printed on it. An identical one with different numbers was sitting in her stomach. A locker in a country club in Chevy Chase with a high membership fee was an expensive place to keep one's money.

She hadn't told Jack about the key. But she was thinking about it.